"THERE'S SOMETHING WEIRD ABOUT THIS STORM. . . ."

Susannah had to shout into her wrist terminal to be heard over the wind. "Remember time-lapse photography? That's what it looks like. Unnatural, you know?"

The reply came mixed with static. "Having trouble . . . ing . . . reports . . . ind of . . . erference. Conditions approaching abnormal . . . and . . . visable . . . turn to . . . ander."

The little terminal went dead.

And suddenly Susannah realized she and her Sawl guide were alone, far from the base, completely cut off from help and caught high on the mountain in the heart of the most violent storm she'd ever seen. . . .

THE WAVE AND THE FLAME

Volume I of *Lear's Daughters*

M. Bradley Kellogg
with
William B. Rossow

A SIGNET BOOK

NEW AMERICAN LIBRARY

Copyright © 1986 by M. Bradley Kellogg

First Printing, June, 1986

1 2 3 4 5 6 7 8 9

FOR BRADLEY LANGDON KELLOGG

With thanks for their expertise
and encouragement:

*Antonia D. Bryan, Claire S. Derway,
Sheila Gilbert, Olenka Hubickyj,
Jarvis P. Kellogg, Jr., and Dr. Katalin Roth*

Special thanks to Barbara Newman Morris
and Lynne M. Kemen

BOOK ONE

"... rain, wind, thunder, fire,
are my daughters ..."

KING LEAR,
Act III, sc. ii

1

The little man huddled in his rock shelter high among the snow-shrouded cliffs. Deep in the curl of a fleece-lined collar, his face was dark, a young man's face in the weathered skin of an ancient. He sat cross-legged and alert in the center of the small domed space, facing a round doorhole that leaked pale light from the white swirling sky. His narrow body was swaddled against the cold by a thick nest of blankets. Fine snow drifted in to lie unmelting among the folds.

His head inclined as if listening, but his back curved at rest beneath the many layers of his clothing. One brown hand smoothed a strip of tooled leather against his thigh. The other held a threaded needle. He matched two edges between thumb and forefinger, eased the leather onto his knee and began to sew.

The wind moaned beyond the open doorway. Outside, the endless snow threw smothering drifts against the thick masonry of his shelter and wiped clean the trail that threaded down the precipitous cliffs. Below his cramped ledge, the white land vanished into the storm. Time passed unnoticed as the leather took its shape in his lap. For hours or weeks he might have been waiting there, perched in his chill aerie. His breath rimed the rough rock with frost. The storm enclosed him in a chaos of white ordered only by the deft logic of his bone needle: hover, like a ravenous hawk, swoop to pierce the resisting leather, pull up, thread taut, to hover and swoop again, in time with the shallow swell of his breathing.

When the wind died, he noted its sudden silence. The spare line of his mouth continued its voiceless count of long neat stitches, but his eyes flicked up and outward. He scanned the whiteness automatically, then returned his concentration to the garment growing in his lap.

3

Then, in the middle of a stitch, his back straightened. From a distance above came a drawn-out warbled cry, so faint even in the utter quiet that it might have been imagined. The bone needle froze in its downward swoop. The little man listened, intent as a huntsman. The cry came again, from high and far away, but repeated now from nearer by. This time he nodded, and unthreaded his needle, folding it into the ornate leather with disciplined haste. He rose, stretching stiffened limbs. His ringleted hair grazed the domed ceiling as he slipped his work bundle into a pouch sewn into the layers of his woolens, then gathered the blankets into a larger pack slung low across his back. He glanced around the shelter, patting at his chest with an absent frown. His thin fingers burrowed nervously among the layers to draw forth a carved blue stone fastened by a worn and knotted thong. Satisfied, he returned the amulet to the safety of his innermost garment. He shrugged his furs about him, stooped, and crawled into the open.

The snow fell gently now, its wildest fury spent. The blind whiteness calmed and coalesced into a landscape. The little man surveyed the cliffs behind him. They towered forbiddingly, then climbed sharply into mountains torn by crevasses and rockfalls, range after range of white crags rising into the whiter distance. One long pace from the door of his shelter, the ragged ledge fell away in a shivering drop to meet a faceless white plain some thousand feet below. The plain rolled softly toward a horizon made invisible by the lowering cloud cover. The little man sniffed the frigid air and waited.

The shrill cry came again, followed by its nearer echo. When a third, still closer voice took up the relay, he answered it with a shorter, trilled reply and heard his own call relayed back, voice by voice, up into the mountains behind. With another, grimmer nod, he fastened his furred hood tightly about his face, pulled on leather mittens and started down the narrow trail.

He moved carefully at first, easing the cramp out of long-immobile muscles, then picked up his pace steadily, his head held low to search the snow for signs of hidden danger. He worked into a stiff-legged lope that sent sprays of powder flying with every falling leap. Arms flung wide for balance, he banked into his turns without slowing. His backpack flapped loosely to the rhythm of his stride as he raced along angled ledges where bare rock broke through the drifted snow. He swerved with each hairpin turn, leaped, raced and swerved again in a controlled fall down the mountainside. Along the lower reaches, the deepening drifts rose about him as he descended, slowing his progress. He plowed through them ungracefully, until his furs and eyebrows were crusted white. His breath puffed out in tiny clouds. His arms flapped like tired wings.

A hundred feet above the plain, the deep snowpack hardened under the weight of its own layers. The trail dropped through the surface drifts into a tunnel that bored into the compacted mass of snow and ice. Its rough-cut walls were glassy with frozen melt. A ghost of daylight filtered in to guide the runner's feet along the rippled floor. The light dimmed with each descending pace. For a distance, the tunnel followed the contour of the cliffs, snaking around outcroppings of rock as pale and translucent as the ice. As it approached the bottom of the cliffs, the tunnel floor was pierced by brittle edges of granite that warmed the icy gleam with glimmers of rose. The little man ran an urgent agile slalom around every twist and obstacle. He slowed only when the floor began to level and smooth out. Then, where a second tunnel intersected at right angles to the first, he skidded to a stop.

The second tunnel was larger, squarer. Yellow sand had been scattered across its glossy floor. A hard white glow reflected along its icy walls. The little man hesitated at the intersection, his face turned away from the glow. He paced in a narrow circle, catching his breath, kicked at shattered tusks of ice lying along the bottom of the walls. Someone taller than he had cleared headroom among the icicles clinging to the ceiling. He stared longingly up the smaller tunnel. Its round cool greenness continued into watery dark as it curved back toward the cliffs and began to rise again. He sighed, pressed his jaw with a balled fist and turned into the light of the larger tunnel. It widened as he rounded a corner, then straightened like a ruled line. He took up a reluctant jog, his delicate features tight with uneasy purpose. Farther along, the ceiling arched into a smooth barrel vault. It threw the chatter of his footsteps back at him in whispering echoes. After a long flat stretch through the snowmass smothering the plain, the tunnel turned a final right angle and dead-ended in a wall of clear blue ice.

The little man halted. The end of a mirrored cylinder protruded through the ice wall. The top of its arc was three times his height. Its open mouth exuded warmth and hard white light. He squinted and shoved back his hood, then edged along the wall toward the opening. He slid off one mitten to touch cautious fingertips to the giant shining curve, then toed its silvered floor as if testing for solidity. His knees flexed as he peered down the cylinder's length, poised for retreat. Less than twenty paces away, bodies moved in a confusion of brightness, bodies larger than his own. He lingered in the shadow and reflected light, hopeful of invisibility, then shivered once and cupped thin hands to his mouth. By the time his shouted message had echoed the length of the cylinder, he had whirled around and was gone.

FTL HAWKING Exploration of Byrnham Cluster
(UWSA/CONPLEX Exp. 23)
Star system PT 6 (KO, 3 p?)

(continued)
       large terrestrial planet for mineral potential
       and possible evidence of ETI artifacts by land-
       ing science team for nine month period.
       (2) Astronomical study of Pop.II late sequence
       stellar system from supporting (in-orbit) SCR
       BOSTON with focus on composition of primary
       and nearby stars.

B. Expedition Complement
  B.1. Ship Complement
    B.1.1. System Carrier - research
           SCR BOSTON   UWSA 036A3
           Configured for: 1 Lander, 4 planetary
           orbiting satellites,4 message drones.
    B.1.2. Lander - research
           LR 14   UWSA 0014C2

  B.2. Crew Complement
    B.2.1. Ship Crew
       Captain Maxim B. Newman   (Commander, SCR)
       Commander Weng Tsi Hua   (Commander, LR: Land.)
       Lt.Commander Jen Wilson   (Master Pilot, SCR)
       Lt. Veronica McPherson   (Pilot, LR: Landing)
       Lt. Bea Suntori   (CRI Specialist)
       En. Ro T. Gobajev   (Propulsion Engineer)
       En.Josei Pilades   (Engineer/MedicalMate)
    B.2.2. Science Team
       Dr. Taylor Danforth   (Ch.Sci., Planetology,L.)
       Dr. Jorge Sundquist   (Asst.Ch. Sci., Astronomy)
       Dr. Susannah James   (Exobiology: Landing)
       Dr. Megan Levy   (Anthropology: Landing)
       Mr. Stavros Ibia   (Linguistics: Landing)
    B.2.3. CONPLEX Team
       Dr.Emil Clausen   (VP, Expl& Dev, CONPLEX:L.)
       Dr. Rye Hobart   (Remote Sensing Specialist)

C. Star System PT 6 Schedule

       The schedule covers the following mission
    phases: star system entry, planetary orbit en-
    try, pre-landing orbital surveys, landing, and

2

Inside the warm white space, the two women at the table looked up from their work, to stare at the silvered entryway. Glare from the overhead lights flashed in a pair of gold-rimmed eyeglasses. The older woman leaned forward on her stool as if to rise, and then did not.

"What was that?"

"Was it Liphar?" asked her companion simultaneously.

A third woman, the youngest, stretched lazily in her low-slung recliner. "Some one of them yelling," she commented, laying aside her reading. "Little buggers never stick around long enough for me to tell 'em apart."

The older woman abruptly shoved aside her sketching terminal. She pushed back her archaic glasses and rubbed at the bridge of her nose in pained disgust. "You'd have less trouble if you gave it some thought, McPherson."

Here we go, thought her dark-haired companion at the table. *Regular as clockwork. The midafternoon battle.* She opened a plastic sample bag and emptied its woody contents on the table. "Easy, Meg. She's only teasing you."

"So who can tell?" Megan complained. She lifted martyred eyes to the landscape of scorched metal above their heads. The landing craft was heat-bruised, sand-scoured and grimed with condensation and grease. Its circular underbelly was crisscrossed with the plastic pipe and looping cables of temporary living. All but two equipment bays dangled open, their contents plundered or replaced with decreasing care as the long weeks wore on. Scattered and uneven stacks of plastic storage crates hinted at a once-orderly partitioning of living spaces that had devolved into haphazard division.

The young blonde flopped around in her recliner with a self-satisfied chortle. "Jeez, Meg, I wish the Lander's buttons were as touchy as yours!"

Megan sniffed. "People are trying to work here, McPherson."

The blonde nodded with mockingly pursed lips. "Yeah? Well, there's good ole Susannah working all right, but you sure ain't getting much observing-the-natives done, Meggies, laying down here on your ass!"

As Megan's heavy features puckered towards a retort, Susannah raised a restraining hand. "Don't, Meg. It's bad enough in here as it is."

Megan sighed and contented herself with a glare at McPherson over the glinting rims of her eyeglasses. Susannah was convinced that Megan had never opted for the standard corrective surgery because she preferred being able to stare at her students over her glasses, just the way she was now staring at McPherson.

McPherson lay back into the curve of the recliner and flexed one trim white-clad leg in the air. "Hell, don't blame you, Meg, sticking down here. You anthropologists don't get shit to sit on when you're working."

"I'm working *now*," responded Megan tightly, then muttered to herself, "I'm just not getting anything done." She resettled the glowing sketchpad in front of her and fiddled guiltily with its keys.

"Ah, the joys of cabin fever," murmured Susannah. She bent back to the mound of dried leaves lying half sorted on the table. She brushed aside crushed twigs and dirt to set out a withered leaf cutting for study, and found herself listening to the silence. She thought it sounded different, in an indefinable way that made her uneasy. She wondered if the runner in the tunnel had been trying to tell them something important. "It probably wasn't Liphar," she commented.

Megan pushed the sketcher aside with a grunt of futility. She picked up a stray leaf which she pretended to examine. "No. He at least stays around for a bite when he ventures down from the Caves. But, you know, delighted as I am to prove his digestive system compatible with ours, I do wish he was a trifle more enthusiastic about my cooking."

Susannah's laugh was gentle. "Mere adolescent snobbery, Meg. I think young Liphar considers our cuisine a bit limited."

"Well, he ain't lying," drawled McPherson from the depths of her chair.

"This expedition never promised a four-star galley," grinned Susannah.

McPherson flexed the other leg. "For god's sake, don't tell Emil. You'll hurt his feelings."

"What feelings?" grumped Megan.

"Not even Emil can do much with freeze-dried soy cake." Susannah grasped her specimen gingerly and reached for her magnifier.

"The Sawls' own diet is just as limited," pursued Megan with a hint of a whine. "How they survive on what's available to them on this planet is a miracle of dietary ingenuity."

Susannah nodded. "True, but if I understand him right, Liphar's real complaint is with our packaging. It bothers him that we use something once and then throw it away. I haven't been able to make the purpose of the recycling unit clear to him." Turning over the specimen on her palm, she frowned and increased the power of her magnifier. "Meg, see the spore cases on the underside of this leaf? It's structured a lot like our *Equisetum*, see? But what would a water plant be doing up here in this frozen desert?"

"Who knows why anything's the way it is on this wretched world," Megan grumbled, but her irritation had ebbed. "Did he actually say that?"

"Who?" Susannah squinted at her leaf, then touched a key on her wrist terminal. "CRI, while you're analyzing the new samples, remember to scan for trehalose."

"Yes, Dr. James," replied the computer.

"Did Liphar really say that about the waste?" Megan insisted. "That's a sophisticated notion for a low-tech society like this one."

"Is it? Well, maybe I'm projecting. He didn't say it in so many words."

"He doesn't know so many words—in English," tossed in McPherson.

Susannah ignored her. "The Sawls are a subtle people," she concluded.

"Polite," Megan corrected.

Susannah shrugged. "If you like."

McPherson snorted, flicking invisible dust from the white spacer uniform that fitted her short athletic body like a second skin. "He's so polite he scrounges a free lunch every time he comes around."

"When you were Liphar's age, I'll bet you were doing the same thing around the Academy cafeteria," Susannah chided with a smile. "Besides, free lunches are hard to come by on this snowball."

McPherson reflexively brushed at the silver figure-eight on her collar. "He ain't so much younger than me. By the time I was his age, I'd graduated and won my first commission. I was buying other folks their lunch!"

"You might remember," intoned Megan, "that food is a time-honored medium for social exchange, here on Fiix as well as throughout the galaxy. Food is a potent symbol of trust and hospitality that crosses all cultures. In fact, many of the smaller Terran colonies, on the harsher worlds where subsistence is marginal, have evolved highly intricate food-based etiquettes. Food is—"

"Phooey." McPherson waved a careless hand. "Save your lectures for the classroom, Megs. It's all wasted on me."

"I'll say," growled Megan.

McPherson bent to retrieve a discarded engineering manual and turned her back. The plastic facsimile pages crinkled loudly as she flipped through them, searching for her place, and Susannah realized what was different about the silence. For the six weeks since their arrival, the storm-strummed vibration of the Lander's shell had hummed a constant accompaniment to the expeditionaries' sleeps and squabbles. Now it had ceased. "Listen to how quiet it is," she said.

But Megan had folded her arms, pouting, and leaned back against the hard trusswork of the landing gear that towered behind her. "Someday they'll fully automate these crates and spare the Sciences from the ignorance of career spacers!"

"Meg . . ." Susannah warned.

"Oh, yeah?" McPherson sprang up from her chair. "You think some machine could have landed us in shit like this? Snow up to the retros? That nice gale-force wind that blew up out of fuckin' nowhere just as I was settin' us down and nearly mashed us against those cliffs? Not your everyday landing, y'know! Even CRI congratulated me!"

"CRI is programmed to be supportive!" Megan retorted.

"Man, when I get my seniority built up, you won't catch me chauffeuring no bunch of scientists around the place!" McPherson exclaimed. "No offense, Susannah."

"None taken," returned Susannah mildly. "By the way, have you got that Sled problem ironed out yet?" Her diplomatic efforts had long ago abandoned subtlety. A moment had come on the long trip out from Earth when she had realized that if she didn't try to keep peace among the seven of them, nobody would. With five such thorny personalities thrown together under a commander whose authority extended only to the physical welfare of ship and passengers (and who took this as a directive not to meddle elsewhere), Susannah was left, as the one determined to remain neutral, to be cast as mediator. She would have preferred to stay out of the battling altogether. Though she was too fed up with the role to remain creative in it, peacekeeping had become so integral to her shipboard identity that it would be difficult to abandon it now. Besides, her success rate was considerable.

The little pilot grimaced, subsiding into her chair to thumb through the manual brusquely. Then she shrugged and allowed herself to be distracted. "Nah. It's not like a thing you can really solve, y'know?" She held up a colored schematic for Susannah's perusal. "It's a joke them things ever got to be called Sleds—that class of skimmer ain't worth a spacer's damn in the snow. But then, we weren't exactly expecting snow, were we. . . ." She waved the manual at two large shrouded hulks parked across the crate-littered Underbelly, alongside the blue-green wall of ice that pressed in against the Lander's encircling force field. One hulk was partly uncovered, exposing an open cockpit. Clothing decorated the windscreen. A wrinkled foil blanket lay in a comfortable nest along one of the triangular wings. The pilot's seat was strewn with printout and plastic eating utensils. Deserted coffee mugs lounged on the control console. "No power in 'em," McPherson mourned, the animation in her round face wilting momentarily. "Not against these winds. Told myself, while they're trapped down here in the ice with us, I'd work 'em up a little, but . . ." She shrugged again. "Phooey."

"Too bad," Susannah agreed abstractedly. She preferred to ignore the Sleds, since a glance in their direction led the eye inevitably beyond to the shifting blue image of the ice. In those private moments when her nerves were most tender, when the bickering gave way to terse silence and the ice spoke in its language of creaks and groans, it was hard to have total faith in the impenetrability of an invisible wall. The ice was a more manifest power, pressing relentlessly inward against the shield, threatening the small space won by the heat of the Lander's descent engines, held at bay only by a slim beam of energy whose source in the Orbiter might as well be a million miles away instead of a few thousand, for all of its current accessibility. The Lander was capable of a single round trip. Once down, the landing party must stay down, until they were ready—or forced—to leave.

Well, I wanted a way out of the laboratory, Susannah reminded herself, but as always, her gaze was snared by the perimeter's stealthy blue dance. In the field distortions, the ice seemed to sway and breathe. It wore a dampness like sweat where ice and forces interfaced. Susannah felt suddenly fragile, under siege on a giant hostile planet, battered not by alien dangers but by more familiar horrors: constant storms, wind, snow, ice and frigid cold. That the preliminary probe had predicted a hot, dry climate made this unrelenting winter somehow harder to bear. She turned away abruptly, back to the meager comfort of her tiny dried twigs, and longed for something living to study, something fresh and growing. She tapped a note into the miniterminal on her wrist and sat back, trying to recall what had seemed so important a moment ago, before the squabbling had sidetracked her. Stretching, she raked her fingers through her straight dark hair to readjust its length in the plastic clasp at her neck, and remembered. "I wonder what he wanted."

"Who?" Megan awoke from some icebound reverie of her own.

"Whoever that was we heard at the tunnel just now."

"Yes, I wonder. Not like the Sawls to run around yelling."

McPherson snapped her manual shut. "Aw, Meg, be real. On the noise scale, they're about a nine. All jammed into their little holes up there, yammering a mile a minute."

Susannah cleared her throat warningly.

"They don't yell at me, McPherson," retorted Megan.

Susannah abandoned persuasion for the direct approach. "I wish you two would work out your mother-daughter competition elsewheres."

Megan glared hopelessly around at the walls of crates and ice. "*Where?* Just tell me where else I can go!"

"Mother, my ass!" bellowed McPherson. "My mother captained the *Orion* for twelve years! The fuckin' *Orion*. You couldn't get a better ship than that in those days!" She cocked her arm and threw the manual hard. As Megan ducked, the flapping plastic missile sailed past her shoulder and slammed into a curtain that closed off a corner of the work space. A moment later, the curtain was drawn aside. A tall white-haired oriental woman surveyed them with stern equanimity.

"Uh-oh." The young pilot clambered up from her recliner.

The newcomer let the silence add dignity to her entrance, a dignity of age and bearing only slightly undercut by the earphone dangling discreetly from one ear. "Lieutenant McPherson, Dr. Levy: I am sure you are both aware of how well sound carries in these denser atmospheres. I see no need for raised voices to make ourselves heard."

"Yes, Commander," McPherson murmured.

Megan shook her head ruefully. "Sorry, Weng. It's just that . . ."

"Yes, Dr. Levy?"

"The usual, that's all."

"Ah. The usual." Weng moved to peer over Susannah's shoulder. Her spotless white uniform hung loosely about her, contriving to make her thin body look full and graceful. She sucked in a parched cheek and poked at a sprig of dried blossoms. "Are we making progress with the Fiixian flora, Dr. James?"

Susannah smiled up at her. "Slowly, Commander. Mostly I'm finding further mysteries in place of answers, so I'm actually grateful for all the extra time we've had here."

Weng's opaque black stare glittered, a hint of amusement mixed with skepticism. "You may be the only one, Dr. James," she murmured, as she retreated towards the relative seclusion of her corner and closed the curtain behind her.

There was a beat of chastened silence, broken only by the ominous creaking of the surrounding ice. Then McPherson whispered fiercely, "She's in there listening to her damn spools again!"

"I prefer Bach to arguments myself." Susannah polished her magnifier on her wrinkled shirttail and laid out another leaf for study. She thought she heard a low distant rumble, more felt than heard, through the soles of her feet, like the passing of an underground train, through her fingertips as they rested on the plastic tabletop. *The wind's come up again*, she decided, though it didn't really sound like the wind at all.

"Isn't it dinnertime yet?" Megan asked suddenly.

McPherson snorted. "It's only sixteen hundred!"

Without looking up, Susannah murmured, "You know, Meg, I was up in the Caves earlier today. It's not so cold in the MeetingHall as it has been."

Megan's mouth tightened. "You going to get on my back, too? Well, how about this? It's not the cold this time. I'd be up there all right, but your friend Stavros is having one of his manic periods. He's hogging the Caveside terminal like it was his personal property!"

"Perhaps we should put in another," Susannah suggested with patience she did not really feel. The Cave terminal's nonavailability was an excuse they all used at one time or another as the lethargy of confinement stole over them.

"Oh, I asked about that, but Stavros refused. He insisted it's too risky to put our only backup on line, and he *is* the Communications Officer, irony of ironies."

"Speak to Weng about it."

"He's got Weng in his pocket. I have a better idea. Why don't *you* speak to Stavros."

The corners of Susannah's mouth twitched. "I have no magic power over the man, Meg."

"So you say, but somehow you always get use of that terminal when you need it."

"Stavros is stubborn, Meg. You have to approach him obliquely if you want to get around him."

"He's nuts," offered McPherson cheerfully. "Sitting in a damp old cave all day like a mole with all that hardware piled up around him. A total obsessive crazy."

"Not crazy," Susannah countered. "Just excessively gifted. Besides, it's his first expedition. He's busy proving himself." Her irritation showed only in her faint blush. She disliked feeling compelled to specially defend her most difficult colleague. Dealing with Stavros was always a messy, ungainly business that left you more challenged than satisfied. His sheltered adolescence as a university wunderkind had not suited the young linguist for the intimate politics of a small scientific expedition. But Susannah admired his unjaded commitment, not just to getting his work done, but to the ideal of the work, to the mystery and wonder of language. Still, as Megan would readily point out, however profound his gift for word theory, Stavros Ibiá had not yet learned to moderate his behavior like an adult. It was just as well he spent most of his time up there in the Caves, out of everyone's hair. "Meg, you remember how it was?" Susannah offered in his defense. "Your first planet is like your first love—it hits you the hardest. You think you'll never care as much about another world, or ever see the first as just one more in the string of worlds you'll study during a lifetime."

Megan grunted. "And you with only three to your credit."

Susannah smiled but continued doggedly. "Why is he hogging the terminal this time?"

Megan had recalled some unfinished charts to her sketchscreen and was toying with them guiltily. "He's recording some major event just getting underway in the MeetingHall: music, tale-chanting, dancing, you know, the works." At her friend's slow look, Megan waggled both palms defensively. "Yeah, yeah, all the more reason to be up there myself. . . . I don't know, some days it just seems like masturbation." Pain crept into her be-mused frown. "Susannah, I *have* been working, up until re-cently. Six weeks I've been trekking up there and back, listening, watching, recording. I have a good book and a half's worth of observations already and I can't give it any shape." Her plump hands flapped around like dying fish. "It just *can't* be as straight-forward as it seems in those caves. It *can't* be so pedestrian. My publishers will have my head in return for their big fat advance!"

"Well, the flora's certainly not straightforward," Susannah offered. "Perhaps when Stavros gets the language sorted out . . ."

Megan made random squiggles with her lightpen that belied the seriousness of her tone. "No, it isn't, I'm sure it isn't. I just can't find the key. Like when I called Liphar's thinking 'sophisticated,' I meant 'modern,' really. I mean, it *looks* straight-forward, like a grade-school text: your simple pretechnical soci-ety, handcraft-oriented, the usual priestly caste, the elaborate guild organization, what you'd call medieval in the old Earth sense, minus the feudal system. But I can't . . . how can I describe this?" She paused, searching. "There's no innocence in their eyes, like when you see a child on the street with a hundred-year-old face. The Sawls are . . . worldly, is that it? Nothing seems to surprise them, even us, dropping on them out of the sky. All my observations say primitive, but my instincts keep yelling, 'old, old!' Yet they seem resourceful and, god knows, energetic, so if their culture is so old, what's held them back?"

She dropped her chin to her chest in an exasperated slump. "You know," she continued, "Deep down, I just can't help thinking that the real problem is *me*. It's been a long time since I've worked with a *living* culture. I mean, maybe my talent is confined to excavations and artifacts. Bones. A little shard of pottery, a well-preserved petroglyph. Inanimate objects." She pushed back her glasses, rubbed her eyes. "A stone hide-scraper isn't going to mislead you intentionally by disguising itself as, oh, say, a water bowl. I mean, what in hell did I think I was doing, so late in life, schlepping all the way out here for the sake of one more book nobody'll read!"

Susannah set aside her magnifier. Megan was spinning herself deeper into the vortex of her depression than usual. "This is nonsense," she began gently. "The Min Kodeh are very much alive and your study of them is considered a classic." She paused, then added significantly, "As well as a best-seller."

"That was years ago, and the Min Kodeh made sense to me."

"But the Min are far less Terran than the Sawls."

"Maybe that's the problem." Megan smiled bitterly. "So close and yet so far?"

"The Sawls will make sense to you, Meg. It just takes time."

"And we got plenty of that," McPherson threw in from her slouch in the recliner.

"Here. Look." Susannah dug among her sample bags and pulled out two desiccated cuttings. One was bulbous and spiny, the other curled and delicate like a fern. "Normally, I wouldn't even classify these two in the same subphylum, but Stavros assures me that the Sawls use the same word for both of them. So who's right? Him? Me? Neither of us? Only time will tell."

McPherson hummed a soapy tune and slouched deeper into her chair.

"Time is useless if you can't even concentrate!" Megan returned. "All this snow and being cooped up all the time . . . !"

"The snow will stop." Susannah summoned her every ounce of conviction and presented the sad dry fern-thing as if it were a candle in the darkness. "This is the best proof we have that the sun will come out. There will be a spring."

But Megan preferred to remain inconsolable. She slumped into silence, chewing on the tip of the lightpen in her fist. The sketchscreen sat forgotten at her elbow. Glancing at it, Susannah noted block capitals scrawled in the margins of the meticulously arranged guild charts. Along one side the letters read, seemingly irrelevantly: "NO WEAPONS. NO WEAPONS. NO?" Along the other, filling the entire margin, marched huge letters reading merely: "WEATHER??"

"Weather, yeah," Susannah murmured, an unconscious echoing that undercut her own offer of hope. *If this weather doesn't break soon, both our tempers and our productivity will be shot to hell*. In the silence, she heard the odd rumbling come and go again. *The wind*, she reminded herself. *Just the wind*.

3

The runner in the tunnel slowed as the grade steepened. His lungs sucked at the cold air in short hard gasps and coughed back puffs of pale mist into the near darkness. His gait was sloppy, his brown face wet with exertion. He had loosed the fastenings on his furs so that his heavy layers flapped about like sodden half-furled sails. He gripped the thong of his blue amulet between bared teeth to prevent its lashing against his chest. At a narrow turn, he tripped on a tongue of rock thrusting through the slick ice, caught himself clumsily, then pushed still harder up the slope.

Ahead, smoother ledges of rock broke the floor ice, climbing in low wide tiers like age-worn steps. Pale gray light washed in to ease the gloom. The icicled ceiling grew steadily higher until, at the top of the grade, the tunnel ended in an arching portal of ice, drifted with heavy mounds of snow. The runner staggered into a high circular well bounded by white-crusted walls. A few large snowflakes floated across his dazed stare. He stuck out his tongue to catch them, then grabbed up a handful of fresh snow to quench his thirst. The deep well was open to the sky, its walls built of carefully fitted blocks of ice. Its floor was a flat white arena. In the center rose a giant conical rock, with a hole piercing its blunt tip. Beyond, opposite the tunnel mouth, a second neatly formed ice arch broke the curve of the wall to admit a steep flight of stone steps. Towering above the top of the wall loomed the sheer snow-swept face of a cliff.

The runner stumbled through thigh-deep powder and gained the bottom step. He lifted one foot to begin the climb, then sank to his knees in the snow. Without pausing for breath, he threw back his head and shouted into the cliff face. His cry ricocheted upward, amplified into a roar of summons.

18

The echoes died into silence. The runner knelt panting in the snow. Then a single voice answered, and a hooded face peered out from a ledge high above the runner's head. He leaned back, squinting up the cliff face, and signaled with one frantic arm. A hundred feet higher, where the single steep zigzag of steps split to climb in opposing directions, a wider ledge filled up with inquiring faces. Embroidered sleeves flapped, fingers pointed. The runner could hear them calling to him all at once, and he waved again and bellowed louder, querulous in his exhaustion. On the lower ledge, the single face withdrew and rewarded him with the slap slap sound of feet hurrying toward him down the stairs.

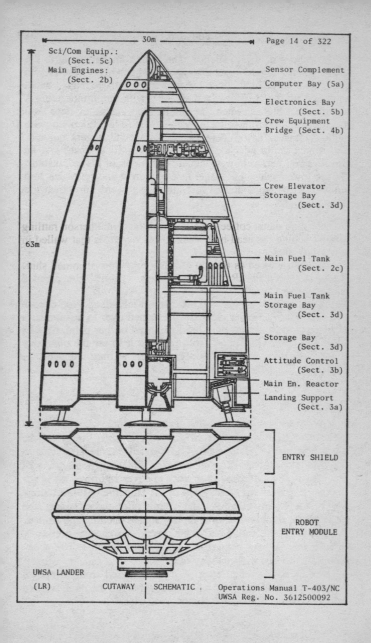

— 30m —

Sci/Com Equip.:
(Sect. 5c)
Main Engines:
(Sect. 2b)

63m

Sensor Complement

Computer Bay (5a)

Electronics Bay
(Sect. 5b)

Crew Equipment

Bridge (Sect. 4b)

Crew Elevator
Storage Bay
(Sect. 3d)

Main Fuel Tank
(Sect. 2c)

Main Fuel Tank
Storage Bay
(Sect. 3d)

Storage Bay
(Sect. 3d)

Attitude Control
(Sect. 3b)

Main En. Reactor

Landing Support
(Sect. 3a)

ENTRY SHIELD

ROBOT
ENTRY MODULE

UWSA LANDER
(LR)   CUTAWAY   SCHEMATIC.   Operations Manual T-403/NC
                                           UWSA Reg. No. 3612500092

4

"There's no damn coffee cups!" complained McPherson rattling around behind the head-high stack of plastic crates that walled in the galley area.

Susannah winced as the top of the storage box slammed shut. Rattle, rattle, slam. Rattle, rattle, slam. "Ron!" she pleaded finally. "Have mercy!"

"If you'd washed one the last time, McPherson, you'd have one this time," Megan gloated. She leaned over to Susannah, a large intricately carved blue bead balanced on her palm. "Did I show you this? Our friend Liphar slipped it to me the other day in what seemed like a fit of concern for my welfare. For luck, he said—I think. 'Khem' is luck, isn't it?"

"I think so."

"That word shows up about six times in the traditional greeting pattern."

McPherson stomped out of the galley, muttering, and headed across the work space toward the litter of dirty mugs on the uncovered Sled's dashboard. She twisted her healthy cherub features into a series of quick frowns, imitating Megan so well that Susannah bent back to her work to cover a guffaw. It did not improve the working atmosphere of the Underbelly to encourage McPherson's clowning. As the young pilot passed under the main hatch, she glanced up at the big square opening and smiled.

"Visitor!" she called out to the others, her cheer restored.

Susannah sat back resignedly. "Seventeen hundred. The work-day seems to end earlier every day."

Over the rim of the hatch, a neatly creased trouser leg appeared, then a second, and a face that surveyed the three women below with mock caution. "Is the coast clear?"

21

Megan's face sagged. "If it's the Commander you're avoiding, Emil, she's busy composing."

"Isn't she composed enough already?" At Megan's answering glower, the man laughed, straightened and dropped gracefully to the ground. The fall of nearly four meters made landing upright a rather showy feat even in the lower gravity of Fiix, especially for a middle-aged man.

"Forgot to warn you, Emil." Susannah grinned. "I'm not much at setting broken limbs—mostly I do research."

"There *is* an elevator, Emil," remarked Megan mordantly, nodding towards the central shaft that housed the Lander's magnetic lift.

"But that would be easy, my dear Megan," the man replied lightly. "And boring besides." The fine net of wrinkles from his permanent suntan smoothed into a manicured smile. The tan was fading toward a sickly yellow, but paler circles remained around his blue eyes where sungoggles had marked him with an owlish expression. He tugged his impeccable sportsman's sweater into place and rubbed his hands together with relish. "Light I bring to your dull day, ladies, relief to your boredom!"

"So who's bored?" grumped Megan.

The man grinned, unperturbed. "Monsieur Emil, *le plus grand chef des dix-neuf mondes*, will prepare a feast for your evening delectation!"

McPherson cheered, balancing a load of coffee mugs between chin and forearm.

"What did you fleece them out of this time, Clausen?" Megan inquired sourly. She shifted her chair around to face him head on.

Susannah gave her full attention to the large twig that formed a scaly brown S against the white tabletop. *Tilting at windmills again, Meg,* she warned silently, as she watched her friend fall into her automatic pattern of assault on the expedition's true power heavyweight. It was Susannah's choice to treat Clausen with respect, the most pragmatic approach, since she then received the same from him in return. But as a beloved treasure of the Academic Left, Megan Levy could not let a megacorporate representative go unchallenged. Susannah suspected that it was only Megan's newsworthy reputation (plus the corporation's public relations fiction of government sponsorship) that had overcome political opposition and won the vocal anthropologist a place in the expedition.

Clausen remained genial, hands at ease in smart, suede-trimmed pockets. "My dear Dr. Levy, I merely offered an appropriate exchange. Your little Sawls are well versed in the intricacies of commerce." He came and stood before Megan, smiling. "I had noticed, you see, that your young friend Liphar was particularly enamored of a certain implement in my possession. It seems that in his priestly studies, the fellow has learned how to write."

McPherson dumped her coffee mugs in the galley and came back crowing with delight. "That old pen of yours, right, Emil? You fobbed that crummy old pen off on him!"

Clausen swung to focus on this more appreciative audience. "A *fountain* pen, McP. A rare and valuable antique. Like Dr. Levy and myself."

"Speak for yourself, Clausen," Megan returned, but one hand strayed unconsciously to her short gray hair. "And how do you think Liphar will like his deal when this antique ceases to write?"

"Status as an antique is proof of one's longevity." Clausen smiled. "Is it not, Meg?"

Susannah reached to pat Megan's fisted hand. "It's all right, Meg. The Sawls make ink. No reason why it shouldn't work in Emil's pen just as well as Terran ink." She stretched and attempted to change the subject. "Listen, Emil, have you noticed how quiet it is out there?"

But Clausen was busy affecting deep personal injury. "I was greatly fond of that pen, Megan. It's seen me through the doldrums of nine expeditions. I even showed the little fellow how to clean and refill it."

McPherson bounced at his elbow. "What'd you get for it?"

Clausen licked his lips comically, blue eyes raised in ecstasy. "The dear boy talked that terrifying mother of his out of a brace of those pheasanty birds she raises up there in a black pit where no self-respecting bird should survive."

McPherson celebrated with rude slurping sounds.

"Sounds delicious," Susannah agreed.

"Those birds are normally reserved for high ceremonial occasions in the guild halls," Megan complained.

"Is that so?" Clausen returned innocently. "Well, that's your specialty, not mine, but if that's the case, then the least we can do is enjoy them with high ceremony. A little ritual sparks any meal, eh? Isn't that what table manners are all about?"

Megan rose once again to his bait. "Dammit, Emil, every-

thing you don't define in terms of profit, you define in terms of
your stomach!''

"Two worthy currencies!" Clausen chortled slyly.

McPherson jeered noisily. "What about earlier when you were
reading us a whole lecture about the politics of food, huh,
Meggies?''

Susannah abandoned all hope of working and began to pack
her specimens away in neatly labeled plastic envelopes. "Come
on, Meg. Ease up. You'll be just as glad for some fresh meat as
we will. Besides, Liphar'll run that pen down to one of his
craftsy older siblings and they'll get a whole work cycle's worth
of entertainment out of trying to reproduce it. That cousin of his
in the Glassblowers' Guild will probably have a fine line of glass
pens available in the Market in no time.''

Clausen considered. "Maybe I should demand a percentage.''

"Paid in foodstuffs.'' Susannah grinned. "No currency here,
remember.''

"Except those stones they're always passing around,'' added
McPherson.

Megan drummed her fingers, dangerously close to another
tantrum. "Official policy is quite explicit in these matters. We
are forbidden to interfere with alien technologies in any way.''

"Quit whining, Meg,'' Clausen yawned. "It's a pen, not a
starship.'' He tossed a smirk in Susannah's direction to see if it
would be returned.

Megan's fist pounded the table. The plastic sample bags jumped
around. Several cascaded to the floor. "It's not the pen,'' she
roared, "it's the principle!''

"Oh. Principles.'' Clausen raised a satirical eyebrow.

Megan rounded on Susannah. "You want to know why I've
had so little experience with living extraterrestrial cultures? It's
guys like this one, with their fast ships and their big corporate
money—they're always there first, hauling in their military and
their machinery, digging up the place until there's nothing left
but slag heaps and mining saloons!''

"Mmmm,'' Susannah replied. She wished that Megan would
not consider her an automatic ally in these confrontations with
Clausen.

"Well?!?''

"Well, Meg, I think that's a little black-and-white, the way
you put it.'' Susannah tried to sound placating, but her determined neutrality only goaded Megan further.

"And you call yourself a xenoscientist? You'll be sorry, you'll see!" Drawing herself up to her most righteous posture, she leveled an accusing finger at the grinning Clausen. "His work here is in direct conflict with ours, Susannah. His very presence on a First Contact expedition is an affront to the scientific integrity of the mission!"

"As well as a prime factor in its funding," added Clausen dryly.

Susannah gazed at Megan steadily. "Sure, I call myself a xenoscientist, which means to me that I collect and observe, and in my case, do a little doctoring when I'm needed. What I don't do is legislate morality."

Megan threw up her hands in disgust. "Glib! *Glib!*"

Susannah shook her head stubbornly. "You have to take it as it comes, Meg. He's here, right? We can't very well tie him up and lock him in a closet!"

Clausen relaxed against a landing strut. His placid smile suggested that the debate was an old and tired one which he had won many times before on many worlds, merely by waiting it out. "Civilization moves in one direction, Meg—forward. Face it, our very presence here, just the seven of us in our shiny metal ship, interferes with the Sawls' technology. Before my first mine is sunk, even before my claim is staked, those little brown folk have a brand-new view of their universe, simply because we appeared in it, out of the heavens. That one event will change them more than any number of mines and machines. It has to. They may be primitive, but they don't seem stupid."

Megan gave up and relapsed into beleaguered gloom. Clausen opened his mouth to deal a final blow, then lost interest as he spotted Susannah's sample bags. He dragged a crate over to her side of the table to pick through the cuttings she had discarded. He crushed one leaf against his palm and held it to his nose with a hopeful sniff.

Susannah could not help smiling. In pursuit of food, Clausen was at his most Gallic and charming. "What do you need, Emil?"

"Would you believe rosemary?"

McPherson drifted over to lean against his shoulder with a rakish grin. "So where's the Ethiopian Prince?"

"You mean Tay?" Sniffing at another sample, Clausen jabbed a blunt finger upward. "I came down here especially to argue with you all because I got bored of listening to Taylor argue with CRI."

Megan rose, stretched, moved away from the table, away from Clausen. "Sort of a Zen sport, arguing with a computer."

Clausen showed small white teeth. "Exactly. You think Taylor's pulling out his curly little hairs for nothing?" He appropriated a small dried sprig and wrapped it neatly in a monogrammed handkerchief. "Actually, what he's doing now is refusing to believe her most recent weather data."

McPherson snickered fondly. "Again?" But Megan glanced up, alert.

"Which is particularly perverse of him this time," Clausen continued, "considering what her data says."

"Yeah," grumped the little pilot. "Snow yesterday, snow today, and tomorrow, for a real change . . ." She trumpeted a fanfare. "*Snow*!"

"Not exactly." Clausen rocked gently on his crate. "It's stopped snowing."

McPherson bolted upright. "What?"

Four long strides brought Megan back to the table. Susannah spread her arms wide in disbelief. "The quiet. Of course! That's what it was! My god, Emil! You stand there for ten minutes rapturing about pheasants when it's *stopped snowing*?"

A smug grin stretched Clausen's jaw.

McPherson threw herself out of her chair with a victory yell and dashed behind the crate wall into the bunk area. Drawers and lockers crashed open and shut. "Where's my therm-suit? Anybody seen my therm-suit?"

Clausen turned his grin on Susannah, reveling in his carefully orchestrated stir, but her attention moved past him with a smile of welcome toward the entry tunnel.

A young Sawl stood there, breathless, cast in dark miniature against the mirrored arc of the giant cylinder. His smile was insecure. One hand clutched at a blue leather bag tied to a thong around his neck. His thick woolen cape was tossed hastily over one shoulder. His beltless tunic had twisted around his childlike body as he ran. He struggled to unbind his arms, then shoved his thick ringlets out of his face in an attempt to make himself presentable.

"Liphar! Speak of the devil!" Clausen boomed. "How's the publishing biz?"

"How, pleezhe?" the young man stammered.

"Have you written the Great Sawlian Novel yet, my boy?"

Liphar smiled again, uncertain.

"Oh, Emil!" Susannah threw Clausen a disapproving maternal frown and held out her hand to the young Sawl as his brown eyes mournfully sought her aid. But her halting attempts in the brusque syllables of his own tongue only puzzled him further. His answer began as a bemused spreading of his open palms and ended in a violent gesture of dismay as he recalled the purpose of his visit. With a yelp, he ran to the table, punctuating incomprehensible chatter with equally mysterious arm-wavings, grabbed Susannah's field pack and thrust it at her. One brown hand snatched at the sample bags while the other pulled frantically at her sleeve. His small pointed features ran through an entire vocabulary of distress. Susannah stood open-mouthed as he continued to tug at her, then slowly she began to stow the bags in her pack. Liphar nodded eagerly, as one would to encourage a child.

"Maybe someone's sick up there," Megan suggested. Her hands dwarfed the young man's shoulders as she reached to still his hysteria. "Liphar, is anyone sick? *Sick*?"

"He's not deaf, Meg," Clausen reminded her.

"But they have their own healers, don't they, Meg?" Susannah chewed her lip. "Maybe it's Stavros. Liphar, I'll come right up. Just let me get my medikit."

Liphar pondered this closely, then shook his head so violently that his long brown curls whipped against his cheeks. "No 'Tavros!" he exclaimed. He pointed a finger at each Terran in rapid succession. "You, you, you, you. Under'tand? Very danger!" He squirmed out of Megan's grasp and ran about slapping at the crates and furniture. "This, this, this thing, out! You, out!" He gathered up piles of printout and clothing from the ground, including the discarded rubbish lying nearby, and tossed it all in the direction of the entrance. When two or three armloads failed to spur his stunned audience into action, he halted, panting, and stared at them over the heap of clutter, his eyes begging their instant comprehension. When they still did not react, he dove back to the table to shove a load into Megan's arms, then recommenced the frantic stuffing of Susannah's pack, railing all the while at high volume.

Susannah grabbed at him. "Liphar. Liphar! Slow down!" She summoned her best bedside manner as she pinned his hands gently to the table. "What do you need? Please explain slowly."

McPherson reappeared from behind the crate wall, shrugging on her white therm-suit. "What the hell's with him?"

"He seems to want us to pack up and leave," Susannah murmured.

McPherson yanked up her zipper with a sage nod. "Oh, right. Ten meters of snow on the ground, the ship encased in ice, and he wants us out on the double. He got any bright ideas how?"

"Ron, will you shut up a minute!" Megan leaned across the table to stare at Liphar intently. "Where is damn Stavros when we need him to translate? . . . Why would they want us to leave all of a sudden?"

Susannah looked thoughtful. "There's one difference between now and any other point in the last six weeks: it's stopped snowing."

"So?"

The mention of snow set off another of Liphar's violent noddings. His face promising patience, he pried his hands loose. Immediately, they began sketching vast dramas in the air. "Okay," he announced. "Snow 'top, yes? Okay. Now, you hear." The brown hands rose and fell like seas. "Snow gone, big water come, oh so much!" His hands stretched wide, then rushed together to grapple madly with each other. "Han chauk! Big fight come, no good! Danger!" His tongue clicked sharply under furrowed brows.

"This is weird," commented McPherson.

"Puts on a good show," said Clausen.

"Liphar, who's going to fight?" Susannah pursued.

Liphar moaned, his hands fainting in frustration. "O rek!" he expostulated finally. "O malaka rek! Han chauk!"

"Rek," Susannah repeated softly.

"Rek," said Megan. "Isn't that . . ."

Susannah nodded. "Pretty sure. . . . You know, that fits right in with Stavros's interpretation of the friezes."

Clausen fished out a silver penknife and began to clean his nails.

"Will somebody clue me in?" McPherson demanded. "What's this rak?"

"*Rek*," Megan corrected primly. "The gods. He's saying the gods are going to war."

McPherson rolled her eyes. "Well, that's useful. For that he's going to throw us out of here?"

Weng Tsi-Hua appeared at the door of her curtained cubicle. "Is there some problem I should be informed about?"

"Liphar claims we're in danger," Megan explained.

"From the gods." McPherson giggled. "Boy, am I scared!"

"It's stopped snowing, Commander," Susannah reported, still gazing intently at the little Sawl. His sincere concern was unmistakable. "Big water," she repeated. "You know, according to Stavros, the Sawls believe that when the gods go to war, the weather turns bad. Do I have it right, Meg?"

"You have *Stav's* interpretation right," Megan conceded.

"He's saying it gonna get worse?" McPherson exclaimed, looking to Clausen. "Didn't you just say . . . ?"

Clausen chuckled. "Worry not, my friends. CRI's new data promises sun and fun. Fortunately for our peace of mind, our ship's computer is not in the habit of consulting the local deities."

McPherson fastened the cuffs of her therm-suit. "Well, I don't know about anyone else, but I'm heading out!"

"I think it would make Liphar feel better if we *all* went out," said Susannah. "Is that all right, Commander?"

Weng nodded graciously. "Though it is not the best idea, Dr. James, I think we could all do with some fresh air and exercise."

"I'll stay with the ship, Weng," Clausen offered. "Taylor and I have business upstairs."

In the disorganized scurry for boots and therm-suits, Susannah kept one eye on Liphar, who danced impatiently at the tunnel entrance. *Why is he so frantic?* she wondered, and then a not entirely unrelated thought occurred to her. *If the silence was the snow and the wind stopping, then what in hell was that rumbling noise?*

5

Outside, the cold land waited. The snow-swept cliffs towered above the smothered plain. The mountains behind bore their crushing weight patiently, snow layered on ice layered on snow. The stillness was like an intake of breath.

Then, overhead, the cloud cover lightened. Paler fissures edged wormlike across the stubborn gray. Billows churned, slowly at first, like a ponderous machine gathering momentum. The frigid air softened. A spear of light dazzled the clifftops with pink and amber. The clouds thinned as a breeze sprang up, revealing widening patches of turquoise sky. A low red sun burned through the last shreds of haze. Brilliant orange set the white cliffs glowing as if they were on fire. At the scarp's eastern tip, a solitary spire of rock blazed like a red-and-white sentinel. Below, the vast rolling plain glittered as the snow moistened under a warm southerly wind.

The cave mouths erupted with activity. From rows of dark recesses high up the cliff face, the Sawls poured out into the sudden sun. Wrapped in layers of leather and wool, their eyes slitted against the light, they tested the wind and hefted their tools, chattering among themselves. Long lines moved briskly along the ledges connecting the four levels of caves, some snaking upward toward the very top of the scarp, some hurrying downward, armed with brush brooms and wooden picks to clear the snow and ice from the ascending steps and trails. Their chatter carried on the wind, high and urgent, mingling with the starting phrases of a work chant, begun at the top of the cliff and relayed down the lines of workers to the bottom. The rhythm of the chant was brisk, the tune melodic. At each arched cave mouth, a small group remained to scour the entry ledge and sing out an antiphonal chorus.

One woman, taller than the rest, thin and hard, set her crew to work, then leaned her pick against the snow-drifted rock to shed a heavy leather outer garment. She stood for a moment, her seamed face set into a frown, listening as the wind's desert yowl delivered the dull thunder of avalanches from the southern mountain range. Her upper lip gleamed with moisture. She blotted her forehead on a knitted sleeve, her frown deepening as she scanned the greenish sky, nostrils flared. She thrust an arm forward, shoved back her sleeve and bent the arm at the elbow, lining it up to measure the height of the crimson sunball that hugged the western horizon. Then she turned northward, to stare for a long time across the plain. The distant wave of mountains was blurred by clouds of steam off the melting snowfields, tinged sunset pink and amber. The woman squinted, straining to see, her grim face caught in a tension between wariness and resignation. Finally, as if she had been resisting it, she let her eyes rest thoughtfully on the blunted cone shape of the Terran Lander where it sat out on the plain, its broad base sunk in thirty feet of snow and ice. From where she stood on the second tier of caves, the Lander's narrow nose was nearly at eye level, though it was a healthy half mile away. The late sun glinted dully on scoured metal broken here and there with patches of a more reflective surface. Her eyes flicked eastward to the sentinel spire of red rock now shedding its damp blanket of white, then back to the Lander. The crooked arm went up again to measure: height, width. The woman muttered to herself, her mouth tight.

The man swinging his pick beside her stopped and joined her at the trail's edge. He nodded at the Lander, made a speculative comment. She shook her head in reply. He nudged her elbow, spread his palms, then held up four fingers. The woman sniffed, considering. The man dug into a hidden pocket and hauled forth a fistful of small white stones, flat and smooth from long handling. He counted, put a few away, held the others out to her. She shook her head, grinning faintly, held up six fingers. The man chuckled, dug again and returned one more stone to his palm. She looked, then finally nodded in agreement and reached for her pick but did not immediately raise it. For a moment more, she and her companion regarded the alien metal shape in silence. Then they exchanged brief, dubious glances and returned to their work.

At the foot of the cliffs, the sound of water could be heard, running beneath the snow.

6

The cubicle was low-ceilinged, a narrow pie wedge atop the starboard engine, tucked inside the Lander's curving shell. In the sickish glow of a double bank of screens and holographic monitors, Taylor Danforth hunched over his console, his long legs cramped into the abbreviated space beneath the keypad. One fist supported his forehead. The other pushed fitfully at knotted muscles in the small of his back.

"Run that by once more, CRI," he muttered wearily.

The center screen blanked and flicked back to dim life as data chattered across it. Danforth stared, glanced at the dimensional wind vector map floating above the holo pad to his right, rubbed his eyes, then returned them to the screen in front of him, wagging his head in reflex negation. "Heat flux profile's building too fast," he sighed. "CRI, forget the cross sections. Give me the hemispherics on holo. I want to try this station by station, just the raw numbers."

"Time period?" The computer offered no comment on Danforth's implied rejection of its data analysis. Its voice mode was thin and scratchy, humanized by undertones of strained patience.

"Just the last five ship's days, local conditions first."

The screens blanked obediently and the holographic vector display vanished, to be replaced by a slowly revolving black-and-white image of a cloud-draped sphere. A broad cut of clear sky crossed the equatorial regions on a diagonal running northwest to southeast. In the northern hemisphere, gray patches of ocean were visible through scattered breaks in the clouds. The geographical features not hidden by clouds were whitened into indistinction by the heavy snow blanket, except in one anomalous area in the southern hemisphere, where a circular upthrust of mountains remained oddly free of both snow and clouds. Between these southern mountains and the clear equatorial band, the holograph was incomplete in several sectors, so that the image was of a partial sphere, a planet missing square chunks of its anatomy.

New figures marched across the center monitor.

"Home station L-Alpha," the computer announced. "Position, Lander. 24.09 degrees north latitude, 31.66 degrees east longitude. Activated ship's day 119, Landing plus one. Functional to present, L plus 47.5, 1600 hours."

Danforth stirred restlessly. "Spare me the calendar, CRI. Just give me the readings. Display the six-week averages on Four."

Ranks of numbers built rapidly across the center screen. A more leisurely listing began on a screen to the left. Watching, Danforth worried his full lower lip with the tip of his tongue. "Include surface radiation with each listing." His hand left off massaging his forehead long enough to tap briefly at the keypad. "Six weeks' average temp, minus eighteen C., and look at it now," he growled. "Okay, store that for the time being and move on. Wait. Shit. Those high winds are back again."

"Excuse me, Dr. Danforth, but Mr. Ibiá is requesting immediate clearance."

"Tell him I'm busy."

"I have done so, sir, but Mr. Ibiá insists that it's urgent."

"Patch him through to the Underbelly." Danforth grimaced, focused on the screens. His fingers hovered over the keypad, indecisive with frustration.

"I have done *that* also, sir, but no one is answering downstairs."

Danforth's hands curled into fists. "So where's Weng? Am I the only one dumb enough to be always available? Tell Stavros you couldn't raise me either."

After a minute's hesitation, the computer admitted, "I already told him you were in your office, sir. He seems very concerned to speak with someone in the Lander. Anyone."

"Tell him I'm in the head!" Danforth's tone threatened retribution. "Move on to L-Beta."

"Is that an order, sir?"

The big man's slippered feet wrestled with each other dangerously. "Don't get sullen with me, CRI. I haven't got time for it. L-Beta?"

"Weather station L-Beta." The computer's words were noticeably clipped. "Position, 25.18 north, 32.46 east. Activa—"

"CRI, just the readings."

New figures slammed onto the screen. Danforth glared at them and entered his notes in silence, working at the pad as if it were resisting his touch. "Where the hell is that south wind getting all its energy? Display the moisture flux alongside, please." He sucked his cheek disconsolately. "Bottomed out. Damn!" He shook his head. "Go on."

"Station L-Gamma. Posit—"

"Goddammit, CRI!" Danforth's hand swung and stopped millimeters above the keypad. His swivel stool screeched with the sudden movement. "L-Gamma's been dysfunctional for two weeks! Get on with it!"

All ten screens went dead and the holographic sphere blinked out, leaving the planetologist fuming in the dark. There was a pause like a sigh, then the sphere popped back into glowing, revolving life and the screens regained their columns of data. "L-Delta," DRI continued stolidly.

Danforth scanned the figures like an alchemist in search of an elusive spell. His head nodded heavily. His shoulders drew up round his neck as if seeking to deny their natural broadness, thereby perhaps avoiding some part of the burden currently weighing on them. "Is L-Delta showing any signs of sensor malfunction?" he complained. "Its temp reading hasn't moved a degree in seventy-two hours."

"Any malfunction would be noted with the data," CRI returned crisply. "This new activity is highly localized. You will note that I *am* registering sharp temp increases from both the western stations, Epsilon and Iota."

The door at Danforth's back slid open noisily. He half turned on his stool, blinking into the glare of the corridor lights. "I'm busy," he growled.

"For Christ's sake, Tay, pull your nose away from your instruments long enough to take a look outside!" Clausen touched the light pad by the door. The room remained in semidarkness. He clucked his tongue and crowded into the cubicle. "Your lights are broken."

"I said I'm busy."

Plastic clattered as Clausen tripped on a discarded meal tray. "Greetings, CRI, my little metal chickadee."

The computer's voice brightened. "Greetings! The reference is to an ancient celluloid . . ."

Danforth groaned.

"You really ought to get out there, Tay," Clausen pursued.

"I'm perfectly aware of what's going on outside," Danforth snapped. "Zero to seventy in eight-six minutes."

"Excellent acceleration for an old car." grinned the prospector.

"Emil, it doesn't make sense."

"Sense in whose terms? Come on, Tay, worry it to death later. The sun's out . . . the sun, which you haven't seen since you set foot on this planet, which is going to set in another sixteen hours and which will then not reappear for another two weeks. Get out and get it while you can! Up in the Caves, the natives are restless. You can almost hear the drums beating." Clausen paused to let his sly grin build. "You'll feel right at home, Tay."

Despite himself, the black man smiled. "My ancestors were ruling desert kingdoms when yours were still trying to figure out which end of a stone ax to use!" He arched his back and stretched, giving in to the prospector's intrusion. "So how're you coming with the radar imaging? Any intimations of paydirt?"

"That's better." Clausen chuckled, then rubbed his hands together. "I do have some promising sites located. Resolution's only decent, at about fourteen meters, but it beats all that blank white in the photo survey. The altimetry and gravity anomaly data seem to correlate interestingly with a few of them." He edged around Danforth's seated bulk to crank open the metal shutters covering the cubicle's single port. They squealed softly on their pivots.

"Oil," CRI muttered absently as late sunlight flooded the tiny space. Bright amber bars slashed high across the smudged gray walls, picking out craterlike dents and graffiti consisting largely of numbers and scrawled Greek letters. Danforth gazed at the liquid warmth as if it were an alien invader. "Oil," the computer repeated.

"Regular use," Clausen corrected. "And, CRI . . . the paint's chipping on your keypad."

"Mr. Clausen, there is no paint on my keypad."

"Figure of speech, CRI. Full of subtle *human* connotations." When the machine remained silent, Clausen added, "The proper response to that remark is 'Up yours, Clausen.' "

"That would be the *human* response, I believe," said CRI.

"*Touché*! You're learning, my girl!"

"Christ, Emil, don't encourage her." Danforth twisted his stool away from the invading sunlight and stretched his legs out through the open door. His dark head sank low into his shoulders. "Really isn't fair," he mused.

"Fair? What's fair?" Clausen leaned against the console, watching the planetologist's back. His eyelids drooped, a watchful lizard sunning on a rock. Though his arms lay folded casually across his chest, his fingers twitched.

"Fair," replied Danforth, "is arriving at a planet and finding some correlation between speculations based on the probe data and what the climate actually turns out to be. Fair is when preliminary modeling offers some success in forecasting. Right now I'd be doing better if I'd brought along an almanac, or a wand and a pointy hat!"

The prospector repressed an impatient sigh. "Relax. It's obvious that the probe wasn't here long enough to record an entire seasonal cycle."

"The probe!" Danforth sneered. "The damn probe lied!"

"Why, Taylor. How quaint and anthropomorphic. And you object to my small attempts to civilize our back-model queen of circuitry."

"Ecch. The only ship's brain in the Colonies with an entire unit devoted to cultural trivia." The black man shook his head disgustedly. "Look, Emil: you want a profitable lithium operation on this planet—how can you pretend this doesn't concern you? Based on the probe data . . ."

"We've been over this . . ." Clausen began.

". . . there shouldn't be ten meters of snow in the first place!"

". . . and over, and over . . ."

"All right. So I spend six weeks chasing whatever indeterminable it is that's been keeping the temp down and the humidity up. Just when I think maybe I got it psyched, the damn temp shoots up, the moisture bottoms out, and we've got a major thaw on our hands!" He spread his palms in exasperation. "Not a hint of it in my long-range data. Emil, how can it happen so *fast*? The heat's even coming from the wrong direction!"

The lizard eyes narrowed as Clausen yawned. "Snow happens. Thaws, too. Assume an unusually harsh winter."

"Gods, Emil, don't you care about anything except what goes on *under* the ground? How about a glacier in the Amazon? Would that perturb you?"

Clausen's tongue flicked, a lizard grin. "It might, if it got in the way of my prospecting."

ICARUS, Vol. 341, No. 4, 78 - 103   292 - 2063

TERRESTRIAL PLANET IN BYRNHAM CLUSTER

J. Sundqvist (MIT, Sol)
T. Danforth   (UW, A.Cent)
T. Riley   (MIT, Sol)
O.D. Bryan   (MIT, Sol)

Received 023-2062, accepted 002-2063.

*A KO subgiant system in Byrnham's Clu
ster was visited by UWSA Deep Probe 6
to investigate a large (radius = 8300
km) terrestrial planet with a massive
(surface pressure 2 bars) oxygen bearing atmosphere, discovered by previous
survey probe. Analysis of flyby remote
sensing confirms a low-density (3.1 un-
compressed) and slow (40 day period)
retrograde rotation. Surface geologi-
cal features are consistent with weak
erosion in extreme desert conditions.
Results suggest a surface mineralogy
dominated by light metals, especially
Al/Mg silicates.*

INTRODUCTION

Byrnham's Cluster has been the subject of intense study for many years because of the opportunity to observe Pop.II systems first hand (see re-
views, Gilbert et al., 2029; Wolf and Akai, 2051).
We discuss in this paper observations and model studies of an unusually large terrestrial planet in a
system visited by UWSA Deep Probe 6. In particular,
several interesting surface mineralogies can occur
in the absence of the heavier metals that usually
form the major ore minerals in the crusts of Pop.I
planets. Lack of iron increases the importance of
magnesium in ore-forming rocks. The role of the
lighter metals in the formation of the volcanic ter-
rains visible in the probe imagery is particularly
crucial in determining the characteristics of the

Danforth pulled himself upright on his stool, heatedly ticking off items on his fingers. "It'd be real easy to dismiss this as winter and spring if we could expect true seasons here, but you know better than that: axial tilt of a mere eight degrees, 281-day orbit nearly circular with the planet right now as close to her sun as her orbit allows, massive atmosphere, slow rotation . . .''

". . . moderate greenhouse effect," Clausen recited tiredly. "Short distance from a cool star that's starting to go red giant and heating up as it moves off from the Main Sequence, blah, blah, blah . . .''

". . . even with the planet's month-long day, the winds should keep the surface temp from varying much, certainly not as much as zero to seventy! Perihelion was thirty-six hours ago. My model says the global average should be 115 degrees, high summer in the desert, and here we are, socked in for six weeks under ten meters of snow! So much for the rational method!''

Clausen glanced languidly over his shoulder. Through the port shutters, the topaz sky glared hot and cloudless. His blunt fingers beat a controlled rhythm against the perfect knit of his sweater. "Look outside, Tay. It *is* high summer in the desert. Right now. Time to get up and about.''

"I didn't come here to do fucking weather, anyway!" growled the planetologist. "Spend so much time wrestling with this damn atmospheric model . . . should have been the easy part.'' He squeezed his eyes shut and surrendered to gloom. "I put my career in hock for this mission, Emil, you know that. When that probe data came in, I thought, man, this is it! A globular cluster we can—I can—get at. Planeted population II stars actually within starship range! A close-up look at a type of planetary evolution we've never been able to touch before, planets near a star going off the Main Sequence, and I'm going to be there first! So. What does it all come to? I can't even get a simple forecast model working, much less a general circulation model. And forget the macro stuff, like a nice climate model or atmospheric and planetary evolution theories, the real publishable material.''

Clausen's attempt at a sympathetic nod went unnoticed. He considered a moment, then pushed himself away from the console, tugging at invisible cuffs and cackling like a mischievious dwarf. "CRI, take a letter. It seems our boy Taylor is feeling a bit sorry for himself. Let's see . . . how does this sound?'' He cleared his throat, the lizard eyes watching Danforth carefully.

"A half a league inside the Coal Sack,
Byrnham's Cluster lies . . .
Clouds of dust and gas obscuring
Taylor's Nobel Prize.
You like it?"

Danforth's look was sour. "Dust and gas are not the problem, but sure, mock away, Emil. Your reputation was made long ago. All you've got at stake here is money."

The easy grin hardened. "All?"

Danforth raised both palms. "I know, I know. No money, no expedition. My acceptance speech will include proper and abject thanks to you and CONPLEX. Don't lecture me, Emil."

The grin fell away like a used skin. "A lecture for a lecture, my boy. You will recall that you put my career in hock as well." Clausen's hands slid into his pockets as he took advantage of the bigger man's seated position to stare down at him. "In my biz, you're only as good as your last strike, and believe me, there are closer worlds than this to go looking for lithium. I had a long list."

"Oh, right. The list. On every one of those planets, CONPLEX'd be sharing mineral rights three, four ways."

"Thirty-three percent of a sure thing beats hell out of a hundred percent of nothing."

Danforth scowled defensively. "There's lithium here. The system's history assures us of that."

"But in what quantity? How pure? How accessible? Will our industries buy it at a higher price than it costs to get it to them?"

"Come on, man! Risks are your business. You cross-checked the data when I brought the idea to you! This is a fucking huge planet! When you strike, you'll strike big!"

Clausen eyed him steadily, unspeaking.

"What, are you getting cold feet?"

Clausen blinked, slowly. "Just reminding you of your . . . our position here. One month into most prospectings, I've made my strike, staked the claim, and ordered the equipment droned in. . . . The Company is going to wonder what's taking me so long, and was I maybe crazy to advise them to buy a whole research mission for some young hotshot, on the strength of a theory."

"It's here. I know it's here."

"Like you knew the climate'd be ideal for mining?"

"Off my back, man! We share the profits, we also share the rap."

"My point precisely." The prospector laughed softly, poised ambiguously enough between ruefulness and condescension to leave Danforth at a loss. The black man retreated into disdain.

"The biggest mining conglomerate in the Colonies can afford to fund a little pure science now and then."

"We do, we do. Our Public Relations Department insists on it. But we don't usually back it up by rerouting our newest and best FTL ship which could be out making billions for us elsewhere." Clausen laid a paternal hand on the planetologist's broad shoulder. "Did you think 'pure' was something like 'fair,' my boy? If so, I have bad news for you." He lowered his voice to a sibilant whisper though his grip remained loose and amiable. "Fair is a fairy tale, and pure science went extinct years ago. This is a deal we have, Tay. You get your science, we get out lithium. It's not take-a-researcher-to-lunch." He backed off then, and smiled. "It's simple, really: CONPLEX pays for what it needs. Of course, if you should happen upon a Nobel along the way, we will happily bathe in the reflected glory. But keep your priorities straight, for your own sake."

Danforth slumped resentfully. "Didn't I make major sacrifices for economy?" He gestured around the crowded cubicle, at the tangles of flatwire snaking about his feet, at the monitors in their noncustomized racks. "Not exactly state-of-the-art, if you know what I mean."

Clausen's sigh was mild. "What an ungrateful wretch you are, Tay."

"Oh? How often have I had to sit here listening to you bitch about having to spend six weeks doing nothing but polishing your goddamned hand-sewn multimillion-dollar imported Italian climbing boots!? With a little more money, just a little, we'd have a Lander capable of more than one lousy round trip, and you could have spent those weeks in the relative comfort of the Orbiter!"

Clausen nodded tolerantly. "I'm surprised you don't blame this unfortunate weather on CONPLEX's funding level. But enough of this bickering. Tell me, Taylor, how good is your practical geology?" He dipped deep into a pocket and produced a chunk of pale granitic rock. "Know what this is?"

Danforth sulked, not looking up. "I bet you can't wait to tell me."

"You should spend more time in the field, Tay. You've been staring at those screens so long, all you can do is whine like a little old lady."

"So leave. You won't have to listen."

"Fresh air and sun would do wonders for your disposition." Clausen tossed the rock in a loop and caught it neatly. "Well, it's granite. I bring it to cheer you up. Pegmatites similar to this are a source of recoverable deposits of lepidolite. Lepidolite is a respectable lithium ore. I would be happy with lepidolite."

"You think raiding your sample box is likely to cheer me up?"

"Taylor, this is local rock. I found it in the Caves, just inside the Fourth Entrance, practically lying on the ground. Imagine what I might find up there, deep inside those cliffs, if the clever little buggers didn't manage to sidetrack me every time I think I'm getting in past the first maze of caverns. I know it goes in deeper than they'd like us to think!"

"You show me this now, *after* you rake me over the coals?" Danforth glowered. "You are one bona fide sonofabitch, Clausen."

The prospector grinned. "Just you keep that in mind."

Danforth massaged his forehead. "I'm the one who should have stayed with the Orbiter."

"Six weeks in parking orbit? That prospect amuses you? They're eating each other alive up there these days."

"Nah. Spacers are used to it. Look at Weng. She's happy as a clam sitting all day long with a plug in her ear. Plus taking up valuable computer time with her so-called compositions."

"Weng's music is actually rather interesting. If I understand her correctly, she's exploring the use of game theory as a compositional rubric."

"Nothing new," muttered Danforth.

"You wouldn't say that if you heard the results. Music of the spheres and all that. Ask CRI to play some back for you sometime." Clausen's stubby hands toyed with his hunk of rock. He held it up to the amber light flooding through the port. Minute specks glinted in tiny ragged crannies, sharp as the gleam of anticipation in the prospector's eye. "So. You ready to go out looking for some more of this?"

"Sure. You bet." Danforth swiveled back to his console without enthusiasm.

"Now."

Danforth chuckled dutifully.

"I'm quite serious, Tay."

The black man shook his head. "It'll take more time than we have till sunset to dig out one of the Sleds."

"Nope." Clausen placed the rock on the keypad, between Danforth's outstretched hands. "Because, one, the snow is melting faster than you can imagine, and two, the way B-Sled's positioned down there . . ." He paused to straighten a forefinger toward the floor. "If we dropped the force field, we could use the hot air from the Sled fans to melt an exit ramp up through the ice."

"Drop the field? Risky."

"Mmmnh."

Danforth steepled his fingers over the rock. "With the melt, we don't know how stable the icepack is."

Clausen shrugged.

Danforth pushed the rock aside. "Get McPherson to help you. She's into risking everyone's life. I've got to stick it out here, with all this new data coming in."

"Ah, Taylor. You do weary an old man's patience."

"That so?"

"And you will force me to say it, won't you?"

"Now what's that, Emil?"

Clausen's jaw twitched. "That you have something I need."

"Yeah?"

"Don't pout, Tay. It's so boring." Clausen moved sharply to the console. "CRI, local wind speeds, please."

"Variable," the computer replied. "Gusting from eighteen to thirty-five meters per second."

"That's thirty-six to seventy mph," Danforth offered automatically.

"I am well aware of that," Clausen growled.

"And I am required to remind you," CRI continued, "that although the manufacturer's safety limit for the Sleds in this atmospheric density is twenty-five meters per second, Commander Weng insists on a limit of twenty."

"Thank you, CRI." Clausen reached to cut off the computer's audio intake.

"Why did you . . . ahhh." Danforth met the other's glance with a sudden schoolboy leer. "You haven't checked this out with Weng, have you?"

The prospector matched his grin silently.

"And where is our Commander at the moment?"

"Up in the Caves."

"So? Go ahead. Go."

Clausen pursed his lips, eyes half-lidded once again. "Due to certain technicalities in the chain of command, I need proper authorization in order to instruct CRI to lower the shield."

Danforth snorted. "Why bother with technicalities? You can fox your way around CRI's programming well enough to get her to do anything you want."

"I prefer to walk the right side of legal whenever possible." Clausen lowered his head and regarded Danforth sideways. "With the Commander unavailable, you can make that authorization."

"So I can." Danforth stretched his legs, leaned back against the pockmarked wall, playing the moment, enjoying himself hugely. "She's not going to like this, you know."

"Tay, do you care? This is a minor insubordination compared to the ones you'd like to commit."

Danforth chewed his lip and glanced unnecessarily at the data screens. "One hell of a wind out there. You'll pilot?"

"Of course. You think I'd trust *you* at the stick?"

"I'm not happy about letting down the shield," Danforth began, "but since you're such a sly bastard . . ." He finished with a grin of appreciation, drew in his long legs and rose. "As Chief Scientist and Captain of the Landing Party in the Commander's absence, I hereby authorize this use of expeditionary equipment." As he stood, the cubicle became too small to hold him. Energized, he swung an abbreviated punch at the air, narrowly missing the shorter man's ear. "Well? Let's get on it, before she comes back!"

"DANFORTH!"

Out in the corridor, the magnetic lift rattled as it bumped up the Lander's central shaft with a slowness obviously maddening to its occupant.

"DANFORTH!"

The conspirators hesitated at the cubicle door. Clausen swore softly as he watched Danforth's enthusiasm twist into a scowl.

"DANFORTH, WHERE THE HELL . . . !" The stream of outrage broke off as the cage rose to level with the floor. The safety grating was slammed aside with a screech and a crash.

Clausen's easy grin reappeared on cue. "Why, Stavros, what a pleasant surprise."

A wiry young man whirled out of the lift and stormed down the corridor, dismissed Clausen with a single glance and glared up at Danforth. His thick black hair fell matted across his eyes as

if he had been tugging at it. Over soiled white ship's fatigues, he
wore a brown knitted Sawl tunic. The wool stretched tight across
his shoulders and the sleeves had been extended in an unmatch-
ing rust color to fit his longer arms. Though his ordinary height
allowed Danforth to tower over him, this did nothing to dampen
his fury. "Since when do you refuse emergency calls?"

"Couldn't have been much of an emergency, Ibiá," Danforth
drawled nastily, "since you're standing here in one piece."

Clausen stood a bit aside, wishing that someone, like the
Commander, would order Ibiá to get a decent haircut. In an
earlier colonial era, the boy would have been disciplined for
setting a bad example to the natives. Clausen's objection was
mainly aesthetic, the welfare of local populations not being high
on his list of priorities. But in addition, Ibiá was always the wild
card in the prospector's machinations. He wore his eccentric
demeanor as if in reproof of the others' willingness to observe
some measure of comfortable convention. Danforth was particularly vulnerable to this goading, perhaps afraid that successes
unorthodoxly achieved might somehow undervalue his own.
Danforth's fragile ego made him an easy target.

But Ibiá was not so easily manipulated. Clausen's pre-expedition
snooping had assured him that the boy was brilliant, that his new
translation programs represented a unique approach to computer
linguistics, but he was also, Clausen suspected, genuinely unstable. It was the prospector's usual habit to encourage such bitter
rivalries, but lately he had found it inconvenient that Danforth,
the older and far better established in reputation, could not
occasionally relax into his seniority. Instead, he rose to Ibiá's
bait every time. In his humbler moments, Clausen doubted that
even his own long-practiced diplomatic skills could effect any
resolution between two men who had hated each other from the
first day out.

Ibiá shoved damp hair back from his eyes. His skin glistened
with sweat even in the controlled dryness of the Lander's air
system. "We've got to evacuate to the Caves!" he blurted. "All
the equipment! Everything we can carry!"

Danforth gave a hard incredulous laugh.

Ibiá hesitated. The lean, stubborn angles of his face, a legacy
from the westerly side of his Mediterranean ancestry, smoothed
under his conscious effort to collect himself and pump more
credibility into his message. "We have to leave, Taylor, you
understand? We're too vulnerable down here on this plain. The
priests say . . ."

"The *priests* say?" Danforth folded his arms across his broad chest with a magisterial air. "Now let me get this straight. You want us to desert ship, uproot the entire base camp into some dank cavern, on the strength of some native dictum?"

The younger man began to pace the narrow corridor, focusing his agitation on the white-tiled floor. "Just listen to me for once, okay? The Sawls say a big storm's coming. Wind, rain, terrible flooding. They're concerned for our safety. They're making serious preparations up there, and they've warned us to do the same." His dark eyes flicked toward Danforth in a resentful pleading. "Liphar convinced the guildmasters that it's their responsibility to offer us shelter in the Caves. You think they'd sacrifice precious space if it wasn't critical?"

"You're nuts, Ibiá. You actually thought I'd buy this nonsense?"

Ibiá blinked, then gathered himself back into strained calm, as if trying to talk a moron out of doing himself harm. "Taylor, you don't know that it's nonsense. This is *their* world. You will grant that they know it a bit better than you do."

Clausen chuckled softly, understanding why Danforth found the young man so infuriating. "Tay, I share your distaste for all that smoke and sweat and dubious sanitation," he put in languidly, "but they do seem to be engaging in some rather extensive efforts to batten down the hatches up there." He nodded toward the sunlit porthole. "Take a look."

Ibiá surprised him with a grateful look in his direction.

"Impossible," countered Danforth. "There is no storm coming." He ducked back into the cubicle. "CRI, display . . ." he called, then remembered. He cut the audio back in. "Display all current weather data from the local stations, up on Six and Seven, then give me an updated short-range forecast on Eight and Nine, long-range on Ten. Oh, and restore hemispherics to holo." As the screens filled, Danforth reached through the door to grab Ibià by his knitted sleeve and drag him into the room. "Show me. Show me any indication of this monsoon you're predicting!"

"*I'm* not predicting it, the Sawls are!"

"Look at the data!" Danforth thundered. He jabbed stiff fingers at each screenful of figures, his hand slicing through the holographic image of a clearing planetary sphere. "Warm wind out of the southwest, bone-dry, temperatures up, pressure steadying . . . or are pictures easier for you?" He fiddled needlessly with the holopad's contrast controls. "See? Not a cloud in the entire hemisphere, Ibiá. Where's your precious storm? Where?"

The young man squirmed in the confining cubicle. As he stared at the ungiving figures, he would have paid dearly for one iota of fact to support the Sawls' claim. "What about the thaw, then? You didn't warn us about that ahead of time."

Danforth's mouth tightened. He stooped to squint at the screens reflexively. Ibiá did not smile as Clausen did.

"That didn't show up in your data, did it?" the young man demanded, less in triumph than in relief.

"It . . ."

"The Sawls knew," he insisted, his voice rising. "The moment the snow stopped, they were preparing for the thaw, before the sun came out, before the wind! They knew! The priests told them!"

Danforth shrugged dismissively. "Coincidence. A local phenomenon."

"NO!" Ibiá swallowed, backing toward the freedom of the corridor. His breath came low and rapid as he rounded on Clausen, who was lounging against the doorframe. "Checked your seismometers lately?"

The prospector nodded, a hint of grudging respect complicating his slow smile.

"And?"

"Avalanches, my dear Stavros, as you are obviously aware."

Danforth stared. "Thanks for telling me. Where?"

"All over the bloody place. Haven't you heard the rumbling? So much for your local phenomenon."

Ibiá's grin was sudden and manic. "See? One morning you're frozen solid and by noon you've got a plague of avalanches! Anything could happen, eh, why not a monsoon? The point is, Danforth, you *don't know*!"

"Avalanches are not unusual in a thaw," the planetologist began.

Stavros knew he would lose control before he actually did. But as always, it was too late to do anything but taste the familiar dry regret at the spectacle he would soon make of himself and wonder if he would ever learn to catch himself in time. He knew the world judged him self-indulgent, but it little realized how close to the abyss such moments brought him. He backed through the cubicle door, brushing past Clausen heedlessly as his voice rose unbidden to a grating squawk. "All right, don't listen to me! I don't give a shit! Better for all of us if you get washed into oblivion!'' He put a hand to the wall. The emptiness of the corridor was not enough relief. He could not escape the shame of his own ranting. ''Stay here as long as you like, the hell with you, but as Communications Officer, I'm ordering every piece of equipment under my command moved up to the Caves immediately!'' He sucked deeply for air. The corridor wall was hard against his sweating back. ''That includes this installation as well, Danforth! I hope you're a terrific swimmer!'' Nauseated, he bolted for the lift. The gate crashed shut behind him.

''You'll need Weng's permission, damn you!'' Danforth roared after him.

''Already got it!'' Ibiá screamed, as the lift descended.

Danforth swore and slammed his stool against the cubicle wall. ''Punk! I'll be damned if I'll . . .'' He whirled on Clausen. ''Is that the best you could do? Some punk fresh from the university with authority over *my* equipment? You could have said something, you know! You could have stopped him!''

The prospector raised a mild eyebrow. ''I?'' He shook his head. ''The odds are always against you when you tangle with a lunatic.''

''Yeah? Well, how's CONPLEX gonna like its equipment being dragged off into the bowels of the earth?''

''Most of our equipment is quite at home in the bowels of the earth. We *are* a mining company, after all.''

Danforth shoved the stool against another wall, adding a long scrape and a dent to its already tortured surface.

Clausen sighed. ''Look, Tay, it's of little import to us *where* our equipment is as long as we have the use of it. Let him move it about if it keeps him occupied. Besides, it'll give us a good excuse to hang around the Caves, maybe slip in further while they're not looking.''

''I can't work in those filthy holes!'' Danforth raged. ''That asshole could have me off-line for hours!''

''Fine. Let him. We now have fifteen and one half hours of light left, and most of that is dusk.''

''It's cold and it's dark and I won't let the little bastard get away with it!''

''Tay. He already has. Now shall we get on with our own business?''

''What business?'' Danforth braced both arms against the console and glared possessively into his monitors.

"B-Sled?"

"B-Sled. Right." He was calming, but his fingers still twitched a brusque staccato. "Hell, it's too late for that now. They'll be crawling all over the ship, with Ibiá on the loose."

Clausen smiled lazily. "So let's have a little fun, then, what do you say? Snatch that Sled right out from under his nose."

Danforth's answering grin came slowly as the possibilities took hold of him. He took a deep breath, straightened, then nodded. "Emil, you're on. We'll do it. Stupid sonofabitch probably won't even notice."

Clausen chuckled. "Oh, I think he'll notice."

7

Susannah hauled herself up into the long shade of a tower of red rock and dumped her pack and camera in an inglorious heap. The hot south wind whipped damp spikes of hair across her eyes as she struggled to appear less breathless than she felt. She glanced back along the trail at Liphar, whose methodical plodding during the upward climb had made her dance with impatience. Now, as he neared the top, she saw that he was barely winded. By rushing the four-hour climb along the rugged scarp, she had exhausted herself, allowed her sample bags to languish empty at the bottom of her pack and left her sketchbook uncracked. But she could not generate much guilt. She had accepted the lower pay scale for xeno field work in order to avoid the claustrophobia of the labs, only to find herself imprisoned in ice for six weeks. This sudden weather change was like a reprieve. She felt catapulted toward the sun and open air.

She mopped her brow with a dirtied white sleeve. The thermsuit was not cooling her as it should. Loosening collar and cuffs let in some air, but the wind was too hot to bring much relief. She stared up at the rock spindle looming beside her, estimating its height at close to thirty meters. It was deep red-orange, a sort of earthy vermilion, a perfect match for the sunball hovering oblate at the horizon. It narrowed in stages as it ascended, as if turned on a mammoth lathe, a giant's table leg. Stavros translated its Sawl name as the "old king," but he offered it without conviction, since the Sawls did not seem to have kings, or anything like a king. Besides, the spindle's smoothly domed summit was more reminiscent of a balding head than a crown. Susannah fancied it a more minor chesspiece, a pawn perhaps, set out on this precipitous rock to await its part in some unknown gambit.

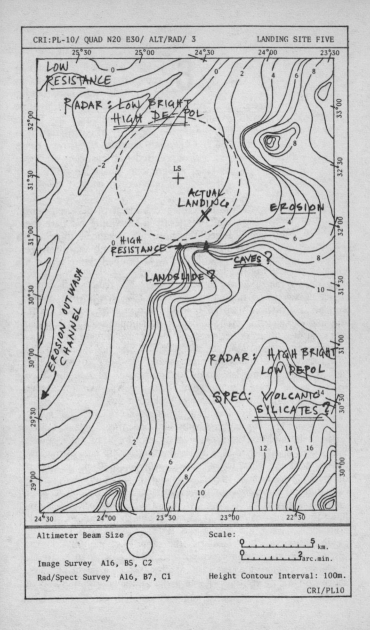

CRI:PL-10/ QUAD N20 E30/ ALT/RAD/ 3   LANDING SITE FIVE

LOW RESISTANCE

RADAR: LOW BRIGHT HIGH DE-POL

LS

ACTUAL LANDING

EROSION

0 HIGH RESISTANCE

CAVES?

LANDSLIDE?

EROSION OUTWASH CHANNEL

RADAR: HIGH BRIGHT LOW REPOL

SPEC: VOLCANIC SILICATES?

Altimeter Beam Size

Scale:
0 ————————— 5 km.
0 ————————— 2 arc.min.

Image Survey A16, B5, C2

Rad/Spect Survey A16, B7, C1

Height Contour Interval: 100m.

CRI/PL10

She circled it, measuring the circumference of its base at a surprisingly slim twenty-six meters. Her booted feet slipped in the melt water sluicing across the terraced rock from crevasses still packed with ice. She scrambled clumsily until she found a cranny deep enough to offer secure footing, then leaned against the rock shaft with a euphoric sigh. Still panting, she found breath enough to laugh aloud for the sheer joy of gazing down on this new planet from such Olympian heights. She loved these fresh worlds, uncrowded and unpolluted—at least they were for the term of her normal field assignment. Susannah placed her faith in a universe big enough to provide an endless supply of them.

Liphar arrived beside her, assured himself of her well-being, then settled down to wait, restlessly intertwining his bare toes. As his dark eyes scanned the horizon, Susannah imagined a sailor searching for a distant sail. Between thumb and forefinger, he worried the azure bead worn on a braided thong about his wrist. Clausen had proclaimed the stone as malachite. It was carved in the shape of a trefoiled blossom, which Susannah took as a sign of encouragement for the botanical sector of her survey. Though the stone was lovely, its intention was not primarily decorative. Its oiled patina hinted at a long history of pressure from nervous fingers.

Susannah smiled down at the young man fondly. Unlike some primitive societies, there was nothing gaudy about the Sawls. With his nut-brown skin, his thick brown curls, his layers of plain clothing in shades of brown and ocher and rust, Liphar was the very color of the landscape that was emerging so rapidly from under its blanket of snow, the same colors smeared so artlessly across Susannah's therm-suit from her reckless upward climb. After so many weeks of watching the Sawls huddle in dark caves, smothered by the blank snow, she thought it was a relief to see such colors, and Liphar's harmony with them.

Time to break out the camera, she thought as she studied her muddied palms for serious cuts and scrapes. Her companion left off his sky watch long enough to extract a cloth bundle from under his tunic. He unwrapped a round loaf of bread, divided it neatly, returned one half to his pocket and split the other between them.

Susannah munched the coarse bread gratefully. It was well after 1900 by the ship's clock, and she had missed supper. She had not thought to bring food for the climb, having been drawn further by the pleasures of sun and air than she had intended.

Studying the Sawls was causing a redefinition of her concept of self-sufficiency. The only life-support system on Fiix was the generosity of a fellow Sawl. She touched the miniterminal on her wrist and called up the ship's computer.

"Susannah here, CRI. I made it all the way up to the White Pawn, except now it's red, with the snow gone. I'm about three hundred meters above plains level. My legs feel like it's three thousand."

The computer was prim. "As Medical Officer, Dr. James, it would be prudent for you to observe your own prescribed regimen of daily exercise."

"Yes, well, as Computer, you can be grateful that you will never have to know how dull calisthenics are. How much time have I got till sunset?"

"Approximately ten hours. Was it necessary to go so far alone?"

"Not alone, CRI. Liphar's with me. He insisted. Wouldn't let me go alone. Besides, we should have a few hours of light after sundown as well, the days moving as slowly as they do around here." Susannah removed the clasp from her long hair and shook it free. "It's no use scolding me, CRI. This view is worth every agonized muscle I'm going to suffer tomorrow. The sky is like a sheet of polished jade and the air is all red and gold and smells like, well, freedom! Oh, and best of all, I spotted something like a lizard on the way up, at least a tail disappearing under a rock. Definitely a living creature. Liphar was not happy when I tried to hunt it down, so I let it pass. Not much else moving about up on the cliffs, though, which is disappointing—there's a limit, after all, to the accuracy of a survey based on a kitchen collection of dried herbs. By the way, my suit thermostat's acting up. I'm sweating like a pig."

"There has been intermittent static on that signal, Dr. James," the computer conceded. "If the problem cannot be solved here in the Orbiter, I suggest you unzip."

Susannah laughed. "Very practical, CRI." As the hot wind billowed into her suit, she giggled like a small child. "Like being inside a dryer! Well, to continue my report, the mountains to the south are still in deep winter. Very forbidding-looking, I must say. The plain is hillier than it looked under snow, all broken up with canyons and arroyos mostly still choked with ice. It's mud-and-sand-colored, yellowish, but this red light and the steam rising off the ice make it look like the whole plain's on fire. Fairly spectacular. The northeastern mountains are just a blur through the steam, but I can see the Lander clearly off to the left, down in the shadow of the cliffs where the snow hasn't melted yet. Liphar's folk are very busy along the cliff top."

"What are they doing?"

"You're a little faint, CRI. Up your volume a bit—wind's drowning you out. It's getting real gusty up here. I'll try for a look over the edge, if I don't get blown off." Susannah knelt on the wet rock and crawled forward as far as she could will herself. Below the ragged edge of the Red Pawn's precipice, ledges of wind-torn stone descended toward the rugged plateau at the top of the cliffs. At the western end of the scarp, scores of dark figures bustled about among the snow and rocks. "Mostly they're moving big stone slabs around with cranes and levers. Liphar couldn't quite make it clear to me when I asked him before. Something about water running into the Caves, or water *not* running into the Caves, I don't know which. Put Meg and Stavros on it. Between them, they should be able to figure it out." She paused with a sigh. "That is, if you can get them to agree on an interpretation."

"Dr. Levy is recording from one of the cave mouths. A religious ritual, I believe. The priests have become very active all of a sudden."

Good. Glad to see Meg's got herself in motion. Susannah waited. Finally, she asked, "What about Stavros?" The answering delay suggested that CRI was pondering a dilemma not easily dealt with in mathematical terms. Susannah retreated from the edge and sat back on her heels. "What's the problem, CRI?"

"There seems to be some difficulty in locating the Commander. Mr. Ibiá is conducting a search. He seems more than usually disturbed, may I say."

"Locating—? Weng's turned off her com unit?" Susannah frowned. Perhaps the Old Lady *had* been on the ground too long.

"Occasionally the Commander desires to be alone," CRI replied quickly. "After serving with her for thirty-nine ship's years, I have learned that she will be found when she wishes to be found. I am not concerned."

Ah, but you are aware, thought Susannah, *loyal servant that you are, that wandering off unannounced could be misinterpreted. You and I both know the old bird's as sharp as a tack, but she is beyond retirement age, and there are plenty of young-bloods back home jockeying for a command.* "She's probably working out some new composition equation," she offered.

"Let me know when she turns up, eh? What are the others up to?"

"Dr. Danforth and Mr. Clausen appear to be trying to dig out around the Lander. The force field has been turned off."

"The shield is down? Is that wise, with all this unstable melt?"

"Dr. Danforth issued the order, in the Commander's absence."

"How convenient. That one doesn't waste any time taking over, does he?" Momentarily, Susannah considered suspicion, then chided herself. This sudden freedom was luring them all into hasty decisions. *I just hope Taylor knows what he's doing.*

"Is Liphar still with you?" asked CRI.

Susannah chuckled. "Much against his better judgment. He didn't want to come up this far, kept trying to get me to turn back. He keeps staring at the sky and shaking his head." Gazing at the young man as he leaned restlessly against the base of the Red Pawn, Susannah felt a sudden guilty start. As a priest-in-training, should Liphar be down at the cave mouth with his brethren? Had her mad dash into the mountains taken him away from his proper duties? She realized that she had not yet learned what his proper duties were. Very soon after their arrival, Liphar had attached himself to the Terran party, hanging around Meg and Stavros when they visited the Caves, venturing almost daily down to the Lander. What she had originally assumed to be childish curiosity now appeared as a dogged determination to make the alien visitors his personal research project. Susannah now suspected he had learned a great deal more about them than they had about him.

But curiosity about Terrans was not Liphar's present concern. His eyes were fixed on the northeastern horizon and the dark crenellation of mountains wavering far across the rugged plain. The tension gripping him would have been expressed in pacing if there had been room enough on the precipice to move about. Instead, his fingers twitched his malachite bead in rapid circles around his thin wrist. He broke into muttered song now and then, and several times he tossed his head and sighed, a short explosive release.

"I'm sure it's much windier up here than when we arrived," Susannah noted into her wrist terminal. "And cooler. It's really barren, too. The rock is worn and brittle, like an old man's teeth. Not much that looks like vegetation, though I did find some dead bushes on the way up, very thick-stemmed and squat. Too desiccated now for me to tell much right off, but a desert type,

I'd guess. I'll get samples on the way down.'' She cupped her hands around the tiny terminal. "Can you hear me all right? I can barely hear myself over this wind!''

"I am having some trouble. Can you find some shelter?''

"Not up here, I'm afraid. Hold on a moment. Liphar . . . ?''

The young Sawl had suddenly mobilized. He grabbed Susannah's sleeve and jabbed a finger in the direction of the distant mountain range. Susannah gasped and blinked. A moment before, there had been nothing out there but jade-green sky and the sunlit amber peaks shimmering through the rising steam. Now the translucent green was being smothered by the black domes of a massive cloud wall. The far mountains were disgorging a storm.

Susannah squinted at it unbelieving. "Say, CRI . . . do you have storm readings to the northeast?'' Beside her, Liphar laced tight the heavy oiled-leather poncho he had packed up the long hot climb.

"I have no readings to the northeast," CRI admitted. "I had loss of signal from both those stations six minutes ago. Still trying to determine the cause. Mr. Ibiá did tell me of a native storm prediction just recently.''

"Well, I don't need instruments to tell you there's a humdinger on its way. I've never seen a storm move so fast! Better patch me through to Megan, quick! I'll bet this is Liphar's 'big water' after all!''

She no longer doubted that the temperature was dropping. Sweat that had never had a chance to dry ran chill rivulets down her back. She zipped up and tucked her hair under her collar. She circled the Red Pawn in search of a leeward side, but the rising gusts chased after her. The storm streaked toward the lowering sun. She shook a resentful fist at it, and Liphar groaned in disapproval.

"Ph'nar khem!" he scolded, making desperate little runs back and forth to the head of the downward trail.

"Ö rek, Liphar?" Susannah called over the howling wind. She pointed at the storm. "Ö rek?''

His head jerked as if the words alone were cause for terror. He bounded to the trail head, then turned back to find Susannah still gaping at the onrushing clouds. His yelp was audible over the wind.

The terminal on Susannah's wrist spat static. She put it close to her mouth and yelled, "Meg? Meg, you won't believe what's going on up here all of a sudden! Remember that nice quiet winter we all bitched about?''

Megan's voice came through scratchy and incredulous. "What, nice? You call that nice? By the way, you'd better get in. It's chaos down here!''

"Nice quiet snow," Susannah continued, unheeding. "A winter wonderland compared to what's on its way now. I'd get a camera to the highest cave mouth to record it, if you can. I'm heading in."

As Liphar took hold to drag her bodily toward the trail, she took a last backward look out over the plain. "You know," she shouted into the terminal, "this is a dumb thing to say about weather, but there's something weird about this storm. Remember time-lapse photography? That's what it looks like. Unnatural, you know? HEY!" She stopped dead and shook Liphar off. "I just saw a Sled take off from the Lander, I swear I did! Meg, can you hear me? CRI?"

The reply came mixed with static. "Having trouble . . . ing . . . reports . . . ind . . . of . . . erference.''

"SOME FOOL'S TAKEN A SLED OUT!" Susannah's voice cracked. "You've got to stop them? There's a storm coming!"

CRI cut in suddenly, barely intelligible through the increasing noise. "Conditions approaching abnormal . . . and . . . visable . . . turn to . . . ander.''

The little terminal went dead.

Susannah felt cold. *Is this my suit still malfunctioning or a touch of panic?* From the moment she had boarded CONPLEX's new FTL ship *Hawking*, she had never been out of contact with her assigned Orbiter's computer. She tapped the terminal with a muddy fingernail as if it were a balky windup clock. "Meg? CRI? MEG? If you can still hear me, I'm coming in!"

Liphar waited in jitters at the trail head. His eyes darted back and forth between Susannah and the approaching storm. She sensed him weighing the potential of anger as a goad to haste, and because she had never seen him angry she was tempted to find further excuse for delay. But the academic value of such observation faded in the face of the young man's fear. Susannah was left no doubt, as the storm swept closer and closer, that Liphar was in mortal terror of it. His loud urgings were collapsing into inarticulate whines. Soon he would lose resolve for anything but flight, as panic overcame even his dedication to her safety.

Should I be in terror of it, too? She relented and hurried to join him.

The advancing cloud line billowed across the sky like pirate sails ripped loose from their stays, fat and black, red-bellied with dying sunlight. The storm's speed was unnatural, the wind inspired with dangerous intent. In this aura of the bizarre, Susannah would not have been surprised to see the orange sun take its own sudden refuge behind the pale western mountains. The plain glowed like a firepit. Its steam-smoke pressed low into the canyons like coiled entrails, then whipped up into reddish shreds as the wind caught and devoured it. The Red Pawn turned the color of dried blood as the clouds swept overhead. When the first heavy raindrops hit, the rock precipice ran red like an opened wound.

Susannah curled an arm around Liphar's narrow shoulders. "It may be weird, but it's only weather," she comforted, perhaps more for her own sake than his. He was beyond comforting.

"O rek! Gisti! Gisti!" he whimpered, and pulled away. His shudder was theatrical in scale. Susannah trotted after him down the darkening trail, repeating his last word to herself. Stavros was convinced that "gisti" encompassed both weather and concepts of deity, but had so far been unable to define the precise relationship, or settle on a Terran word that seemed to suit its apparent complexities. *The gods' weather*? Or *godlike weather*? Susannah tended to side with Occam even in matters of linguistic theory, thus "weather gods" seemed the most logical. Megan agreed, from an anthropological standpoint, but Stavros insisted that language was devious in ways that the physical world could never be. It was Stavros who had first stated that the Sawls were a subtle people.

The cloud billows screamed past, reaching for the sun. Liphar leaped down the trail, screeching like one possessed, gesturing wildly to hurry Susannah along. The Red Pawn disappeared behind a rim of wet rock. The young Sawl glued his eyes to the treacherous terrain, avoiding even a moment's fearful glance at the roiling sky and its blood-hued clouds. The light turned bilious and ruddy, and too faint to show the path clearly in the shadow of the rocks. Susannah slowed as the scattered raindrops exploded into a vicious downpour. Liphar was barely visible through the sheeting rain. Feeling again the chill of panic, she picked up her pace. A march of ragged boulders rose out of the dimness as suddenly as specters. The trail swerved sharply around them. then sliced downward, nearly vertical and awash with muddy water.

The storm swallowed the sun at last. A gray-umber darkness overtook them. Rain lashed at Susannah's eyes. She reached too quickly to fasten her suit hood. Pebbles rolled beneath her feet. She fell skidding down the gravel-washed path, across thin razor edges of rock, past the fleeing Liphar. He grabbed at her reflexively. His bare feet found hold on the brittle stone but his weight was too slight to break her fall. He let go just as momentum would have dragged him after her. She slid hard into a ledge of granite that rose, as if by a miracle, to one side of the trail just where it switchbacked to avoid a deep cleft in the mountainside. Susannah huddled against the ledge in shock until Liphar scrambled down to pull her to her feet. He hurriedly checked her for injury and patted her sympathetically, but pushed on downward without further pause.

Susannah was too numb to protest. The tough skin of her therm-suit had protected her body but her uncovered hands and face were scraped raw. She touched a hand to her face and could not tell if the welling blood came from her palm or her cheek. Her doctor's instincts told her these were only surface wounds, but the sight of her own blood flowing so freely frightened her unreasonably. She tore her eyes away from the dark cleft and the vision of herself lying shattered on the icy rock fifty meters below, and tried not to cling to Liphar like a dream-waked child. As soon as she could hear the wind and rain again, over the pounding of her heart, she cursed her foolishness. Weng had once observed that only a complete understanding of a world can render it harmless, no matter how benign its outward appearance.

Did I think of that, when the snow stopped? Susannah scolded. *No. I go charging off into the hills like some giddy schoolgirl on a picnic. If I had listened to Liphar . . .*

As she stared at the lithe little shadow bobbing ahead of her, it dawned on her that his reluctance to make the climb had been no mere habitual caution. Liphar had *known*. He had known enough to pack a rain poncho up a hot mountain trail on a cloudless day.

How did he know?

She hurried along behind him with chastened concentration. She observed him scrupulously; when he slowed, where he looked, where he put each foot. She took note of each protruding rock he used for balance. The wind mounted into swirling blasts that pressed her into a crouch. She could see no more than five meters ahead of them, but Liphar moved securely along the trail as if he could have walked it blind. He led her around two more steep switchbacks, then the trail cut through a towering pile of stone rubble that clogged the upper end of a canyon. Knife-sharp chunks of granite pressed in from either side, and the wind howled down the cut. Blood washed down the rock where Susannah grasped for support. The torn surface was like fire on her palms, and she realized she was tiring rapidly.

They struggled out of the boulder pile. The canyon widened. The path dropped sharply toward the canyon floor. Liphar hesitated. The bottom was invisible behind a curtain of rain. The roar of wind and falling water sang a demon's chorus within the canyon walls. The young Sawl stood in anxious indecision, listening. His body was still but for his hands, working tirelessly at his azure bead.

Suddenly he swerved to one side and leaped up onto a ledge that snaked high along the wall, just below the canyon's rim. Susannah clambered up after him, wondering why he chose not to retrace the easier route through the canyon. The ledge was narrow, too narrow for a Terran to negotiate comfortably. It was littered with rock debris and split here and there by the same thick root she had noticed on the upward climb. She struggled along fearfully, looking forward only, never down. Liphar raced ahead, waited for her to catch up, then pointed out a line of handholds chipped into the crumbling rock. When he was sure she understood his shouted explanation, he raced away again.

The canyon took a sharp curve. The ledge wall undulated sickeningly. Susannah had to scramble along half-bent to make use of the handholds, cut at a height optimal for a Sawl. She had eyes for nothing but her feet and the rock beneath them. Her fingers were stiff and cold. She blessed the imperviousness of her therm-suit. Ahead, the ledge ended abruptly where a side wash broke through in a jumble of collapsed strata. The roar of water echoed down the steep walls in a directionless bombardment that seemed born of the air itself.

Liphar halted again, blinking into the rain. He rocked on the balls of his feet and stared up the wash. It was wide and bottomed with oddly rounded stones whose symmetrical smoothness reminded Susannah of an oriental garden. But it was more like a river of rock cascading down the mountain. Liphar beckoned her close to him. His hands slashed swift straight motions across the wash to where the ledge picked up again.

"Go much quick, you," he shouted into her ear. "Most quick! I go one time, next time you go."

Susannah nodded, shielding her eyes from the rain. His continuing anxiety confused her. Surely they were past the worst, being off the top of the scarp? He clutched his bead, his thin cheeks sucked in with doubt. Then he slipped the thong off his wrist and pressed the bead into Susannah's hand.

"Khem khe!" he declared and sprang away. She watched him jump down into the wash and fly from rock to rock, his feet barely touching down on one before he was on to the next. His poncho flapped around him like a leather sail, his skinny arms outstretched like unfeathered wings. He did not look back until he had gained the other side, where he hauled himself up onto the ledge, panting, and quickly waved her on.

Susannah climbed down into the wash carefully. She tried to move as he had done, but her booted feet slipped on the smooth wet rock. She fell once, caught herself, fell again and cried out as the rock smashed into her shoulder. She pulled herself to her knees, tucked the talisman into a pocket and began to crawl, using hands, feet, elbows, whatever helped to move her along. In the middle of the wash, she glanced up to see Liphar gesturing with renewed fury from the ledge. His eyes were on her as he screamed unintelligible encouragements, but a telling bias in his stance made her look sidelong, up the broad rubbled wash.

Susannah froze, like a startled deer.

A man-high wall of water thundered toward her. Deep in its muddy boil, stones ground and clattered like dragon's teeth.

Time slowed. The roar and clatter faded. The giant wave bowed gracefully into its downward rush, garlanded with a delicate wreath of bloody froth. Vast boulders danced and turned inside its curl, an endless freefall, slow as the movement of continents.

Susannah's own scream broke the spell. She launched herself across the wash in a scramble for her life.

8

The Lander sat lifeless, shuddering in the storm.

Stavros set his battery lamp on the corridor floor. Leaning against the doorframe, he gave the looted cubicle a final survey. He dragged a damp palm across his brow, wiped both hands on his bared chest, then on his grimy white fatigue pants. He missed the comfortable cycling hum of the air system. Weng had kept the ship powered up on the emergency batteries until it was finally time for them to be disengaged and carried up to the safety of the Caves.

He ran through a mental catalogue of the salvaged equipment: those items which were intended to be portable, others he had spent ten sleepless hours cannibalizing, others he must leave behind. He tried to picture each emptied niche and cabin but his exhaustion confused their images in his mind.

He regretted that Danforth was not present to witness the rape of his coveted instruments. Or better still, to be forced to admit that the Sawls had predicted the abrupt weather change with uncanny accuracy. Perhaps, during those long last moments before B-Sled had gone down in the storm, as Stavros was certain it had, perhaps *then* Taylor had allowed this recognition a foothold in his rigid brain, an inkling at least, a brief suspicion that he should have laid aside his habitual contempt, and listened.

Stavros prayed that he had.

The glare of the battery lamp stung his tired eyes. He left it in the corridor and moved into the darkened emptiness of the cubicle. The sounds of the last stages of the evacuation, the general clatter and human voices, the rattle of cartwheels, floated up the central service shaft, softened by distance. The rain beat a hard staccato on the outer hull, percussive, regular.

SONG # 13 (VALLA)

Work chant, recorded L+41.
Tunnel maintenance crew, Entry 6.
CRI:file 386-49 Sawlsong.
Translation: CRI/Ibiá

ANTIPHONAL: 1, 4, 6, 7 - single voice
alternating

EDO VALLA DULVALLA-NI JELA
(When Valla comes ∧ from DulValla)
          DOWN?

MAR-RI-EH   KE-DO
(?)
                    CHORUS ⎤ RHYMING
                            ⎥ GIBBERISH
MAR-RI-EH   KE-DO   ⎦ ONLY?
(?)
                    RARE DIPHTHONG : PRON?
EDO VALLA NHE (JUON) SIVELA
(When Valla her (?) ~~puts on~~ NO.

MAR-RI-EH   KE-DO
(?)

E LAGRI NHE CHEKE
(Then Lagri her sister) (FORMAL FORM)

NANIN-NHO O LEKH
(Answers the challenge)
          ASKING?

MAR-RI-EH   KE-DO
(?)

SRI DEMRA

SRI DEMRA

SRI DEMRA JEO
(We are the weak)

               AU?
         MAUR-REI- KE-DO - L. NO TRANSLATE
   COMPARE W/ LAGRI SONG 5 - CHORUS?
   DEFINE TENSES.

Like a Sawl work chant. Stavros pondered a possible connection.

In the shaft of lamplight slicing through the doorway, the cubicle's gray walls confronted the linguist balefully. He chose to read reproof in their smudges and stains, resentment of being deserted, left behind to brave the storm alone.

You're not ready for this, he told himself. *Not prepared to take people's lives in your hands so soon.* But in his heart, he knew it thrilled him. He drank deeply from the clay jug dangling at his waist. The water was sweet relief from the heat of the Lander's upper levels. He felt it drop to his stomach and spread its chill down into his groin. It excited him, as the storm excited him, and the smoothly coordinated evacuation of the Lander. The taste of crisis was as pungent as the acrid smoke from the cookfires burning in the Underbelly. It was adventure myth come alive, all he had dreamed of in his narrow dormitory bunk on Earth. He stood in awe of their power as he discovered these atavistic joys, and he surrendered to them with a lover's trembling helplessness.

He took another step into the room, resisting the impulse to search its shadowed corners. Danforth's presence lurked invisibly.

For the loss of Emil Clausen, the young linguist felt not a moment's regret. It was his one point of agreement with Megan Levy, that the prospector was a menace to all life-supporting planets. University gossip made CONPLEX responsible for the loss or adulteration of at least seven alien languages before linguists could document them properly. Stavros had thought long and hard before accepting a post on a CONPLEX-funded expedition, but even a wunderkind could not afford to turn down a good first assignment.

His quarrel with Danforth had been more a clash of personalities, but in addition, Stavros felt challenged by Danforth's reputation. As he measured himself against the older scientist's expertise and found himself wanting, he sniffed out Danforth's weaknesses and worried them like a terrier in defense against his own insecurities.

Should be easier to write him off, Stavros mused, but shame resurfaced to challenge his excitement. Not even Danforth, for all his arrogance, deserved to die in the rain on some alien mountainside.

He rattled a stray bolt across the shelf of a stripped utility rack. He felt uneasy about leaving the racks behind. *Taylor would . . . no*. The racks were too tall to fit into the lift cage, and there was not enough time to disassemble them or drop them down the shaft one by one.

Taylor gone. The reality of it settled around him at last, like a chill fog. *And Susannah missing*. McPherson had brought that news.

Susannah . . .

Stavros snatched up the bolt and surprised himself by stuffing it into his pants pocket.

Out in the corridor, two sweating Sawls grunted over the last of CRI's monitor screens. The lift cage was packed tight. Their comradely debate over where to add to the load was escalating into an argument. Stavros heard fear in their voices. They were not happy being away from the Caves in such weather. The plastic sides of the cage creaked as they tried to shift its load.

At the bottom of the forty-meter shaft, a giant wooden winch substituted for the crippled lift system, a Sawl winch hauled down from the Caves to meet the emergency. Storm gusts howled about the bottom of the shaft, spiraling upward to rock the cage to an unfamiliar lullaby. The hum of the magnetic lift field had given way to the groaning music of rope on timber. In the cubicle, Stavros clenched his eyes in sudden dizziness. He touched his forehead to the cool plastic of the racks, seeking a better balance within the confusion of sound. He felt perilously near the edge, loving the anticipation of the terror, knowing he would hate it when it overtook him. He shook his head, distracted by a slap-slap rhythm like the flap of a window shade on a windy evening. Sounds billowed like sails. The rain drummed against the Lander's shell but his ears were full of the ocean's roar and the snap of storm-lashed canvas. The singsong shouts of the winch crew echoed up the lift shaft. Stavros saw himself salt-drenched, hauling at shredded rigging. Far below, the big machine moaned in its labors, brave wood straining at the upper limits of its strength. Stavros moved to the doorway as the music sang through him. The steamy odor of his own fear wrapped him in a heated embrace. His body rocked in communion with the taut hum of the ropes, with the creak of leather, with the sinuous motion of the naked backs of his Sawl companions as they struggled to heave their burden to the top of the pile. Ecstasy sang in him like a siren, luring his sanity. Reaching for a mast of pain to lash himself to, Stavros slammed his fist against the doorframe, yet still swayed off balance as the great ship beneath him rolled into a wave. His bare feet gripped for weathered planking. Another bash of his fist and his mind accepted that the deck he stood on was the smooth plastic of a twenty-first-century ship. But the stark terror in the faces of the two Sawls told him that the motion was not imagined. A monitor slid from the top of the lift and crashed to the floor.

Forty meters down, the winch crew fell abruptly silent. The only sound was the pounding of the wind and the rain on the outer hull.

Then a cracking like the cry of a rent glacier echoed up the shaft. The Lander shuddered.

Stavros sprang toward the lift. The two Sawls clung trembling to the safety grating. He wanted to be brave, to offer them calm in the face of this nonimagined danger, but his fear made him move too fast. He shoved them stumbling into the cage, tossed them the emergency lamp, then grabbed the top rail of the gate. He swung up to wedge himself in on top of the load and crammed his body against the ceiling grate. The lift bucked, dropped precipitately and stopped short with a jolt. The updrafts whistled like police sirens around the cage. The Sawls hung on with eyes shut tight.

The lift steadied. Stavros reclaimed his lamp and yelled down the shaft for the winch crew to lower away. A chorus of warnings drifted upward as the Lander swayed again, then settled at a tilt. The laden cage slammed against the shaftway. Stavros renewed his bellowed pleas, waving the lantern like a beacon. He heard McPherson's voice below, raised in command. Painfully, the cage edged downward to the screech of metal against metal. Stavros managed a smile of encouragement for his companions on the lift. He raised the lamp at the entrance to each floor as they descended, flashing the beam into darkened corners and calling out to assure himself that no one had been left behind.

Megan waited at the easternmost cave mouth, closest to the trail that Susannah had taken to climb the cliff face. The tunnel mouth was an invitation to chaos. Raw gusts reached in to snatch at Megan's legs. She chewed her lip and watched the mist bead up on her therm-suit. The world outside was darkening as the long slow night began.

"Where *are* they?" she moaned helplessly. After losing contact with Susannah and Liphar, Megan had busied herself for a while by helping with the evacuation of the Lander. A long ten hours later, she could only pace and worry. In another few hours, darkness would be complete, and there would not be light again for several weeks to guide the wanderers home. Megan saw malice in the creeping twilight.

"Stupid. Stupid!" she grumbled, then thought that Susannah's foolishness paled in the face of what Danforth and Clausen had done. Muttering, she massaged her wrists. The cold damp had awakened her arthritis.

A Sawl woman sat a few paces up the tunnel at the foot of the inner stairs, cross-legged on the damp stone floor. She wore a knitted shawl over rough wool trousers and tunic. Even in the gloom, the soft drape shone blue as the water of a summer lake. A thick knotted fringe bordered it like a darker shoreline. The woman worked from a ball of brown yarn, turning her needles into the light of a small oil lamp that rested beside her knee. The lamp was of blown glass. Its glass chimney was faceted in an aesthetic rather than practical manner, for it reflected the light as a cut jewel would, flashing and irregular. The woman held her knitting close to the flame while tiny prisms danced and sparkled along the walls, and the tunnel remained for all useful purposes in darkness.

Megan paced in and out of the light, stiff with standing. The Sawl woman had said her name was Tyril, and Megan was grateful for her willingness to wait out the long hours at her side. Clausen would have said that Tyril's unspoken duty was to keep Megan from straying too far into the Caves. Megan did not care. Tyril's quiet presence was sympathetic, if uncurious, and Megan hoped she would be a friend. After six long weeks, Megan still knew none of the Sawls well, except Liphar, if one can ever be said to know a shadow well. Only Stavros could remark that a friend had said thus and so, and mean Sawl as often as Terran. More often, for as the weeks went by, he spent less and less time with his Terran colleagues.

She glanced about the plain stone walls of the tunnel. *Why do they keep their distance so, these Sawls? A habit of privacy, within the overcrowding of the Caves?* Susannah had remarked, "They are waiting until they know us, know what we are." But Megan wondered if the Sawls were trying to deny the existence of a universe beyond their own world by appearing unconcerned by the presence of visitors claiming to represent it.

Whatever their reluctance was, that caution that barred the
Terrans full access to Sawl lives and living places, the Sawls
seemed willing to put it aside in a crisis, to find space for the
visitors in the already crowded Caves, to help with the salvage of
the alien equipment. Megan was moved by their generosity. She
would not like to be descended upon by a pack of strangers,
poking, proding, recording, demanding explanations for this and
that. *Our intrusion is just as presumptuous as Clausen's*, she
admitted privately. *It's simply less harmful.*

Covertly, she studied Tyril's face. The same fine-boned angu-
larity that seemed delicate in the Sawl men shaped the women's
faces with strength. The mouth was wide and firm, yet sensuous.
The nose was a straight line that met heavy arched brows promising a seriousness of mind. She sat very still, cheek half turned
into the soft light of the lamp, her jawline chiseled with shadow.
But for the flick of her bone needles, Tyril might have been
carved from fine brown marble. Megan thought her very beautiful. The men were as well, but more in the way that a child is
beautiful: sexless and unripe. *But watch that Terran bias*, she
reminded herself.

Megan let her eyes travel up the wall to focus on the niche
above Tyril's head. It was the entryway's only hint of decoration, shallow and long, and crowded with tiny clay statuettes. In
the dim light, Meg could barely distinguish their outlines, but
she knew from the hours spent poring over her photographs that
the entryway friezes contained mostly grotesques: stocky little
gnomes with smoothly misshapen limbs, or wraithlike stick figures full of ribs and elbows. Each was a nightmare of anguish or
deformity, bent, twisted, dwarfed or overgrown, as if an embod-
iment of a specific agony. The figures were painted in rich
polychrome, the hues deepened with the gloss of age. The
hundred tiny eyes glittered with shards of black glass.

At the back of the niche, carved from the natural stone, two
larger figures dominated the composition. The clay grotesques
bent toward them in a shared gesture of obeisance. Megan often
joked that this particular Sawl art form had been inspired by a
malicious muse who bore a grudge against anthropologists. Stavros,
irritatingly, found the friezes resonant with meaning, though
even he was willing to admit that it was frequently elusive. In
the odd dancing light, the little statues seemed to be dancing too.

Danse Macabre. Megan shivered and turned her back on
them.

"No sign of them as yet, Dr. Levy?" Commander Weng came silently down the inner stairs followed by a grandmotherly Sawl bearing a steaming jug and a small stack of clay drinking bowls. A sweet scent of boiled herbs invaded the tunnel's damp. Tyril smiled but continued with her knitting

Megan shook her head dispiritedly.

Weng poured hot tea and set the bowls on the bottom step. "Mr. Ibiá has managed to explain the situation to that tall woman who never speaks."

"Aguidran? The master of the Ranger Guild, yes?"

Weng nodded gravely. *There is a lot of Tyril's calm about her*, Megan thought. "She is willing to mount a formal search, but most of her workers are occupied down at the Lander."

Megan stared into the howling grayness at the tunnel mouth. "I suppose we should be out there searching for them ourselves."

"An inefficient solution, Dr. Levy. It does no good to indulge our survivor guilt in such a fashion. I have already had need to resort to orders to keep Lieutenant McPherson from rushing out there herself."

Megan shrugged. "Well, you know how she feels about Taylor. . . ."

"The Ranger woman is far better prepared to direct a search around her own countryside." Weng turned to leave, then paused and said over her shoulder, not unkindly, "Food is being prepared in the Meeting Hall, Dr. Levy, if you could see fit to leave off your vigil for a spell."

"Thanks, Weng. I'll keep it in mind."

"As you wish." Weng remounted the steps as silently as she had come.

As Megan resumed her pensive pacing, Tyril laid aside her knitting. She reached for the steaming jug and poured two bowls of pale green liquid, then unfolded a cloth bundle stuffed with bread and a cold cheese pie. She held a bowl out to Megan, who remembered in time her own dictates on the etiquette of food. She accepted the hot herbal tea and a chunk of bread. She would have preferred the cheese pie, but she was unwilling to break her penance completely, noting that Weng's remark about survival guilt had been well placed. Penance was a habit borrowed from her second husband, a Neo-Catholic psychiatrist. They had not renewed the contract beyond the first year, partly because Megan had begun to see Neo-Catholicism and psychiatry as inherently contradictory and could not understand why he did not.

But the rite of private penance she had taken into herself like a drug, to tranquilize the guilt that often assailed her so unaccountably that she wondered if guilt might possibly be gene-linked. What other than genetic habit could make her feel guilty for Susannah's being lost in the storm?

She sipped her tea, smiled at Tyril, and continued to pace.

With a final screech and fall, the lift cage jarred to the ground. Stavros and his Sawl companions jumped off as efficient hands reached to snatch the cargo to safety. The winch crew locked their machine and swarmed up over the cage. Stavros allowed himself a moment to stop shaking.

The Underbelly was in an uproar. Shouts and chanting and the clatter of loading and carrying competed with the throb and yowl of the storm. The air was chill at ground level, and smelled of soot and wet wool and the strong herb tea brewing on the cookfires.

The crate partitions had been dismantled to be repacked and carried up to the Caves. A few smaller metal boxes remained, scattered about open, half filled. Two hastily strung emergency lights swung overhead, casting mobile shadows across the milling crowd. Stavros noted with relief that the entry cylinder was still firmly encased in ice, though the ice wall enclosing the perimeter had shrunk severely since he had gone uplevel. A leaden band of twilight interceded between the Lander's heat shield and the top of the ice that held back the floods outside. The rain lashed in, melting the wall unevenly into a circle of blunt teeth. Tongues of dirty froth licked up into the spaces between the teeth. The water noise was deafening. Stavros eyed the ice dike with foreboding. Moisture was weeping through in several places. He longed for the protection of the force field. The cylinder was funneling a two-way stream of traffic in and out of the tunnel to the Caves. The ice must hold. The tunnel was their only escape route.

He shouted to McPherson through the cooksmoke and bedlam. She finished lashing a plastic crate to a wooden Sawl handtruck and sent the child who manned it on his way with a quick pat. Stavros thought she looked tired, strained, but enviably in control for one so young. The crowd eddied around her as she made her way toward him like a small freighter steaming upcurrent.

Behind him, the winch crew gained the top of the cage

and picked frantically at the great knots attaching it to their machine. The ropes were as thick as a wrist. A woman called out, and passed up a lantern with a jug of water.

A Sawl backed into him with a cart piled high with seismic equipment. *Clausen's stuff.* Stavros considered telling the woman to leave it behind. He wondered if he would have to answer for the loss of CONPLEX property. *Besides, who knows what we'll need in the days to come?* He helped the woman jockey the cart about, then noted as she dragged it toward the tunnel that the wheels bumped sharply along the ground.

Stavros frowned. Two months earlier, when the Lander's descent engines had seared through several meters of snow and ice, the top sandy layer of soil had been fused into flawless glass. A flat floor had been created under the Lander's belly, perfect for setting up the base camp.

Now that perfect floor had developed cracks and slants. Stavros pointed this out to McPherson as she joined him. She shrugged and nodded. He wanted to object, to badger her into sharing this new worry, but had to admire her pure and uncomplicated refusal to bother herself with problems she could do nothing to solve. While he faced crisis torn between terror and relish, McPherson got on with business.

"Cleaned out upstairs," he reported, trying to echo her efficient solidity. His voice was hoarse above the din. "Much more to go down here?"

"Nothing much we need," she replied. " 'Cept her."

Stavros followed her gesture toward the perimeter. Fresh, ragged freeze blocked a Sled-sized hole in the ice wall. The remaining Sled waited like a beached whale. Stray clothing still decorated its windscreen; a damp lab coat, a lone thermal sock. McPherson's intent blue eyes blinked in frustration.

"How're we gonna get her outta here?"

He had given up on the Sled and should have known that she would not. Perhaps the decision was not his to make, but Weng had directed him to recover what he could *safely.* He glanced up at the smoky, slanting belly of the Lander, thought he saw its maze of pipes and wires and hatches wheel above him. "We're not," he stated quietly.

"*What?*"

"We're not!" he snapped. The irritation flared so suddenly that he wondered why he'd thought he had the taste for command. In his imagination, he was never faced with this constant questioning of his authority.

McPherson flinched into a fighting posture. "Whadda ya mean, NOT? We got two crewmen to rescue!"

"Three," he reminded her.

"You wanna tour this damn planet on your feet?" yelled McPherson.

Stavros shook his head furiously. "I'm thinking about now, Ron, and how we'd better get ourselves and all these people out of here!" He jabbed a finger at the wrinkled floor, at the melting ice wall. "*Now!*"

With a cheer, the winch crew got the big knots loose and hauled the ropes free of the top of the cage. A woman jumped down, calling to the others to clear the shaftway. The weathered cross-timbers of the winch towered over her as she bent her back to the crank handle.

"Where's Weng?" Stavros asked, drawing calm from the steady rhythm of the crank.

"Up in the Caves, keeping tabs on where they're stowing all our stuff. Stav, about the Sled, we could . . ."

His voice gentled as the winch and its crew won his full attention. "Ronnie, forget the Sled." His shoulders tensed as the ropes jerked up and rumbled through their pulleys at the shaft head, then thundered into a heap at the bottom in a cloud of mist and hemp shreds. A second handle was fitted to the opposite side of the crank. Manned by four groaning Sawls, the big slatted drum began to roll, winding the rope around itself. Stavros left McPherson's side to help feed in the tangled ends. The braided fibers grated across his blistered palms. He loved the secure tightness of the weave. The sinuous coiling onto the drum made him smile with sensuous pleasure. The winch gleamed with a polish of hard use and age. It spoke to him of history. I am a treasure, it said. I am the finest of my kind.

Stavros envied its builders. Their hands were schooled to work more than computer keys. The winch belonged to the Engineers' Guild. Stavros saw it as the apex of their art, which he honored with a romantic's blind nostalgia. It was constructed of thousands of small lengths of wood pegged together into stout beams. The wooden wheels were a foot thick, five layers laminated at cross-grain to each other. The Sawls' response to a metals-poor environment was the creation of miracles with a nearly as inadequate supply of trees. Not a single nail or bolt had been used throughout the entire frame. Wooden dowel alone held piece to piece.

"Just think what they'd accomplish with iron available to them," Stavros murmured.

"Huh?" demanded McPherson, coming up to dog his shoulder.

Stavros lingered by the machine, stroking its oiled beams as if it were a faithful draft animal. The crew scrambled over each other to pull fat stone wedges out from under the wheels, then braced themselves to start the winch rolling toward the exit.

McPherson grabbed his arm. "They taking that away?"

A shuddering crack like a volley of pistol shot rang out. The glassy floor vibrated. Stavros shook McPherson off and waved at the winch crew to hurry.

"Stav, we could use that winch to haul the Sled out! Shit, at least we gotta try!"

Before he could answer, the ground wailed and shook again. The floor buckled at his feet. Black water shot up through the cracks. The sudden cold and deadly gurgle around his bare ankles lanced a buried nightmare. Now Stavros paid dearly for hunting the thrills to be found along the edge of the abyss. His grasp on reality, ever encouraged to be fragile, gave way to an upwelling of panic. His worst imaginings took hold. He foundered in a vision of shattered ice floes and dark frigid seas.

"Out!" he shouted. "Everybody out!"

He whirled on the Sawl nearest him and pushed her toward the exit cylinder. Her bundle of plastic dishware went cascading across the floor. Ignoring her astonishment, Stavros turned to gesture wildly at McPherson.

"Get them out! *Now*! This thing's gonna come right down on top of us!" He ran at a group of Sawls dividing a crate of tools into smaller loads. "Out! OUT!" he bellowed. The Sawls gazed back at him unblinking.

McPherson charged after him. She planted her stocky little body firmly in his path, arms outstretched.

"STAVROS!" She whacked him hard across the jaw.

He stopped dead, stunned. His eyes widened, then slid past hers as clarity returned. He withdrew into himself like a turtle into its shell.

McPherson dropped her hands to her hips. "For god's sake," she muttered.

Stavros averted his head with a shamed growl. "Aren't you going to say 'Get a hold of yourself, man' or something military like that?"

McPherson eyed his naked wet torso and feet. "I'm going to

say, get some proper clothes on and help get these folks out of here quietly. I ain't got the language, Stav, so if you crap out on me, we've had it.''

Shaken, shivering with the cold, he nodded, but could not make his tongue form the angular Sawlish syllables. The Sawls who had witnessed his outburst glanced at each other and went back to work of their own accord. As cold water washed around their feet, and the towering alien hulk swayed above them, each resumed his burden and joined the now orderly stream toward the exit. The empty-handed picked up the nearest object they could handle and followed.

I have become a liability, thought Stavros wonderingly. He was used to being a danger to himself, but not to others. This panic was neither thrilling nor romantic anymore. He was grateful that Susannah had not been there to witness his unmanned behavior.

"Susannah," he murmured, remembering the floods raging on the other side of the ice.

"Stav? Stav!" McPherson shoved some clothing at him, his boots and woolen Sawl tunic. She watched him carefully as he rolled up his wet pant cuffs and pulled the boots onto his muddied feet.

"Serve you right if you get frostbite," she observed evenly.

"Not cold enough." He wrung water out of his tunic, then returned her measuring stare. "Leave me alone, Ron. I'm all right now."

"Better be." She gazed over his shoulder. "Crowd's backing up at the cylinder. You ready to go back to work?"

"I'm ready."

"Then let's do it. I wanna get outta this joint alive!"

I might have had a clue about the weather, Megan mused, *if I hadn't been so preoccupied with my fortress theories*. She turned her mind from wild images of Susannah's body battered by the torrent.

The theory had been a strong one, on the whole, but an understanding had come to her during her vigil, one so obvious that she was shamed to have missed it before. She stared gloomily at the stone depressions flanking both sides of the entryway. The probe data had led them to expect a desert planet. *But these are obviously gutters, and I didn't even* notice *them until they were awash with rain*!

She had developed the fortress theory to explain why the
Sawls lived high up on the cliffs. There were lower, more
accessible caves. And why the steep entry tunnels, with their
long flights of steps that led upward to where the warren of
living quarters nestled deep in the rock? Megan climbed the
curving tunnel to where Tyril sat at the bottom of the stairs.
Beyond there, the cave mouth was hidden from view and the
rough-hewn walls were dry. A draft flowed downward, laden
with the musky odors of the upper caverns. Out of the circle of
lamplight, it was dark and comforting, like a womb.

*Taylor did suggest climate as an explanation, but I put that
down to professional bias. Defense, I said! Peoples choose
inaccessible dwellings for purposes of defense!* Even Susannah
had been unable to shake her loose from that, try as she might to
point out the apparent lack of large predators.

"And the gift you all seem to have for settling your differences peacefully," she added to Tyril, as the woman offered her
a final corner of the cheese pie. "You have no armies, no
uniforms, no police. The guilds all seem to discipline themselves." Megan stared at her with genuine curiosity. "How do
you do that, Tyril? We Terrans can't even keep the peace within
a community of seven!"

Tyril offered a smile of patient commiseration, having understood nothing more than the misery in the other woman's tone.
Megan felt a rush of warmth. They were women together,
separated by a vast cultural rift, yet joined in waiting. *Perhaps
later in mourning?* Megan rejected that horror and resumed her
monologue.

"The Sawls, said I, have gone to a lot of trouble over what
would appear to be a very long time to carve out these caves—
what else but defense could encourage such an effort? Well,
defense it is, but it just didn't occur to me that the real enemy
might be Nature. I invented a fierce past for you, Tyril, out of
which, I proposed, you are just now maturing. When we fully
grasp the language, I said, throwing the ball neatly into Stavros's
court, we will find such a history hidden in the legends of the
Warring Gods." Megan paused, dropped her arms heavily to her
sides. "I had myself quite convinced."

She slouched back toward the cave mouth with a ponderous
sigh, to let the rain batter her face and punish her unscientific
rush to judgment. " 'Now,' Susannah kept saying, 'remember
the pueblos.' " Her shrug was a wave of both arms, like a big

bird trying not very hard to fly. "Built above the spring high-water mark, shaded in summer, sheltered from wind, rain and snow by the canyon walls, placed to catch most of the low winter sun . . ."

Her hound-dog face drooped as her chatter ran out of steam. *Weather*, she mused. *Did I say that the enemy might be* only *Nature? What more formidable enemy could one wish? Man at his worst cannot match Nature's ferocious unpredictability. Wind and water, heat and killing cold. Taylor thought to reduce it to a formula, but it had him baffled here. Here,* WE *are reduced to the humble state of our ancestors: at Nature's mercy in our ignorance of her. No wonder the Sawls find gods in the weather— better to endow the storm with intention, however cruel, than to believe it random and face intimations of a chaotic universe. . . .*

Megan shook her head. The gray void outside was a long shade darker than before. She envisioned the expedition come to ruin, worn down by hostile weather, like sand dunes, like eroded rocks. *I am getting morbid*, she declared. She turned back to Tyril, for even a one-sided conversation was less depressing than her private thoughts.

But Tyril had set her knitting aside. Her head was cocked, listening. Megan could hear only the roar of the storm, but suddenly, Tyril smiled and rose. The edged contours of her body softened as she stared at the cave mouth with expectant relief.

A shadow appeared across the screen of mist. Liphar staggered into the opening. His brown face was haggard, his clothing soaked through. He was plastered with mud from head to foot, the exact image of the clay grotesques crowding the frieze niche.

Born out of the void, breathed Megan. and her heart stopped momentarily until she saw Susannah's hooded form struggle in behind him. The pair scrambled up the tunnel like two drowning rats in a last effort to save themselves, fell stumbling past Megan as she was opening her mouth in relieved welcome, and collapsed at the foot of the stairs, choking and shivering. Megan ran to kneel beside them.

"Thank god!" she said. "Are you all right?"

Her chest heaving, Susannah nodded weakly, unable to speak. Tyril helped Liphar to sit up and began to swab mud off his face with a corner of her shawl. Susannah dragged herself up to lean against the bottom step. She caught Liphar's eye and they gazed at each other with exhausted pride.

"We made it!" she gasped.

"Thought for sure you were dead," muttered Megan gratefully.

Susannah fumbled to unsnap a mud-soaked pocket. She pulled out Liphar's blue talisman and raised it in victory, then returned it to him. Tyril nodded approvingly.

Liphar took on a worn, self-satisfied look. "Khem khe!" he exclaimed, tapping at his thin chest between attempts to wring mud and water out of his clothing. Still fighting for breath, he chattered at Tyril compulsively, as if to tell the tale was to relieve himself of its terrors. Tyril listened with folded arms, now and then shaking her head with maternal sympathy.

"You look awful," said Megan. "Dry clothes, first. Can you walk?"

"Not just yet, I think," mumbled Susannah. She shuddered convulsively and sank back on the steps, trying to coax her numb face into a smile. Megan helped her push back her hood. Mud dripped from her shoulders onto the stone. Her forehead and cheek were streaked with blood. Her hands were raw and bleeding.

"Are you all right?" Megan asked again.

Susannah winced as she tried to shrug, then sighed, a shivering intake of breath. "Yeah. I guess so. Most of the way, the trail held up, but here and there . . . Meg, did you ever think it was trite when someone claimed they'd seen death staring them in the face?"

"That bad, huh?"

"That bad." They were silent a moment, listening to Liphar's chatter. Tyril was trying unsuccessfully to get him out of his wet clothing, blotting at his cuts and scrapes, scolding softly. Finally she gave up and rose, laid a reassuring hand on Susannah's shoulder and headed up the stairs. Liphar lay back on the cold stone and closed his eyes.

"Did you ever find Weng?" asked Susannah fuzzily.

"I didn't know she was lost."

"But CRI said . . . ah, never mind." Thinking was like trying to wade through deep water. Susannah wondered how much of what she remembered of her fourteen-hour ordeal was real and how much imagined.

"Weng's seeing to the salvage of our gear in the Lander before the floods carry it off to parts unknown. It's Taylor and Emil we can't find. One of the Sleds is missing."

"Oh, my god!" Susannah jerked upright, remembering. "It took off! I saw it! I was up there with the storm coming and I tried to warn CRI but there was all this static and—'' She fell back weakly.

"Easy now," urged Megan. "They're idiots to have done it, but we'll find them, soon as the weather lets up."

"But it's not going to let up! Ask Liphar. According to him, it's going to get worse."

Megan glanced behind her, glad that the darkening void was hidden from view by the curve of the tunnel. "How much worse can it get?"

"Ask *him*. Have you noticed how he seems to know about these events well ahead of time?" Her head sagged to her knees.

"Well, I . . ." Megan pursed her lips dubiously and went on. "Also, we've lost contact with CRI."

"Completely?"

"Even the main terminal in the Lander. Haven't been able to raise her since we lost contact with you up on the cliffs. Stavros is in a state."

Susannah's bruised mouth twisted. She pushed at the wet hair clinging to her face. "I'll bet he is. You don't lose contact with a system like CRI just because of a little weather."

"It was odd—the last transmission we could distinguish, she was complaining about outside interference. Now there's nothing but noise on all frequencies. The force field's out, of course. We're on emergency power." Megan fingered the small power pack on her belt. "Haven't used one of these in years."

"I *told* CRI there was something wrong with my suit," Susannah began. Then she frowned. "What did she mean, outside interference?"

"Who knows. Sunspots."

"Visitors?"

"In this weather?"

Susannah's grin was halfhearted. She held up her bloodied hands. "Great, Meg, it'll be just like the good old days, when they dropped you in the bush with nothing but a canteen and matches. Some fun, eh?" She stretched, tried to sit up and fell back with a groan. "I think my body's coming apart."

"Even I don't remember *those* good old days," Megan returned. "Come on, I'll help you up the stairs." She pulled herself up from the step and struggled to raise Susannah to her feet and hold her there. "How bad is it out there, really? How much chance do those two have?"

Susannah took a pain-filled breath, wavering on rubbery legs.

"Oh, it's not so bad. What snow was left, the rain is melting, and between them, the canyons are six meters deep in angry rock-filled water. The plain is being torn to ribbons, the cliffs are one mammoth Niagara Falls with a full-blown river raging at their feet, complete with one-ton chunks of ice. All in all, it's terrific flying weather. Wanna hear more?"

She paused, blinking as if the rain still battered her eyes. "They'll make it back, Meg. I did, didn't I? Like for instance, you know that network of ledges carved into every rock face around?" She mimed a weak little dance step and caught herself with a hand against the wall. "Would you believe they're *all* above flood level? Liphar and I would be dead without them."

Megan grasped her friend about her waist to support her up the stairs. "I know, I know. Remember the pueblos. . . ."

The giant winch sat at an angle to the opening of the mirrored cylinder entry to the Underbelly. While the crew struggled to maneuver it into position, it blocked the exit completely. The crowd fell silent as forward motion ceased. The stoutest set down their loads. They shouldered in to grab hold and lend their strength as the crew struggled to pivot the winch around.

A single alto voice began a work chant. Its simple minor-keyed melody spread through the crowd like a fire in dry brush. The shriek of the storm was subdued to atonal accompaniment. Stavros wished for his recorder. Like many of the Sawl ritual songs he had been studying, this chant took the form of a three-part dialogue. Two of the voices were always sung solo, but the responsibility was passed around from verse to verse. The third voice was a resounding choral answer to the first two. The language of the songs differed from spoken Sawlish in ways that made Stavros suspect that a more ancient version of the tongue was preserved in the ritual. He listened rapt as the melody rose and fell with the wind.

The winch rocked and creaked. Inch by inch, the vast rear wheels edged about until, with a final swell, the chant broke into a cheer. The machine lurched and rolled ponderously forward into the cylinder.

As the crowd began to move again, Stavros and McPherson made a last hurried circuit of the Underbelly. Icy water bubbled up through the shattered floor. Sodden paper and clothing squished underfoot. The deserted cookfires hissed into ashes and sad plumes of smoke.

McPherson stared at the remaining Sled for a long moment, then impulsively ran to sweep the junk from its windscreen onto the wet ground. Then she turned on her heel and followed Stavros to the exit. At the rear of the line filing through the cylinder, he halted.

"Wait. The emergency lights."

She caught his sleeve. "It'll take too long."

"We're going to need them."

"That's what I said about the Sled."

He would need her help to retrieve the lights, and knew he would not get it. In Danforth's memory, she would refuse him that last indulgence. As if in protest, the ground shifted again and rose in a prolonged quake. The glassy floor began to separate like a cracked ice floe. Edge screeched against edge as the looser sand beneath was washed away. The emergency lights dimmed and lashed about on their cable. The Lander's support struts cried out in metal anguish. The squeal vibrated through Stavros's jaw. McPherson grabbed his elbow and yanked him into the cylinder.

The tube was clear. They ran down the silvered length into the gray light beyond. The ceiling of the ice tunnel had collapsed. The laden Sawls threaded a slow path through the ruins. The walls ran slick with water as the rain pelted in. Frigid slush puddled in the hollows. Above the ragged edge of the walls, the sky was disappearing into night. The Lander's sixty meters of metal loomed over the struggling caravan at an uneasy tilt. Stavros prayed again that the ice walls would hold.

McPherson pulled at his sleeve. The wind tore the words from her mouth before he could hear them. He blinked away rain and his premonitions of a tumbling Lander, and looked where she pointed, up the wall. All along the top, as far as they could see into the darkening downpour, towering sprays of water and foam reached into the wind, scattering into mist. Stavros put an ear to the ice. A symphony of roaring assaulted him. The wall seemed to bulge under the pressure of the tons of raging water and rock beating against its other side.

"Water's way above our heads out there!" he shouted to McPherson. Ahead, the long caravan had slowed. Patient Sawls crowded the broken tunnel. Stavros shifted uneasily, feeling the walls close in again, but McPherson was watching him. The steady pressure of her hand at the small of his back helped him catch his panic before it could run away with him. He glanced again at the surf breaking along the wall, his high excitement souring in his throat. It was for him, at his urging, that the Sawls were down here risking their lives without complaint to rescue objects whose use or value was unknown to them. It was he who had asked that the winch be brought down from the safety of the Caves, the winch that kept blocking their escape route. Why had the Sawls gone along so willingly? Had his self-indulgent hysteria convinced them that these objects must be somehow essential to the Terrans' survival?

Stavros was astonished by his own selfishness. There was not, would never be a way to repay such generosity, unless it be to dedicate himself to them with a loyalty that spoke of his gratitude.

The crowd stirred into motion. The line moved steadily along the flat for several minutes, winding among the ice chunks from the broken ceiling. Stavros remained at the rear, urging the stragglers along like an anxious sheepdog. As the tunnel curved into a bend, rock outcroppings appeared in the cliffside wall. The pace slowed again as, up ahead, the winch stalled on the incline. Once more, the work chant rose to drown out the storm. Stavros danced in place, adding his own whispered urgings to the chorus. He breathed a little easier with each small gain in elevation that lifted them farther out of the path of the flood. The floor ahead was rock, solid ground at last. Over the crush of rain-drenched heads and burdened shoulders, he could see the ice walls spreading apart to open into a circle. The familiar cone shape of the ballast stone, with its pierced tip, loomed in the darkness, and beyond, the safety of the cliffs.

The Sawls strained and sang. The winch inched up the last steep slope and lumbered across the rock terrace to nudge against the ballast stone. Rain pelted down. Spray arched over the walls. From the twilit upper reaches of the cliff face, cascades rushed outward into space and smashed down onto the wide stone steps that ascended to the Caves.

The winch crew gathered around the stone. Several strands of stout rope passed through the hole at the tip in a loose knot. The long ends ran straight up into blackness at the cliff top, holding taut against the storm. The wind strummed at them madly, and Stavros hoped that Weng was listening to this wild music for Fiixian solo bass.

The crew loosed the hanging ropes and wrapped them around the winch in a sling. When the ends were secured and the knots double-checked, they joined the end of the line struggling up the steps. McPherson followed, dodging the avalanche of falling water. Stavros lingered on the bottom step, unsure of what kept him there.

The great circular well was now empty, but for himself and the winch waiting trussed and silent in the downpour. He climbed a flight, then halted. From this higher vantage, he could see over the ice wall. The Lander was a darker shadow against the deepening night. The surrounding snowpack had melted. A stubborn circle of ice around the Lander's base was all that held the flood at bay. From that faint halo, two pale thinning ramparts snaked in tandem toward the cliffs across the no-man's-land of angry water that separated Stavros from his passage Homeward.

Stavros struggled to identify the emptiness that haunted him. *What am I missing? What have I left behind?* He shivered. His tunic was soaked through. The last Sawl was disappearing up the stairs.

My self-respect, he decided, in a rare surge of irony, *washed away in the storm*.

He shivered again, uncontrollably, and took the next flight of steps at a gasping run. Halfway to the lowest cave mouth, he slowed to ease the pain in his lungs. The winch rose past him, swaying in its harness like a slow pendulum. The cries of the crew slid down the rocks, faint and satisfied. Stavros pushed himself upward, panting, flight after flight. Strong hands pulled him up the last few steps into the shelter of an overhang. A blanket was draped over his wet shoulders. A steaming mug was thrust into his fist. His numbed fingers curled reflexively around the heat. He stood dazed with relief to be out of the punishing rain. He was conscious only of the rough wool of the blanket wrapping his cheek and the warmth spreading inward from his palms.

"That was very well done, Senhor Ibiá."

He was being spoken to. Probably an answer would be expected.

"Was it?" he mumbled, squinting about vaguely for McPherson, who knew better but would be unlikely to give him away. The cave mouth swam into focus. All around him, Sawls busied themselves with the last of the rescued cargo. Oil lanterns flared from hollows in the rock. From the niche above his head, the hundred obsidian eyes of an entryway frieze winked lamplight back at him.

Weng stood in front of him, with eyes that might also have been obsidian. She wore spotless white. Her rank insignia was a glint of gold at her collar.

"Very well done indeed," she repeated. "You might like to know that Dr. James has rejoined us safely."

A smile curled his lips before he could bid it away. "Ah," he said merely. "And Liphar?"

"As well."

He shrugged the blanket closer and tried to stop shivering. "Danforth?"

"No."

He shook his head. "Where's McPherson?"

Weng nodded behind her. To one side of the cave mouth, the little pilot hunkered down, staring out into the storm. A Sawl blanket draped her shoulders. Her blond hair was plastered to her head like a skullcap.

Suddenly she stood, and called out sharply. "Commander!" The blanket slid to the ground.

Weng and Stavros joined her at the edge. The Lander held its ground bravely out on the plain, a tall sentinel wreathed in ice. But as they watched, the flood claimed a victory. The ice encircling the Lander's base groaned and crumbled. Water rushed in, carrying a flotilla of icebergs to swirl about in the Underbelly.

"Shit," growled McPherson. "There she goes."

A-Sled swept out from beneath the Lander, buoyed aloft on the crest of a wave. The current tossed it like a toy boat on a string, then swallowed it altogether. The Lander tilted crazily. For a moment, it seemed to bob in the water, a dark renegade berg loose among luminous brothers. It rocked back and forth, as if recalling a habit of equilibrium, then lurched up abruptly.

McPherson cried out, and Stavros was stunned by the spasm that tightened his throat as he imagined a burst of flame, and the valiant engine rising like the phoenix from the flood that it was now sinking into.

The Lander dropped and tipped to one side, falling. Just as the tension must break that held it in its slow deliberate collapse, it halted midway and settled, angled but still standing.

McPherson cheered. "Atta girl!"

A glance at her hopeful face finally identified the loss that had plagued Stavros back on the wet stairs. Both McPherson and Weng saw the Lander as their lifeline, though the older spacer had the weathering of many past crises to help her remain unruffled through this one. For them, the number-one priority was knowing that escape from this alien planet was still possible.

That's what's missing. If terror comes so easily to me, why don't I feel threatened by the loss of a Sled, or even Lander? Why does the regret feel more like relief?

Stavros left them there at the entry. Confused and weary, he climbed the long stairs to lose himself in the firelit welcome of the Caves.

BOOK TWO

" 'Tis a naughty night to swim in."
KING LEAR,
Act III, sc. iv

9

The storm settled in with the night. The rain-dashed cliff sank
into blackness, then came alive again as a faint brave glow
awoke in each cave mouth. In the stone shelter at the side of
each entry, an oil lamp was lit as the storm watch took up its
stations. The shelters were hive-shaped and small, the masonry
clean and tight, but the door holes remained open to the weather.
The storm was merciless in its intrusion on the watchers' comfort. They wrapped themselves tightly in woolens and oiled
leathers, hugged warm jugs of tea to their chests and prepared
with stolid patience to gaze for endless hours into the wet
darkness.

A tall woman draped in leather as dark as the storm appeared
at the lowest cave mouth as that entry's watcher crawled into his
shelter and lit his lamp. Water roiled in the gutters flanking the
entry and raced off the edge to swell the flood roaring a meager
distance below. The rain beat at the woman's face as she bent to
exchange a word with the sentry. She laced her hood more
tightly about her lean dark head, then moved on to the next
watchpost. She carried no light herself, braving the night and the
storm to use the exterior stairs that were the shortest route
between each cave mouth. The wind snapped her leather poncho
wetly against the cliff rock as she paced up the stairs, taking
them two at a time without haste.

She gained the second entry and crouched by the lit doorway
of the watchpost. Her leathers glistened in the lamplight like the
carapace of a drenched insect. She spoke, listened, then nodded
and moved methodically on to the next.

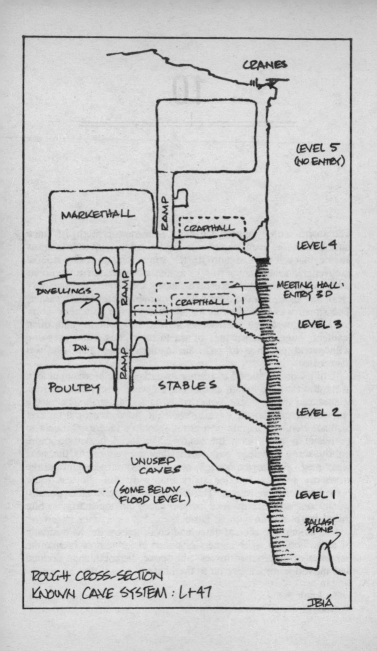

CRANES

LEVEL 5
(NO ENTRY)

MARKETHALL

RAMP

CRAFTHALL

LEVEL 4

DWELLINGS

RAMP

CRAFTHALL

MEETING HALL:
ENTRY 3 D

LEVEL 3

DW.

RAMP

POULTRY

STABLES

LEVEL 2

UNUSED
CAVES

(SOME BELOW
FLOOD LEVEL)

LEVEL 1

BALLAST
STONE

ROUGH CROSS-SECTION
KNOWN CAVE SYSTEM: L+47

JBIÁ

10

Susannah's knees sagged at the top of the steep flight of entry stairs. "Can't make it, Meg, not without a rest." She slipped from Megan's grasp into a limp pile on the stone floor. Liphar stumbled up the last step and collapsed beside her, his final reserves of energy burned out in chatter and worry.

"I'd go for help but I hate to leave you alone," fussed Megan.

"I'll be all right," Susannah murmured thickly. "Liphar's here."

Megan eyed the dazed and bleeding little Sawl. "He's hardly in any shape to . . . wait, here comes someone."

Tyril padded around the corner bearing a large bowl of hot water and strips of clean linen cloth. The man who followed was a stranger. He was tall for a Sawl, with the stoop-shouldered posture of one uncomfortable with looking down on the rest of his world. His glance met Megan's at eye level. He studied her with brief intensity while she hesitated protectively between him and Susannah. Then he smiled reassuringly.

My god, he's beautiful, this one, thought Megan with some surprise.

He had a long, thoughtful face dominated by a wide mouth. He did not wear his hair in loose ringlets like most Sawls, but pulled back and knotted at the back of his neck with an air of precision. He wore a long linen tunic, unbelted, with many pockets. The soft unbleached fabric bore the ghosts of laundered bloodstains. He carried a lidded wicker basket slung from a canvas strap. He nodded to Tyril, who urged the uncertain Megan aside to let him pass.

He knelt between Susannah and Liphar. The younger Sawl greeted him and answered his murmured questions with wan cheer. He uncovered his basket and took out a corked ceramic jug, then gestured to Tyril to bring the cloth and hot water. Megan moved to kneel at Susannah's other side.

"One of their healers?" she muttered as the Sawl uncorked his jug and poured warm amber liquid into two small bowls. He put one into Liphar's hands and after the slightest hesitation, offered the other to Susannah.

Susannah blinked and struggled to sit upright, but the Sawl laid a restraining hand on her shoulder and held the bowl to her lips with such gentle and professional solicitude that she could not bear to insult him by refusing his aid. She took only a meager sip but he seemed satisfied.

"How do you know what he's feeding you?" hissed Megan, who had seen her fill of local witch doctors.

"It's just an herbal tea," returned Susannah. "Besides, what harm can he do? This is hardly major surgery."

"I don't know—you're bleeding pretty badly."

"You could go get my medikit," suggested Susannah to distract her. Meg nodded but did not budge an inch as the Sawl healer fed Susannah another sip of tea, then wrung out a cloth over the steaming bowl and prepared to wash the mud and rain from her face. "Really, it'd be a good idea, just to be sure," Susannah insisted. Her tongue felt thick and lazy. The warm cloth was soft on her battered skin. Though she winced as the healer probed the deeper cuts for ground-in dirt and gravel, his touch comforted her with its skill. He was no brash inexperienced youth, and was, in a way, her colleague. Susannah felt she owed him at least the beginnings of trust but wanted also the reinforcement of her own medicine.

"Meg, please . . ."

"Oh, all right. I'll get it." Megan rose stiffly. "If I can find it in all that mess coming in from the Lander." Reluctantly, she plodded away up the passage, followed by Tyril, her patient shadow.

The Sawl healer murmured to himself and put his cloth aside. He poured hot water into a flat dish, tempering it with cold from another jug. He held it in his lap to help Susannah wash her hands. The scent of the water was reminiscent of mint and lemon. It tingled in her wounds but did not sting. When he was done, he presented the tea bowl again with such authority that Susannah drank deeply this time, even as she realized that more than simple warmth was seeping through her frozen limbs and dulling the ache in her bruised joints.

What has *he fed me?* she thought with a sudden thrill of fear. She tried to ease it by reminding herself that he had given Liphar the same concoction. She was too weak to do otherwise, feeling herself begin to float. She leaned back against the rough stone wall and smiled uncertainly at Liphar as the healer rinsed out a clean cloth and went to work on him.

Some time later, she awoke lying on her back. Liphar was gone. She was cradled in a leather stretcher that creaked rhythmically to the step of its bearers. She was being carried down a narrow shadowed tunnel. She could not move or call out, but to her surprise, it was not an uncomfortable sensation. The Sawl healer glided beside her. He seemed to loom very tall in his rough linen smock. His hand lightly clasped the pulse point on her wrist. Susannah lay quietly, wrapped in the wooly cocoon of his mysterious sedative, listening to passing voices, to the bustle of people moving through the tightness of the passageway, to the occasional rattle of cartwheels at tunnel intersections.

The stretcher tilted as they climbed a ramp. When it leveled again at the top, the tunnel walls were no longer visible even from the corners of her vision. She studied what her eyes received, as one will mechanically study the details of a dream, with scant belief in their reality. The ceiling confused her. It was a delicately chiseled barrel vault, a graceful arch of pinkish stone too lofty and finely finished to be the tunnels she had spent the last six weeks in and out of. Greenish light pooled along the shadowed vault from sources outside her range of view.

Her absence of fear interested her in the same languid way as the unlikely vaulting. She wondered again, with a more professional curiosity, what magic local ingredient the tall Sawl had added to his herbal tea.

The walls closed in again as Susannah was tilted up another long incline. The passage wound a tight spiral and opened into another, taller corridor. Susannah would not trust her counting in her present state, but she thought that they had ascended one more level than she had known existed in the Caves. The bustle and cart noise increased, but voices were hushed, in a way that was somehow familiar to her. The pools of light on the ceiling were broader, closer together. The vaulting was finished to a high polish that brought out the serpentine rose-and-lavender graining of the stone. *What a pleasant dream*, she thought, bemused.

The stretcher bearers took a turn. The semicircular reveal of an arch passed above Susannah's head. She had a fleeting impression of elaborate carvings that made the friezes at the cave mouths look like the crude dabblings of an amateur, and then there was no ceiling overhead, only blackness and two long rows of hanging oil lamps. Each was a great wheel with a central ceramic reservoir and a broad circle of lighted wicks at the ends of wooden spokes. The air was dry, a refreshing mixture of cool and warm. It smelled exotic but again, familiar—of strange herbs cooking, of hot wax and steam and blood. Sounds were muted within the vast space but resonant with urgent comings and goings. Dimly, Susannah heard a baby crying.

Then in her dream, the crying faded. Walls rose to either side, tiers of long shelves lined with thick books and tall glass jars. Blue flames burned under steaming kettles. Liquids bubbled up in transparent flasks. Susannah gave herself up to the dream with a slow unresisting smile. Her drowsiness was overpowering. The stretcher was laid on a smooth surface whose hardness through a thick layer of padding suggested stone. A huge lamp wheel burned overhead. She heard soft orders being given, the clink of glassware, the rustle of clothing. The Sawl healer leaned over her, adjusting the oil lamp so that its light fell more evenly. The light haloed him in gold. Gazing down at her, he had the solemn smiling face of a da Vinci angel. He brushed a strand of damp hair from her face as if she were a child, and went away.

Susannah understood the familiarity at last. She was somehow back home on Terra and in the doctors' care. All would be well. She fell asleep to the well-remembered sounds of a surgeon washing his hands.

11

In the MeetingHall, the wagonwheel chandeliers were unlit. From a vast fireplace at one end of the cavern, orange firelight danced across the bare stone walls and flickered into the shadowed corners. Stavros added another category to his list, stacked three crates together and pushed them against the wall.

Sounds of chanting and cracking ice still rang in his ears. He kept his back to the temptations of the roaring blaze. The great stone fireplace was one of two that dominated the short walls of the hall. The heavy sculpted mantel framed an opening twice the height of the average Sawl and wide enough for twenty to stand shoulder to shoulder within it. The entire wall above the mantel was carved in shallow bas-relief: a crudely represented landscape of rugged mountains, a faceless crowd milling about lost in their shadow, and a single giant figure striding among them with seeming unconcern. The darkened fireplace at the other end of the hall was also surmounted by a wall-sized frieze. The composition was identical but the background was a storm-tossed ocean. Feeling similarly lost among the piles of crates and loose equipment in the middle of the cavernous space, Stavros shivered.

I wonder what penumonia feels like.

Scattered groups of Sawls lounged on the stone floor warmed by the blaze, their chatter subdued by exhaustion. Several had fallen asleep stretched out on the stone benches that lined the deep angled sides of the fireplace. One of the men called to Stavros and waved at him to join them in the warmth, but he shook his head with a gesture at the mess that surrounded him. The slightly sour smell of hot Sawl beer cut through the smell of burning dung cakes. His eyes watered and his lungs hurt, and more than anything else he wanted to sleep. But as he put the jumbled salvage to order, drawing up lists, making piles, decid-

ing what could stay in the MeetingHall and what must go to
their new living quarters, he could pretend to put himself to
order, of a sort, and at the moment he needed that pretense very
badly. *If I could just get on with life as easily as the Sawls do.
They take a risk, they're scared, but it's business as usual.*

His shivering rendered his handwriting more illegible than
usual. His wool Sawl tunic clung with clammy insistence to his
aching shoulders. It dripped on the minute scrawl of his inventory so that the paper wrinkled and the ink ran. Stavros threw his
clipboard down on a box and shed the tunic to knot a somewhat
drier blanket around his neck. But the blanket's weight was
worse than the tunic. He shrugged himself free in exasperation
and continued his stacking and counting half-naked in his ship's
pants, leaving muddy puddles on the floor as he moved about.
He hefted a huge spool of nylon climbing rope and felt the
muscles in his back rebel.

"But Commander!" McPherson dogged Weng's elbow as
they came into the cavern. Two Sawl women followed a few
paces behind, shaking their heads at each other. "How do we
know there's even gonna *be* a break in the weather?"

"Lieutenant, I cannot allow you to risk your life out there
until we are sure there is no other option."

McPherson struggled against her habit of respect for a superior
officer. "Commander, they could be dead by then!"

Weng crossed the hall, stiff-necked, to the piles of equipment. "The living quarters are a trifle dank, Mr. Ibiá. Not much
in the way of amenities, but they will certainly do until the
Lander is available to us again. Dr. Levy is getting them organ-
ized as best she can."

"You can fly it outta here just as good as I can, dammit!"
McPherson exploded. "You don't need me around to do it!"

Weng turned to face her calmly. "I think I am the best judge
of that, Lieutenant."

McPherson glowered. "Yes, Commander."

"Our first order of business will be the homing beacon," said
Weng. She returned her attention to Stavros with a nod toward
the waiting Sawl women. "I've located a decent site at the cave
mouth. These ladies will help carry the equipment if you have it
sorted out, Mr. Ibiá."

"Right over here, Commander." Stavros handed two neatly
packed carryalls to the Sawls and shoved a third into McPherson's arms with a glance of sympathetic reproof. The little pilot
returned a sullen glare but said nothing. Stavros suspected she

was on the verge of tears. He did not want to see that. He needed
McPherson to be, like the Sawls, an image of stability. He
pushed her gently in the direction of the door.

He was relieved when they were gone. He had gotten used to
having the Caves and the Sawls nearly to himself, his private
laboratory. His constant presence in the Caves and his gift with
the language had by default put him in a position to control his
colleagues' access to the Sawls. This might require a more
conscious effort, with the other Terrans moved into the Caves.

He sneezed and could find nothing but the back of his hand to
wipe his nose on. The chill in his feet was creeping into his
knees. The fantasy element of this adventure was dying fast. To
his relief, he did not mourn its demise. He sneezed again and
brushed his knuckle across his face with self-conscious intent.

*The Sawls manage to survive here . . . we're going to have to
learn to live as they do.*

He moved on to the next heap of unsorted salvage. On top was
a file drawer of Danforth's papers. Stavros had packed it himself, thrown in everything loose in the cubicle. He sifted through
the top layers of photos and data printout, and pulled out a
bundle of notes. He leafed through pages of quick hand calcula-
tions and annotated data sheets. Danforth's numbers were neat
and precise, his script the drawn-out scrawl of one easily made
impatient with the slowness of writing by hand.

Though the figures meant nothing to Stavros, his linguist's
instincts could read the subtler signs, the language of scale and
placement of marks upon the page. Apparently, Danforth had
been worried about the calibration of his instruments. He had
spent time hand-checking the accuracy of his incoming data,
falling back on his trust of his own brain when all else seemed to
be in doubt. Stavros could feel his struggle with the data in the
brutality of his cross-outs and underlining, could see where
incredulity had weighted the pen as Danforth resisted results he
didn't want and couldn't explain.

A note scrawled on the bottom of one page read:

"CRI—crosscheck all ground stations against orbital measurements."

and then:

"Run model with known data sets: Earth. Yirkalla. VENUS??"

The first two names had been crossed out, and Venus scrawled
in later. Stavros tossed the pages back into the drawer as a

quartet of tired Sawls arrived with the last load of salvage. Two
of them lovingly cradled a monitor screen from Danforth's cubicle. One led a small goatlike beast which the Sawls called a
hakra. Its larger, more placid relations, the hekkers, made up
the dairy herds housed in the lower caverns. The hakra was
harnessed to a two-wheeled cart that was piled high with a
rattling cargo which the fourth Sawl struggled to keep in place.
The first two set down their burden to help unload bins of plastic
eating utensils and bundles of sectioned eating trays. Underneath
lurked a portable sonic cleaner from the Lander's galley. Stavros
shut his eyes in a spasm of confusion.

*I'm not doing this right. If we're going to learn to live like the
Sawls, why in hell did I make them drag all this shit up here?*

He tapped the sonic indecisively. Perhaps it was not totally
useless. Perhaps he could scavenge its power supply.

His self-recriminations were broken by an impatient tug at his
elbow. A still-bedraggled Liphar stood before him, his long
ringlets caked with drying mud. A heavy knitted blanket covered
him from neck to toe. He had gathered it like a toga over one
wrist. "Look for you, I! All everywhere!" he expostulated.

Stavros stared. "What happened to you?" Then he remembered. He cuffed the little Sawl gently across the jaw, then
threw an arm around his shoulder, careful to avoid his bandaged
chin. "Bad shit out there, Lifa?"

"Bad shit, Ibi!" the youngster agreed delightedly. His fists
rolled and his teeth gnashed in imitation of the storm until
Stavros laughed aloud and pushed him playfully aside. "Na
mena, Ibi," he continued eagerly. "To sukahir le gin Susannah.
To min!" He assumed a hero's stance and beamed proudly.

Stavros's grin twisted. "Not *my* gin, Lifa," he murmured.
"Not yet, at least. But I'm glad you saved her." He took up his
clipboard and pen again, "You better go get cleaned up."

Liphar shook his head. "Come you, Ibi."

"Lifa, I've got work to do here."

"No, no, no." Liphar grabbed Stavros's wrist and rubbed it
with his own warm hands. "Cold you. Be sick, ah?" He glanced
across the cavern toward the main entry where the four helpers
were leaving with the emptied cart. He lowered his voice. "Come
you, Ibi." His head twitched in negation. He corrected himself.
"You come."

"Where?"

Liphar put his palm to his mouth. "No say, you, ah?"

Intrigued, Stavros repeated the gesture, promising secrecy. He let himself be lured away from his precious cache of hardware, grateful in his exhaustion for Liphar's insistence. A left-hand turn at the archway to the outer corridor confirmed his hope: Liphar was leading him inward, where remained those parts of the Caves still unknown to him.

It was Stavros's secret that he had been allowed to wander far deeper into the maze than any of his colleagues. Because Liphar had chosen, often at the risk of disciplining from his elders, to return the linguist's obsession with the Sawls with an adolescent devotion amounting to total trust, Stavros was not led the merry chase that the others were in order to confuse them into thinking that they had been everywhere in the Caves that there was to go. As far as the others knew—though Stavros was sure that Clausen suspected the truth—each cave mouth led up a flight of stairs to one or two of the halls, which were large caverns occupied by the guilds or given over to a specific purpose such as the MeetingHall and MarketHall. Around these, a warren of corridors connected the adjacent living quarters.

But there was more, much more. For reasons he did not yet understand, certain areas remained off limits. While he went eagerly as far as Liphar would take him, Stavros honored the Sawls' need for concealment, whatever it might be, and therefore could only guess at how extensive these ancient burrowings might actually be.

They hurried along the wide tunnel past the elaborately carved and paneled doors of the Woodworkers' Hall. The floor was paved with broad square stones, smoothly level but for two faint cart tracks, one reflecting the wear from inbound traffic and the other, outbound. Stavros recalled Clausen pointing out, in a rare moment of bothering to connect physical and social phenomena, that the rock used for paving was not particularly soft, thus the Sawls must have been using carts with the same wheelbase for hundreds of years.

Hundreds? thought Stavros. *More like thousands. The language alone could tell you that. But how many? How often has the Stonemasons' Guild repaved these tunnels?* Stavros had asked that question once, in an attempt to find an indicator of societal age that did not rely on a shared standard of time. Liphar had replied that the masons' guild books would contain all such records but that he would have to find a guildsman who both could and would search them for such useless information.

Beyond the guildhall, they skirted a residential area inhabited by members of the one of three work shifts that was currently in the sleep part of their cycle. Solid doors were rare in the Caves, wood being too precious to waste in the name of privacy. An embroidered fabric or tooled leather drape more often served to shut off a Sawl domicile from the public corridors. Stavros followed Liphar quietly past the rows of darkened doorways. A thought nagged at him. When they were into the wide lateral corridor that ran behind the living quarters, he touched the young man's shoulder as they stood aside to let a train of carts rumble by.

"So where did the Council put us, Lifa?"

Liphar read his subtext accurately. He tossed a conspiratorial nod in the direction they had come. "New cave. Away. More good landur."

"Land-er," Stavros corrected. "Better than the Lander?"

Liphar nodded. "Bettur wokind home."

"Better?" *Wokindu-moten* loosely translated as "heads-above-our-own." The Sawls had settled on a shortened version of the phrase as their nickname for their uninvited visitors.

"Away," repeated Liphar.

Stavros hoped that "better" and "away" in this case implied that the new cave would put the Terrans where the Sawls could more easily keep an eye on them. He could not recall when he had decided that the Sawls needed protection from the other Terrans. Something Danforth had said, or Clausen, had tipped the balance. It did not take him long to realize that the Guild Council was way ahead of him in this regard.

Liphar turned right at an intersection, heading farther inward. Stavros was now in unfamiliar territory. The corridor twisted and narrowed as they left the heavily traveled areas. They met no passersby and crossed no other tunnels for a long stretch. The floor was unpaved, unevenly worn. The walls met the rough-hewn ceiling in an imperfect curve. The only breaks in the stone were the regularly spaced lamp niches. Along this section of tunnel, as few as every third or fourth oil lamp was lit.

Then they passed several intersections in a row. Liphar slowed at the last, hesitated to gnaw at his fist in sudden indecision, then made a quick turn into the unlit opening. The rock pinched in so closely that they could not proceed side by side. Stavros sensed a low ceiling in the darkness. He reached and touched sharp-edged stone only inches above his head. He could barely see Liphar ahead of him. He sneezed in the cold and dust. His exhaustion was returning, dragging at his limbs, slowing his pace.

"Lifa!" he called softly, overpowered by the need to sit down.

Liphar came back along the tunnel murmuring Sawlish encouragements together with what sounded to Stavros like an apology for taking him in the back way. And then, around a corner so tight that Stavros's bare shoulder was scraped raw by the rock, there was amber light pouring through a small archway.

The air moistened perceptibly. Stavros felt a blessed warmth caress his skin. Liphar halted, staring ahead.

"No say, you, ah?" he whispered. "No say wokind?"

"You mean, don't tell the others?" Stavros raised a palm. "Lifa, I won't, unless you say I can. Okay?"

"Okay." Liphar shot him a nervous grin and a here-we-go shrug.

Stavros could see a crowd milling about beyond the opening. He could hear noise, a good-natured commotion of talk and song and children at play. He wanted to be there, in that rich golden light, but was immobilized by a sense that he was intruding. He felt like a small boy at the top of the stairs, spying on his parents late at night. This ritual, whatever it was, was not intended for his viewing or participation. He put out a hand to hold Liphar back, but the young Sawl had survived his own moment of doubt. He grasped Stavros firmly by the elbow and guided him through the archway.

At first Stavros was sure his imagination was playing tricks on him again. The transition from dark to light, from cold to warm was too sudden to be credible. He squeezed his eyes shut and opened them again. The remarkable vision remained intact.

He stood at the top of a narrow flight of stairs, staring out into a vast golden cavern, as wide as three or four MeetingHalls and so long that the far end shimmered in an amber blur. Tall arched colonnades marched along the walls, framing white-tiled alcoves. The columns were wrapped in fluted ceramic, painted with colored glazes that gleamed in the light of countless chandeliers of porcelain and glass. The ceiling above the chandeliers was masked by a maze of fat white pipes and a haze of steam. Stavros looked up. The pipes were as big around as his own shoulders. He could see no joints except where a pipe angled to vanish into the damp shiny tile of a side wall. The pipes were utterly seamless.

Stavros squinted down into the golden brightness. The flat glassy floor was broken by a neat arrangement of broad shallow pools lined with brilliant multicolored tile. The huge space echoed with the splash and tinkle of water and the hiss of escaping steam. Mist rose from the surface of the pools.

Sawls lounged everywhere, young and old, dressed and undressed, all those who had chilled and dirtied and exhausted themselves evacuating the Lander. They sat around the pools chatting as they washed and soaked, or gathered at the stone gaming tables in the alcoves. Some luxuriated under warm jets issuing from the center of the pools. Children played tag around the shining columns and ran laughing in and out of the water.

"Wow," said Stavros quietly. "Baths." His brain struggled to fit this new information into his previous assessment of Sawl culture and technology. Pipes, steam, pressurized hot water, a vast system centralized around a single heat source, he assumed, as no heat source was visible in the cavern. But after six weeks closed in by the dark, rough-walled caves, the clean symmetry was the most disorienting, the sharp corners of the tile and the golden glow of the lamplight on the hard white glaze. It shook Stavros badly to have been so wrong, or so misled.

Liphar urged him forward, onto the narrow stairs. A sweet-scented heat enveloped them. Stavros became aware of a stillness growing within the vast space as the youngster dragged him insistently downward. The crowds on the floor turned to stare in surprise and dubious welcome. He froze at the bottom of the stairs, suddenly breathless with embarrassment. His intrusion on their nakedness was inexcusable. He felt blinded by the sharp breasts of the women, the rounded bellies and the parched limbs, the chests of the men so thin he could have counted every rib. Beside them, he felt obscenely soft and well-fed. He pulled back against Liphar's grip and groaned in genteel panic, wanting nothing more than to be invisible or to have never come.

But it was too late to undo the intrusion, and Liphar held to his decision stubbornly. He hauled Stavros into the midst of the astonished bathers, toward the steam and the water. In the pools, the children stopped their games, cowed by the resonant silence.

The crowd parted for Liphar and Stavros to pass, then closed behind them in a solid wall. For the first time since his arrival, Stavros feared for his life in Sawl hands, but he shook it off in shame. He must return the trust that Liphar showed by bringing him to this astonishing place.

They reached the edge of the nearest pool. Liphar stopped. He turned to stare at the crowd in nervous challenge. Having brought matters this far by his own hand, he now seemed to be waiting for some sign from the others. Stavros felt dirty and oversized

and pale as a grub. He had taken Liphar's risks on his behalf too
much for granted up until now. He tried to stand a little straighter,
to be less of a disgrace at his young friend's side.

A whispered discussion passed through the crowd. Several
older Sawls whom Stavros recognized as guildmasters worked
their way to the front ranks to draw each other into what sounded
like stiff ideological debate. But the crowd continued to murmur
around them and the murmur rose gradually into a groundswell
of unofficial approval. Liphar nudged Stavros and grinned. Tentatively, Stavros returned the grin, and the tension in the cavern
broke as sharply and noisily as spring ice.

Spontaneous cheering broke out, and laughter, and then everyone wanted to welcome him at once. Acquaintances and friends
who had hung back now pushed forward to touch his hand and
introduce other friends and families. The children charged about
in circles, responding to the energy that rushed through the gathering like a warm breeze. Liphar grinned more broadly. Wild
with relief, he rained little pats of celebration on Stavros's back.
Stavros smiled back, out of the depths of his amazement, greeted
those he knew and many more that he didn't. He thanked them
for their help with the salvage of his equipment. The language
seemed to roll out of his unconscious, neither grammatical or
precise, but with a fluidity that astonished him.

Meanwhile, he struggled to right his capsized understanding of
Sawl society. He had thought himself more generous than his
colleagues in his estimation of Sawl technology.

But this . . .

Each newly noted detail amazed him further. From along the
edges of the pool came the telltale sucking sounds of a circulating water system. The floor was a sheet of ridged glass imbedded
with a grid of pipes. The glass was warm to the soles of his feet.

He wondered how they managed such feats without sophisticated tools or machines, then realized that it was not so much
the Baths themselves that shook his preconceptions. It was what
the Baths implied about the rest of the technology. He had
assumed that the Sawl habit of concealment expressed tribal and
social taboos until now, when he had a glimpse of what they
were really hiding.

Is there more? If they are capable of this, what else . . . ?"

It did not occur to Stavros to question his own reaction, which
was not to rush back and inform his colleagues of this wonderful
discovery. Instead, he felt even more protective of the Sawls
than before, more convinced that their secrets must be kept. He

was obscurely aware that in conspiring to this concealment, he journeyed into the heart of the dangerous no-man's-land of divided loyalties on whose outskirts he had been lingering for six weeks.

But for now all that mattered was the heady rush of the Sawls' approval. He watched as Liphar unwound his togalike drape and tossed it aside to ease his slim brown body into the pool with a long sigh of pleasure. Stavros reached to undo the Velcro fastening at his own waist, then hesitated. He glanced down at his pants as if they could offer some understanding as to why he found it suddenly so difficult to part with them. They were damp, grimy and totally synthetic. Ship's issue. Plastic rivets at the seams.

He had never felt more alien in his life.

Waiting in the pool, Liphar mistook his hesitation for an attack of modesty. The little Sawl laughed and let loose a sidearm swing that sent hot water cascading into Stavros's face. He coughed and blinked and shook his head like a dog.

He undid his pants. As they slid down across his buttocks, over his thighs, past his knees, he lived through a long terrifying second. On one side of it he felt utterly exposed and alone. On the other, he stepped out of the muddy huddle of his ship's clothing with a sense of release that exploded into laughter.

He stood at the edge of the pool, hands on hips, laughing. His laughter was contagious. The children squealed with delight as the crowd joined in. No one knew quite why they were laughing, least of all the off-worlder who had started it, but they knew it felt good.

To Stavros, it was better than good. It was miraculous. Almost as miraculous as the clear hot water washing around him as he slid into the pool, as heat and laughter brought tingling new life to his frigid limbs.

12

Susannah's dream woke her with a fit of coughing. She lay on a pad of blankets spread in front of a smoking fire. Megan knelt beside it, blowing into the coals and swearing softly. She pushed several dung cakes at it as if she were feeding a wild animal, then sat back on her heels, embarrassed by Susannah's laugh.

"I used to be good at this Girl Scout stuff, would you believe?" she complained. "How do you feel?"

Susannah stretched cautiously. To her surprise, her body did not cry out in immediate protest. "Pretty good. Not too stiff . . . the bruises are tender, of course, but . . ." Her hands were immobilized by thick linen dressings. "How long have I been out?"

Megan considered. "Not long—eight, ten hours."

"Whew. Whatever the doctor, I mean, that healer gave me, it sure worked." Susannah sat up, less carefully. "I actually feel terrific. And boy, you know, I had the most amazing dreams up there."

"Up where?"

"Where he took me."

Megan shrugged, poking again at the fire. "Must have been dreaming, all right. Two of them brought you down here on a stretcher pretty soon after I left you in the tunnel. You've been sleeping like a baby ever since."

"No. Really?" Susannah lay back, confused. "But I distinctly remember . . . oh, well." She peered into the darkness surrounding the fire. "So where is here?"

"Welcome to our new quarters." Megan gestured grandly around. "McPherson and I call it the Black Hole. Weng of course refuses to sink to our level, but then she's still insisting it's only temporary."

"It's still raining?"

"Oh yes." Megan nodded grimly. "With a vengeance."

"No sign of . . . ?"

"No."

"Have you been able to contact CRI?"

"Nope."

Susannah sucked at her cheek and glanced around pensively. "Sure is dark in here."

"Oh." Megan turned up the battery lamp at her side. "Sorry. Conserving power, you know."

The light revealed a good-sized cavern, longer than it was wide, with a lowish uneven ceiling. The walls were only crudely finished but for a section near the front, where smooth stone met flat floor in a gentle curve and the beginnings of a lamp niche echoed the curl of the entry arch. The cave was empty but for a jumble of familiar crates and equipment cases.

"This is a new cave," Meg explained with a wave at the pile of stone rubble that had been hastily swept into a back corner. "They were still digging it out. Part of the western expansion, they tell me. Stav says Tyril has promised to get her cousin the brickmaker to fix us up a proper firepit, and Weng's worked out some plan for using the crate lids to build a sleeping platform in the rear there. This lying on stone is hell on *my* old bones."

"I notice they've left us alone."

"The Sawls, you mean? In here, yes. But step two feet down that corridor outside and there's someone right at your side. It's going to be hard on them now we're here all the time. They'll have to do shifts."

"They *have* been keeping track of us, haven't they. Like Emil said."

"Certainly. I would too, if I were them."

"Why should they suspect us of meaning them harm?"

Megan gazed at her friend with bemused incredulity. "Susannah, I swear, I look at you sometimes and ask myself, can she really be that naive? It's like with Clausen, you . . ."

"Don't start, Meg. I feel good, but not that good."

Megan shrugged and returned her attention to the still-smoking fire.

After a while, Susannah murmured, "I wonder if I could talk Tyril or Liphar into taking me up there again."

Meg raised an eyebrow, shook her head.

"Well, I know I was somewhere, Meg!" Susannah sat upright. "Somewhere like a hospital ward, I swear! I wasn't *that* out of it!"

"If you say so."

"It would be great to work with that healer for a while, see what Sawl medicine is like."

A light bobbed in the narrow entry tunnel leading to the main corridor. Weng's voice called a strained but polite thank-you to someone outside. She snapped off her lamp as soon as she entered the cavern, and made her way slowly to the fire. She sat down on a nearby crate without speaking, tucking loose strands of hair back into her silver bun. Belatedly, she noticed that Susannah was awake.

"Ah. Dr. James. A relief to have you back among us."

Susannah smiled with professional concern. "None too soon, I see. You look exhausted, Commander. Are you neglecting that regimen I gave you?"

Weng forced her back into a straighter line. "I keep up as best I can, Dr. James, given the situation." Her mouth drew itself together and she gave a small sigh. "Lieutenant McPherson has disobeyed my orders," she reported to Megan finally.

"She went out by herself?"

"No. Interestingly enough, the Sawls proved more successful in preventing that than I did. She has gone with the RangerGuild search party."

Susannah groaned, remembering.

"One of us should be out there with them, Weng," said Megan reasonably.

"I had planned, as soon as we were settled in here . . ." Weng fell silent. Then she said, "Of course, you're right, Dr. Levy. Ship's regulations are not always appropriate to the situation."

Susannah drew up her knees and hugged them. "What do the Sawls say about the weather? Has anyone asked?"

Megan made a wry face. "Sure, but it's like the old joke, you know? Everyone talks about the weather but nobody does anything about it."

"But what do they say?"

"What do they say?" Megan exchanged a glance with Weng. "At the moment, they won't say. When questioned on the weather, mostly they just look at you, and shake their heads."

13

"These folk are obsessed with weather," Megan muttered to herself as she settled to observe a group of Sawl priests. She was only mildly surprised at how resentful she sounded. She had decided the only defense against slipping back into her recent lethargic depression was to invoke a strict schedule of study. That she had done and was the better for it, as it also reinforced the fading distinctions of her Terran day and night, morning and afternoon, concepts that had no physical reality in the depths of the rock. It did not help that the Sawls lived around the clock, in three revolving shifts dividing what approximated a thirty-hour day. Thus, the Caves were never quiet, and there was always something going on that would not find a place on Megan's schedule if she wanted to leave time for sleep. And with each further day spent in humid darkness, though it was yet barely midnight by the Fiixian clock, the oblivion of sleep became more and more alluring.

So far Megan had resisted bravely. But as she constantly consoled herself, it was nowhere written that she had to be cheerful about the discomforts her schedule of study might place her in. She derived a certain energy from the very act of complaining.

This particular moment, afternoon by her schedule, the priests had chosen to gather at the narrowest of the cave mouths. But the storm was at a singularly vicious peak. Despite the protected entry, cold rain and wind hammered in from the darkness. The stone floor was drenched and the gutters roaring. Megan tucked her foil blanket higher on her neck. The very thought of exposed skin set her shivering. She draped the foil in a silver tent around her lap to keep her borrowed sketchbook from the blowing mist. This normally wise move blocked the light from the oil lamp above her head. She adjusted one side of the tent, but then the winds swept in to chill her ribs through the scant protection of her unpowered therm-suit. Megan let out an exasperated sigh and tried to concentrate on her drawing. The lamp flame swayed in its niche above and made her crude stick figures leap and stutter like an antique film. She thought with longing of the inner caverns and the warmth of her bedroll, but bent back to her sketch like a proper student.

The eight priests stood in a shivering circle several paces inside the overhang of the cliff face. There they would usually have been in the lee of the wind, but the wind was blowing in all directions at once. They drew their circle tighter to shield the oldest and frailest as best they could. Megan thought them a ragtag bunch in their damp layers of brown knits and woolens. The two of the eight who seemed to have given some thought to dressing as might befit a priest had thrown sleeveless embroidered robes over their warm clothing. One wore hers open, the other had laced his casually at the neck. The embroidery on front and back resembled a guild seal in design: a red-and-orange flame suspended over blue-lavender waves, encircled in green and brown.

In fact, Megan suspected that what kept the priests from being just another of the many guilds was that matters of weather seemed to fall particularly under their jurisdiction. This, more than any presumption of authority, gave them their central focus in Sawl society, for as Megan was fond of noting, the Sawls were obsessed with the weather.

For this, she could not blame them. She was becoming obsessed with it herself, as were the other Terrans, when they were not hiding ostrich-like in their work. Stavros never left the inner caves but was compulsively collecting a weather language and mythology. McPherson faced the weather daily with the Ranger-Guild's search parties, keeping Danforth alive in her mind long after the others had given up hope. Megan did not feel guilty for staying behind. In such fearsome storms, she would be a liability to the searchers and probably kill or maim herself in the bargain. But it had required the efforts of both Susannah and Stavros to convince Weng similarly. Megan thought the situation particularly hard on Weng, who felt the greatest responsibility and could do the least about it. The Commander had finally given up on her attempts to reestablish the communications link with the Orbiter, left the homing beacon running and buried herself in her music.

Megan's attention was drawn abruptly back to the priests. The gathering, which had begun as a discussion, was evolving into a heated debate. The young apprentices hovered about, listening in avidly. One held a lamp suspended from a supple pole to light the center of the circle. Megan sketched the gentle curve of the pole, held the pad up to assess the result. She had borrowed the sketchbook from Susannah, who often put aside the camera to do her own drawings. The front half was filled with botanical details shaped with intimidating skill, but even her own inexpert hand was convincing Megan that at times, the pad is mightier than the screen. Though she missed her computer terminal, she was becoming fond of the editorial quality of line that a human hand could produce. She erased the curve and drew it again.

Tyril, her faithful shadow, sat beside her, absorbed in her perpetual knitting. Megan had wanted to sit closer to the priestly huddle, for a better view of the mysteries inside, but Tyril had persuaded her to leave them some private distance. Tyril never ordered or insisted, but somehow always got her way where Megan was concerned. Now, as Megan sketched, Tyril looked over her shoulder occasionally to nod and smile encouragingly as the work on the page progressed.

Megan drew in the lamp at the end of its pole, and began on the circle of backs bent in earnest consultation. Their curl inward toward the lamp was softened by the layers of knitted shawls and scarves and heavy cloaks and overtunics. The nodding, murmuring heads were rounded by woolen caps, some with long flaps that hung down like hound's ears.

Megan heard nothing ritualistic emanating from that huddle, nothing like prayer, no chanting or singing. The debate rose and fell. Every few minutes, one of the younger priests pulled herself away from the group to venture out onto the ledge, attended by two soaked and worried apprentices. The wind threatened to topple her into the abyss as it tore at her garments and she, heedless, strained her ears and eyes outward. Megan wondered what the woman could possibly hope to see in such total blackness. She was relieved when the apprentices succeeded in urging their distracted mistress to retreat to the comparative shelter of the overhang. The young priest returned to the circle frowning and thoughtful, her long curls swinging as heavily as the rain-weighted hem of her cloak. But then, a few moments later, she was away again, pacing toward the edge.

As she pulled away, a space was left in the circle. Megan's mental ears pricked up as she spotted fat books changing hands inside the huddle. She caught tantalizing glimpses of yellowed sheets pressed between slats of wood, of sewn bindings in cloth and cracked leather, of parchment and vellum pages. To one side, an apprentice waited with an additional armload swathed in a triangular drape of pale suede. The drape was embroidered with the same circular design, the flame and the wave, but nothing further. Megan had decided already that the Sawls had little taste for meaningless decoration.

Megan eyed the books hungrily. Her interpretation of Sawl society had taken a new turn the day she had learned about the guild libraries. The Sawl literature was still oral, but like proto-bureaucrats, they were compulsive record keepers. Megan longed to hold just one of those books in her own hands. One did not even have to be able to read a book to glean a depth of information from it. But the Sawls were protective of their records, and Tyril had made it quite clear through sign and scattered word that these were sacred books of a very great age: surely Megan would not wish to assume the risk of harming such treasures. Megan had not noticed the priests handling the books with much more than the normal care, but when Tyril offered a trip to her own guildhall, where books pertaining to the proud craft of weaving would be found to be (she implied) of equal interest, Megan acquiesced. Such an offer had not been made before. It indicated, she thought, a relaxing of at least one Sawl's attitude toward the Terran visitors.

The Min Kodeh, she recalled, *were miraculous weavers as well. Maybe I should forget this weather-prediction stuff and concentrate on the Sawls as craftsmen. A nice artsy book. Lots of pictures. It would certainly be easier. . . .*

She wrenched her concentration back to the priests. Observing body language and the cadence of voices, she tried to determine a hierarchy within the group. But they were all speaking at once, and flipping through the pages of several books at a time (with no great reverence, she noted) to point out this reference or that. It reminded Megan of a meeting of the trustees of a Terran university, any one of the several she had taught at during her lengthy academic career. If one voice occasionally soared over the others to be heard above the roar of the wind, its owner won a moment's domination over the discussion. But fast talking was also necessary to get the point across before the voice was lost again among the rest.

As she squinted to see the nearest book in greater detail, Megan noticed that the palms of the priest holding it were utterly

smooth, almost shiny, as if layered with scar tissue. She glanced
to another for comparison and found those palms similarly smooth.
Curious, she leaned over to peer at Tyril's hands and found
nothing unusual beyond her weaver's calluses. Megan took a
note in a corner of her drawing to remind herself to look into this
further.

Still the debate raged on. The apprentices without a specific
responsibility to the circle stood about in twos and threes, chatting or listening, their ears open for a summons to duty. A few
clustered around an older boy who was counting out a pocketful
of thin stone disks, dividing them equally among his companions. Megan had a few of those disks in her own pocket. They
represented one of at least three unofficial currencies employed
in the Caves. The official currency was Trade and Barter. Megan
had traded a resealable plastic bag for her handful of disks, and
noticed that the trader seemed inordinately pleased with the deal.

*If Emil can go around handing out pens, one little plastic bag
won't hurt anybody. At least my trade was for the purpose of
study, not merely to pamper my palate.*

The memory of Clausen made her shoulders sag in sudden
exhaustion. She supposed it was inevitable that a prospector
would lose his life to one of the planets he was bent on raping.
Men like Clausen did not die in bed. In the abstract, Megan
could appreciate the poetic justice of it, but the actuality saddened her. For once, she permitted herself to contemplate the
question that always lurked, no matter how hard, with insistent
busyness, she might try to keep it at bay.

*Is this it, then? Are we really to be stranded on this cold and
dreary world?*

Until the night and the storm ended, the answer could not be
known. The Lander might be functional, and if it was not, it
might be repaired in time. According to the mission plan, there
were still seven earthmonths before the Orbiter must leave Fiixian
space to rendezvous with the mother ship *Hawking* for the return
jumps to Earth.

Worlds have been won and lost in seven months.

But if the Lander was dead, so was the possibility of the
landing party's return to Earth.

Away, such thoughts!

The priests were stirring. The huddle had fallen silent. As if
by mutual consent, or simply through mutual fatigue, the priests
ended their debate. With a series of hollow thuds that rang the
closest thing to a formal coda Megan had yet heard from this

clergy, the books were closed and passed to the apprentices to be rewrapped in their protective finery for safe passage back to the priestly library. The group stood about for a moment, aimless, their brown faces sharing an expression of frustration and deep foreboding.

Megan folded up the sketchbook and stuck her pencil behind her ear. *It's almost suppertime, anyway,* she concluded hopefully. Whatever purpose this gathering had served, it had not satisfied its participants. As the priests passed by her on their way toward the inner stairs, they allowed her pleasant but distracted nods.

If anything, she decided, *they look less happy than when they came down here an hour ago.*

She stood up with some effort and stretched her stiffened legs. The wind invaded the folds of her blanket and set her shivering again. Tyril stowed her knitting in a pouch at her waist and wrapped her own thick shawl more tightly around herself.

"Coold," she ventured.

"Cold," Megan agreed, and led the way up the stairs.

14

Susannah ducked her head and squeezed the heavy water bag into the narrow entry corridor. Warm air and a little light from the cavern inside strayed along the rock walls. She sniffed, analyzing the separate odors.

All right, nose. Tell me who's home.

She could not scent out each individual, as the Sawls claimed was possible, but the smells generated by specific personal activities were easy enough to identify. She paused and set down the bulbous leather sack to sniff with greater concentration. She smelled lamp oil and burning dung, both uninformative for her purposes, as they were ever-present background odors of the Caves, as was the barn smell of the woven straw matting that softened the stone floors in the domestic spaces. There were cooking smells as well: the flat odor of soy stew, the metallic tang of instant coffee.

And there!

The slight hot-paper scent of photographs being studied too close to the fire.

Megan's home.

Susannah struggled with the waterskin in the near dark and emerged into the cavern slightly breathless. She lugged it across the matting to the newly bricked-in firepit and lowered it with a sigh.

"Just think what great shape we're going to be in when we get out of here," remarked Megan from the comfort of the fire's circle of warmth.

"Yeah." Susannah knelt beside the waterskin. It gurgled as she leaned against it to use it as a pillow. "Any word from the Outside?"

Megan drew a red circle on the top photo in her lap, then set

113

the whole pile and her notebook aside. "Ronnie's not back yet."
She reached over the fire to stir a large pot with a long-handled
wooden spoon. "Every day for a week, she's out there in this!
She comes back looking worse than you did."

Susannah touched the pink healing skin on her wrists and
chin. "At least one of us hasn't given up on them."

Megan tapped the miniterminal she still wore on her wrist.
"Six and a half days, to be exact, by the ship's clock. My
chronometer still works, even if the rest is a piece of junk. So.
How goes the search for the witch doctors?" She laughed at
Susannah's reflex frown. "I call them that mostly to annoy
Stavros. Actually, I thought they patched you up just fine. I've
always had a secret faith in homespun medicines."

Susannah's frown deepened. "It's frustrating. I'm beginning
to think going through Stav is not the way to send a message
around here."

"Even yours? I know he stonewalls me at every turn, but I'd
have thought you'd get better treatment."

"He's too preoccupied with his own quest to help with someone else's."

Megan pursed her lips. "You could read it that way. But don't
you think he's been even more secretive than usual since we
moved into the Caves?"

Susannah gave an uneasy shrug. "I've hardly seen him since
then. Except to ask what the words for 'doctor' and 'hospital'
are. He says he doesn't know."

"I'm sure your request has been conveyed. They'll come to
you when they're ready. It's often like this with a First Contact—
takes time for things to open up."

Susannah wrapped her arms around her knees, hardly consoled, and sighed again. "What are you up to?"

Megan sorted through a handful of photos, laid a few out on
the notebook and moved her oil lamp in closer. "Been trying to
put these pix of the entry friezes into some kind of order."

"Chronological?"

Megan shook her head. "Don't know enough yet to do that.
I'm trying to sort according to reappearing themes and characters. It's unenlightening so far, but I figure you gotta start
somewhere." She raised an eyebrow. "Well, look who's here."

Stavros slipped in at the entrance and padded barefoot across
the mats to crouch by the fire. He gave Susannah a quick smile
that tried to look offhand, then blinked darkly at Megan. He held
a metal ship's wrench in one hand and a complication of ceramic

tubing in the other. He wore a ship's-issue shirt over his Sawl tunic and baggy Sawl pants. The shirt and his fingers were black with grease. "Any sign of McPherson?" he asked.

"Not yet," replied Megan as she ladled stew into a clay bowl. "You better not let the Commander see you using that shirt as a rag."

Stavros gathered his shirttail and wiped at the threaded end of the tubing. "Ron promised she'd help me with this."

"What is it?" Susannah asked.

"Faucet." He pointed into the darkness by the doorway. Thick ceramic pipes hung by new leather fittings bolted to the rock wall. "That's what that stuff's all about. The guildsmen don't like to set plumbing before a living space is finished, but they're making an exception in our case." Stavros had kept the secret of the Baths as he had promised, but had managed to obtain for his colleagues the same more primitive gravity-fed cold-water system that served every Sawl domestic space. He held his handful up to the lamplight. "See how clean the cast is? Virtually seamless. The Sawls have a genius for ceramics. You couldn't find workmanship like this anywhere on Earth! The pipes along the wall are sealed off now, but when I attach this, it'll break the seal and we'll have running water!"

"Or so the theory goes," said Megan dryly into her bowl of stew.

Susannah smiled at Stavros's enthusiasm. "Hot and cold?" she joked.

Stavros frowned.

Megan chortled. "What do you think this is, the Ritz?"

Stavros looked away from Susannah's smile and eyed Megan critically. "How can you stand to eat that stuff?"

Megan grunted. Her mouth was full of soybean stew. She lowered her spoon and swallowed. "Didn't used to bother you before you went native on us." She looked to Susannah. "Wait till he gets one of those expeditions where you have to wear a mask and analyze everything you touch."

"I've never done one of those either," said Susannah. She stirred the fire gingerly with a long metal spike she'd found lying on the mats. In the rekindled blaze, she recognized it as a piton scavenged from Clausen's climbing gear. She set it aside guiltily. She assessed the diminishing fuel supply, counted three dung cakes off the stack and fed them into the fire. "Listen, about this weather. Is anybody besides me getting the impression that it's worse than usual out there?"

Megan balanced her bowl on her knee, a mild gleam coming into her eye.

"We haven't really been here long enough to tell," Stavros muttered.

"But I mean, what do the Sawls have to say about it?" Susannah pursued.

Stavros glanced around the high-domed cave as if searching its unlit recesses for someone to call him away on urgent business. He specifically avoided Megan's smirk. "They say it's worse than usual," he allowed finally.

"They're worried because their predictions have been going wrong," stated Megan with an assured wave of her spoon.

Stavros bridled. "They haven't been making any."

Megan turned to Susannah. "The priests gather regularly. I've timed them. Every twenty-nine and a quarter hours."

"Once a cycle," Stavros added sullenly.

"Each time it's a different cave mouth—maybe they're making sure the whole population knows they're on the job—and they look out at the storm and confer at length, and then . . ."

"Then nothing." Stavros was finally lured into the debate. "No prediction. If the weather were going to change, they'd make a prediction. What's got them worried, Meg, is that it's not changing."

Megan gave a dubious snort. "Another chicken-or-the-egg dispute," she said to Susannah. "I still say it'd give their folks more confidence in them if they presented a positive front."

Stavros made a vehement gesture with his wrench and nearly lost his balance. "It's not some kind of cover-up, Meg! The priests have a responsibility to let the population know what the weather's going to do. The FoodGuild is getting worried about their supplies. Rationing procedures were announced last cycle."

"All the more reason to eat the food we brought with us," murmured Megan, dipping her spoon into her bowl.

Susannah frowned gently. "Is it really as bad as that? Even if the dry supplies run low, there're still the dairy herds, and the fowl."

"And the mushroom cellars," Megan added with gloomy humor. "Think what Emil could have done with those! Rock-fungus quiche, the geologist's dream meal!"

Susannah smiled patiently. "I was talking about a more general anxiety . . . that sort of manic energy that hides a desperation you're trying to pretend you don't feel?"

Stavros rose abruptly from his crouch. "You want psychol-

ogy, try Dr. Levy here. She's got lots of theories.'' He brandished his pipe construction. ''I deal with what the words mean.
One by one. Period.''

Susannah flicked Megan a knowing eye. The anthropologist
was chasing the last morsels of rehydrated bean curd across the
bottom of her dish with utter concentration. Susannah sighed.
''Okay, I get it. The disciplines are at war again, right?''

Her spoon halfway to her mouth, Megan looked up at Stavros.
''If the priests aren't making predictions, what's keeping the
gamblers so busy?''

The linguist drummed his foot against the matting. ''That is a
side issue, Megan.''

She shrugged. ''So that's where we disagree.''

''Gamblers?'' asked Susannah.

Megan tossed a nod in Susannah's direction and a sly grin at
Stavros. ''She's hopelessly naive, but we love her anyway, eh?''

Stavros gave a dark growl of exasperation, snatched up Megan's
lantern and stalked away from the fire, wrench and faucet clenched
tight in hand. He set the lantern down along the wall where the
water pipes angled and dropped into a square stone trough. An
impromptu sleeping platform filled the back of the cavern, constructed from disassembled crates. Damp blankets strung on
lengths of climbing rope provided a minimum of privacy.

Over the ensuing grinding of the wrench against the hard
ceramic, Susannah cocked her head at Megan. ''Explain?''

Megan chewed for a moment, swallowed, then took a breath.
''Well, it all started when I dared to suggest that the Sawls and
their priests have no special gift for weather prediction beyond
your usual rural body of empirical knowledge. As in, for instance, the farmer's almanacs that are common to agricultural
societies.''

Susannah considered. ''Seems reasonable, so long as you'll
admit they have a stunning record of success so far.''

''Yes, until the past week. You see, what they do have a gift
for is observation. They're objective, they record assiduously,
they apply the proper data when a known circumstance recurs.
Those priests'd make great lab techs. But to listen to Stavros,
you'd think there was magic involved!''

''Intuition!'' Stavros roared from the far end of the cavern.
The racket of the wrench increased.

''Get back here and present your case yourself, if you're going
to eavesdrop!'' Megan leaned toward Susannah, shaking her
head. ''It's weird,'' she whispered. ''The lad has become a total

literalist. He's so involved in his 'absolute meaning'—like he said, each word, one by one—that he takes the whole sentence merely as the sum of its parts. He's forgotten how to read between the lines.'' Megan tucked her thick legs up under her as she hitched herself closer to the fire. "It's like this: you ask a Sawl how come he knew it was going to rain. Well, he says, the priests said so. But then he says that it was obvious anyway because the hot winds—you recall we had hot winds for about an hour?—the hot winds are the battle fires of Lagri, and Valla Ired always responds with the same strategic defense, that is, by throwing an ocean at him." She sat back to let the image sink in.

"Rather poetical, don't you think?" Susannah ventured.

"Exactly! But Stavros, he says, right, and then what . . . ? As if this made some kind of literal sense, like there were actual gods out there trying to brain each other with thunderbolts!" Megan threw her hands into the air. "He's letting metaphor become reality!"

"And your interpretation?"

Megan spread her palms. "It's what we've seen on a dozen different worlds, including our own. Lagri and Valla Ired are god constructs of the sort that primitives have always invented to explain natural phenomena. As for this business of predictions . . ." Megan cleared her throat, and Susannah knew she was about to be dealt a full-fledged lecture. "Look at the evidence. The RangerGuild has this remarkable system of lookouts and couriers to provide round-the-clock vigilance. Then there's that Sawl ability to mobilize on the instant that so astounded us during the Lander evacuation. So. When the earliest signs of a change appear, too faint for our urban senses to detect, the rangers note them, relay them, report them to the priests, who base their prediction on their study of the collected lore of generations of devoted weather-watchers. It's brilliant, but it's not magic. Even the priests don't pretend it's magic. You should see them hot and heavy over their books out there in the cave mouths!" Megan dusted her hands together as if the issue was closed, then added, "They wouldn't be such inveterate gamblers if they thought they were always going to be right . . . right?"

"I guess," replied Susannah neutrally, still in the dark about the gambling.

Stavros returned to the fire with a determined air, wiping his hands on his shirttail. He knelt to fish among Megan's photographs, pulled one out and passed it across the firepit to Susannah. She held it up to the firelight. It was a detail of two frieze figures facing each other with great formality, as if in ritual preparation for hand-to-hand combat. One was thick and helmeted, with finlike protrusions curling up from rump and shoulders. It was terra-cotta-colored, with traces of polychrome on its squarish visor. The other figure was smoothly contoured, carved in a cool white stone shot with green and lavender.

Susannah traced a finger around the print. "Ferocious, aren't they."

Stavros edged minutely closer. "You know what 'Lagri' means?" he asked as if laying out some mystery for her. When she shook her head and looked encouragingly interested, he stood and came around the fire to crouch behind her. He reached gingerly over her arm to touch the head of the red figure. "It means 'drought,' as best as I can tell." His fingertip slipped along the serrations of the brighter fins, a gesture so like a caress that Susannah felt suddenly distracted by his nearness. "Flames," he said intensely. "See them?" His finger shifted. "The white one is Valla Ired, which means 'the ocean bottom.' " He stood and looked down at her. "Interesting?"

Susannah kept her eyes on the photograph, lest they betray her distraction. "All the gods' names have literal meanings, then?"

He moved away, into the shadows. "They're actually goddesses, as it turns out, and there are only the two of them: Valla and Lagri. The Sisters, they call them."

Susannah raised an eyebrow at the fiercely combatant figures. "Sisters? Some family."

"Perhaps I should investigate the Sawls' views on sibling rivalry," Megan commented.

"I think I've detected a third figure," Stavros continued, beginning to pace. Susannah could feel his tension radiating like heat behind her. The deeper he got into his subject, the more defensive he would become, as if sure that no one could care to listen, but unable to stop himself from telling them anyway. *He's so used to people thinking he's crazy,* she decided.

"She shows up with some consistency," he went on, "but only as a victim, never as a deity. Often she appears as a multitude, especially in the big friezes, like those in the Meeting Hall. But the Sawls seem to have no distinct name for her."

"Two goddesses. Not much of a pantheon."

"He is right about the number," Megan offered. "That's all I've come up with as well. The Sawls appear to be ditheistic, a first in my experience."

Stavros paced out of the shadow and hunkered down across

the firepit from Susannah. She saw the flames reflected in his eyes and for a moment wondered if Megan was right after all to worry about his sanity.

"We all have our own methods of getting at the truth," he began with quiet assurance. "The only way I can approach a total understanding of a language is by setting aside all, and I mean *all*, personal or cultural preconceptions. I must try to see this world the way the Sawls see it. I must learn to think the way they do." He paused, looked down, then fixed Susannah with a challenging stare. "If the Sawls say that the rains come out of Valla Ired's arsenal, then so do I."

Susannah leaned to the side on one elbow, backing off from his stare. "This is a methodological skirmish," she decreed.

This time, Megan resisted. "Wrong! When you do things his way, you throw objective distance to the winds! And you know what happens? You wind up, as he has, selling the Sawls short with all this talk of magic and superstition. Because, you know, it's all a kind of literary exercise for the Sawls, this speaking in poetry and metaphor, like most of the superstitions *we* still give lip service to. They know the weather is just the weather, but to personify it with names and histories promotes a richer understanding of their place in Nature. Mythologies impose order on Nature's chaos." She smiled and shook a finger at the young linguist as if he were one of her students. "They make damn good stories, too, and the Sawls adore telling stories. Did the ancient Greeks, your own ancestors, actually believe that the pictures they saw among the stars represented the physical bodies of the gods and heroes they named them for?"

Susannah chuckled, but Stavros remained unsmiling. "The ancient Greeks *knew* that gods walked the earth," he asserted.

"Knew?"

He nodded with dark conviction.

Megan glanced at Susannah. "See what I mean?"

Susannah sat up, brushing her long hair behind her. "But aren't you both saying the same thing in the long run? That the Sawls have developed a psychic defense to cope with the weather that goes hand in hand with their physical defense?"

"Maybe," allowed Megan.

"No," said Stavros. But behind his stubborn gaze, Susannah saw a young man pleading for her understanding. "Megan assumes the Sawls have the same relationship to superstition as she does," he pursued. "But there's a gulf of difference between believing and *knowing*." He rose and stood for a moment as if daring them to continue the debate, then slouched back into the darkness to the more comfortable company of his pipes and sink. He moved the lantern to a shallow ledge above the stone trough and bent over to rub grease into the pipe threads. He fitted the faucet into place and rotated it cautiously. "Should have water any minute," he called.

Susannah smiled, mostly to herself, and stretched her legs in front of her, brushing straw splinters from her therm-suit. "So what's all this about gambling, Meg?" She fed another dung cake into the fire.

Megan's gesture would have been familiar to her Jewish grand-mother. "Haven't you noticed? These people will gamble over anything!" She tossed a covert glance into the shadows, then leaned forward. "But their real passion is gambling over the weather. Sure, they hold ceremonies and they carve their gods— that is, goddesses—into every surface available, but they don't *pray*. What do they do instead? Invoke their luck. The traditional greeting, 'Rhe khem,' means 'Your luck.' The appropriate response, 'Khem rhe,' means 'Luck to you.' "

"Luck can also mean fortune, as in 'Be fortunate,' 'Be well,' perhaps asking the goddesses for good fortune. That's a kind of prayer."

Megan shook her head. "It's the element of chance, of the random occurrence, that's important here. I ask you, how devout can they be? They've got pools, odds, the whole setup, a mini-Vegas without the glitz."

Susannah laughed. "Farmers have been gambling on the weather for eons!"

"Not so formally," said Megan. "You see, the wagers are laid whenever the priests promise an official prediction. I mean, goods change hands at the drop of a hat around here!"

"The drop of a priest's hat." Susannah's grin was fond. "You sound a little shocked, Meg. I thought I was the innocent one."

"Well, I suppose I am a little shocked, though not half as much as Stav is. He's got the Sawls so romanticized he can't even deal with the notion of a nation of gamesters. And listen to this." She paused dramatically. "Guess who holds the bets."

"Do tell."

"Now this is no idle gossip," Megan reproved. "This is serious."

"I'm listening . . . seriously."

"The priests' apprentices."

"Hold the bets?"

Meg nodded significantly. "They take note of the stakes when the bets are laid, then settle with the winners when the priests send them around to announce the predictions. Not only is this gambling officially sanctioned by the priesthood, it's administered by them as well."

"I'm confused. They bet on the prediction or on the actual weather?"

"Both! All Sawls know enough weather lore to make educated guesses based on the reported signs. So they bet on what the prediction will be, then there's another round of betting on the final outcome, how the weather actually turns out."

"Whew!" Susannah was starting to giggle. "Do the 'prentices take commission?"

Stavros let out a yell from the sink. "We've got a trickle here!"

"Tips," confided Megan, frowning.

The giggle burst into a belly laugh. "Liphar!" Susannah choked out.

Megan's nod was insistently severe.

"Our good friend Liphar," Susannah repeated between gasps, "is a numbers runner!"

"I fail to see what's so funny," Megan replied stuffily.

"*Water!*" Stavros exulted, as a coughing gurgle echoed from the dark end of the cavern. "*Water!* It works!"

"You guys leave me any supper?" called McPherson from the entrance. She limped stiffly to the firepit, kicked a blanket closer to the flame and dropped onto it carelessly. Her therm-suit dripped wet ocher mud onto the matting. Her round face was drawn but for the high color of exertion spotting her cheeks. "Who's a numbers runner?"

The mood of manic cheer died like a bad joke, but Susannah obligingly explained.

The pilot gave an offhand shrug. "Oh yeah? Glad someone's clearing a profit around here."

Stavros shut down the faucet and brought the lantern over to the fire. With unusual gentleness, he said, "Never mind, Ron. Just keep thinking of the fortune CONPLEX is paying into your account back home."

"Won't do me no good if I'm stuck here forever and ever." She ran her fingers through her sodden curls, fluffed them a little, then slumped down listlessly.

"Did you spot Weng on your way in?" asked Megan.

McPherson shook her head.

"Where does she *go* when she's not here?" Susannah marveled.

Megan waved a hand. "The realm of the abstract. She'll be here soon enough. The Commander always comes up for meals."

"She just never eats anything," McPherson muttered.

"What's it like outside?" asked Stavros abruptly.

McPherson shrugged again. "Same old shit. Black as pitch and blowin' like hell." She rubbed her eyes with muddied fingers. "When's this gonna stop?"

"Only another week until dawn," Susannah offered.

The others just looked at her.

"Well, it'll help with the darkness, at least," she defended weakly.

Stavros knelt beside the lantern, making his fingernails greasier by trying to clean them on his shirt. "Got running water now, Ron."

McPherson grunted.

Megan searched out a clean bowl and dipped it into the stew. Juice dripped hissing into the coals as she passed it over to McPherson. "No sign of them, eh?"

"Sign? Shit." The pilot dug into the stew without looking up. "We could walk right by 'em in this crap and never know it."

Megan sat back. "Tyril says the Master Ranger doesn't think there's much point prolonging the search," she told Susannah quietly. "She doesn't want to risk any more of her people out there."

"Aguidran's an idiot," McPherson growled between swallows.

Stavros glanced up sharply but kept his rebuke to a monotone. "She's an idiot because she won't let you go out there alone?"

McPherson threw down her half-empty bowl. It spun around, splattering stew, and clattered into the bricked firepit. She leaped up and bolted the length of the cavern to the raised sleeping platform. She yanked aside a blanket partition and pulled it shut behind her.

"Nice work, Ibiá," remarked Megan.

"Not my fucking fault," muttered the linguist. "You'd think that goddamned Sled was the Holy Grail! She should let it go for a few days and get some sleep!"

"You of all people say this?" Megan barked. "You, our resident lunatic?" She contemplated a tirade, but sighed deeply instead and said with patience that she did not feel, "It's not the Sled so much, you know that. It's Taylor. Have some sympathy for her feelings."

Stavros drew up his shoulders sullenly.

"Besides, there *is* still hope," Susannah put in, without much conviction. "Emil was a veteran pilot, and the Sleds are provisioned for at least a couple of weeks."

"They're gone," Stavros stated.

"Weng's kept the homing beacon broadcasting, bless her heart," Megan observed.

"They're gone," repeated Stavros more loudly.

Megan gave him a sour eye. "You're working real hard at being a creep today, Ibiá."

"Meg, they are gone." He spread his palms like the most reasonable of men. "Why is everybody pretending otherwise? Two weeks out in the open, in *this*? We're wasting precious resources running after dead men!" He stood, visibly restraining his indignation. "We should be digging in, maximizing what we have left to us! We need McPherson *here*, not out on some wild goose chase! We *need* the emergency power that's feeding that damned beacon! When are the rest of you going to wake up to the fact that we've got to take an active interest in our *own* survival on this world? We're probably going to be here awhile!" He clenched his fists, then released an explosive sigh and stalked from the cavern.

Megan stared after him but could only shake her head.

Susannah studied her fingers and the even regiments of colored thread marching across the weave of her blanket. The dung fire crackled, its coals crumbling into ash. "He'll be sorry soon as he's calmed down," she murmured.

Megan stirred finally to add more fuel to the dying fire. "In a way, he's right, though I hate to admit it. Leave it to youth to be so unsentimental."

"McPherson's younger than he is," Susannah reminded her.

"McPherson was in love."

"Ummm." Susannah sucked her cheek, thinking: *The hard thing about Stav is that he's always at his most unreasonable when he's right.*

know they think I'm crazy to keep watching out but its them who are crazy if they think I'm gonna sit down in the Black Hole with them all day, nobody beeping shiptime anymore and them always arguing, Meg and Stavros, about some shit that don't matter, when all that matters is getting out of this joint ALIVE!

I think the Old Lady's given up already, not just on finding Jay and the Sled but on the whole damn thing! Like maybe she's been looking for an excuse to sit back with that MUSIC of hers that nobody ever listens to but her. You'll love this one now. Meg says to me, that music's serious work and it takes patience, and when I understand about patience, I'll understand the Commander! Ha! If patience is some other way of saying sitting around on your ass, then I'd as soon never understand that one. Well hell, you know how it is. The Commander's a good enough Capt and she's seen a whole lot of shit in her time but she's not much for shore leave, I guess. You know, like Bob used to be when he was home without you. He spent all day in the workshop making those rings he was always giving out to everyone, remember, with all the space junk set in them?

Well, now the Old Lady won't even talk about finding Jay and the Sled anymore. And now Agidran quit on me too, but she at least gave me good reason. I mean, she's got her job to do and she's got her men to watch out for. That last time she took us out, shit, it was blowing! We nearly lost the whole bunch of us into a big ravine and A. says it wasn't there before this storm came. And then when we were almost back to the caves, we got hit by this amazing whirlwind, and the rain

15

Stavros regretted that he must go empty-handed into Kav Ashimmel's presence, but he had requested the audience, thus he must observe its requirements. The battered canvas pack that had carried his recorder and notebooks throughout his university career was set aside at the blunt-columned entrance of the PriestHall. It was not, Liphar assured him, that any threat was seen in the little gray box that repeated every word it was told. A subtle Sawl eye roll implied that priests and even apprentice priests lived elbow to elbow with mysteries equally as unfathomable. But tradition dictated, he explained, that everything but the body and its coverings be left behind upon entering the place of priestly studies.

Stavros had to discard another expectation once inside the hallowed portal. The PriestHall held a prime location in the Caves, being on the same level and only one entry to the east of the great central MeetingHall. He anticipated a cavern on the same grand scale, with lofty vaulting and enormous walk-in fireplaces. Instead, Liphar ushered him with great excitement and ceremony into a smoky warren of a hall, bustling with comings and goings, humming with the sounds of lecture and debate. The low-ceilinged space might have been the crypt of a Romanesque cathedral, though considerably more lively. It was divided by a dozen long rows of smoothly cylindrical columns, each as thick as a man's arm span. They were set much closer together than their great girth and the low vaulting would seem to require. In each shaft, a small oil lamp burned in an eye-level niche. Straw matting rustled underfoot as Stavros followed in Liphar's circuitous wake. They threaded through several rows of the fat stone cylinders, avoiding the clots of priests and student priests who sat in cross-legged discussion while bending over mugs of hot

126

tea and musty books, waving chunks of crusty orange bread to emphasize a favorite point.

Stavros wondered when he would discover some concrete trace of mysticism in the Sawl religion. His instincts insisted that the Sawls' relationship to their goddesses was not so pragmatic as Megan proposed. But so far, his only real evidence lay in the weather mythos which pervaded every aspect of Sawl life and language. When he was honest with himself, he would admit that it was not simple mysticism he was after, but a hint at genuine power. A part of him wanted to believe that the Sawl priests were more than skilled guessers. He longed for proof that they could actually foretell the vagaries of the Fiixian climate by means of their magical relationship with the cosmos.

But he was not likely to discover magic in the PriestHall, he decided as he peered about. This was not a place of worship or even meditation. Stavros recognized the stolid aura of academia drifting among the pillars with the lamp smoke. He felt both at home and suddenly claustrophobic. At any moment, his old semiotics professor might come wheeling out from behind a nearby column. Stavros laughed aloud to relieve a creeping panic, and several apprentices turned from their studies to stare at him as he passed. Ahead, a seated gathering blocked their path. A trio of priests were conducting a highly vocal seminar with several dozen older students. Liphar turned aside, but their presence had already caused a lull in the intense debate. Stavros wished he were shorter and slimmer. His Sawl clothing was not enough disguise to allow him to pass among the Sawls unnoticed.

Ignoring the stares, Liphar urged him onward with quick little beckonings. One long wall of the hall was now visible as a tapestry of muted color striped by the darker silhouettes of the columns. As they moved closer, Stavros could see that the rock was honeycombed with niches, longer, deeper and more regular than the usual lamp niches. They mounted one on top of the other like a legion of shelves. They were crammed with wrapped parcels of every conceivable size and description. Wooden ladders propped against the shelves accessed the higher stacks.

Stavros gazed through the dim smoky light at the rows and rows of leather- and cloth-shrouded bundles. He knew those wrappings. The wave-and-flame seal of the PriestGuild decorated every one.

Megan would kill to see this, he thought with satisfaction. *This is the PriestGuild Library*.

Liphar waited at his elbow with unusual patience, savoring his awe.

"How many, Lifa?" Stavros asked, a little breathlessly.

Liphar considered his ten fingers, struggling with the newness of Terran numbers. "Hunderd hunderd, maybe," he stated finally but then splayed both palms in the Sawlish shrug.

Stavros delighted him with an amazed whistle. "Are they very old?"

The young Sawl shook his curls indignantly. "Ibi! Give mo't good care, we!"

Stavros smiled. ET linguistics theory had warned him that concepts of age might be tricky to communicate, time being among the most relative of phenomena. The Sawl astronomical year was roughly equivalent to 209 Earth days, little over half a Terran year, and the Sawls did not use it as a significant time marker. Instead, they measured long time periods in generations. Stavros had not yet been able to determine the formal duration of a generation, as he and Liphar still lacked a common yardstick. He was left with only the more physical markers of age to point to, which inevitably led Liphar to misunderstand "old" as meaning "damaged" or "disabled." Stavros collected such near misses. His favorite character in all literature was Mrs. Malaprop, though this was a secret that would die with him. These glancing errors were not only funny. They taught lessons about the relationship of language and perception. Liphar seemed to appreciate this as well, since nothing could start him giggling faster than Stavros attempting to choose, from a battery of at least a dozen separate words meaning "rain," the one word that properly described a particular kind of rain falling at a particular moment. Stavros's senses were not yet tuned to the fine distinctions that a Sawl naturally applied to an issue as critical as the weather.

He moved closer to the wall of swaddled volumes to inspect a particularly shredded and fading wrapping. He drank in the musty smell of aged leather. Libraries were always his favorite places of refuge. Liphar sighed and looked troubled. He pointed at the bundle but did not touch it.

"Make new very soon, we," he offered. He cycled his hands one around the other, carefully enshrouding an invisible treasure. "New itra."

"Itra?" Stavros repeated the gesture, and Liphar nodded. Stavros wondered how many times this particular ancient text had been rebound, had had new wrappings made for it. He noted some interesting variations in the wave-and-flame designs between the older and newer-looking itras. He would happily have lingered, having forgotten Kav Ashimmel for the moment, but Liphar tugged his sleeve and continued onward. This time, his palm was to his mouth, bidding silence.

They followed the last row of columns toward the deepest corner of the cavern. Stavros heard the voice long before he could see the speaker. It was the voice of a woman who clearly did not care if her lecture disturbed any other nearby gatherings. A good deal of open space surrounded her group as if others had moved off out of range.

As they slipped into the outer edge of the gathering, Liphar found space on the floor among the listeners and signaled Stavros to do the same. "Kav Ashimmel," he said, nodding at the speaker.

Stavros settled cross-legged on the matting with his back against a column. Now his un-Sawlish height allowed him an excellent view over the heads of the others. Kav Ashimmel was a brusque and stocky priest with graying curls. She wore her guildseal robe neatly fastened from hem to embroidered collar, but the long wide sleeves of her undertunic were rolled up to her elbows to allow for the greatest possible freedom of gesture. The smooth blank palms of her hands shone like silk in the lamplight. She paced as she spoke, and seemed occasionally to slip into a private distraction, out of which she broke with renewed vigor for her argument.

Stavros ached for his translator. This was far more complex than everyday conversational Sawlish, or even than most of the tale-chants he had begun to translate. The cadences of Ashimmel's presentation suggested an almost Talmudic disputation on the interpretation of a certain piece of text. Much of the vocabulary he was familiar with, having mostly to do with the goddesses and the weather. But her use of tenses left him in a muddle, and now and then she would pause for emphasis to repeat a long and carefully articulated phrase that was totally incomprehensible to him. It did not even sound like quite the same language.

A corrupt form? Stavros thought that unlikely. *A more formal form, for ritual use?*

He leaned close to Liphar. "Lifa, what's she saying?"

Liphar's eyes widened in distress. His palm flew to his open mouth.

Stavros drew in his shoulders in apology and nodded his promise to be silent. He heard Lagri's name mentioned then, and seconds later, Ashimmel growled the name of the sister-goddess,

Valla Ired. A rustle breathed through the gathering as the listeners rubbed their talisman beads. As the storm continued into the second half of the long Fiixian night, most laymen avoided speaking Valla's name for fear it might add to her strength. Stavros noticed that many wore smaller red clay beads alongside the usual green malachite, and that Kav Ashimmel was now using words from a vocabulary that Liphar was just beginning to teach him: the terms used to describe the various climatic weapons used by the goddesses to fight the arrah, the weather war. The word "arrah" was itself ambiguous. It did not seem to mean war per se, but rather "struggle" or perhaps "wrestling," which is what Liphar did to define its meaning, or even simply "game." What "arrah" did seem to imply was the condition of endlessness, not as in "eternal," Stavros decided, but as in "for-goddamn-bloody-ever."

Then, as Kav Ashimmel once again intoned her untranslatable bit of text, Stavros heard within it familiar syllables, a phrase that might have been "atoph phenar." Liphar often used this phrase to explain to Stavros what would happen if one of the Sisters ever defeated the other. Stavros had it loosely translated as "stillness of death," but however large his margin of error, he knew it meant bad news.

With this final repetition, Ashimmel ended her lecture. Her sober eyes surveyed her audience warningly, raking back and forth until they met Stavros's unflinching Terran gaze. They narrowed, then moved on until she had made eye contact with each and every listener. Then she dismissed them with a few brisk exhortations, waited solemnly as they rose and filed away, then stalked across the floor to confront Stavros with her arms folded.

Liphar remained seated, looking cowed. Stavros elected to follow suit. He did not want to stand and be forced to look down on this impressive priest. Ashimmel stared for a moment, then barked a question at Liphar. The young Sawl answered eagerly and at length. Stavros heard his own name mentioned with that of Kav Daven, whom Liphar called the Talesinger. Kav Daven was the priest whom Stavros really wanted to see. Within the PriestGuild, Daven was the informal keeper of myth and ritual. He was also extremely old, said Liphar (as in "disabled"), and secluded by the other priests like a precious treasure. Thus Ashimmel, as GuildMaster, dispensed or withheld any permission for an audience with Kav Daven.

But frail as he was, Kav Daven, Liphar had implied, very

much maintained a will of his own. The same iron stubbornness that kept him moving and breathing at such an advanced age also encouraged him to prolong his refusal to settle on a permanent apprentice. The entire Guild agreed that it was long past time for young blood to begin training in the ancient complications of the ritual lore, eventually to succeed the old priest, who surely could not manage to live forever. Many candidates had been offered. But when challenged, Kav Daven (said Liphar) would smile and nod and nod and continue to turn away each hopeful apprentice as unsuitable for this reason or that. Stavros contemplated the politics of the gesture, then decided that perhaps it was simply an old man's way of clinging eagerly to life.

Ashimmel asked Liphar another curt question, one that Stavros understood and that caused him to glance up at her in surprise.

Since the Wokind appeared in snow, she demanded of the young man, what proof does *this* one offer that he is not some new strategy of Valla Ired's?

Stavros had been wondering when that suspicion would be voiced. Liphar drew himself up somewhat and offered the defense that there was no proof the Wokind were not sent by Lagri to weaken Valla Ired at a time when she seemed to hold the planet in a deathgrip.

As humbly as he could, Stavros returned Kav Ashimmel's stare. "I am human, Kav," he said. "*Kho sue epele*, as yourself."

Ashimmel blinked and looked interested at the sound of her language on the alien's tongue. She stared a moment longer, then nodded abruptly to herself and stalked away, her sandals flapping authoritatively through the forest of pillars.

Liphar let out a deep sigh and sprawled a little easier on the matting.

"Will she let me see him, Lifa?"

Liphar opened his palms. "Kav Daven say yes, say no. If he want, you come."

But how will he ever know if he wants it, worried Stavros, *with a tough old soldier like Ashimmel standing in my way?*.

He stood, and Liphar scrambled up beside him.

"O cilmillar, Ibi?" The young man grinned eagerly.

Stavros laughed. Liphar was coming to know him too well. "Okay, Lifa, you're on. What better way to forget your troubles, eh? To the Baths!"

16

Susannah followed Megan and Tyril through the entry corridor. As Megan's oil lantern disappeared around a bend, Susannah felt her way along in darkness, avoiding the drip from the new water pipes hanging just above her head. The comfort of their new home still had room for improvement. The entry needed widening. The larger access tunnel that joined this westernmost excavation to the rest of the Caves was rough-hewn and unlit. When the Sawls had offered the (as Megan insistently called it) Black Hole to the Terrans, their apologies for its unfinished state had included the eager assurance that it lacked only a generation or so until completion.

"Have you noticed these?" asked Susannah as they emerged into the dark outer tunnel.

Megan raised her lantern. The sharp-edged rock around the mouth of the entryway was hung with many long strips of cloth. She moved the lamp closer. Even in the dim light, the colors of the cloth showed clearly: sun-bright yellows and flaming oranges, smoldering vermilion and strong, deep reds. Susannah drew one strip gently through her hand. The fabric was soft and fine. It had several small terra-cotta beads worked into a knot tied at the end.

Megan turned to Tyril. The Sawl woman was watching their puzzlement with impassive unease.

"What's this all about, Tyr?" asked Megan, though she recognized that careful blankness that came into Tyril's manner when she didn't want to understand what was said to her. Tyril's brown eyes lowered briefly, flicked to the doorway and back to Megan. Megan had an image of a smooth lake rippled by disturbance from below.

132

Susannah balanced the little clay bead on her palm. "For khem?" she asked hopefully. "Is it for khem?"

Tyril nodded slowly, unconvincingly. "Lagri embriha. Nho arma Lagri."

Megan's eyes lit. "Ah, right." She stroked the bright streamers. "These are Lagri's associated colors. The colors of the Flame. But I hadn't noticed them decorating doorways before."

"Something special for us?" offered Susannah.

"Umm." Megan lowered the lamp thoughtfully as Tyril moved on ahead. "But why should we be in particular need of Lagri's attention?"

"And why just Lagri? Why not the other sister as well?"

"You weren't listening to Stav's lecture. Rainstorms are considered part of Valla's weaponry. She's a bit unpopular at the moment, as you can imagine." Megan's brow furrowed. She fell into a pondering silence. Susannah let her think in peace. She'd only be grouchy if disturbed.

They reached a more inhabited sector of the Caves, turning into a wider throughfare with high barrel-vaulted ceilings. Here the floor was worn smooth. It dipped toward the center where generations of Sawls had walked a path into the stone. Large oil lamps with painted bases glowed in regularly spaced niches, showing the walls to be of a pale, granular rock, enlivened with sculpted textures. In some sections, the rock appeared to be woven, in shaded strands that crisscrossed or herringboned. In others, a thousand tiny scorings dipped and swelled with the contours of the wall, like the furrows of a wheat field.

"Imagine what they could do in bronze," Susannah murmured. She reinterpreted the phrase "living rock" as she trailed a hand across age-softened stone that seemed to breathe in time with the slow flicker of Megan's lantern.

The big tunnel became brighter and more crowded as they went along. Guildsmen bustled by with big baskets strapped to their backs. Cartwheels rattled up ahead.

"Everyone's up and about," said Megan, emerging from her ponder. She extinguished her lantern and checked her chronometer. "This'll be the second shift, if I have it right, or actually, the second just heading home to eat and the third going to work."

"It's a sensible way to organize things. Think how overcrowded the Caves would feel if they all lived on the same schedule," said Susannah. "Earth could learn from the Sawls' example."

"Perhaps," grumped Megan. "If you were brought up with it. I for one long for the old middle-of-the-night lull. Used to get my best thinking done then."

The Sawls who passed smiled pleasantly or waved but did not stop to chat. A slim man wearing the sign of the WeaverGuild on his chest paced beside Tyril briefly for a murmured exchange, then bid goodbye and sped off down a side tunnel. The congestion of people and carts increased. They filed around a slow-moving two-wheeler laden with stacks of grain bags, hauled by a bright-eyed cart hakra the size of a large sheepdog. Its fleshy calloused hooves made no sound on the stone floor. Susannah was reminded to revisit the lower-level stables where the dairy herds were housed. Liphar had rushed them through that leg of his tour, showing a distinct dislike for the big cowlike creatures.

They passed through a residential area, where smaller corridors intersected at regular intervals. Children played a Sawl version of tag at the crossings, or gathered against the walls, engrossed in games that involved brightly colored stone counters being passed back and forth. Susannah saw one boy hunkered over a huge pile of stones. He sported a victorious grin. She nudged Megan.

"Even the children are gamblers," she laughed.

Megan made a sour face. "So it would appear."

Down each smaller corridor, five or six dwelling caverns opened onto a common tunnel. Old men leaned in their doorways, calling across the corridor to each other. Householders swept up the cycle's deposit of straw and manure to dump into bins at the corners. A father called his children in to wash. Balls and small curly-haired animals tumbled underfoot amid shouts and laughter. The sounds and smells of cooking drifted down the side streets. The stares as the Terrans passed were brief or covert. There was no longer the pregnant hush that used to follow them wherever they went in the Caves.

With still-increasing traffic and bustle, they approached a major intersection. The crossing tunnel was as wide as an urban boulevard on Earth. Its arching vaults sharpened and magnified the clamor of voices, groaning axles and wheels clattering on stone. The racket was overwhelming.

"I always feel at home in the MarketHall," Megan remarked.

"I always feel like I just got off a cruise ship," Susannah returned.

Megan laughed darkly. "Fiix *is* a little out of the way, but it could make a proper addition to the commercial tours, I suppose.

At least that would prevent CONPLEX from digging it up down to the bedrock.''

The MarketHall stretched several hundred yards to either side of the intersection. A honeycomb of two- and three-storied shops clung to the high cavern walls. Cloth awnings and banners hung from upper windows; signs painted above on the naked rock proclaimed product and proprietor in colored pictures and spiky lettering. Oil lamps flared from giant spoked rings suspended from the vaulting. They lit mountains of wares spread out on tables and carts. Susannah squinted like a surfacing mole. The open-fronted shops were bright with lamp glare, showing off shelves of glassware and ceramics, handwoven cloth, bright embroidery, paper and leather goods, wooden tools and painted toys. The raw materials were also offered: bulk wool and yarns, dyes, hides, select woods, clay, stones, and the strong plant fibers used for rope and straw matting and wickerwork.

"Don't you find it odd to see no food for sale?" asked Susannah. "I mean, think of the cult of food-selling at home."

"Food isn't exactly a pastime here," replied Megan. "Has to be more carefully regulated than that."

Susannah made a circling gesture. "You think all this is what satisfies their commercial yearnings, which we know they have? I mean, enough to allow them to practice their classic Marxism where the food is concerned?"

"I'd guess survival here dictates a controlled distribution system. Communal food stores feed the greatest number most fairly, and allow for the kind of long-range supply planning they need to make it all last. What impresses me is how little corruption there seems to be within the FoodGuild." Megan shrugged and smiled. "All that gambling helps satisfy the old commercial yearnings as well, I imagine."

They moved through the midst of the bustle. Shoppers crowded in with baskets and multicolored two-wheeled carts, exchanging greetings and news and comments about the merchandise, but Susannah noticed very little buying going on. The proprietors lounged in the doorways of the various guild shops. They gossiped and listened to the reed-and-pipes of the street musicians, and watched dolefully as the shoppers fingered their wares and moved on. Some essentials were being purchased, a new wooden bowl or a wicker back basket to replace one falling apart at the seams.

"The buyers are in a cautious mood," Susannah commented. Rations of the local green-amber beer were being distributed from the FoodGuild's tentlike kiosks that were spaced regularly among the stores. It was sour and low in alcoholic content. Among the Terrans, only Stavros found it worth the trouble. Among the shoppers, it was going like hotcakes.

"Cautious, but cheerful," Megan replied.

At the far end of the MarketHall, the cavern broadened even further into a vast interior plaza. Above it rose an open shaft that sliced upward through the many living levels of the Caves, all the way to the top of the cliffs. A clever system of deflectors and baffles drew out the stale, smoke-laden air without letting in the rain or snow.

In the center of the plaza, a deep stone well gave up crystal water into a long stone trough. Animal and Sawl alike lined up to drink from the cold green sparkle. The air was rich with the smells of beast and manure. Tyril led the two women through the jam of carts and wagons. A priests' apprentice stood in the center of a group of men wearing the Wheelwrights' guildseal. His young face was sober as he collected a handful of bulging leather pouches.

On the far side of the plaza, the market boulevard split to drop toward the lower level on the right, and climb up a wide ramp to the left. Shallow flights of steps hugged each wall. Tyril turned upward, out of the hustle and noise. The incline was long and easy. At the top, she stood aside with an anticipatory smile to let Susannah and Megan pass by.

The light was dim, the air fresh and cool. It smelled of stone and wet clay. The walls opened up around them. Susannah stopped and let out a sigh of delighted awe. Her every sense was compelled upward, as in a Gothic cathedral, where wonder and architecture merge into a single experience. But the hall's enormous loft gave an impression of narrowness that was misleading. It was uncolumned and as wide as the base of the Terran Lander. From where Susannah stood at the head of the ramp, it stretched resolutely into blackness to both right and left. Despite being carved of solid rock, it gave a sense of both lightness and light: in the faint shafts thrown low through open doorways, in the receding glimmer of a high row of blown-glass chandeliers that marched into the darkened distance.

Tyril murmured softly from behind, pointing upward. The chandeliers hung unlit but for a single lonely bluish flame that kept vigil in the center of each shimmering cluster of spheres.

"Something about when the lamps are lighted, I think," said Megan in the same hushed tone.

Susannah imagined a Sawlish festival graced by a thousand blazing galaxies of glass. Each chandelier was individually shaped, like the galaxies, and each nearly as complex, a froth of opalescent bubbles caught in flight.

A look of peace smoothed Tyril's brown face. She ushered them smiling into the hall. The marble floor was as smooth as a lake at twilight. It was set with square tiles of pale green and white and blue, in a large repeating pattern of three interlocking circles. Each center circle was missing some random section of its arc. The stone gleamed with the satin patina of age, spotlessly clean as if recently mopped.

A wainscoting of polished white marble ran along both walls, as tall as the average Sawl. It flared out into a bench at sitting height. On the seat, the high polish was worn away. The stone was warm to the touch, like skin. A painstakingly sculpted geometric band finished the top of the wainscoting with a gentle roll. Above that, the Friezes began.

Susannah gaped upward at a vast wall of sculpture. It was broken into separate panels and levels, one above the other, mounting into the darkness beyond the chandeliers. The figures were life-sized or bigger. They sprang into motion as if born from the rock itself. With precisely imagined detail of expression and anatomy, they laughed and wept and danced and stumbled along the walls. They moved in families or in multitudes, never alone, muscles straining, faces vivid with momentary joy or anguish.

Susannah had to back up against one wall to see the highest friezes on the opposite wall. There were stories to be read in the stone. Some were easily made out, a simple telling of a domestic event: a particularly rich harvest, a contest of athletes, a gathering of musicians and dancing. Other sequences were more obscure. They were haunted by dark imagery, by violence and suffering, anger, bewilderment, outraged innocence.

She felt Megan draw closer as if in reaction to the darkness marching through the Friezes.

"Don't they look like they're all waiting for something?" Megan whispered. "Even as they go on about their business? It's like that in the entry friezes, too."

"Waiting for what?"

"What do you wait for on this grand a scale? Either salvation or some final disaster."

Throughout the dark chaos of the Friezes, two recurrent figures stalked in tandem, ever together, ever in conflict, always

dominating the smaller figures of the multitudes. One was stocky
and angular, the other sinuous as smoke. They fought without
visible weapons, but the signs of unsettled weather shadowed
them wherever they appeared: great billowing waters and towers
of cloud carved in the rock, lightning scoring a ravaged stone
landscape, fire, hail, wind and ice.

"Guess who," said Megan, pointing.

The goddesses' eyes burned dim malevolent fire.

Tyril did not look too closely at the Friezes as she drew her
party down the hall. A distance along, a thin scaffold of lashed
timbers climbed one wall. A rail-thin apprentice burrowed in the
depths of a large wicker basket, then tied a slim leather-wrapped
object to a rope hanging from the upper level and tugged on it
gently. Atop the scaffold, a Sawl artisan perched with a lantern,
chalking a new design across a stretch of virgin rock. The
scaffold quaked alarmingly as he moved about, pulling up the
rope to untie the little bundle.

The apprentice grinned shyly as Tyril greeted him and went
back to burrowing in the basket. Susannah noticed a tunic-clad
figure seated cross-legged on the shadowy bench along the opposite wall. She did not recognize him until he spoke.

"Hello," called Stavros quietly, without getting up. "Welcome to the FriezeHall."

Susannah thought he looked very much at home, and rather
put out by their intrusion. This was obviously not his first visit,
as it was theirs. She wondered how long he had known about
this magnificent hall but could not think of a way to ask that did
not sound accusatory.

"What are you doing here?" demanded Megan, not caring
how she sounded.

"Watching," he replied blandly.

The scaffold shook again as the stonecutter set aside his chalk,
rearranged his light, then reached for his wooden mallet and
tools. He unwrapped the leather bundle and took up a stout little
chisel as if it were a sacred object. Stavros rose from the bench
and ambled out of the shadows, pointing upward.

"See that tool?" His expression shared some of the artisan's
reverence for the rough-hewn sliver of black metal. "Probably
belonged to his great-great-grandfather, at least. Back in his
guildhall, there will be a record somewhere of all the different
panels carved with this particular tool."

"History as totem magic," said Megan. "The tool's past

deeds surround it with good medicine, as my Indian friends
would say.''

"It's admirable, really," he continued, his manner as ungiving
as the rock itself and totally at odds with his subject matter. "So
little metal available to them, and they use it not to make
weapons or currency but to tell their stories, record their myths,
to explain themselves to the future.''

"Very poetic, Ibiá," said Megan dryly.

His jaw tightened stubbornly but his reply was to direct Susannah's attention upward once more to the sculpted panel next to
the artisan's sketch. Two familiar figures carried on another
phase of their endless battling. Touches of fading polychrome on
hair and drapery hinted at an original brilliance of color, but now
the natural pallor of the stone muted all but their eyes.

"Lagri has the red eyes, of course," Stavros lectured. "And
the lavender is always Valla, though sometimes she's blue.''

"I noticed," said Megan, "that most of the goddess figures
have cabochon jewels, but in a few that look more recently
carved, the eyes are faceted. We should be able to use that as a
yardstick for at least one technological advance.''

Susannah studied the wall more carefully. "Jewels, did you
say? Precious stones? Not glass?''

"Based on my layman's knowledge," answered Stavros with
forced nonchalance, "I'd guess the lavender is amethyst; semi-
precious, at least on Earth. But there are more exotic minerals
that can produce a crystal that color. As for the reds, well, garnet
has iron in it, which is rare on Fiix, so maybe they're ruby. And
the blue could be sapphire.''

Megan clucked her tongue. "Definitely not glass. Can you
imagine what . . .'' She glanced at Stavros then, and fell silent
with sudden understanding.

Susannah was still peering at the dark sparkle above her head.
"Whew," she breathed, and decided that she no longer cared if
she sounded accusatory. "How long have you known about this
place?''

Stavros shrugged. "Awhile.''

Her suspicions blooming, she turned to face him sternly,
wondering at Megan's uncharacteristic restraint. "A *long* while?
Since before the storm?''

His eyes met hers briefly, then shied away as if it hurt to hold
her gaze.

"You told the Sawls not to let us in here, didn't you?" she
pursued.

He opened his mouth in automatic denial, then shut it. "You'd have preferred a diplomatic incident?" he growled. "Before we had half a chance to do what we came here to do? You know Clausen's attitude toward the Noninterference Code! He would have been up on a scaffold prying out eyes in a second!"

Megan watched with interest as Susannah decided it was time to get angry. Tyril's placid features slid toward concern.

"And I used to think Emil was paranoid to insist that the Sawls controlled our access to the Caves!" Susannah exclaimed.

"Our welcome here is less secure than you think," Stavros defended. "So far, we've been accepted because we've behaved ourselves!"

"Or you've made sure we behaved ourselves. Kept us out of trouble, is that it?"

"Clausen was the problem," Stavros insisted. "I couldn't risk him knowing."

"*You* couldn't risk!" Susannah caught herself on the verge of shouting, sighed with the effort and backed off. "Look, I'll assume you were looking out for our interests, and for the Sawls, but . . ." She stopped, finally unable to express herself without outrage.

Megan took up the issue in an attempt to defuse it. "Stav, its naive to think that Emil Clausen would ever have done something so blatant. Taylor maybe, on impulse, but not Emil. Not unless he was absolutely sure he could get away with it."

Stavros's chin jutted righteously. "Who could have stopped him but us? Who but someone who knew what he was about?"

Megan nodded reluctantly. "He's got a point there."

"Maybe." Susannah turned away, uneasy in her own ambivalence. "But the point is, Stav, you're interpreting each of us for the Sawls as if we were mere bits of language. I am not a word. I am more complicated and, yes, more willful than any word. If you misjudged Emil, who else might you be wrong about? Can't you let the Sawls make up their *own* minds?"

Stavros scowled but without real confidence. A voice rose in complaint from the top of the scaffold. The apprentice stonecutter's mournful eyes bounced from Stavros to Susannah and back again, begging for silence so his master might concentrate. Susannah lowered her voice guiltily, but her words still burst from her like whispered explosions. "Stav, I feel cheated! Is *this* why I can't make contact with the Healers?"

"No! Why would I warn them away from you?" he blurted unhappily. "Or anyone, except Danforth and Clausen?"

Tyril stirred, and Megan offered her a reassuring smile. She suspected that it was equally clear to both of them that this debate had taken on a decidedly personal tone. "Let me put it this way," she interposed, amused to find herself the arbitrator all of a sudden. It was not that Susannah's objection was unimportant. But in exploring her own lack of indignation, Megan realized that her agreement with Stavros over the threat represented by Emil Clausen overrode her natural objection to being pigeonholed by a presumptuous colleague. "If you're going to manipulate the Sawls' vision of us, Stav, remember we have no defense until we're as fluent in Sawlish as you are. By then, the damage, if there is any, will already be done. The best we can do is beg you to interpret with a clear head."

"And conscience," threw in Susannah.

Megan could see Stavros building up to his usual solution for ending a losing argument. She waited for him to level his nasty parting shot, then flee before Susannah had a chance to respond. Megan was more familiar with this technique than Susannah was, as Stavros did not pick fights often with Susannah and Susannah rarely picked fights at all.

But Stavros surprised her. He leveled no parting thrust. He raked a hand through his ragged hair, muttered an unintelligible oath, then turned and staged a pensive retreat down the long hall into darkness.

He's hoping she'll call him back and all will be forgiven, Megan decided. *Fat chance.*

Susannah watched him go in silence. "Sorry I lost my temper," she muttered to Megan.

Megan grinned. "A rare sight, that. Surprised him, too, I think."

A woody groan resounded through the hall. It ended with a series of sharp cracks and a shout of alarm as the stonecutter's foot crashed through a rotting board. The apprentice squealed as the legs of the scaffold unsupported by the wall bent outward, quivering like drawn longbows. A length of planking tumbled to the floor. A narrow ladder snapped free from one of the curving legs and fell in a long graceful arc, narrowly missing Tyril as she roughly pulled Megan out of range. The stonecutter scrambled for the wall-side supports. He wrapped his arms and legs around a leg and clambered down as fast as he could manage. His high platform of timbers tilted, spilling tools and chalk. A ceramic water jug smashed into dust at Susannah's feet. The apprentice dove under the creaking scaffold to snatch up the tools he had taken out of the basket. Fragments of rotten wood rained around his head. Susannah yelled at him to run clear, but he grinned wildly and uncomprehendingly and continued madly stuffing bits and pieces into the basket.

The scaffold quaked as one outside leg bent to its limit and snapped. The stonecutter jumped free from several times his height and landed moaning on the marble tiles. Susannah lunged for the unwitting apprentice but had the wind knocked out of her as an arm shot around her waist, jerked her away and flung her clear of the falling timbers.

Breathless from his return sprint, Stavros whirled back for the apprentice just as the second unsupported leg gave way with a splintering crack. The boy shrieked, pushing and tugging at the heavy basket. The end of a thick plank struck his shoulder as he abandoned the basket and tried to scramble away. He staggered, looking confused. Stavros grabbed for him but had to shield his own head with his arms as the remains of the upper platform thundered down on top of them.

Tyril was into the wreckage instantly, heaving broken boards aside and shouting for help from the Terran women, who stood frozen in shock. The lump of splinters that was Stavros stirred and fell away as he staggered to his feet and went to work beside Tyril. Susannah shook herself into motion. She dropped down at the side of the dazed stonecarver and took his hand. He was not a young man. His landing had jarred him badly. He winced with each breath but he was not in agony. When he focused at last on the collapsed scaffold and the searchers frantic in the rubble, his eyes widened in horror and he struggled to rise and join them.

Susannah soothed him and made him lie back. Gently, she began to probe for broken bones.

"Is he all right?" demanded Megan at her side.

"Shaken up, a few cracked ribs, I'd say . . . a bad ankle here, maybe a sprain, probably a fracture. What about the boy?"

Megan looked over her shoulder. "They're just getting to him now. . . . Oh, my god. Poor little thing."

Susannah continued her examination. "Meg, I'm going to need water and . . ."

"*Susannah!*" Stavros's shout was shrill. "Get over here!"

Susannah rose calmly as Tyril sped past at a dead run. Megan looked faint. "Meg, find this man some water," she said firmly. "And don't let him move!" Then she looked toward Stavros.

The apprentice boy lay spread-eagled in a pool of blood. Stavros had stripped off his tunic and was pressing it in an awkward bundle to the boy's thigh. His hands were wet. The blood had already soaked through the fabric. Two deep gashes on the boy's shoulder and forehead bled heavily. His left arm was crooked at an unpleasant angle. He lay as limp as a broken doll.

Susannah knelt at Stavros's side. "How bad is it under there?"

"Open from groin to knee," he muttered. "Like with a carving knife."

"Okay. I need you to take that cloth away and tear it into strips as fast as you can."

"Whenever you're ready."

Susannah took a breath. "Been a long time since I've done emergency medicine." She opened her pocket knife. "Ready."

Stavros pulled away the reddening bundle. Blood welled up from a ragged slash as long as his arm and bone-deep. Torn fabric twisted with turned-back flaps of skin as if the child's leg had been split open by a plow.

"Jesus!" breathed Susannah. "What did that?" She sliced at the blood-drenched pant leg, wrenched aside the fabric, then quickly folded the loose skin and muscle back into the wound. She grabbed up the strips as fast as Stavros could tear them and wrapped the thigh as tightly as possible. Her fingers slippery with blood, she ripped the end of a final strip, tied a quick knot and began a second layer.

"It's slowing a little, I think," she said. "When you're done tearing, wrap the head wound just like I'm doing. Did Tyril go for help?"

Stavros nodded. He brushed blood-damp hair from the boy's forehead and then from his own. A slow trickle stained his cheek. He laid a strip of his tunic on the boy's head gash.

"He'll need fluids," Susannah muttered as she moved to cut shredded wool away from the shoulder wound. "You'll have to explain to them about transfusing and then we'll need to test for the right blood type." As she bound the shoulder, her hand brushed a hard-edged object pinned under the boy's body. She grasped it and yanked it free. It was the stonecutter's chisel. It's long flat blade was shiny with blood.

"Think I've found the culprit." She tossed the chisel aside with far less reverence than the stonecutter would have used. "Metal has a way of becoming a weapon all of its own accord," she added tightly.

She knotted the bandage and sat back on her heels. "Now we've got to get him down where I can treat him properly. The

old man, too. Meg . . . ?'' She turned to see Megan standing
aside while two sturdy Sawl women lifted the stonecutter into a
leather stretcher. Another woman holding a second stretcher
waited next to a tall linen-smocked Sawl with tied-back curls and
a dignified stoop. His intent gaze was fixed on Susannah.

She knew him instantly, and smiled with relief and welcome,
then sobered as she realized that he might view her with suspicion or even jealousy. She backed a bit away from the injured
boy and gestured to the tall man to come and look for himself.

"Is this your healer?" murmured Stavros.

Susannah nodded nervously. She watched for a reaction as the
man knelt beside the boy. His brown hands were large and
long-fingered but delicately built. They explored and probed
deftly, traveling the length of the boy's limp body without haste,
seeming often to hover just above the skin. Glancing up with
some impatience, Susannah saw that the healer's eyes were
closed, his thin handsome face gone slack with concentration.

When he opened them again, he looked straight at Susannah,
his wide mouth held in an expressionless line. Then he nodded,
as if in approval. When he spoke, his voice was soft and light.

"He thanks us for our efforts on the boy's behalf," Stavros
translated stiffly.

"Ask his name," whispered Susannah eagerly. "Tell him I'm
. . . a healer, too, and I'd like to study with him."

The healer listened, his long head politely inclined.

"Tell him the boy needs blood," Susannah continued in a
rush, "but if we take him down to our cave, I can get him sewn
up in no time. And, Stav . . . please tell it to him straight."

Stavros stared at her, then drew back and replied coolly, "If
you want to work with this guy, you'd better let him treat the
boy himself."

"But how do I know he can deal with injury this serious?"

"How do you know he can't?"

"Are we going to sit here arguing while this boy dies on us?"

"No." Stavros grasped her wrist and rose abruptly, as if
having made a decision he was not quite happy about. He drew
her firmly aside. "I wouldn't make it look like a struggle, if I
were you. That's not likely to impress him." He nodded to the
healer, who waved over the woman with the second stretcher.

Susannah looked to Megan.

Megan shrugged and shook her head. "It's not our place."

Helpless, Susannah watched the two Sawls ease the broken
body onto the leather sling. Stavros loosed his grip on her wrist

as the stretcher was raised. He spoke rapidly to the healer. The tall Sawl listened, holding one end of the stretcher, but his reply was brief and then he was gone with his patient down the dark FriezeHall. When Susannah made a move to follow, Stavros grabbed her arm again.

"What did he say?" she demanded.

"Said he'd think about it," he replied. "More or less."

Susannah wrenched her wrist free with the strength of rage. "You can stick to your purism about the Noninterference Code when there's a life at stake? Both of you! You too, Meg!"

"Are you going to be around here forever to supply the knowledge and technology they lack?" Stavros returned, his usual defensiveness surfacing as the crisis passed. "Or do you just want to dazzle them with a few miracle cures and split, leaving guys like him feeling inadequate?"

"And forever dissatisfied," murmured Megan.

Susannah stared and then dropped her eyes. She had the grace to admit when she was outmaneuvered. "All right. I'll accept it but I don't agree with it," she stated finally.

Now it was Stavros's turn to look down and shift uneasily. Megan laughed inwardly. He knew how not to lose an argument but he didn't know what to do when he won. In the end, he fell back on his habitual solution.

"Fine," he growled, then turned on his heel and walked away.

17

Stavros exhausted his frustration by swimming laps for twenty minutes, while Liphar soaked in the shallows and looked on in tolerant disbelief. The pools in the Baths were ill suited to aggressive swimming. Steaming water roiled over the tiled edges and sluiced across the glass floor. A pair of elderly Sawls at the next pool glanced up in mild irritation and began to wring out their piles of clean laundry all over again.

He hauled himself up on the steps beside Liphar. "Out of shape," he panted. He had an odd flashing memory of his high school swimming team, of a comradery reminiscent of his hours with Liphar in the Baths. For the first time, it seemed significant that he chose to spend so much of his time with a near-child. Certainly Megan would think so, he decided.

And Susannah? He felt that he'd handled himself badly in the FriezeHall, yet had only done—and said—what he thought was right.

They soaked for a while in silence. Liphar let his toes float up and stared at the fat white pipes suspended high above like tubular clouds. He watched the occasional droplet of condensation take the long fall into the pool.

Stavros studied the other bathers. The golden cavern was crowded as always, but the mood was unusually subdued. A relative of the injured stonecutter described the accident to her fellow guildmen in vivid secondhand detail, but the clatter of the stones across the gaming tables was louder than her emphatic murmur. Even the children had withdrawn to the farthest corners to play their quietest games. Stavros saw many families enter the Baths, wash themselves and their clothing, then leave without the usual socializing.

"So Kav Ashimmel still refuses to give us an answer?" he ventured at last.

Liphar grunted his assent.

"I guess she has some reason for not wanting me to see him?" Stavros prompted.

The young Sawl's shoulders hunched as he drew his knees up to his thin chest and hugged them. The green water sloshed gently. "O rek," he muttered. "Gisti."

"I know she said that," said Stavros, "but I don't get it, Lifa. Why should she think the Wokind have anything to do with Valla Ired?"

Liphar glanced about anxiously. His fingers toyed with the amulet on his wrist. "O wokind, kurm arma . . ." His voice dropped to a whisper. "Valla Ired."

"Us?" Stavros exclaimed. "*Helping* her?"

Liphar edged closer, pulled in a long breath and launched into a rapid explanation so mumbled that Stavros had to make him slow down to catch even half of it. What he did understand appalled him.

"She actually thinks the storm's gone on so long because the Wokind have come to help Valla? Why would we want to do that? We've already lost two of us to the storm and nearly lost a third."

Liphar squirmed miserably as if he didn't want to be identified with the suspicions he was passing on, but wouldn't mind hearing them disproved. "Not like it, you," he warned.

"Try me," Stavros persisted.

"Okay. Wokind help Valla, then all Sawl gone. Wokind all here."

Stavros was stunned. *Who put that idea into their heads?* And then he knew. *I did. With my warnings about Clausen and Danforth. Ah, Christ.* He dropped his head into his hands. He had planted seeds of territoriality and distrust where the ground might have been free of them. So much for the purity of his Noninterference. The best he could do now was to try to squelch the weed before it ran rampant. "Lifa, please. We don't want you gone! Clausen might have, but he's gone himself, killed by Valla's own storm! You are the reason we came here, to learn about you, from you. Nothing else! Do you believe me?"

Liphar spread his palms mournfully. "Not important, I."

Stavros turned on one knee to face him. "There is no truth in Ashimmel's accusations, I swear. With Clausen dead, Fiix will

come to no harm at Terran hands.'' He held out a flattened palm.
''My own life on it.''

Belatedly, he realized that he meant it. Eventually, if they
ever made it back to Earth, he would have to discourage
CONPLEX from sending a follow-up expedition, but he thought
he could count on Megan's help in writing the appropriate
report.

Liphar solemnly covered the open palm with his own. ''Embriha
Lagri,'' he intoned. Then he sat back, elbows against the tile,
and looked at least momentarily relieved.

Time to get the others more involved, thought Stavros. *Susannah is right that isolation leads to misunderstanding.*

And yet, he had his doubts. His self-assumed role of cham-
pion of the Sawls could not be shed between one bit of insight
and another. He was unsure which of his colleagues could really
be trusted to keep the Sawls' best interests at heart. He stirred
the water with limp fingers, then cupped his hand to feel the heat
run out of it slowly.

''Lifa,'' he said finally, ''there's two things you could do for
me. First, think of a way that we—the Wokind—can make a
show of support for Lagri, to dispel Kav Ashimmel's suspicions.
Second—and this may be the hardest—would you dare to speak
to Kav Daven for me yourself?''

18

In the middle of the Terran "day," the Black Hole was usually deserted. Weng had retreated to her secret ivory tower and the company of her now handwritten scores. McPherson always left early to begin her daily vigil at the highest cave mouth, where she passed the hours by filling a notebook with a supposed letter to her mother back home. Megan had gone off with Tyril to the WeaverHall several hours ago, and Stavros hadn't been seen in two days.

Susannah reveled in a rare moment of solitude.

She raised the wick of her oil lamp to a scandalously wasteful height and reread her most recent list. She was amazed by the variety of edibles the Sawls managed to produce in the virtual darkness of the Caves. Her current and rather long list only covered the fungi.

That fungi were a staple was not surprising, given the Sawls' cave-dwelling habit. What was remarkable was the range of shape, texture and taste. Some were grown in a compost that was nearly a hundred percent aged hakra manure. Other varieties grew on rotted wood or in damp sand, some on the naked rock. The slim translucent bells like Indian Pipe were Susannah's favorite so far, but she had also liked the tiny spherical mil, and the giant cushion mushroom, whose thick broiled slices tasted just like Terran chicken.

Susannah giggled. *Why are all indescribable tastes said to be just like chicken?*

The guildsmen in the mushroom caves had warmed to her interest in their craft. Her new wicker sample basket overflowed with multicolored fungi. She chose a morel-like cone, fished a scalpel out of her medikit and sliced the fungus neatly in half.

She laid the rough-skinned sections out on her sketchbook and settled in to draw.

Meanwhile, she let her mind sift through possible explanations for the amazing variety. There was no such range of dark-growing edible fungi on Earth or any planet that she knew of. It could be an evolutionary response to the long Fiixian night, or it could be that the Sawls were unsurpassed hybridists. The same questions could be asked about the several dozen breeds of fowl, or the various small mammals that were raised for food in the Caves, or the schools of pale slow-moving fish bred in unlit pools at the back of the stable level.

Astonishing, really, she thought, as she outlined a warty cone shape on the page.

A soft cough came from somewhere near the entryway. Susannah's hand jerked, marring the precision of her curve. Though he carried no light, his gentle stoop identified him. She wondered how long he had been standing there in the shadows.

"Please come in," she said, laying aside her pencil.

The healer nodded, and like a teacher observing a pupil's homework, he came to look over her shoulder at her sketchbook. He murmured something that sounded like approval, then picked up her pencil, studied it, set it down, felt the texture of the paper, tested its thickness between a slim thumb and forefinger. Then he reached for the scalpel.

This he held up to the lamplight, let the high flame flash on the mirrored stainless steel. As Susannah watched anxiously, he laid his thumb to the blade with professional caution. She saw knowledge in his eyes, and interest, but nothing like envy. He clearly understood what he held in his hand.

He kept the scalpel with him as he settled on the matting a few paces in front of her. He held it up delicately by both ends, his elbows propped up on his knees, and regarded her over its shining length.

"Kho jeu Ogo Dul-ni, Ghirra min," he offered gravely.

An introduction. Susannah knew enough Sawlish to understand that. His name was Ghirra, then, and there was an unusual prefix, "Ogo Dul." The Sawls called their cave city DulElesi, and each took the name as an accepted prefix to their own. Ghirra then either followed a different custom or was from somewhere else.

Somewhere else? The thought of other settlements hadn't yet occurred to her. *But why not? Of course there must be other settlements.*

Thinking about it, she decided "Ogo Dul" had a familiar ring to it after all. She was sure the Master Ranger Aguidran used a prefix something like that. She had just never thought to wonder about it before.

"Kho jeu James-ni, Susannah, min," she returned. It didn't quite correspond but she felt she couldn't very well give her last name as "Earth." She knew her accent was atrocious, but Ghirra's polite nod showed that he had understood perfectly.

"Zuzhanna," he repeated with satisfaction.

Susannah had judged her own assessment of the Sawls to be the most generous of all her colleagues, even Stavros, who she thought tended to glorify their primitive purity way beyond what was flattering. But now she sensed that she had better do some quick reassessing, or this intelligent Sawl was going to be two steps ahead of her all the way and would tire eventually of the insult of waiting for her lower expectations to catch up with the reality. She wished they could somehow dispense with the usual introductory formalities, which would be awkward anyway, without a common language between them. She wished Stavros there and then was glad he was not.

Because maybe this Ghirra and I do have a language in common. . . .

On impulse, she grabbed up her medikit and set it open on the floor in front of him. Ghirra looked at it, looked at her, then began to lift instruments out one by one and lay them in a careful row along the matting.

How badly will this *sit with Stav's noninterference policies?* Susannah mused, with only mild regret.

19

The WeaverHall was low and wide and divided into corridors by four rows of sturdy wooden looms. Megan counted ten in each row. Their workings and construction were similiar to old Terran looms, though not as refined (she was obscurely happy to note) as the great bronze looms her friends the Min Kodeh had developed.

Large bowled lamps hung between each work station. As they followed Tyril between the rows, Weng pointed out that every single loom was in use. The weavers chatted and sang, trading jokes and gossip across the rows. The looms clacked and eighty small hands flew back and forth among the colored threads. The noise was deafening, though Megan thought the chatter had dulled just slightly as they entered the cavern.

Wooden racks along the outside walls sprouted endless fat spools and long looping skeins of fine yarn. Bolts of finished cloth lay piled according to color and the weight of the weave. Tyril urged them to feel the smooth texture of the fabric and admire the tight regularity of the threads. She showed them her own loom, where she was working on a length of yellow wool as soft as cashmere. An apprentice in the next station wove with a thicker thread, like a heavy reddish cotton. He glanced uneasily over his shoulder at the Terran women, and the patient journeyman who was showing him how to introduce a second color into the weave rapped his head lightly to return his attention to the work.

"Did you notice," Megan whispered to Weng rhetorically, "that they're only using Lagri's colors, or am I seeing signs now where there are none?"

Beyond the ranks of looms, intricately colored hangings curtained off a portion of the hall. Narrow strips of every possible weave, material and color had been sewn together in a giant sampler of the guild's craft. Tyril led them through a slit in the drape. A long wooden table sat crosswise in the space. Behind it, taut rope netting slung between thick posts supported the several hundred volumes of guild records.

Tyril gestured the women to a bench at the table, then chose a volume at random. She hauled it down from its woven shelf and laid it open on the table. It looked old but not ancient. Its parchment leaves were caught between stiff leather covers and sewn with a waxed string. The pages were crowded with spiky Sawlish lettering written in many differing hands: names, numbers, unintelligible notations. Tyril flipped over the leaf. The next two pages looked the same. She ran a finger down the lines and stopped near the bottom.

"Na," she announced proudly. "O kemma-ip khe."

"Her eight-mother," Megan explained to Weng. "We've been working on generational terminologies. All the guilds keep very exact membership records, you see." She leaned over the page myopically. "DulElesegar-ni-Suri-min," she read haltingly. Tyril clapped her hands in delighted approval.

"Suri," she repeated, nodding. "O kemma-ip."

"DulElesegar is an older form of the cave name DulElesi. Eight-mother is a grandmother seven generations removed," said Megan. "Great-great-great, etc. They record matrilineally within the guilds. The women are encouraged, though not forced, to carry on the mother's craft. The sons are encouraged to train out in a craft of their choice. Marriages are required to cross guild lines, however. There aren't many sexual taboos here, but that one is strictly enforced. I guess it helps prevent inbreeding."

"Two hundred years," Weng calculated, then added, "Earth years."

"And Earth generations. A generation seems to be a little longer here, in real time."

Tyril flipped two more pages, searched and pointed out another entry. The ink on this page had browned slightly but still read strong and clear.

"O kemma-seph," she said.

"Fifteen-mother," said Megan.

"Three hundred twenty-five," offered Weng. "More or less."

Tyril left the book open on the table and returned to the shelves for another, older volume. This one was bound between thin planks of dry wood. Its leather lashings creaked as she slowly levered it open. She turned several yellowed pages with extreme care. Her finger hovered over but did not touch an entry that preceded a short list. "O kemma-lef seph-ip khe."

"No . . ." Megan's eyes widened.

Tyril nodded emphatically.

"It seems she's saying her forty-eighth."

"That's over twelve hundred years," said Weng with admiration.

"Not possible. I must be getting the numbers wrong."

"Of course its possible," Weng replied sternly. "I can follow my lineage back nearly that far."

Megan stared at her.

"Well, nine hundred years," Weng conceded. "Nearly that far."

Megan gestured abruptly at the crowded shelves. "But look how many still older books there are!"

"Yes," smiled Weng. "Isn't it wonderful?"

Guild membership figures are approximate only:

Dyers   (130)
  pigment, paint
  ink
  dyes, dyeing
Engineers   (300)
  winchcrew
  plumbing
  tunnel maint.
  excavation
Weavers   (180)
Glassmakers   (125)
Potters   (210)
  pottery
  brick, tile
Keth-Toph (250) ("LifeGuild":
  lamp oil   'Heat and Light')
  dung fuel
  candles
  soap
Woodworkers   (200)
  toolmakers
  coopers
  wheelwrights
  cabinetry
Stonecutters   (300)
Basketry   (215)
Rugmakers   (75)
Papermakers   (60)
Leatherworkers   (285)

PriestGuild   (100)
Rangers   (130)
  weatherwatch
  trail guides
  mapping
Physicians   (27)
  healers
  midwives
  nursing
  herbalists
FoodGuild   (750) ?
  agricultural:
    mushroomers
    seedsmen: seed
          fertilizer
  husbandry:
    fisheries
    fowl
    small mammals
    herdsmen: dairy
            draft
  brewers
  breadmakers
  curers & smokers
  picklers & preservers
  icekeepers
  storesmen
  distributors
approx. 3337 working members

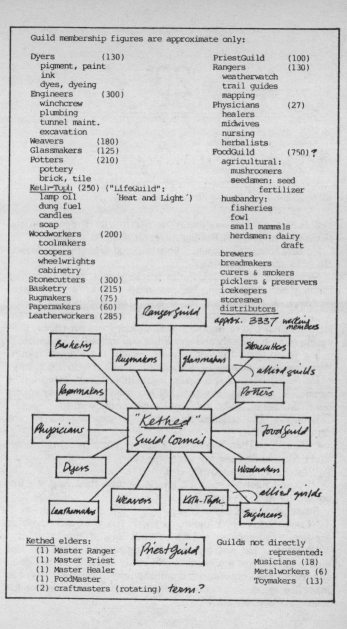

"Kethed" Guild Council

RangerGuild
Basketry
Rugmakers
glassmakers
Stonecutters
allied guilds
Potters
Papermakers
Physicians
FoodGuild
Dyers
Woodmakers
Weavers
Keth-Toph
allied guilds
Engineers
Leathermakers
PriestGuild

Kethed elders:
  (1) Master Ranger
  (1) Master Priest
  (1) Master Healer
  (1) FoodMaster
  (2) craftmasters (rotating) term?

Guilds not directly
        represented:
  Musicians (18)
  Metalworkers (6)
  Toymakers (13)

20

The lantern clinked too loudly as Stavros set it down on the sleeping platform. *Am I going to regret this?* he wondered.

He bent low. "Susannah!" he whispered urgently. He leaned closer to her ear. "Susannah!"

She stirred, deep in sleep. In the lamplight, with dark hair framing her lucent skin, she reminded him of a Caravaggio madonna, at rest but not yet at peace, her lidded eyes mobile with waiting energy. The suddenness of his desire confused him. He nearly reached to smooth a wisp of hair from her cheek, then caught himself abruptly and shook her arm instead. "Susannah!"

She jolted upright in her sleeping cocoon and blinked at him. "You are in my bedroom," she remarked with convincing clarity.

He pulled back on his heels awkwardly. "Hey, mine too. I mean . . ." He realized with relief that she was not really seeing him. "Susannah, wake up! You have to come with me!"

Belatedly, her reflexes activated. "Is someone hurt?" she demanded shrilly.

"Shhh! No. There's something you've got to see, right now! Wake Meg while I get my stuff together."

"Stav, it's . . . what time *is* it?"

"Doesn't matter—you won't want to miss this! And it's important for us to be there."

Susannah slumped groggily.

"Look, Susannah, I know you . . ." His voice trailed off as she finally came awake enough to really look at him.

"I what?" He was trying to apologize, she could see that much, but he was too impatient to really work at it. Susannah considered his contagious excitement reward enough, but was interested to see if he could actually make it to the end of his sentence. "I what, Stav?"

"Never mind. Meet you by the fire."

He shot away, leaving her in blackness. Susannah peered sleepily around the canvas partition to watch his lantern bob from sink to firepit. "I hope he's putting on coffee," she muttered.

She unzipped her cocoon and dragged herself across the dark platform as quietly as she could to jostle the sleeping huddle that was usually Megan. She hoped there hadn't been any unannounced changes in sleeping areas.

Megan woke quickly. "What is it now?" she grumbled worriedly.

Susannah tried to look awake. "It's Stavros. He's having an event."

When they joined him at the firepit, he held out hot mugs to both of them. Susannah smelled shipboard Nescaf. Normally he would have made the bitter Sawlian equivalent and looked down his nose when they refused to share it. She nudged Megan. "He's trying to be nice to us."

"Watch out," Megan agreed, but she grasped the mug gratefully. "I've been looking for you, Ibiá," she complained after downing a third of her coffee in one long gulp. "Need you to take a look at some of this stuff from the WeaverGuild archives." She glanced at her chronometer. "I hadn't counted on five a.m. to be the time for it, but the implications are amazing, really."

"Later, later," he replied.

"So what's so all-fired important?"

Stavros looked smug. "Only the Dance of Origins, that's all. What you might call the Sawl Genesis." He kept his voice low but his whole body danced with excitement. "The key to their entire racial history might be found in this one tale-chant!"

"Whoa, slow down," said Megan. "Who and where? When is patently obvious."

Fidgeting, he leaned on the white plastic cases stacked at his side. "The who is Kav Daven, the Ritual Master. Where is somewhere near the FriezeHall. Liphar's coming to take us there. The old priest suddenly decided to perform this chant, out of the blue. Liphar's been working on him for me and finally got him to agree to let me record it."

"Behind Ashimmel's back?" Megan noted. "Congratulations."

"And I need both of you there." Stavros allowed Megan one of his rare half-grins. "To preserve my objectivity, of course."

"I wouldn't miss it for the world," returned Megan dryly. "If only to make sure you don't interpret this 'Sawl Genesis' as literally as the Old Testament version has been in the past."

"Good. Oh, and there's another thing," he added casually. "Our being there will be seen as a sign of support for Lagri."

"Is that good?" asked Susannah.

"At this point, I'd say it was necessary."

"Certainly couldn't hurt," Megan agreed. "What about Weng and McPherson?"

"The Kav is a very old man," said Stavros quickly. "I didn't want to throw too much at him all at once."

Megan nodded speculatively. "Unh-huh."

Stavros knelt and busied himself with his cases. "Liphar should be here any minute."

"Remarkable, isn't it?" Susannah yawned. "Eight hundred and ninety-nine hours in their day and they still manage to be on time."

The slap of leather on stone announced Liphar at the entry-way. He trotted up to the firepit. "Khem, Ibi," he murmured to Stavros. He patted the plastic cases with a proprietary air, then crouched beside Susannah. "Rho khem, Suzhannah."

"Khem rho," she replied, completing the ritual greeting.

"Not see, you," he complained. "Keep you alla time uplevel."

"That's for sure," agreed Megan. "Lucky if we see you for meals the last few days."

Susannah smiled. "Doctor's hours. The Physicians' Hall is only one level up, Meg. You should come visit sometime."

"One level up but all the way at the other end of the cliff."

"Nice hot water in Physicians'. Ghirra's got his own supply somehow." Susannah sipped her coffee, not noticing the look that Stavros gave her. "You know, I'd forgotten how much I love plain old-fashioned doctoring. Working with Ghirra may turn me into an herbalist yet."

"I be alla time with 'Tavros now, you know?" said Liphar proudly.

"No, I didn't."

"Like you be with Ghirra." He let out a huge chuckle. "Easy work. I talk, maybe sing. He listen, Ibi." The young Sawl's tongue clicked and his fingers danced through a passable imitation of Stavros intent at his keypad. "Later, maybe, he talk, I listen, ah?"

"How does Kav Ashimmel feel about this? Aren't you miss-ing your training?" Susannah studied him carefully for a clue to what he had given up by removing himself from the apparently profitable weather racket. *Perhaps he's still taking bets on the side?* But Liphar looked puzzled and Stavros translated for him in a quiet aside. Liphar grinned and waved a dismissive hand. Susannah thought it an oddly Terran gesture.

"Kav Ashimmel has released him from his guild duties," Stavros explained. "She's finally decided she needs someone fluent in Terran as badly as we need to be fluent in Sawl."

If the other women heard this as a reproof, neither allowed him the satisfaction of a response. He stood and grasped the handle of the largest case. "Is Kav Daven ready for us, Lifa? Are you sure he understands."—he patted the aggressively white plastic—"about all this?"

"Ready, yes." Liphar scooted over to heft the smallest of the equipment cases. With his arm extended under the weight, the case bumped along the ground, but he refused to be relieved of it.

Stavros picked up the third and nodded toward the entryway. "Shall we?"

The MarketHall was quiet. In the lighted shop doorways, Sawls gathered in murmured conversations that fell silent as the Terrans passed and then picked up again with a louder, more directed grumble. For the first time, Susannah began to believe Stavros's warning about the tenuousness of their welcome in the Caves. The Physicians' Hall was its own little kingdom, a protected environment isolated by people's natural aversion to illness, and Ghirra had an apparently inexhaustible curiosity for things Terran.

What would the Sawls do to us, she wondered, *if they finally decided they didn't want us around?*

Crossing the open plaza, passing by the groups around the well, she felt too many eyes on her. They were not hostile, but the friendly curiosity she had grown used to was definitely gone. She was glad to ascend the long ramp to the FriezeHall, leaving the restless crowd behind.

Liphar set his case down at the top of the ramp. Gazing about, he let out a peaceful sigh, just as Tyril had done on Susannah's first visit to the FriezeHall. He let the quiet settle around them for a bit.

"This is the reverence that draws him to the priesthood," Susannah murmured to Megan.

Megan scoffed quietly. "Priest*Guild*," she reminded. "Around here, it's a craft, like weaving or glassmaking or anything else."

Liphar picked up the case again. He looked to Stavros. "Ready?"

"Ready," nodded the linguist.

They proceeded down the hall in silence, but for the whisper of their footsteps echoing from wall to wall. The wreckage of the fallen scaffold had been cleared without a trace. The marble floor gleamed.

"How's the boy doing?" Megan inquired.

Susannah shook her head in admiration. "Ghirra seems to have pulled him through." She gave a self-deprecating chuckle. "Even without benefit of Terran medicine."

They walked for several minutes, passing no one but the stone multitudes thronging the walls. At last, Liphar halted beside an arched doorway. Intricately carved flames of ruddy marble licked about paired portal columns as thick as twin oak trees. The tall arch was fitted with heavy wooden doors. The doors were paneled with miniature frieze carvings. They had no latch, just a huge pair of elaborate iron pulls. They were shaped as tongues of flame rising out of the familiar trefoil, the motif of the three interlocking circles.

Megan bent to study the ironwork. "The first bit of decorative metal I've seen in the Caves," she noted.

Liphar stepped forward and knocked respectfully on the oiled wood. They waited only a moment, then the giant doors cracked and swung open on superbly balanced hinges. A golden-skinned child appeared, bathed in ruddy light, and motioned them inward.

21

Stepping into the doorway, Susannah recoiled.

Fire!

The glare beat at her eyes so that she could not focus. The child was a wavering silhouette retreating calmly into the roaring heart of the inferno. Susannah dared not breathe, dared not cry out. The heat would sear her lungs. She braced for the screams and the horror of burning flesh.

Stavros was beside her. "I could use some help setting up," he suggested and moved briskly into the fire with his cases, all dark efficiency against the brilliant red.

Susannah forced her eyes to adjust. The room was not on fire. The fire was in the center of the room, contained to a circular hearth of glazed brick. The hearth sat in the middle of a circular floor, which was laid with the same brick. Six concentric brick tiers rose around it to form a horseshoe-shaped amphitheater whose opening faced the doors. The brick was glazed with a hard reflective gloss that magnified the firelight, tossing it from surface to surface, up the rise of the tiers and around the surrounding wall. The wall rose and curled overhead into a dome. Wall and dome were smoothly plastered. The flames that appeared to be consuming them were painted on their curving surface. They began low on the wall, sinuous tongues with bright yellow cores and sinister darker outlines. They raged through gold and orange and vermilion to scarlet at the apex of the dome. In the high center of the vault they flickered into sooted crimson around a well-used smokehole.

The sharpness of burning dung was a calming familiarity. Susannah gave the hall a more leisured careful study. The red light reflected on the faces of a group of apprentice priests sitting on an upper tier. The rest of the tiers were sparsely occupied by families with wide-eyed children and several elderly men and women.

"What is this place?" Susannah whispered to Megan.

"I think it's a StoryHall. Dedicated to Lagri, I'll bet."

Susannah's throat was as parched as if the flames were real. "I can see why. If this event is so special, where's everybody else?"

"Most of them have probably heard this tale at one time or another," shrugged Megan. "Would you expect the world to show up for a staged reading of the Bible?"

Still encumbered with equipment, Liphar waved them to places on the lowest tier. When she was finally seated, facing the central hearth, Susannah noticed the old man on the far side of the fire.

He too was seated on the bottom tier. His hands rested lightly on his knees. His brown garments draped around him softly, like a layer of autumn leaves. His head was shriveled and hairless but for a silver stubble dusting his sunken cheeks. His back was ramrod-straight, which seemed like a miracle to Susannah. She thought that she had never seen an older human being, certainly not one who could still sit upright. The tawny child waited at his feet, one hand laid lightly over his. Susannah for a moment could believe that should he but stir or the child remove her hand's feathery restraint, the old man might be swept up by the fire's draft to drift and swirl into the sooted vent at the top of the dome, set free with the smoke.

Her hand touched Stavros's knee in unconscious imitation. "Does he live here?"

He frowned, unlatching his cases, and moved slightly away. "Of course not. He lives downstairs with his family. That little girl is one of his great-granddaughters."

She resented that he made her feel stupid, when it was only the illusion of inferno still clinging to her that slowed her responses. "This is Lagri's hall?"

"Yes," he replied, as if it were obvious.

"Does Valla Ired have a hall as well?"

"Do *not* say that name in here," hissed Stavros. Liphar threw a shocked glance over his shoulder as he struggled with the latching of his own case. In a lower voice, Stavros added, "She has one at the other end of the FriezeHall."

"What's it like?" Susannah wondered if it would be as dank as this one was dry.

"It's been locked up tight since we've been here—only locked door in the Caves, that I know of." Stavros passed her the plug ends of several cables. "They won't set foot in it now, not until Lagri shows signs of a comeback."

"The Sawls feel it's in their best interests to promote an even balance," added Megan skeptically.

"So, performing this tale-chant is a pitch for Lagri?"

"Performing it *here*," he replied.

"It's what the Sawls would call hedging their bets," Megan needled. "Have you heard what happens if V—if she wins?"

Susannah looked to Stavros, who was matter-of-fact. "The legends call it Phena Cilm," he said. "The Wet Death. Total devastation. The world will drown." He adjusted his keypad on his knees and leaned over to plug it into the translator's screen.

"I can certainly sympathize with that anxiety," remarked Susannah, thinking of the flood that had nearly meant her own wet death.

"If Lagri wins, it's Phena Nar, death by fire. The Two Deaths."

Megan raised her eyes to the flaming dome and sang softly, "Lord said a fire not a flood next time . . ."

Stavros's jaw twitched but he held his tongue. He took the plugs Susannah had been holding uselessly and fitted them into the battery pack. "You mentioned sensing a general anxiety a while ago?" he said to her. "Well, the specter of a Wet Death is in everyone's mind at the moment, as all signs indicate that Lagri's losing ground more rapidly and for a longer period than usual. They think our arrival may have something to do with this, which is the real reason we're here."

"Is this like a prayer to Lagri?"

"More like an homage, a show of support. The Sawls don't pray, exactly. The Sisters aren't likely to listen to that sort of thing."

"Oh." Susannah felt a vague prickle chilling her urge to smile. The fiery magic of the hall and the still presence of the frail old man lent credibility to the linguist's tone of utter conviction. She envied Megan her reflex skepticism and retreated to the safety of scientific objectivity. "Has that ever happened before, one goddess winning? I mean, is there any historical basis for the legend?"

Stavros shot a give-me-a-chance glance at Megan, and Susannah prepared herself for another bit of disputed information.

Stavros set his keypad aside. "We know that the five thousand or so in the Caves don't represent the total Sawl population on

Fiix, but Liphar has given me estimates for the other settlements, and even allowing for a large margin of error and the various social structures to prevent inbreeding, the figures seem abnormally small for so large a world.'' He looked to Megan, who nodded her agreement with his report thus far. "So I asked Liphar why that was the case, and he said that every hundred and thirty generations, more or less, a near victory for one of the Sisters wipes out most of the population.''

Susannah raised an eyebrow at Megan, who shrugged. "That *is* what he said. I was there.''

"He also implied,'' Stavros continued, "that a hundred and thirty generations is usually the time it takes for the population to build up again to excess levels.''

"An interesting correlation,'' remarked Megan.

"Excess for what?'' asked Susannah, unable to fathom such a possibility on Fiix.

"That's not quite clear,'' admitted Stavros. "More people than they can feed, I guess. Liphar just says 'too many people.' '' He nodded at the ancient priest, who still sat as if unaware of their presence. "So you can believe Kav Daven will be pouring everything he's got into this performance.''

He beckoned Liphar to him and strapped a small power pack around the Sawl's narrow waist. Liphar received the little video gun and cradled it in one arm nonchalantly while stealing a sidelong glance at Susannah to be sure that she noticed how expert he looked.

"Ready?'' Stavros powered up the translator without waiting for affirmation. "Our silence will tell him we're set up.''

Megan and Susannah settled themselves. Liphar moved a few paces out onto the brick floor and dropped to one knee, video gun aimed at the central hearth. They waited in the brilliant room for long unmoving minutes, listening to the fire snap and spit. Around the edges of the coals, spent dung crumbled into ash. The flames sank into blue and lavender, and the hall darkened until the dome pressed in like a midnight fog. Susannah started when the old priest moved. It was ever so slight, just the raising of a hand, but in such mesmerizing stillness, it had the power of a scream.

The hand lifted from the knee, a bird of bones floating independent of its body. The smoothly scarred palm gleamed in the firelight. The child stood quickly and crossed to the big double doors. She barred them with a beam that seemed too heavy for her to lift, then padded to the hearth. Digging her hands into the peripheral ash, she raked great chalky mounds onto the brick floor. With practiced sweeps, she spread the ash in a thick even layer, forming a perfect disk. She stood, scrutinizing her work, then retreated to the far side of the fire and nestled down beside a stack of dung cakes. Her delicate face was solemn as she fed several cakes into the sunken coals. She leaned and blew gently into the glow. The fire sputtered. A miasma of black smoke billowed toward the dome, and as the flames rekindled, Kav Daven rose.

Stavros poised his hands above the keypad like a concert soloist awaiting his cue. Liphar adjusted the video gun in the crook of his arm. Susannah realized that she was holding her breath.

The old priest's rising was liquid, a flowing of spirit from one bit of flesh into the next, boneless and unmuscled, as if gravity disdained to drag on so insubstantial a mass. He did not acknowledge his visitors, but glided across the glossy brick to the disk of ash. Its whiteness vibrated against the ceramic orange. He circled it without looking at it, his bare feet tracing its circumference with intimate familiarity. He seemed to hardly move his arm, yet from some concealment produced a long tapering reed. He brandished it at the fire. The gesture was both an introduction and the conducting of an opening cadence, a rise and fall that took its tempo from the reaching flames.

The girl fed in more fuel and the blaze rose higher. Kav Daven began to dance a subtle crooked minuet around the disk of ashes. He hummed tunelessly and his bony shoulder dipped toward the fire, then toward the center of the ash, then back again. The tip of the reed and the silken folds of his garments flirted with the leaping heat as if his floating body could be the bridge to bring fire back to lifeless ash.

His hum slipped into a murmur. Syllables came and went like whispers. Stavros touched his keys, impatient, enrapt, then held back, chewing his lip. His breath came short and tight.

The old priest stilled. The tip of his long reed drew every eye as he dropped it to the disk to draw in the white ash. In the center he raked the outline of a human figure. He lifted the reed and resumed his circling. Then, in a conversational tone, he began the tale, like a neighbor man relating the local gossip.

Stavros bent to his keypad. The old man illustrated his words with floating one-handed mime and a widening spiral of tiny scratchings in the ash. Eyes glued to his screen, Stavros waved

Liphar in for a close-up. The translation unfolded in green phosphor turned sallow by the fire's brilliance.

The words came slowly. There were frequent gaps. Severed from CRI's master brain and library, the little translator could only stagger along like a cripple. Still, Susannah was impressed as she and Megan crowded in to peer at the screen. Stavros's word-substitution program managed to nearly mimic the machine sentience of a vast data cruncher like CRI.

Stavros's hands danced in frustration over a word he could not transliterate. "There's words I've never heard before in this tale," he muttered. "It's always the priests . . ."

"Priests often have a secret or ritual language," Megan reminded him quietly.

Stavros grunted, his fingers flying again, and the thought was lost as the translation picked up after a lengthy gap.

"In the very earliest generations," the screen read, "before the five great (destructions) (deaths) (?) . . ." The translator added its own question mark here to indicate dissatisfaction with both possible meanings. ". . . the great (large) king (parent) ruled the land (planet) (world)." All word choices but the preferred one were put in parentheses. "The king was wise and skilled in the ways of (power) (weather) (?), and the kingdom prospered without sickness or (war) (destruction) (darkness) for one thousand generations . . ."

"King?" said Megan.

"Sssh!" said Stavros.

Kav Daven paused to draw three new figures in the ash, in careful detail. Those on either side were looking away from the one in the middle, who was smaller than the other two. Across the fire, the silent girl added more dung cakes.

". . . the king had three beautiful children (daughters). The three were as one to the king. The eldest was tall and white (cold) with eyes of shining ice. The youngest was dark with eyes of fire. The middle child was mild and practical (craft-skilled). The middle child was . . ." Here the translator registered a complete blank, but as Stavros watched Kav Daven dig parallel furrows in the ash, he revised the data. ". . . a farmer . . ."

There was a soft knock at the double doors. The girl glanced up, frowning slightly. A sharper rapping followed and voices could be heard through the thick wooden panels. The apprentices on the back tier murmured, but Kav Daven ignored the disturbance and no one made a move to answer the knock.

The translator continued its stumbling interpretation. ". . .

though the middle child was weakest, she was much loved by the king, and the king charged her stronger siblings (sisters) with her protection . . .''

The knocking at the door had ceased. Kav Daven withdrew into himself, cringing before the fire. Suddenly he sprang up, then danced aside to rail and slash his reed at the space where he had been. His yell echoed around the dome like erupting thunder. His body seemed to shed decades with every whirling step. Building her pace with his, the girl threw dung cakes at the fire as if slinging stones. The flames roared and reached for the ceiling. Water trickling down the smokehole lent a rhythmic hiss of annihilation. The translator stuttered as the girl took up a thin staccato chant that underscored the priest's wailing with tones of threat. Liphar, still manning the video gun, chanted along with her under his breath.

Stavros's fingers rippled over the keys. Lost to the rhythm of the chanting, his body moved to Kav Daven's movement. His lips tried to form the words as the old priest sang them.

''. . . and then it happened,'' read the translator, ''that the war (darkness) arrived (neared) and the king grew old (ripe) (dark). Not the healers or the priests could save (heal) him/her . . .'' The translator showed a sudden confusion about gender. ''. . . The king divided the land among his three children, and bade the two strong siblings to protect the weaker. But when the king died (darkened), the world fell into strife. The eldest child and the youngest child were blinded by the warring (darkness) and disobeyed (forgot) the king's charge to them. They grew dissatisfied (bored) and battled (wrestled) (gamed) . . .''

Stavros shot a sudden finger to the screen. ''That's 'arrah' there, the verb form. You see the ambiguity?''

''. . . for control of the whole kingdom (world). Their battle-ground (arena) (gaming board) was the lands of the middle child. War (darkness) settled over the world. The war (game) had begun.''

Kav Daven halted and for the first time looked straight at his audience. Susannah ground her fingernails against the hard brick to steady her surprise. The old priest's pupils were milky white.

''Blind!'' breathed Megan.

The girl's chant rose like an animal howl, then ceased midnote. The priest's opaque eyes commanded even the taking of a breath. Behind him, the fire wheezed and sighed. Stavros raised his head from the screen, eager for the next line. The priest's whole body swiveled until he faced Stavros directly. Stavros stared back, transfixed, his jaw sagging open. Kav Daven lowered his reed and after a frozen pause, he offered a dazzling smile that crinkled his sightless eyes with elfin humor and showed a mouth full of strong yellow teeth.

Then brief as a bird shadow, the smile was gone. His years settled over him again. He turned away and shuffled across the brick, scuffing a trail through his pictures so carefully drawn in the ash. One leg dragged a little behind. The girl went to his side and helped him to sit.

Megan leaned back with a spent sigh that was echoed by the Sawls on the upper tiers. Liphar remained kneeling on the brick. The video gun lolled forgotten on his arm. He gazed at Stavros with admiration and then back at the old priest, as if searching out his own future in the old man's image. Even the fire seemed to recognize a culmination. It sank down exhausted. The inferno dimmed and became a round room painted with flame. Stavros did not move.

"Why doesn't she fight back, the middle one?" Megan queried reasonably.

Susannah smiled and shook her head, moved to silence by the performer's magic and the shock of his sudden vanishing smile.

Liphar stirred and brought over the video gun. He knelt with it at Stavros's side. "Ibi?" he inquired in a whisper. "Tel khem, Ibi!"

Stavros turned to him slowly, his jaw still slack. His awe relaxed into bewilderment. "I sure hope so," he muttered hoarsely. With mechanical efficiency, he stored the recording and the preliminary translation in the permanent memory, then pulled all the plugs. His slump was pensive.

"It isn't exactly a creation myth, is it?" Megan began. "But what's interesting is that all over the explored universe, it's the *youngest* child who gets ganged up on in the ancient legends. Significant?"

"Why isn't it a creation myth?" asked Susannah.

"There's nothing about creation in it."

"You mean, no void or firmaments?"

"No creator."

"The king?"

"Creators don't usually grow old and die," Meg reminded her.

Stavros made a noise of distracted protest, then seemed surprised when both women turned to him expectantly. "What? Oh . . . well, the translator's not clear on that point. About what happened to the king. If it was a king." His reply was more than usually disjointed, though he was clearly struggling to appear collected. "He grew old *or* ripe *or* dark. I think we can exclude 'ripe' as a possibility for now." He unbuckled the power pack from Liphar's back and handed it to him to put away in its case.

"Perhaps he simply left," Megan proposed. "Not an unfamiliar variation, the god who creates a world, then splits."

"A sorry excuse for a god," Susannah murmured.

"But he was 'skilled in the ways of power' . . . or 'weather,' " mused Stavros, regaining his focus. "You recognize the warring siblings, of course."

"Fire-eyed Lagri," said Susannah quietly.

"And she of the lavender ice." He rolled the words in his mouth like a lyric.

"The middle child must be your unnamed multitude," said Megan. She sighed. "Truthfully, I'd hoped for more. It's like a piece of mythical reporting, really, without much moral comment."

"Oh, I think the part about the sisters betraying the father's charge implies moral censure," said Susannah.

"Betrayed or *forgot*," reminded Stavros.

Susannah frowned. "How could you forget such a thing?"

"There is an interesting sense of the original trouble coming from the outside," said Megan. "Even before the king died, war or darkness fell on the land, am I remembering it right?"

"Let me refine the translation," said Stavros. "There must be a frieze somewhere to match it. That'll answer some questions. Meg, about this idea of a separate ritual language . . . I am beginning to think there is a kind of language within a language here—" He was interrupted by the return of the knocker at the doors. This time, the appeal was more insistent. The apprentice priests chatting on the back tier fell silent. The girl left Kav Daven's side and whispered across the brick to draw back the heavy beam. The doors flew open.

Kav Ashimmel waited in the archway, with a retinue of priests behind her. An unfamiliar gray-white light crept past the threshold. It etched Ashimmel with a pallid halo that left her face in shadow. Liphar gasped, then sprang to his feet and dashed past Ashimmel and the crowd of priests to stand in the middle of the FriezeHall, staring straight up. The same pale light caressed his face, which slowly broke into a joyful grin.

Stavros rose, laying aside his keypad. "My god," he murmured.

"What is it?" demanded Susannah. Shouts and singing rang in the farther corridors. The other watchers on the tiers gathered themselves and their children and surged down and across the floor, sweeping the Terrans along with them. They joined Liphar in the middle of the patterned floor, where the blue and green circles were waking to new life, and all looked up.

The hovering darkness above the chandeliers had transformed into a realm of light.

"But where's it coming from?" asked Susannah.

Stavros pointed. "From the clerestory, below the vaulting."

"No, I mean . . ." Still she could not comprehend.

Liphar dropped his eyes from the light to send an awe-filled stare through the flame-carved archway, past the silent Ashimmel, whose message was demonstrating itself, past the astonished little girl, over the embers lowering on the brick and straight into the heart of an old man's blind smile.

"It's the dawn," said Stavros. "The sky is clear."

Beside them, Liphar exulted softly, "Embriha Lagri!"

BOOK THREE

"Thou, Nature, art my goddess . . ."
KING LEAR,
Act I, sc. ii

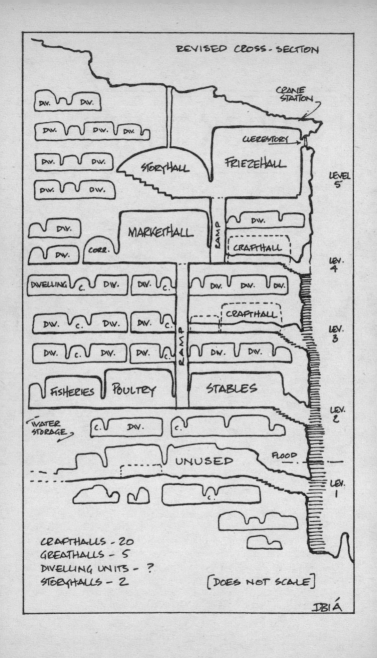

22

The jubilant families and apprentices gathered up Ashimmel and her retinue and carried them away down the FriezeHall in a sudden burst of cheers and laughter. Liphar danced around the astonished Terrans like an excited terrier. He snatched at Stavros as the linguist spun back to grab his equipment where it waited in the StoryHall, hard white against the fiery brick.

"No, no!" Liphar exclaimed. "Later, that. Come now, you!" He turned and sped away. The now-empty FriezeHall echoed with the rumble of distant celebration. Stavros gave his cases a single bewildered glance and bolted after Liphar.

Megan and Susannah followed, pacing down the long hall past the rows of glowering friezes. Susannah held back for Megan's sake, though she longed to be running with Stavros, with the others. She heard singing now and the marble floor vibrated like a drumskin with the passage of thousands through the tunnels below.

The dawn! She wished for Megan to hurry, to be younger, lighter.

The dawn! She rejoiced, while another part of her brain scolded her for allowing the irrational possibility that she had just witnessed a true feat of priestly weather magic.

Is logic really this fragile?

"Coincidence," she muttered aloud.

"No way," replied Megan, who was not supposed to have heard. "That old priest was out checking the signs. He knew the dawn was coming, even we knew that. And he knew the weather was going to break. Why else would he decide to start his performance in the middle of the night?"

"Probably wasn't the middle of the night for him."

"I'm telling you, he arranged the whole thing."

The Sisters glared down at them from a frieze that rose the full height of the hall. Stavros and Liphar were distant shadows fleeting in and out of dim pools of light, flying toward the ramp head. Susannah's stride lengthened unconsciously.

A setup. Now that's a nicely rational explanation. Why didn't I think of that? She found herself dancing in place, like Liphar, to slow her pace. "But why would he need to do that? To convince *us*?"

Megan chuckled, as if Susannah's innocence were the quaintest thing imaginable. "Of course! It won't hurt his credibility with his own folk if the Wokind appear to be impressed by this show of power. Remember, Stav said Ashimmel's been accusing us of being pawns of Valla Ired. Kav Daven could now claim to have brought us around to the other side. Don't you know Liphar's going to be spreading this tale for many days to come, about how Kav Daven stood at the right hand of Lagri while she brought back the sun?"

"And you used to say the Sawls didn't really believe in their myth!"

"I exaggerated for emphasis. They do and they don't. It's complicated."

"Well, they certainly believe in some of it. When Liphar and I were caught in the storm on that mountain, he wasn't invoking his gods for my benefit."

Megan scoffed. "Liphar's in training to be a priest—what do you expect?" Then she slowed, considering. "Besides, how do you know he wasn't?"

"Oh, Meg." Faint music and cheering floated up the FriezeHall. Susannah fidgeted. Sometimes she pictured Megan as Sisyphus' rock. "Sometimes you just have to trust your instincts." She peered ahead into the near-darkness, wondering if they had missed the turning at the ramp head.

"Of course, there's some belief," Megan continued, plodding along at the measured pace of her words. "Despite the seeming lack of a system of religious ethic, this *is* a society structured around a religion: the weather. The priests would have no power at all if there were *no* belief." Then she added significantly, "And no income. The real question is the exact nature of that belief. Are the goddesses, as Stavros claims, incarnate or not? Do the priests have a hotline to them? Remember, the priesthood is often the police force in a primitive society, using superstition to keep the people in line."

"Except here, the Guild Council holds the civil authority, not just the priests."

"Well then, a dual authority," amended Megan. "Church and State. Hearts and Minds, or in this case, Hearts and Bellies."

Ahead, Liphar suddenly reappeared, passing through a shaft of light falling from the clerestory. Susannah resisted the urge to grab Megan and run. "Weng claims Sawl society's structured like a ship's crew, with every Sawl doing his or her job in support of the whole. But she's also having trouble deciding who the captain is."

"Weng's viewpoint on that subject is hardly objective."

"It's as objective as any of ours."

Megan sniffed. "Well, all I'm saying is that the levels of belief are more complex than Stavros would have it, with all his mystic cant about 'knowing' that gods walk the earth. The Sawls are a pragmatic people."

We keep laying down these generalizations, Susannah thought uneasily. She tensed her shoulders against the chill that tickled the back of her neck. Liphar had stopped to wait in the shaft of gray light. On the walls, jeweled eyes glimmered like morning stars. "I think Stavros also exaggerates for emphasis, to fuel his argument, just like you."

"Not just like me," Megan insisted. "I ponder. Stavros acts. I question. Stavros accepts."

Susannah let the tired subject of Stavros's methods pass. "I don't know with Kav Daven, though: if this was planned, his timing was impeccable."

Megan's shrug was confident. "That's why he's a successful priest."

They caught up with Liphar in the light of the clerestory. Stavros was nowhere in sight. The young Sawl beckoned them eagerly toward the ramp head, toward the shouts and singing below. As they stood at the top of the slope, Susannah felt as if the very air were in motion, drawing them down into the teeming mass of rejoicing Sawls.

"Come, you!" Liphar called, and danced away down the ramp.

The crowd flowed like a living river across the vast market plaza. Many had come straight from their guild halls, with the clay drying on their hands or the dye still fresh on their leather aprons. Others wore whatever their hands had found first when the joyous alarms had waked them from a sound sleep. Children chased each other through the throng with high-pitched squeals.

The youngest rode wide-eyed on their elders' shoulders. Grand-mothers and grandfathers perched in the front of little two-carts, with fat canvas sacks jostling in the box behind them. The shaggy hakra hauled their loads with a jauntier step than usual, their bright eyes eager, their noses working.

"Exodus!" Susannah murmured.

The two women hesitated at the bottom of the ramp. Liphar waved, his guide duty done, and bounded off into the crowd. Megan was already breathing hard. Susannah awaited only the proper moment to plunge in. Once into that current of humanity, it would drag her along irresistibly. There was no sign of hostil-ity toward the Terrans now. Men and women called to them, laughing, gesturing them onward. Susannah took a step forward, and the current swept around her as gently and firmly as an arm laid about her waist. She grabbed Megan's hand to pull her along. They were carried around the wide plaza in a spiral. The new light of dawn filtered like dust down the huge ventilation shaft to touch the curls of two small children splashing in the stone water trough. The throng moved on toward the bright signs and lanterns of the MarketHall.

In the MarketHall, the shops stood empty. The proprietors and their customers had gone on ahead with the first wave. The signboards and painted banners swayed as if in a breeze, presid-ing over a wake of scattered gaming pieces, handcarts heaped with merchandise, deserted toys and the occasional lonely broom parked unceremoniously beside its pile of litter.

Susannah knew from the reproof in Megan's eye that she was grinning like a fool. She started to try to explain her sudden giddiness but was happy to be drowned out by voices around them raised in boisterous song. Two songs were begun at once, and the singers faltered in laughter and began again, each choos-ing to sing what the other had started first. The singing was throaty and disorganizedly cheerful, at times inaudible over the cheering and chatter and rattle of cartwheels as the throng swept along. Small bands of reed-and-pipers marched among the sing-ers, their sweet shrillings attempting a more disciplined music.

An intersection approached, where another ramp fed in from the upper levels. Susannah spotted three of the midwives, down from the Physicians' Hall with their apprentices. The Head Midwife, Xifa, still wore her stained linen smock with its many pockets, baggy from use. The women's drawn, hardworking faces were glazed with relief, as if the coming of the sun and the change of mood could affect some of the cures that they had been unable to. Behind them came the Master Healer, who returned Susannah's fisted victory salute with a wan smile and a wave.

"That's Ghirra, you remember?" Susannah said loudly into Megan's ear. "The one who patched me up after the storm?" She pointed him out as the crowd carried them by.

"I remember," replied Megan, craning her head back with interest. "You don't forget a face like that."

Susannah laughed. "Yes, well, there is that. Quite a beauty, is Ghirra." She grinned at Megan teasingly. "Unattached, too, as far as I can tell. And not *much* younger than you are."

"Big for a Sawl," Megan commented.

"Like Aguidran, you know, the Master Ranger? Ghirra's her twin brother." Susannah sidestepped a teenager pulling a cart laden with bulging sacks. "They're from the northeast, apparently, another settlement called Ogo Dul. They came here on a trading trip when they were babies and lost their parents in a mudslide. One of the herdsmen raised them."

"Guess they've done all right for themselves here," observed Megan. "Both Masters of their guilds."

Susannah nodded. "Ghirra is a gifted healer," she replied simply.

"And Aguidran is a powerhouse," Megan added. "Quite a pair."

They overtook a lumbering high-wheeled wagon. It was stained berry-red. Clusters of white streamers were tied to its corner posts. Megan peered through its slats as they passed. Inside, a leggy wooden device wound with leather strapping sat on top of another load of canvas sacks.

"Plow," she remarked, then caught at Susannah's sleeve and shouted over the din, "Plow!"

Susannah shrugged an inquiry. The noise swelled as the tunnel narrowed.

"I just noticed . . ." Megan yelled.

Grinning, Susannah burlesqued deafness. The Sawls' joy was too contagious to dampen it with serious discussion. She thrilled to the roar of a thousand voices echoing along the rock, to the pressure of moving bodies all around her. The reed-and-pipes urged her to hurry. She took a little skip, childlike, laughing.

Megan caught up to yell into her ear. "Don't you feel you should be carrying a rake or something?" She pointed at the ranks of poles sticking up from the crowd like a forest of porcupine quills. "That's what I just noticed."

Everyone, no matter what age or guild affiliation, carried some sort of digging tool. Susannah saw rakes and harrows of all shapes and sizes, broad-bladed shovels and fat wooden picks lashed to their handles with heavy oiled thongs. She saw even an occasional pitted iron hoe, carried reverently aloft like a relic.

"Now you can really see how crowded the Caves would feel if they all worked on the same shift," she said.

Megan nodded. "It was a mob armed like this that stormed the Bastille," she joked, and slapped the heavy wheels of the wagon. "Tumbrels and all."

Susannah found the image hopelessly inappropriate.

"You wait, though," Megan pursued. "We'll see that this is no act of spontaneous celebration. I mean, when was the last time you took a plow to a party?"

Ah, Meg. Always analyzing things. Suddenly Susannah envied Stavros. Why should she not lose herself impulsively in the crowd, as he had done? Why be immune to such contagious joy? She let the human current carry her forward a little faster, turning to look at Megan, who plodded along, absorbed in her ponderings of priests and plows. The throng flowed around her like water around a rock. As she glanced up to discover herself being left behind, Susannah waved guiltily but did not fight to slow her forward drift. Megan waved back and settled in to move along at her own pace.

Alone among the Sawls, Susannah felt lighter, relieved of sharing the burden of Megan's more cynical vision. *Realistic, Meg would say,* she reminded herself. She fell in step with a young musician who shot her a friendly glance over her pipes. Her brightly colored guild tabard was slightly askew, donned in haste and never adjusted. The narrowing of the corridor compressed the crowd so that Susannah walked shoulder to shoulder with her. The hoarse singing around them coalesced into a more unified voice and a single song-chant surfaced through the random cheering. Susannah swung her arms to the rhythm as the chant was repeated through verse after verse. Though she could not pick out the words, the melody soon became familiar. She began to hum along, to the delight of the young musician beside her, who leaned toward her and piped all the louder. Susannah reveled in not caring for the moment where she was going or why.

The human river slowed at a bend to stream thickly down a wide ramp that dropped in a spiral through two major levels with their additional half-levels. From each joining passage, a tributary flow swelled the river further. With a final banking turn, the ramp opened into the lowest level still in use. Here, the animal smells were damp and rich, and the lighting dim. The strong downdraft made the lamps flare and gutter in their niches. The main tunnel was low and wide, with countless barrel-vaulted corridors leading off to both sides. The dairy herds bellowed from their stable caverns and the side corridors bustled as the herdsmen led out huge broad-shouldered beasts that strained against their halters with excitement, nostrils flared to catch the changed air.

The great beasts threw gigantic lunging shadows on the wall. Susannah was confused, thinking she had not seen them before. She pulled herself out of the flow to study them and realized that these were the hjalk, the heavy draft animals. During his tour of the stable level, Liphar had shown even less of a fondness for the hjalk than he had for the somewhat smaller dairy beasts, or hekkers. He had been disinclined to hang around while she observed them more closely. She had assumed them to be just oversized members of the dairy herd, but now, in the open tunnel, they loomed far larger than when she'd glimpsed them stamping and steaming in their chill dark stalls. They were several hands taller than the average hekker and much more muscular. Their bulky withers were level with their herdsmen's heads. Their coats were a mass of short tight curls that lengthened into golden ringlets gathering in a thick mane around the neck.

Like a cross between a goat and a camel, thought Susannah. *And maybe an elephant.* But she had used the goat-camel cross before, to describe the little hakra, and it could apply to the dairy beasts as well. In fact, given the differences between the three in size and musculature, the similarities were remarkable.

The same low rounded rump, the same high-boned shoulders, those same fleshy, horn-bottomed camel feet.

She studied the golden giants as the crowd jostled around her. A loaded two-cart moved into her line of sight. A little cart hakra stood side by side with a towering hjalk.

Hakra, hekker, hjalk . . . even the names sound alike. More coincidence? You could interpret it as the same basic morphology overlaid with adaptations for specific function. Phew! If I didn't know where I was, I'd congratulate them on some very efficient gene engineering!

Susannah resolved to have a long chat with the herdsmen about their breeding program, which she was beginning to think she had underestimated. But that would have to wait until they got their celebrating out of their systems. Meanwhile, she would check with Stavros about the apparent similarity of the names.

If I can find him.

She backed away as one of the hjalk in its excitement swerved its rump toward her. She jumped to avoid being trampled or kicked, but the herdsman at the beast's head laughed. He gestured to several of his apprentices, who threw down armloads of leather harness to slap the huge animal's behind or bounce their slight bodies against its giant shoulders. The harness was draped across its back and several squealing children were tossed up to dig their hands and feet into its golden curls. The hjalk settled down the moment it felt their weight, and rolled itself forward like a slow furry wave.

The herdsman let it go off on its own and, still laughing, dusted his hands on his tunic. His FoodGuild insignia was faded behind layers of dander and golden hjalk hair. He grinned at Susannah and dove into the nearest stable corridor to bring out another eager beast.

Susannah rejoined the throng. As they passed the entries to the dairy caverns, the deserted hekkers lowed their complaints. Squawkings and crowings echoed out of the poultry warrens. The tunnel darkened, and Susannah stumbled along with the help of strangers to either side of her until at last the cave mouth registered as a faint glow far ahead.

The inflowing draft was chilly but overlaid with a promise of warmth. Susannah gratefully inhaled the scent of wet earth. Out of the company of midnight and downpour, it was a fresh and hopeful smell. The rough walls brightened as the tunnel dipped toward the cave mouth. The pace slowed at the inner stairs. The laughter and singing quietened to a more businesslike excitement. Rake handles and cartwheels clanked against stone. A hakra balked at the shallow steps, then compounded his offense by trying to descend them two or three at a time, his cart rattling behind him. Sawls scattered to either side of him until he finally reached the bottom and halted just inside the overhang, looking confused and shamed.

This lowest cave mouth had a large open terrace protected by the overhanging rock. It was still cool and in shadow. Guildsmen milled about, unhitching carts. The lighter ones were being carried down the long outer stairs by hand. The heavier loads were parked along the edge to be lowered by winch. The animals were set loose to negotiate the precarious flights by themselves.

The triangular seal of the Engineers' Guild was everywhere in evidence as they manned the winch ropes, loaded the pallets. Crowds filled the inner cavern and massed along the wide ledge outside the overhang. Brown-tunicked rangers directed traffic and kept the crowd moving down the stairs three abreast. A deep musical bellowing resounded from somewhere out on the cliffs.

Susannah pulled to one side to watch the procession descend. Wary now of the depth of her impulse toward open space, she forced herself to make a slower contact with the outdoors than she had on her first outing on Fiix. She noted that the Sawls did not pause, as she did, to exclaim over the ringing turquoise clarity of the sky or the salmon glow of the sun just peeking in a startling half-moon over the distant mountains to the east. Sawl eyes were focused on the dangers of the still-damp steps, or if they bothered to look at the sky, it was in brief glances of assessment and speculation. But Susannah stared unabashedly, counting lingering stars, and wondered what new surprises the Sisters might be preparing for them.

She saw McPherson standing to one side with Aguidran. She snaked through the crowd, between the stalled carts and bleating animals, to join them. The Master Ranger was a giant by Sawl standards, taller than her twin Ghirra, taller by two handbreadths than Susannah, and rangy and brown as a weathered tree. Her thin body was cased in well-worked leathers more closely cut than was the usual fashion in the Caves. She nodded a sober greeting as Susannah came smiling toward them, then returned to watching the procession move down the steps as if her will alone could prevent a stumble.

McPherson was buckling on a huge field pack. A fresh coil of Clausen's nylon rope swung at her waist. The solid bulk of the pack weighing down the little pilot's back was sobering. Without comment, Susannah tightened the rear lacing and helped to adjust the load. Then she stood aside to gaze out into the impossibly slow dawn. The coming light revealed a devastated plain, all gullies and canyons choked with rock and yellow mud as far as her eyes could see. The tall needle shape of the Red Pawn rose against the greenish sky just to one side of the half-moon sun. It echoed the blunter shape of the Terran vehicle stalled below it on the plain. The Lander waited bravely at its incongruous tilt, reflecting a glimmer of pink dawn from its scoured nose.

"What a mess," Susannah murmured. Her ballooning giddiness deflated rapidly. She watched McPherson zip up the front of her therm-suit. The suit was no longer remotely white, after two weeks of venturing out into the storm. "You're going out again?" she asked, trying not to sound disapproving.

McPherson's cherub face hardened as she prepared to defend yet another of her hopeless forays into the treacherous sodden hills. "First decent search weather we've had," she began tightly.

Susannah kept her tone sympathetic. "Hope it stays that way."

McPherson's jaw relaxed. "Aguidran's coming with me."

Susannah backed against the rock wall to make room for a giant hjalk as it lumbered past toward the outer stair. She trailed a hand through the golden curls on the beast's flank and found them surprisingly soft. She also felt what was not so easily seen, that beneath the thick ringlets, the animal was bone-thin. *So food rationing extends to the herds as well,* she mused.

"Glad you and Aguidran have finally made friends," she said to McPherson.

The pilot drew her shoulders together with more hope than a shrug would have had. "Yeah. It'll be just the two of us out there, since they can't spare any more hands from the planting. But that's okay—we'll move faster that way."

"Planting?" Susannah looked incredulously at the devastation of mud below.

McPherson tossed an impatient gesture at the crowd armed with its tools and the carts loaded with bulging sacks. "Whadda you think this is all about?"

"Well, I thought . . ." *Why not just celebrate the dawn? Maybe Meg is right. Maybe I am a hopeless innocent.* "They don't waste any time, do they?"

"Smart," nodded McPherson.

At the far end of the ledge, an Engineers' apprentice swung out on a set of winch ropes, using his weight as an anchor while his guildsmen positioned a load. The taut ropes hummed, dark against the brightening sky.

"How long will you be out?" asked Susannah.

"Long as it takes, lady," McPherson drawled with a hint of her old mischief. She swaggered a step or two, then sighed. "That or a little under two earthweeks, what Aguidran calls ten throws. That's all we got supplies for, and she tells me we can't live off the land."

"Not unless you can learn to eat mud." Susannah was encouraged by the new respect that colored McPherson's tone when she spoke of the Master Ranger. She suspected that the pilot had found herself a new role model. "That ground will take a week of drying before anything will grow in it."

"Nah, she says the stuff out there's poisonous, even when it does grow."

"Oh?" Susannah wanted to hear more of this, but decided she would ask Ghirra instead. His answers were willing and precise, even if they didn't always seem to make scientific sense. *Like planting?* she wondered to herself. *Planting now?*

A shadow slipped across her face, falling from above to cast its elongated plow shape on the sunlit wall behind her. The winch ropes sang. The image of tossing good seed into a plain of ocher mud struck Susannah as movingly optimistic. *Devastation and fertility, death and birth, loss and renewal.* She pictured the lost Sled lying bright and broken on some muddy rockslide, with new green shoots poking up around it. She regarded McPherson more gently. "I hope you're prepared for what you might find out there."

McPherson looked at her oddly. "You really do think I'm a baby, don't you?"

"No, Ron, I . . ."

"Look, I just gotta know I did my best, that's all. If they're dead, they're dead. But we need that Sled."

"Even what's left of it?"

"Even that."

Susannah shuffled a booted foot against the rock. It seemed that the subject was closed. They stood in silence for a moment, using a close attention to the winch operations as a cover for their private thoughts. Finally Susannah roused herself, remembering.

"Did you see Stavros come by this way?"

McPherson's nod was more like a shake of the head. "Sure did. He came charging out here, stood gawking up at the sky like a moron, glanced over at the Lander, then zipped around and took off back into the Caves. Looked in his usual panic, but my guess is he's gonna try raising CRI now the weather's cleared. Won't work, though. Look." Her hand knifed the air in a neat diagonal as she pointed to the Lander where it was firmly settled in the mud. "Main antenna in the nose was sheared right off. The dish probably wound up in the next county." She glanced into the crowds still streaming out of the shadowed overhang. "Shit, here comes the Commander. Gotta get going or she'll want me to climb right up there and fix the damn thing with my bare hands and her silver chopsticks."

"If you did fix it, CRI's scanners could find the Sled in less than an hour." But Susannah understood that this was not the real issue.

"Let Stav do it," McPherson fired back. "He can scavenge parts as good as I can." She was already moving away. "Besides, if they're mobile, they'd be back by now, so even if CRI did find 'em, somebody'd have to go out there on foot to bring 'em in anyhow. If I start now, I'm ahead of the game."

"But you don't even know which way they went."

"I know where Aguidran and me ain't looked yet!" McPherson held up a banded wrist. "I'm hooked in, 'case we do get back on line. You call me, eh?" She adjusted her pack again and nudged the Master Ranger's arm. Aguidran took a last quick look around, then led the way up the narrower flight of stairs that climbed from the cave mouth to the top of the cliff.

"Rhe khem," Susannah called softly after they had disappeared, and thought it interesting that the phrase should so readily leap to mind. Though she had not considered going with them, she felt absurdly left behind. *They'll need more than two to bring the bodies back.* . . .

She shivered. The air was still cool. Suddenly the Caves looked warm and inviting. She contemplated going back up into the tunnels to search for Stavros, but could not convince herself that anything was worth being inside again, no matter how threatening the outside might seem. She took advantage of the transitional area of overhang and ledge, no longer dark and closed in but not yet out in the open. Susannah sighed. She had always been fond of weather, happy to indulge in pathetic fallacy, let the weather reflect her mood. It saddened her to have to think of it as the Enemy.

She leaned against the slowly warming rock, stealing a moment to bask while the touch of Fiix's sun was still gentle. She would need dark-lenses when the sun rose to its full height later in the week.

"That is," she murmured, "If the weather holds. . . ."

Stavros raced along an inner corridor as if demons were chasing him. He slowed only when he reached the unlit newer section of tunnel where the floor had not been smoothed by generations of use. He stubbed his bare foot against an invisible lip of rock, but only briefly considered turning back for a lantern. The nearest light station was several hundred yards back in the main corridor. He picked his feet up higher and continued his plunge into darkness with his hands outstretched.

Embriha Lagri! Liphar's words echoed in his brain.

"Even if the dish is gone," he muttered to fill the black silence, "the omni might still be working. No power maybe, but at least we could get the comlink reestablished."

Embriha Lagri!

When the tunnel narrowed, he eased sideways to guide himself along the wall. The blackness was as suffocating as his dreams of night drowning. It sent a worm of panic burrowing through his gut. But almost instantly, he knew it for an old reflex, a habit of imagined fear that he would no longer indulge. He was in the Caves, he knew he was safe, and he was not afraid, though once he would have been, uncontrollably.

"Then why am I in such an immortal hurry?" he growled.

Embriha Lagri! his brain replied, and Stavros pushed the thought away until he had time to deal with its implications.

His probing fingers found an end to the rough wall. He felt for the overhang of the narrow entry to the Black Hole and ducked instinctively as he turned in, although he himself had helped the Sawl masons hammer away enough stone to raise the opening to Terran head-height. The darkness ahead took on a reddish cast.

Good. They've left a fire burning. He would not have to feel his way to the terminal like a blind man. He had not used it since he had set it up over two weeks ago, nor could he remember where in the cavern he had last left a lantern.

The coals were ruby, nearly spent. He crossed to the firepit and placed several dung cakes in a careful pyramid around the brightest coals, blew gently and waited, squinting impatiently into the shadows, hoping for a lantern to appear. The dung popped and flared, then died, but he had seen a brief glimmer on the edge of the sleeping platform. He stumbled toward where he guessed it to be and was rewarded when his hand touched ceramic and glass.

He grasped the lamp triumphantly. It was one of the largest sizes the potters made, and it weighed full. He felt around the bowl and found flint and tinder in a recess below the handle. He struck a spark into the tinder and lit the wick, a recently learned local skill that gave him uncommon satisfaction. He carried the lamp to the nest of plastic crates in the rear of the cavern where he had set up the least portable of the scavenged terminals. It was Danforth's terminal, but Stavros was sure that the planetologist was in no condition to care. He set the lamp on a tall crate, checked the cable to the emergency battery and pulled up a smaller crate to perch on as he powered up the terminal.

When the screen glowed ready, he tapped in CRI's call code and held his breath.

Nothing. His own inquiry glared back at him unchanged.

He tried again, a routine repeat. But his fingers trembled.

Again, no reply.

He stared for a moment at the screen. Then he put the call on repeater and sat back to wait, while he pondered what to do with the anticlimax that was seeping through him like a soporific.

"Well, the relay's out," he explained to his own words on the screen. "And the omni's gone, too. But no problem. Easy enough to fix."

The oil lamp flickered. He jerked as if out of sleep. He had been staring at the screen mesmerized by its refusal to respond. Meanwhile, Liphar's voice in his brain still whispered its refrain.

Embriha Lagri!

Stavros roused himself and shut down the terminal. CRI would pick up the homing beacon and know at least that someone was still alive down here. That would have to do until he got the antenna fixed. Reaching for his lamp, his arm dislodged a stack of printout from the top of the monitor. Damp papers fluttered in the lamplight. Stavros stooped, gathered and came up with more of Danforth's notes. Scrawled across a charted data sheet he read, "Venus model run outputs nominal Venus data," followed by a numbered list headed "Possible Tinkering." Venus, again. He wondered why Danforth was so concerned with Venus all the way out here on Fiix. Down in the corner was a tighter scribble. Stavros held the paper up to the lamp. Danforth's impatience snarled at him from the page.

It read: "Explore possibility of large-scale dynamic instability mode—probe data resolution too low?"

Then, a scrawl that spoke of infinite frustration: "MORE DETAILED MEASUREMENTS!!"

And finally, more purposefully: "CRI: new wind data. Increase resolution of model to check for possible instability mode."

Stavros neatened the papers and replaced them on top of the monitor. His hand lingered on them briefly. He knew now that he missed the energy that Danforth had brought to their group.

Should have been just Clausen, he thought, and turned away from the darkened terminal.

He took the lamp to light his way. He could return it to the local light station as he passed by on his way to the cave mouth.

CRI - PL - 10:   TEST VEN / FORCAST MODEL 3A / OBS: ORB IR / MICRO / 361 - 2

TIME STEP = 31200,   TIME = 0.8 TEQ

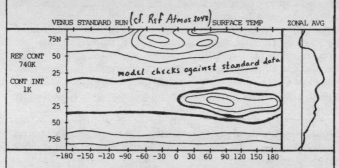

VENUS STANDARD RUN (cf. Ref Atmos 2048) SURFACE TEMP   ZONAL AVG

REF CONT
740K

CONT INT
1K

model checks against standard data

75N
50
25
0
25
50
75S

-180 -150 -120 -90 -60 -30 0 30 60 90 120 150 180

CORR = 0.93   MAX DIFF = 0.75 (65N,30W)   AVG DIFF = 0.09   AVG TEMP = 738.3
DW SOL=30.1   UP SOL=4.3   DW IR=16801.5   UP IR=16837.2   TRANS = 841.9

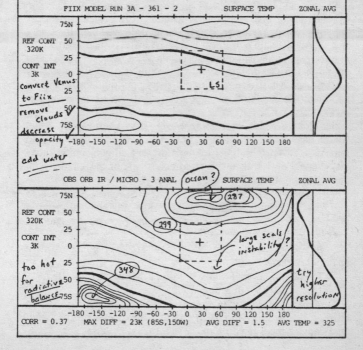

FIIX MODEL RUN 3A - 361 - 2   SURFACE TEMP   ZONAL AVG

REF CONT
320K

CONT INT
3K

convert Venus
to Fiix

remove
clouds

decrease
opacity

add water

75N
50
25
0
25
50
75S

LS

-180 -150 -120 -90 -60 -30 0 30 60 90 120 150 180

OBS ORB IR / MICRO - 3 ANAL ocean? SURFACE TEMP   ZONAL AVG

REF CONT
320K

CONT INT
3K

too hot
for radiative
balance

75N
50
25
0
25
50
75S

287
299
large scale
instability?
348

try
higher
resolution

-180 -150 -120 -90 -60 -30 0 30 60 90 120 150 180

CORR = 0.37   MAX DIFF = 23K (85S,150W)   AVG DIFF = 1.5   AVG TEMP = 325

He hurried along the outer corridor, preoccupied with a mental inventory of the parts he would need to repair the antenna. He reached the lighted sectors and extinguished the lamp. As he passed through an area of living quarters, he noted the lack of the usual bustle and noise. He found a light station at an intersection, where a high-vaulted tunnel led to the MarketHall. The intersection, normally a jam of two-carts and pedestrians, stretched wide and empty. Stavros set his lamp on the long stone shelf in a row of similar lamps with large brown-glazed bowls and stubby chimneys of thick utilitarian glass.

As he turned from the shelf, he heard the echoes of his footsteps returning along the vaulting, then dying away into an unprecedented silence. He could not hear a whisper of sound but his own.

The Caves were deserted, and he was alone in them.

"Susannah!"

She started guiltily. She had been daydreaming in the sun. She searched about and saw Megan waving from beside a two-cart bumping down the inner stairs. Weng followed her in stately step, her white ship's uniform bright against the shadowed walls. A man from the PaperGuild paused ahead of them to take a child up on his back. Megan climbed around them, automatically offering her arm to Weng. The old spacer put out her hand so as not to refuse the kindness but negotiated the obstacle on her own.

Susannah smiled. *How very Weng.* The Commander's feet would have to be agile on those stairs if her attention was to remain fixed on the object of their present all-consuming interest. Weng's eyes sought the tilted coneshape of the Lander with the concentration of the single-minded.

"Hedonist!" Megan accused, as the two joined Susannah in the weak sunlight. Susannah checked to be sure she had meant it playfully. Megan raised a hand to shade her brow as she squinted over the tortured plain.

"Mud soup," she observed. "How are they going to plant anything in that?"

"I'm adopting a wait-and-see attitude," Susannah replied.

"What's that booming noise?"

Susannah had forgotten the basso howl from the top of the cliffs. "Horns. Big wooden horns that the priests are blowing. You can see them if you look up right from the edge."

"Later," replied Megan with an uncertain glance over the precipice.

Susannah smiled at Weng. "Good morning, Commander."

Weng withdrew from her long-distance inspection of the Lander long enough to be civil. "Ah, Dr. James," she replied a bit myopically, as if Susannah were a pleasant intrusion on deeper, more important thoughts. Though Megan's eyes were still slitting, Weng did not seem at all bothered by the pale glare. "I suppose one must indeed call it morning, for that is the sun rising, even though one has just recently finished lunch."

Lunch? marveled Susannah. *Were we that long in the StoryHall?*

"Was that our young pilot with you just now?" Weng's tone was genial but the question obviously rhetorical.

"Um-hum. Want me to go after her?"

Weng folded her hands at her waist, her eyes straying back toward the metal cone glinting on the plain. "No, I think not, Dr. James. Off into the hills again, is she?"

Susannah nodded briskly.

The officer chuckled. "No need to look guilty, Dr. James. A pilot needs her vehicle, and so do we."

Susannah's nod was gentler. *This pilot needs her man.*

"So it's better she be out there finding it," Weng concluded, "than pining around here underfoot."

Megan moved farther away from the edge as a loaded winch pallet swung too close for her liking. "I just hope she's selective about what she brings back," she commented sourly.

Weng toyed with the adjustment of her braid-trimmed cuff. "You surprise me, Dr. Levy . . . Mr. Clausen was such a cultured gentleman. I would have thought you would find each other quite congenial."

Susannah studied Weng carefully but only the slightest deepening of the soft lines around the officer's chin betrayed her. *Why, Weng, you old fox!*

Megan grinned appreciatively. "Yes, if ever there was a threat to your authority, I guess it was that one, eh? Bad influence on Taylor, too."

Weng's hint of a smile did not change as she replied coolly, "My authority was not endangered, Dr. Levy. Besides, any crew is a threat to a captain's authority if they're worth their salt."

"Very noble and archaic, Weng," Megan countered airily, "but first of all, Clausen was hardly your ordinary crewman."

"But like Dr. Danforth, he was crucial to this mission."

Weng's tone was suddenly stern, as if reminding Megan that she too was considered "crew." Susannah also noted her use of the past tense. She hoped that Weng would not get started on the subject of The Mission. Music and the Mission were the Commander's own sister-deities, and the latter particularly encouraged her to indulge in a knee-jerk rhetoric that Susannah found embarrassing in an otherwise so admirable figure.

"We are one machine," Weng continued, "not self-sufficient parts. If we have lost some of our parts, we cannot go home a success."

"I know, I know. Dammit, Weng, you brought it up." Megan sulked in complaint of being encouraged to vent her loathing of Clausen and then unfairly taken to task. "I'm sorry about Taylor. I wished him no ill."

Susannah pulled herself up from her slouch against the wall. She suspected that Weng's real objection had been the questioning of her hold on the captaincy. "Were you headed down to inspect the Lander, Commander?"

Weng accepted the diversion gracefully. She could easily slide from leadership to companionship, as her expression of both was equally formal. Susannah now understood that the Commander's fabled calm was not relaxation but collected and controlled vigilance.

"I was indeed," Weng replied. The square of her thin shoulders directed their gaze over the ledge. "The sun may be shining at last, but we are still far from an optimum situation. There is considerable question as to the possibility of getting ourselves aloft again." She paused to glance back into the cave mouth. Laden Sawls still poured down the inner stairs, but there were fewer animals and heavy carts coming through. "Will you join me, Dr. James? Dr. Levy?"

"Sure, I'll come along." Megan made a halfhearted attempt to make up for her diplomatic blunder. "The Sawls'll put me to work in the mud otherwise."

Weng nodded graciously.

The Old Lady, thought Susannah. In the sunlight, Weng looked more nearly her true age, information privileged only to the ship's computer . . . and the ship's doctor. *Yes, Weng, I know. But I'm not telling. Besides, look at you. Skin like fine Chinese silk. Untouched by worldly weather for most of your years.*

She thought it odd to realize that she had never before seen Weng in natural light, except of course starlight, that faint supernatural light that bathed the Orbiter's bridge during night watch, when all but the running lights were down.

Susannah could not keep her eyes from drifting upward. *Seems so long ago now . . . I wonder how they all are up there?*

"Dr. James?"

"Coming, Commander."

He had never been alone in the Caves before.

The realization stopped Stavros dead while he considered the ramifications. He had free run. He could go where he liked. Either the Sawls had forgotten about him in the heat of their celebrating, or they had decided to trust him at last.

Because I was there . . . ?

Embriha Lagri!

Standing in the middle of the deserted intersection, Stavros lost his inner battle with the thought that had been yammering at him, demanding attention.

He did it. Kav Daven changed the weather.

No, that wasn't quite right.

His dance changed the weather   by lending power to Lagri.

Impossible, of course. But hadn't he seen it with his own eyes?

No. Coincidence.

His knees wobbled. He tottered over to the stone bench at the light station and dropped onto it, his head in his hands.

It had been easy, up until now, to play the game of belief. Stavros was practiced at it from a solitary youth filled with holos and fantasy games. Later, he found it a useful tool in his work, a technique for which he had developed the philosophical defense he used so successfully to goad more orthodox colleagues like Megan Levy. It was often vertiginous to hang along the edges of belief. It led to unstable behavior. The empathetic gift that made him a superior linguist also left him vulnerable to the worldviews that infuse all languages. But he had learned ways of dealing with that. He played games of logic and semiotics with their symbolisms while pretending to accept, and coexisted with the supernatural while allowing it to remain unrealized in his mind.

But Kav Daven's dance and the clear dawn that followed called out for more than technical belief.

ACTUAL *belief?*

His head sunk deeper into his hands. What, after all, had he seen? An old priest did a dance and the sun came out. *Simple. No problem.*

A soft moan escaped him as a vision of Kav Daven's brilliant blind smile swam into his consciousness unbidden. Stavros had not really known the profound potential of belief until now. He had not known that it could wrap itself around your soul and take you unwilling prisoner.

There was nothing technical about the Sawls' belief. There was also nothing symbolic. To believe with them, he must accept the actual existence of the sister-goddesses, not as spirits, not as disembodied energies, not even as the icons of a more abstract faith which rational societies tended to let their deities evolve into. Nor were they mere mortal representations of a deity, like a prophet or a pharaoh.

He must accept them as actual beings of incomprehensible power.

Goddesses incarnate.

He was surprised that his mind balked so at a concept that his neoChristian grandparents had accepted wholeheartedly. But their acceptance had been required long after the supposed fact of that particular incarnation, when time and faith had pulled a veil over history and there was no longer a physical body around to muddy the waters of their mysticism. The Sawl goddesses still walked the planet.

He remembered his reckless statement of conviction to Megan on the part of his Greek ancestors, and tried a laugh that came out as a strangled sigh. *Bad enough to have gods messing with the weather, but if you have to think of them as people . . .*

Knowledge and Belief, Ibiá. Your own argument.

He could not yet accept the *knowing.*

He was stalled at the point of being ready to *believe* that he had seen a miracle occur, but was unable to go further. He was unsure of what definition and degree of deity he could persuade the rational part of his mind to accept. The less rational part and the good old unconscious would travel willingly down any path, but past experience suggested that an inner split would not benefit his sanity.

Again, the strangled laugh. *Well, they've always said I was crazy. . . .*

But the thought of it made Stavros sweat.

For he was sure that he would rather risk a tumble into the abyss of belief than let stubborn unbelief sever the umbilical of trust that even playing at belief had helped establish with the

Sawls. *Actual* belief might threaten his balance but it would make him a truer interpreter of the language. To lose the trust would render him useless.

He thought again of Kav Daven's smile, a very *knowing* smile, directed at him, as if the old priest were interpreting *him*. He rocked a little on the cool stone bench, then raised his head and stood. His weakness had passed. He stretched as if his exhaustion were merely physical.

This need not be immediately resolved, he comforted himself. Yet he stood immobile. He had intended to head for the cave mouth, for the outside and the sun and other people. He was unable to make a start. The silence and the emptiness urged him in another direction. It drew him inward and down, toward the center of the rock.

All right, then, he thought. *A compromise*. The antenna repairs could wait awhile longer. He decided to climb up to the StoryHall to retrieve his translator units.

While at the back of his brain, Liphar's voice kept repeating, *Embriha Lagri!*

23

Susannah swore as she sank into ocher mud up to her knees.

Clever me, volunteering to lead the way. . . .

The cold mud resisted with obscene sucking noises as she wrenched her legs free. Silted clay clung to the ridges of her bootsoles so that her feet weighed heavily, like some larger creature's feet. Behind her, Weng and Megan gingerly steered clear of the sinkhole she had blundered into. When she did not need both arms for balance, Weng lifted both white trouser legs as if protecting the hem of a skirt.

Beyond the layered terraces of rock at the base of the cliffs, the solid areas of the plain were rock-strewn and broken by frequent rivulets flowing between murky puddles as big as ponds. The rest was as treacherous as a swamp. Where she was able, Susannah chose a path across the high ground, avoiding the bottoms of ravines and gullies, with their promise of quicksand and flash floods. Even on the upper flats, the mud was so deep that they left a trail of rubbery footprints clearly visible all the way back to the cliff face. The shallowest slopes were slippery, the steeper ones were perilous. Susannah led her party down a long hill sideways and stopped to rest beside a pile of boulders after the ground had begun to rise again. Megan sighed and lowered herself to a rock. Weng remained standing with her hands on her hips, gazing over the plain like a sea captain on the forward deck.

"Mr. Ibiá tells me," she said, "that the Sawls call this plain the Dop Arek, the Gaming Board."

"The *Goddesses*' Gaming Board," Susannah added.

"More like a washboard," snorted Megan. "You know, I was in a flood once, back home. When the water went down, it was like all the color'd been bleached out of the landscape. Fences, houses, signs, cars, everything the flood touched was turned the same dreary gray.''

"Be the same here if there was anything left upright for the flood to touch," said Susannah. "Except it's yellow. Look behind you.''

The cliffs towered above them, even from a quarter of a mile away. The white rock shimmered amber in the dawn. Over the muddy rise of the plain, the terraced base was barely visible. The cliff face wore a band of ocher mud two stories high.

"Now that's one hell of a flood," said Megan.

Susannah only shivered.

The rising sun threw the cave openings into deep relief against the pale brilliance of the rock. Wind-sculpted alternations of shadow and striation were broken at intervals by the dark zigzags of vertical clefts. Four long rows of openings pierced the sheerest drop, joined by a herringbone pattern of ledges and stairs. Susannah counted twelve to fifteen openings per level, spaced more or less regularly. Since this was her first opportunity to see the cliff unobstructed by either snow or floodwaters, she had not realized that the big main flight of stairs they had just come down actually climbed to the second level of caves. The first level was well inside the band of mud.

"Look," she pointed out to Megan. "There are caves lower than the stables. Must be abandoned now. Could the floods have been rising that much over the years?''

"Umm. You know, I'd bet there weren't even the beginnings of natural caves here," said Megan. "Those energetic little folks searched out a cliff that suited their needs and went to work. Imagine how long they must have been at it!" Her sigh was as weary as if she had been at it herself.

"And there they are busily moving out," Weng commented.

Susannah laughed. On the broad rock ledges that spread out from the base of the cliff, a huge contingent from the FoodGuild was setting up a small city of tent canopies and cookfires. Wagons and two-carts were being unloaded and hauled off to one side. The little hakra ventured to the edge of the terraces on their own to sniff the mud, while the hjalk stood in a patient huddle, being harnessed. "It's just temporary, I'm sure," she replied. "Got to feed those diggers!''

Without seeming to pace, Weng contrived to place herself in their line of view. "Are you rested, Dr. Levy?" she inquired.

Megan roused herself with a sigh, and they continued across the slope to the top of the rise. From there, they followed a ridge that skirted a ragged gully. Thick yellow water oozed through the boulders piled along the bottom. Susannah dallied along the edge, scanning the shallows hopefully for signs of life. Even on urban Earth, the dirt would be squirming after a good rain. But then, two and a half weeks was more than just a good rain. It would be a miracle if *anything* survived.

Have to run high or burrow deep to make it on Fiix, she decided.

The yellow mud did not smell like the earth she knew, yet when she rubbed it between her fingers, it seemed rich with particulate organic matter. She was surprised. She had expected a desert soil, sandier and with fewer organics. On Earth, organics would have made the soil dark.

They hurried in and out of a narrow dip where a side wash fed into the gully. Slipping on the slopes, they gained another rise. The Lander loomed before them. Weng's head mirrored its tilt as she began her close-up assessment of the damage.

"Our very own Tower of Pisa," Megan quipped.

The gully snaked around, then ran under the Lander's belly. The number-three landing strut was sunk in the streambed, with a mare's nest of rocks and vegetable matter tangled in its trusswork. All four struts and a good three meters worth of hull wore a thick coat of drying mud. A shallow trench ringed the entire craft, an artifact of the ice wall created by the melt-and-freeze between the snowmass and the force field. The trench was filled with muddy water, like a moat. The only way across it was through it, and Weng did not hesitate. She pulled her trouser legs high as if at a Victorian beach party and waded in.

In the shadow of the Underbelly, it was dank and chilly. Because of the tilt, the clearance toward strut number three was reduced to less than two meters. The struts were mottled yellow. Working at it with the edge of a sharp stone, Susannah could barely crack the surface. Mud spattered the Lander's underside as well. One man-sized hatchcover dangled by its remaining hinge. The doors on two of the small storage bays had been ripped away entirely, and the contents captured by the flood.

"The Sawls are unlikely to be able to assist us with the manufacture of any missing parts," Weng mused, looking up at the empty bays.

The main hatch gaped wide, now a scant three meters above. Weng stood in the ankle-deep mud beneath the opening and studied its hovering darkness as if she could coax it to speak to her of its miseries and provide a list of damages.

"We will need a rope," she stated finally. Terseness was often her only visible sign of impatience.

Susannah craned her neck for a look. She could not tell how far the mud and water had risen into the hatch. Besides, Weng's main concern would be for the precious ascent engines, and the state of their health could hardly be determined by staring into their muddied exhaust cones. She wondered how McPherson had managed to get up to the nose so fast to check the antennas, and then decided that she had done her checking long-distance. Susannah was disappointed. She rather liked her image of McPherson scaling the Lander's outer shell like Sir Edmund Hillary. "Perhaps the Sawls could build us a new ladder at least," she suggested.

Weng glanced her way, blinked, then nodded briskly. "We can trade for the materials."

"What have we got that they want?" asked Megan.

But Weng's back was a little straighter than it had been a moment before. "I will arrange for it right away." She turned to start the half-mile trek back to the cliffs. A tired groan from Megan halted her only briefly. "Ah, Dr. Levy. Do stay and enjoy the air." Her smile was a sly flicker of an eyelid. "I'll see myself home."

24

Stavros padded through the FriezeHall looking neither to right nor to left. When he noticed that he was shunning the light pooled beneath the chandeliers, he also realized that he was scudding along on the balls of his feet, a sort of speeding tiptoe.

Nobody's here . . . who am I avoiding?

But out of the corner of his eye, he caught the red-and-lavender jewel-sparkle from the Friezes, and the accompanying chill told him that Belief was creeping up on him of its own accord.

Breathless, he halted at the open doors of the StoryHall. The old priest had gone, to rest or to celebrate. The fire was ash. The room was dark but for a cool steady glow coming from somewhere in the upper tiers. Stavros slipped in and found his cases waiting in a neat line just inside the door, not as he had left them, scattered in his surprise, but as some meticulous Sawl had placed them, ready for his return. He was ashamed to have worried about leaving them.

He took the two larger cases into the outer hall. Returning for the third, he glanced about for the source of the odd glow. He expected to find a hidden window or a light shaft in the dome, but instead, he saw a faint spear of light on the back wall, at the level of the highest tier. He squinted to make it out clearly, then climbed the tiers for a closer look.

In the wall, just opposite the great wooden doors, was an arched niche that had escaped his notice when the surrounding tiles were ablaze with reflected firelight. A thin flame burned in the niche.

Oil lamp? he wondered as he approached. But the flame was the wrong color.

The niche was tall and narrow, a semicircle bowed into the

wall. The curve was set with a mosaic of tiny lozenge-shaped tiles. Its beaded pattern was like a fiery lizard skin: glossy crimson, salmon, vermilion and garnet. Black inlaid letters curved in bands around the back of the inset. Stavros could just make out Lagri's name, though the lettering differed here and there from the Sawl alphabet he was learning. Some of the tiles were chipped or missing. Moving in as closely as he could without singeing his cheek, he noted hairline cracks in the grout and minute webs of fracture in the glaze. It reminded him of the texture of ancient pots in museums on Earth.

He decided that the niche was very old. The letters excited him with their differences. But the flame itself . . .

The shelf was tiled in concentric rings. The outside ring was deep wine red, and the colors moved inward through red and orange. The central ring was a raised ceramic collar glazed in golden yellow and set with blood-red cabochon stones. The collar enclosed a small hole. From the hole sprang the flame.

The flame was slim and blue. It burned clean and hot without a trace of soot. Leaning in close, Stavros heard a gentle hissing.

He stared at the flame as if it were alive, then stepped back and explored the tiled surfaces for a seam or a hinge, anything that would indicate a hidden vessel of some sort, a refillable reservoir. He found nothing. The flame apparently burned on its own.

And what would burn with such a flame? He knew and did not know. That is, if he were home on Terra, he would know it as a gas flame. But here? How could the Sawls, without metal or machinery, harness a flammable gas?

He thought of the steaming, pressurized water in the BathHall. He had known how wondrous that was but had accepted it rather than explore further to learn how it was accomplished. He thought of the warm, circulating air throughout the entire cave system. The list was lengthening. Apparently more than he had guessed remained to be revealed about the Sawls' capabilities. And, he thought with relief, this time it had nothing to do with magic or weather. These purely technical mysteries he could delve into without worrying about side issues of sanity or belief.

In a sudden flurry, he scrambled down the tiers and ran into the FriezeHall to grab the case containing the video gun. Pictures, first, then he would tell the others. He bent to lift the little gun from its housing but came up slowly, sucking his cheek.

No.

He couldn't tell the others, not until he was sure that the revelation would in no way harm the Sawls.

Secrets again, Ibiá?

But it had to be. Secrecy was his only weapon. Megan's warnings not to become involved were well meant, he knew that. But she had seen many planets in her lifetime. Her long experience had jaded her into protest without action. Stavros could not bear the thought that everything that was the Sawls, their industrious fatalistic cheer, their rich mythohistory, their generosity and ingenuity, might be lost to him if the rest of the galaxy decided to take further notice, for one reason or another, of the planet Fiix. He was not sure he could just stand aside when it happened, and he certainly wasn't going to do anything to encourage it.

This secret he would keep for his own sake, as well as for the Sawls'.

Weng would call this a mutiny and have my hide, he thought. His crooked smile belied his awareness that he had just made one of those rare turning-point decisions. *Thus are the lines drawn, and fatal choices made.*

Stavros took up his new loyalty as easily as he shouldered the little video gun, and went about his secret work.

25

A soft wind sprang up as Megan and Susannah watched Weng retrace the rugged path through the mud and rocks. Susannah sniffed at it warily, reminded of the hot desert blast that had foretold the earlier disastrous thaw. She wondered how long it would take to run the return distance to the Caves. Once, proximity to the Lander would have meant safety, and might again, if it was found to be in working order. For now, it was only a vulnerable metal shell parked on an open plain. For now, safety was in the Caves.

"A nice spring breeze," she remarked to Megan, as if they stood on the terrace of a friend's country apartment on Terra. "Think I'll go for a stroll." She moved out from under the Lander's oppressive shadow, needing the comfort of the sun. She splashed through the shallow moat and walked to the top of the nearby rise. From there she had a nearly full panorama. Facing south, to her right, muddy hillocks and ravines led to the flat rock terraces beneath the cliffs. Ahead of her to the east, more mud and hillocks, and the cliff curling around to meet a towering scarp dominated by the Red Pawn. To her left stretched the vast ravaged expanse of the Dop Arek, with its sawtoothed edging of distant mountains.

Megan struggled up behind her, slower and out of breath.

"Well, look at that," she exclaimed, pointing toward the cliffs.

Susannah nodded. The wide stone stairs were deserted. Gray smoke curled up from a dozen cookfires among the forest of newly erected tents. The harnessing of the hjalk continued, but already a long procession of people and carts and animals snaked down from the rock flats, fanning out into the ravines, their digging tools shouldered like weapons.

Susannah clambered up on a high boulder for a better view.

One arm of the procession moved toward them along the bottom of the gully that ran under the Lander. At the head of the line, a wizened FoodGuildsman walked in intense gesticulating consultation with two Engineers, one of whom broke away to wave directions to the others behind them. They divided into work details and attacked the sides of the gully with rakes and hoes. Each detail started at the top of the slope and worked its way steadily to the bottom, shoveling the yellow mud into semicircular terraces that followed the contour of the rise. Four giant hjalk hauled flatbed wagons along the stream bed. Stones pulled out of the mud were tossed down into the gully to be sorted by a horde of Stonecutters' apprentices and stacked on the flatbeds according to size. When a wagon was full, its hjalk drew it back up the gully to where the terracing began. There, a detail of journeymen wearing the Stonecutters' Guild hammer-and-chisel seal raised a low stone dike to contain the bottom terrace. Fat earthworks edged the higher tiers. As each terrace was carved out and flattened, the runoff water was gathered by the earthwork, until a series of narrow stepped ponds lined the gully sides.

From the top of her boulder, Susannah could see the same process being carried out in several dozen gullies or ravines. The terraces took shape with astonishing speed. The largest were nearly an acre square, though most were a third that size or smaller, as the contours of the land dictated. Every available inch of ground was being shaped and put to use.

The mood of wild celebration had dissipated. The party transforming the gully nearest to the Lander worked with a concentration that was almost grim. The foreman from the Engineers' Guild tramped about in the mud offering advice and encouragement to workers too intent on their task to really listen. The elderly FoodGuildsman paced the top of the slope with his mouth set tight. Occasionally he halted to study the sky, with particular attention to the northeastern horizon.

Susannah and Megan watched for an hour, admiring the care and speed of the work. When both sides of the gully had been terraced for several hundred yards, the work detail took a break. They passed around the water jugs, shed a layer or two of clothing and moved on to carve up the next section of water-logged slope.

Susannah chewed her lip. "Usually you plow first and *then* flood a paddy. I mean, terracing is normally used to keep water from running off, but, here, you'd think they'd *want* it to run off."

"Apparently not . . ." Megan began.

The wall-building teams now climbed to the top of the finished terraces. Working down the tiers under the watchful eye of the Engineer foreman, they opened a shallow sluice in each earthwork. A small amount of the water collected in each terrace ran off onto the level below.

"Equalizing the water level," she concluded.

The finished terraces did not stand vacant for long. More hjalk appeared along the ridge, each hauling a double-shared wooden plow. A young herdsman sat high on each beast's burly shoulders, feet twined in the curly mane. They urged their mounts into the top terraces and drove them back and forth in the shin-deep mud and water. When one terrace was plowed, a digger was on hand to help lift the heavy blades and rollers over the earthwork and onto the next level.

Susannah shook her head. "Gods, they're efficient."

"Mmmm. Too efficient. I'd say they're in one hell of a hurry."

Susannah frowned, thinking of the Sawls' uncanny nose for weather. The old FoodGuildsman too was staring at the sky. The oblate salmon sun still rested between the peaks of the eastern mountain range, as if gathering itself for that precise moment of separation from the horizon that would signal an official sunrise.

This sun is not a friendly color, Susannah decided. The orangy pink was acidic, and the sky around it was tinged a faint green that progressed through a watercolor wash of turquoise and aqua as it rose to azure at the zenith. It deepened again to the heavy green of malachite where the western sky met the sharp white profile of the cliffs. "Why do you think they're in such a hurry?"

"Sawls hurry," Megan stated dogmatically. "Whatever they happen to be doing, they do faster than we would do it, so to us it looks like hurrying. Actually, it's their natural pace of existence."

"Even though their day is longer and you'd think they'd work slower?" Susannah laughed. "Is this Levy's Law of Special Relativity?"

Megan looked wounded. "I'm serious."

Susannah worked at concealing her grin. "Well, I have noticed that their metabolisms run a little hotter, but . . . Oh, my. Look at this!"

The hjalk and their plows had moved on to the next sector of terraces. The mud stood in high furrows that just broke the surface of the water. A long-haired dairy hekker was coming over the rise. A solitary figure perched on a pad of blankets strapped to its back.

"Kav Daven!" Megan breathed.

The old priest sat erect and smiling on his barrel-chested mount. In the sunlight he seemed to have gained substance. Susannah no longer worried that he would shatter like crystal in the slightest breeze. He stared straight ahead as the hekker plodded along the ridge. His bald head was slightly cocked, as if he were listening to the ground. Behind him strode an apprentice, the tawny child from the StoryHall. She led a double line of younger children who were trying unsuccessfully to appear adult and solemn.

At the first flight of terraces, Kav Daven raised his hand and the hekker stopped. The animal was as thin and gray as the old man himself but it had a willing softness in its eye. Mud and splashing had plastered its long coat to its ribs in matted strands. It was hardly tall enough to be a proper mount. The priest's bony legs hung long at its sides, his toes skimming the water.

The tawny girl came to stand at the animal's head. At a sign from the priest, she led it down into the highest terrace. Kav Daven carried a huge loose sack slung from hip to shoulder. The sack bulged with shifting weight. He dipped in, drew forth a brimming handful of seeds and raised them to the sky in salute. Then with a sweeping gesture, he cast them at random into the mud. The line of children began a high-pitched hum.

The girl twined a hand in the hekker's shaggy mane and led it up and down the field. The younger children followed in a vee formation, humming their shrill monotone, stalking along the furrows like a flock of water birds. Kav Daven scattered the seed from side to side and sang out in a voice that seemed to fill the nearby plain. The children answered him, and the rhythm of their chant mimicked the swing of his arm and the swish of their own feet as they pressed the seed into the mud.

Susannah climbed down from her boulder, stiff from sitting still. "Let's find out what they're planting that's all going to rot in this waterlogged soil!" She scrambled down the wet bank into the gully and waded along the streambed.

"This you call a wait-and-see attitude?" Megan called after her but rose to follow unwillingly. "Maybe it's like rice, eh? Rice grows in water."

"It's the rice seedlings you plant in water, not the seeds.

Besides, what about Taylor's 'desert climate'? Rice won't grow in a desert.''

"Irrigation? From what they've done here, I'd guess they were capable of it."

Susannah recalled the last plant sample she'd been working on before the snow had stopped. She had never completed her analysis of that sample. *It was structured like a water plant. . . .*

She left the stream bed and climbed the opposite bank, dragging Megan up after her as if she were a troublesome child. She struck out across the rutted ground to intercept the gully where it curved back on itself. The land sloped gently into a puddled depression and rose again. The old priest and his entourage had progressed to the next set of fields. Others moved along the ridges now, seedsmen from the FoodGuild and long lines of apprentices behind them, to finish the bulk of the sowing.

Susannah came to the edge and looked down into the first level of terraces. The water stood knee-deep and still. The furrows had been flattened by the children's feet. She crouched and plunged both hands into the mud. "Whew! Cold!"

"What do you expect?" said Megan. "It's been pitch-black night for two weeks."

"And those children walking in it barefoot!" She scooped up a handful of silt and let the water drain out through her fingers. She sifted the mud back and forth until she had sorted out a dirty pile of seeds. She rinsed one in the water and held it up for Megan to see. It was chunky, triangular and the size of her thumb pad.

"What does that remind you of?" She turned the seed to catch the pale sunlight. Under its coating of yellow mud, it was pale magenta.

Megan took it in her own palm and poked it. "Kind of looks like big corn."

"Go to the head of the class." Susannah fished in her thermsuit pockets with a muddy hand. "Forgot to come equipped. Not even some old sample bag with a hole in it. Oh well." She dropped the dirty seeds into her breast pocket, leaving smudged fingerprints all over the flap. "It isn't corn, of course, but it might resemble it. We'll take a look under Ghirra's lenses in Physicians'. They're more powerful than my kit scope, would you believe? Damn! If we had CRI on line, she could do . . . well, we don't, do we." She took the single seed back from Megan and tried to break the seedcoat with her thumbnail. "Now, you don't usually sow corn by broadcast, but . . ."

"I don't recall eating any corn here," mused Megan.

"It's not corn," Susannah repeated with a trace of impatience. She rubbed her fingertips together, testing the soil texture. "*Like* corn. It could be feed grain for the animals. Or perhaps it's only used when ground into meal. You know, I still haven't done that full diet breakout. What the hell have I been doing these past two weeks?"

"Practicing medicine, a perfectly valid pursuit," Megan replied, thinking that she ought to have done the diet study herself. "How long should it take such a seed to come up?"

"Depends. On the temperature, on the moisture. Corn will begin to show within a long week, earthtime, if the conditions are ideal. Takes longer if it's wet or cold," she added significantly. "Also, even the earliest of our corns need a solid month and a half to ripen, and those are our newest bioengineered hybrids. Either the Sawls are very sure of the weather this time, or . . ." She paused to let the sweep of her arm include the rising sun, which had finally vaulted clear of the sawtoothed horizon. The terraces were a descending flight of mirrors reflecting the malachite sky. "Or all this is a magnificent gamble."

Megan grunted, smiled.

"I thought you'd like that," Susannah continued. "But it's true. They could be just taking a chance that the weather will hold. If they lose, this whole effort will be wasted, washed out, blown away, frozen solid or whatever by the next natural disaster this world has in store for us."

Megan's smile twisted ever so slightly. "No wonder they're hurrying."

26

Thrust from the familiar darkness, Stavros felt out of phase.

Like being born, he thought fuzzily.

Not a thing he was altogether sure he had liked in the first place. Liphar had found him in the Black Hole, sunk in a drift of Sawl paper and Terran photographs. Amid joyful cries that the Planting was done and the Feast being laid, the young man had bullied him out of his protective shell of concentration and dragged him forth with irresistible merriment into the building pressure of the midday heat to join the celebration.

Stavros felt as if he were floating in light. His eyes watered. He sat hunched on a thick rug that softened the rock edges beneath him. At his back, the cliff face was blindingly bright. The sun seemed too fat and too close. Its amber glare filtered through the open-weave canopy to rest like palpable weight on his head and shoulders.

Stavros could not remember if he liked the heat of the sun. Surely his ancestors, both the Greek and the Portuguese, had flourished under that other sun, Earth's sun, in the days when it had still shone on them clearly.

Should I lie down in the open and bask, like a lizard? . . . Fitting for one who lives his life as a cultural chameleon.

He liked the thought that this sun would quickly burn his skin as dark as the Sawls'. He felt his muscles uncurling petal-like to its warmth. During his three-day bout of manic concentration, he had slept only in snatches. His confusion hinted at deep exhaustion. His brain was as blurry as his eyes, both still cave-adjusted.

He heard water, he thought, ripples on a lake. But it was the soft lapping of the multicolored banners tied to the tent poles. An ocean of billowing canopies brightened the rock terraces as far as he could see. A thousand guy ropes had been laced with silken

streamers, yellow and red and orange, so that Lagri's colors
dazzled him wherever he looked. Joyous crowds wrapped in
rainbows milled about in the shadow and sunlight.

Stavros shut his eyes as his brain threatened a sensual overload. His shutdown was like irising in a lens. The confusion was
manageable if he restricted the incoming data. He concentrated
on the knobby beige and gray wool of the rug, on the subtle
twistings of the unbleached fibers.

*They must have hauled out every rug and cushion in the Caves
for this,* he thought.

A mug of chilled herb drink sat beside him, one ice chunk still
afloat. The pale clay sweated in the heat.

Ice. Another Sawl wonder. He had not known about the
ice-storage caverns until now.

In his lap was a platter of food that he dimly recalled being set
before him by a flushed and laughing cook's apprentice. The
platter was a satiny wooden oval, divided in quarters like a
Terran child's dish, but the size of a serving tray. It was wide
enough to balance securely on his knees as he sat cross-legged.
Stavros inspected its contents distantly, as if it were a museum
display or a piece of conceptual art. He nudged a pile of boiled
yellow roots. One toppled and jumped its wooden corral, rolling
into a lump of white mash next to several thick chunks of dark
orange bread. He twisted an experimental fingertip in the mash.
It was lukewarm but tasted spicy, like a cooked radish, or a
turnip with pepper in it. He recognized it as specially prepared
kamad root. Comforted, he ate a little more.

Food is so very real.

He widened his iris to admit sound. His ears were used to
sorting out the worst kind of cacophony in the Caves. He did not
worry that they would overload and betray him, even though
sound was different here, outside of the stone echo chambers.
Uncontained, it was allowed to fade with distance or drift away
with a passing breeze.

He heard music around him, many instruments pursuing many
different melodies. Conversation hummed across the several acres
shaded by the canopies, gossip and debate, broken by laughter
and the clatter of dishes, by a child's excited giggle, and here
and there by satisfied mutual silence. The many tunes were
muted. The softened tones of the chatter told him that the huge
gathering was feeling well fed and mellow. Yet there was still
the crisp bustle of the cook's apprentices, busing their loaded

trays from tent to tent, calling out the menu in a song of endless mouthwatering stanzas.

Beyond the music and conversation, he heard cheers and cries that brought a stab of homesickness with memories of summer afternoons and ball games in the local park. As he listened, a groan of disappointment surged through the distant spectators. Stavros pictured a great tidal wave sweeping fortunes in stone counters to the winds like so much sea foam. But the Sawls did not possess fortunes, only their own handmade goods and the promise of services, many of which would be traded back and forth by the time this Planting Feast was over.

Stavros grinned privately. Among his many concealments, there was one he continued for his own amusement alone. He had not been honest with Megan about the gambling. Any fool could see the Sawls were inveterate gamblers, that games of chance dominated substantial portions of their meager free time and that any issue open to question was fair game for a wager. But what Megan saw as born out of boredom, greed and tradesmanship, he saw as a brave metaphor for the Sawls' battle for survival on a hostile planet. If he proposed this interpretation to her, she'd just call him a romantic and think she had won the argument.

Their whole lives are a gamble . . . why shouldn't they make light of it if they can?

The food and the cool tea steadied him. In addition to not sleeping, he had also forgotten to eat regularly during his seclusion. His fear of overload was ebbing. He decided to admit words to the data flow, and the conversation nearest him resolved itself out of former nonsense.

"When you were little and you saw programs on the vid about the Land of the Midnight Sun, didn't you want to go there right away to find out how the Scand kids knew when it was bedtime?"

Susannah's voice was husky with ease and memory. Stavros sensed a slippage inside him that he knew for a warning sign, but the light and the heat sapped his resistance. He tuned in to the sound of her. The wash of pleasure was greater than he had expected. She had been on his mind during the last few days, he deep in the caves, she out with the Planting. He was forced to admit that he had missed her.

Megan, by contrast, sounded forlorn, despite her answering chuckle. "Every time I called up one of those cultural shows, my mother would hang over my shoulder and editorialize. So I

stopped watching. She always seemed to have better, fresher
data than the journalists did."

There was a small clatter, as of wooden objects tipping over.

"Is that your move, Dr. Levy?" Weng's voice held subtle
mischief, and accompanied the clink of wooden objects being
righted.

"Does it help to fondle the bishop like that?" Susannah
rustled. He pictured her stirring, lying back perhaps.

"I wish it did," replied Megan distractedly. Stavros heard a
tentative clunk. "No, wait. There's got to be a better move than
that."

"There are a number of them," offered Weng mildly.

It was an easy guess who was winning, but Stavros wanted to
watch it happen. He raised his head carefully. His eyes had
stopped watering. He blinked and focused.

Weng and Megan sat upright on two red cushions as thick as
little ottomans, for all the world like two colonial pashas at tea
among the barbarians. A third pile of cushions set between them
supported the chessboard. A quick survey told him that endgame
was fast approaching. Megan sent her remaining rook halfway
across the board with a defeated sigh.

"Liphar says the priests will dance later, in the fields." She
twisted sideways on her cushion. "He seemed particularly eager
that we be there, Susannah."

Cautiously, Stavros followed Megan's gaze. Susannah reclined
in a tumble of soft pillows at the far corner of his rug. Her head
lolled back lazily. Her dark hair fanned out against the bright
yellow, red and orange of the pillow fabric. She had shed her
unwashed, useless therm-suit for a loose Sawl shift that the
lender had not had a chance to lengthen. Stavros's discovery of
her knees and ankles was as disturbingly arousing to him as it
would have been to a Victorian gentleman. It was as if he had
never really seen her before. The sudden summer seemed to
encourage a sensuousness in her that he had known only in his
fantasies. Gauzy shadows played across her cheek. She stretched
luxuriantly among the pillows. The arch of her back and her
body's unconscious preening tied knots in his gut. He had to
look away.

He focused on the chess game, on the hot green-blue sky, on
the food drying out in his dish. He remembered the papers at his
side and felt for them blindly. Sandwiched between pages of
rough hand translation and a sheaf of stills of the Dance of
Origins were his secret photos of the StoryHall flame. He snatched

up the papers and planted them in front of his nose. The blind face of Kav Daven smiled back at him from the top of the stack. His ardor cooled with the leaden weight of the secrets held in his hand that he could not share with her. She had disapproved of his running interference between Clausen and the Sawls. How would she feel about this?

Megan heard the crackle of his papers. "Put that work away, boy. Get over here and win this game for me!"

"I'm afraid it's too late for rescue, Dr. Levy," Weng assured her.

Megan sighed.

"Still working on the Dance of Origins translation?" Susannah asked him lazily.

"Mmmm." Guilt and desire left him inarticulate.

"It might help to take a break, if you're having trouble," she suggested.

"Mmmm," he muttered again. He heard her rustling among her pillows again and imagined himself among them with her.

"But if you insist on ignoring the most glorious weather that ever was," she continued, "meant only for relaxing, there was something I wanted to check out with you."

Stavros glanced up with what he hoped would read as polite interest and found he could not meet her eyes.

"Would you say that the words 'hakra,' 'hekker' and 'hjalk' are root-related in any way?" she asked.

Genuine interest offered him an anchor. He repeated the words experimentally in his head, then cleared his throat, fully expecting his voice to be as dysfunctional as the rest of him seemed to be. But speech was still within his grasp. "If similarity of sound were enough to go on, I'd say yes, but etymology is often less logical than that. Why do you ask?"

"Well, they've all got the same body, more or less, in three different sizes. Yet within the three, the range of size is minimal."

Stavros nodded. "I'll put a flag on it in the translator's glossary. Part of the program searches possible roots and derivations. What's your guess?"

Susannah sucked her cheek. "That they were all the same animal once. Which would suggest that the Sawls have been fiendishly clever at breeding for desired characteristics, for a very long time. These are not short-generation animals, these sturdy beasts. It would take a while to get them the way you wanted them."

"Couldn't they have evolved that way in the first place?"

She considered. "Possible. But not likely."

A young Sawl wheeled in under their canopy, balancing a steaming tray on one shoulder. His gray apron bore the ubiquitous double red and blue stripes of the FoodGuild, topped by the thin yellow band of an apprentice cook. He greeted them cheerfully, spun the tray down and presented it to the chessplayers with a flourish.

Weng studied the food closely without appearing to, then pincered a small dumpling between delicate fingers. She rewarded the apprentice with a gracious nod and laid the dumpling beside the neat file of chessmen she had captured from Megan. A chunk of uneaten cheese and a thin roll shared this relegation to obscurity.

Stavros watched her fondly. *That must be the sort of smile they used to teach queens to make.* Weng's children had children his age. He was grateful to be able to love her without confusion.

Megan looked the tray over and shook her head definitively, then as the apprentice turned away, she changed her mind and snatched a fat pastry off the edge of the tray. Susannah roused herself eagerly, reaching for her battered notebook to take the tray's inventory. She pointed to a baked casserole and asked what it was.

The little cook smiled proudly and reeled off a list of ingredients. Susannah made a few rapid scrawls, then foundered. "Stav, are you listening? Translate, please?"

"Eggs, butter, three cheeses: kidri, voss and nahrin; those onionlike shoots, blue fungus, kamad root, you know, like a turnip, flat noodles, uh . . ." He still could not look her in the eye. Perhaps it was just the brightness of the light.

I've never had this problem before.

He asked the Sawl to repeat the end of his list. "The rest are mostly spices that I think you already have in your listings. And by the way, your asking made him very happy. That recipe is one of his own that the cooks are allowing him to try out during the Feast."

Susannah scribbled frantically. "Kamad, noodles . . . jeez, writing by hand is slow!"

He chose to read subtle rebuke into her remark. "I'm working on that. Liphar tells me that some of the terracers found what's left of the main antenna out in a gully." His awkwardness with her made him talk too fast, sound too businesslike for a festive occasion. "Now that Planting's done, they can help us haul it in and I'll see what can be done about getting it pushed back into shape and mounted in a proper send-receive position. But that'll take a while. First thing is to get the omni working again.''

She smiled a puzzled apology at him. "Stav, it's all right. I didn't mean . . ."

"Liphar also mentioned an old metalsmith in Engineers' who might be able to help with the welds, if he can get his forge hot enough. He works in high-temp ceramics mostly but he also does all the repairs on metals in the Caves."

Susannah laid her notebook aside and took a square of kamad casserole onto her platter. The apprentice went away beaming. "It's all right, really," she soothed. "I just get impatient sometimes. Actually I'm managing just fine without a computer, though I never thought I'd hear myself say it."

Weng made a small noise that was not quite a grumble, and then looked embarrassed that she had let anything so inadvertent escape her.

Megan laughed. "Maybe you're doing okay, but I think the Commander misses her music. What is it now, Weng, two weeks' worth of numbers playing around in your head that you haven't been able to listen to yet?"

Weng's embarrassment deepened. She pointed a thin finger at the chessboard. "If CRI were on line, Dr. Levy, you would not be so often required to allow me to lay *your* armies to waste."

Megan swiveled back to stare at the board. "Is that what's happening?"

Susannah chuckled mischievously. "Game theory has its practical applications, I see, Commander."

Weng nodded. "An enlightening system of analysis, Dr. James."

Other visitors followed the apprentice cook. Tyril stopped by to show off her baby, a plump five-month-old girl. After the women had cooed over it and let it grasp their fingers, Tyril invited them to visit her family's canopy later, before the priests' dance ended the celebration. As she left, Weng's eyes followed the baby. She gave it a grandmotherly wave and went back to her chess game.

The Master Healer came along next, dressed still in his linen smock.

"Rhe khem, Suzhanna," he murmured with a smile as he ducked under the canopy and folded his long legs beneath him on the rug.

"Khem rhe, Ghirra." She offered a mug of cold tea, then made the introductions. Weng smiled. Megan became positively girlish. Stavros let his attention wander. The Sawl physician's soft voice and stooping, gentle carriage did nothing to detract from his dark good looks, and Stavros did not like the way his long-fingered surgeon's hands fluttered around Susannah as he praised her skill in the infirmary. He brought no wife or companion visiting with him, nor did it help Stavros's pride that Ghirra was mastering English without the aid of the official Ship's Linguist and Communications Officer. Stavros sucked at his lukewarm tea and watched his neighbors.

Under the adjacent canopy, a large and jovial group had been raising their mugs in semimusical unison, emptying endless trays of food. Leather dyers, he thought, looking at their hands. He recognized a woman who worked a stall in the MarketHall, trading exquisitely colored pouches and strapping. Now the more boisterous of this group rose and sauntered away to watch the games. Others drifted off to wander from canopy to canopy on the expected after-dinner rounds of socializing. A single couple remained, and as Stavros watched from the corner of his eye, they snuggled themselves among their pillows and began to make quiet love. Stavros nearly groaned aloud. Circumstances were conspiring to keep him from tranquillity. He decided it would be less painful to listen to Ghirra charming the ladies.

The Master Healer was discussing remedies for arthritis with Megan. As he detailed his preparations of certain herbs, Susannah lounged next to him, smiling, attentive to every word. Even Weng seemed enrapt. Stavros retreated to the consolation of his notes and photographs.

Then if she won't have me, I'll find someone else.

Who, then? He could not imagine himself and McPherson as lovers, but he did know many Sawl women who were interesting and desirable. Taking a Sawl lover seemed both a positive solution to his dilemma and a natural extension of his work. The Sawls would have no objection. Their sexual taboos centered around avoiding inappropriate childbirth and inbreeding. Liphar had already nosed him in the direction of a lovely young weaver, though Stavros suspected him of excess generosity in that case. He guessed that Liphar was interested in the girl himself.

He enjoyed a moment of sudden calm, during which he convinced himself that his apparent infatuation with Susannah was due mainly to a lack of initiative. He just hadn't done enough looking around. He pictured an everyday life in the Caves. It was a saner, more placid vision than the passion and drama heating his dreams of Susannah. He relaxed. He laid aside his paperwork, his decision made, and looked up to find Susannah watching him. His calm vanished.

Damn! Why didn't I see this earlier when I could have stopped it!

Her smile was warm and lazy. "You do realize you're making us all feel guilty, sitting in a corner working while we play."

"Stavros never learned to play," muttered Megan. "Deprived childhood."

Ghirra refilled their mugs from the tall misted pitcher he had brought with him. His brown eyes rested on Stavros for the first time.

"Check," said Weng.

"Again?"

"If you'd pay closer attention, Dr. Levy . . ."

Stavros pretended deep concentration, but Susannah would not let him off the hook. "Surely Kav Daven's tale will keep till tomorrow," she teased, and for a moment he thought her smile acknowledged his confusion.

She knows! He thought that was probably the last thing he wanted but wasn't sure.

But then she yawned and stretched, merely friendly, and turned away as Ghirra asked a question in his gallant halting English.

Stavros lapsed into relief, happy for the time to let the Master Healer's insatiable curiosity for things Terran occupy Susannah's interest. He was not ready. He still retained romantic visions of waiting until the Right Moment, which of course only he would recognize. Part of it was needing to be sure he would not be refused.

"Mate," declared Weng without much satisfaction.

Megan slumped away from the board with a thankful sigh.

Weng gathered the venerable ebony and teak chessmen into a drawstringed pouch of threadbare velvet and tied it to her belt. "Oh-one-hundred. It's late," she commented, squinting up through the open-weave tenting. The fat sun hovered halfway to zenith, midmorning by the Fiixian clock.

"It's late, said the White Queen," Susannah murmured.

"That was the rabbit," Megan corrected.

"Ah."

"The White Rabbit. The guy with the pocket watch."

"I remember."

Stavros smiled. He too preferred Susannah's image of Weng as the looking-glass queen, with that wisp of silver hair straying from the neat bun at the back of her neck, insisting that nonsense made sense, that it could be late though the sun was still rising.

"I think I shall retire," said Weng. Ghirra rose as she did, exhibiting a sensitive eye for Terran manners. "Tomorrow work must begin in earnest," she stated.

"Yeah, no more of this fartin' around," said Megan in a passable imitation of McPherson's comic drawl. She rolled her eyes at Susannah. "Weng, sometimes I wonder what part of the universe you operate in! We've all been busy as bees since the snow melted!"

Weng straightened her spotless uniform as if camouflaging a shrug and turned to Stavros. "Perhaps you might have the comlink reestablished within the next ship's day?"

Stavros blinked. "Uhh . . . I'll try, Commander."

"Excellent. If the lieutenant returns, I assume someone will inform me?"

"Of course, Commander," chorused the civilians like three loyal ensigns.

Ghirra took advantage of her leaving to excuse himself also, murmuring of further social obligations. Megan gazed after him wistfully, as one gazes upon the unattainable, but commented only, "I wonder if that stuff he was describing really works."

"Ghirra and his herbalists could give most pharmaceutical houses a run for their money," smiled Susannah as she took a long cool sip from her mug.

Weng's leaving removed a certain tension. In an easier silence, they watched her weave a slow and stately path among the canopies, pausing only to smile at the children she met along the way. As she passed out of the woven shadow into the sun, she blazed white like a vision of angels. She headed down a wide dirt track, newly graded but already rutted from cartwheels. From the edge of the rock flat, it wound among the still-muddy acres of open field and the repeating tiers of mirrored terraces. A half mile out, a smaller side track would lead her to the Lander, where she had once more taken up residence.

The Lander's solidity and improbable tilt made it look pasted on against the background of plain and sky. Stavros thought that the gleaming cone of scoured metal had never looked more alien.

"That's a long walk in this heat," said Megan.

"She'll make it," Susannah replied with admiration. "Tough old bird."

"How long did McPherson say they'd be out?"

"Supplies for two earthweeks, she said. More than a week left still."

"She won't come in before she has to," Stavros put in.

"Not unless . . ."

"Not a chance."

"I suppose not."

Megan shrugged and stood, shaking out her legs with a series of groans. "Got to get me some of Ghirra's magic potion. Well, I'm off to pay Tyril that return visit. Don't forget to go watch Liphar dance."

"We'll be there," Susannah replied.

Megan wandered off. Susannah lay back on her pillows with a contented sigh. The cries from the games had quietened. An old man snored several canopies away. Stavros watched Susannah covertly, hoping for a sign. She seemed both beautiful and terrifying to him now, lying in the dappling sun.

Is this the Right Moment? he wondered. If it was, he feared he was going to have to let it pass. He was not yet up to it. It seemed the worst kind of injustice that he should suffer this sensuous attack when he felt least prepared to make good on it.

Susannah turned on her pillows and regarded him slyly across the emptied stretch of carpet. For one horrifying moment, he thought she was going to steal his moment from him. In all his fantasies, he was the seducer, not the seduced. But she tilted her head and the look in her eyes was coolly speculative.

"Are you happy here?" she asked.

He was startled out of his silence. "That's a weird question."

"And that is an evasion."

She was always more direct in person than in his memory. "Why do you ask?" he countered.

She sat up and shook her long hair behind her. "Because instinct tells me you're in no rush to get the comlink fixed."

He caught his breath. The sensation inside him was that of a well-oiled bolt sliding into place. "You mean, do I want to stay here?" he asked, trying to sound incredulous.

Susannah's shrug was indulgent. "Well, for a while at least. I didn't mean forever." Then she leaned forward as if reconsidering. "Did I? Is that what you want, Stav?"

He shook his head, but less in denial than in awe of the hidden realms of possibility that were suddenly revealing themselves. His attempt at a careless grin stiffened on his lips. "What ever gave you that idea?"

Susannah let silence and an appraising stare be her reply.

Stavros was again aware of the heat of the sun and the thick knobby texture of the rug. *Is that what I want?* Her stare weighed down on him as heavily as the sun. Defensively he met her eyes and knew that he had suspected correctly the first time. She knew. She knew everything about him. His desire, his secretive guilt were as clear to her as if he had shouted them out loud.

"Susannah . . ." he began hoarsely. It was not at all the moment he had imagined, and now that he thought about it, her directness intimidated him far more than her beauty. His own romanticizing had remained simple, centering around bodies and bed. The realities had been neatly avoided, that painful delicious tension inevitable when two individuals attempt to share the same point in space and time.

How did this get so complicated? All I wanted was a roll in the hay . . . I think.

"Susannah," he began again, and again he failed and fell silent. In the distance, from over the fields, he heard singing.

Susannah rose, smoothing her short robe, tightening its braided sash. "I'm going to walk some of this meal off," she announced in a tone that was not quite an invitation. A rejection, he wondered, or was she giving him back his solitude because he so obviously needed it? "It looks like the priests are starting their dance down on the plain."

She passed deliberately close to him as she left, and trailed her hand across the top of his head so that his glossy hair slipped through her fingers. He jammed his eyes shut in pain and to keep himself from grabbing at the billowing hem of her robe to pull her down beneath him.

I should. That would settle it, one way or the other.

But he did not, and she said nothing more, only moved away beneath the rainbowed canopies, following Weng's path toward the new roadway. Stunned and miserable, Stavros remained hunched in the half-shadow. The singing drew him with its rising joyful cadence but he could not move.

I will not run after the woman like a sorry puppy.

All around him a new bustle arose with the singing. There was a general stretching and moving toward the fields amid building happy chatter that echoed in minor key the euphoria of the Planting exodus. He heard his name called. He gazed blankly at Megan as she lumbered across the scattering of carpets and cushions.

"Aren't you going down?" she called. From the cliff top boomed the first deep notes of the ceremonial horns.

Stavros knew it would be childish to shrug.

"Nobody will tell me what it's all about," she complained as she reached him. "They all just smile and say, wait, see."

Megan would be his escort, he decided. No lovelorn pursuit, but two colleagues arriving to observe the local rituals. He scrambled up, mobilized. He packed his photos and notes away in his field pack and slung it to his shoulder, then thought again and extracted a small notebook and pencil.

Megan lifted her empty hands. "How come I never come equipped?"

"I'll take notes for both of us," he promised, his brisk edge returning as purpose renewed itself.

At the edge of the rock ledges, they fell in with another long procession to the fields. In place of tools this time, many carried full mugs of beer. The woodworker next to Stavros munched a thick slice of kamad-root pie while his friends nudged him and joked about the size of his belly.

They followed the new road as it dipped from the plateau at the base of the cliffs. It wove across the tops of the flooded terraces, then curled past the Lander and continued outward. Weng's small footprints broke the thick mud of the turnoff. Stavros saw her standing in the shadow of the Underbelly, hand shading her brow.

Megan pointed ahead. "It's really too far to tell, but I think they're gathering around that field Susannah and I watched Kav Daven planting."

"The Kav sowed the first seed because it was his song that gave Lagri the strength to drive back Valla Ired." Stavros reflexively slipped into the dogmatic tone he had always used to tease her, but as he spoke, he heard more in his voice than teasing. He heard conviction, and saw Megan glance at him swiftly as if she too heard something different, something new.

"Right," she said, eyes narrowing.

Beyond the turnoff to the Lander, they spotted Susannah working her way back through the crowd. She signaled frantically when she saw them. "Hurry!" she cried over the singing and the boom of the horns. She turned and dove back into the throng. Stavros edged through the joyful mob to the side of the road and broke into a run. Megan struggled along behind him gamely.

At the top of a rise, the procession backed up into a tightly packed and sweating mass. Politely but firmly, Stavros forced a pathway through. No one seemed to mind, for cheerful hands patted him and helped him along, while those at the edges of the throng balanced carefully to avoid stepping down into the planted terraces. Ahead, the road dropped into the bottom of a gully. Down in the crowded hollow, Stavros could see Susannah head and shoulders above the others. He called to her, had to call three times before she heard him. She turned and gestured him forward, whirling back again so quickly that her face, glanced at only briefly, left him with an image of eyes wide with confusion and amazement. Then she dropped from view completely, as if she had knelt or fallen.

The singing distracted him. Its throaty volume and richness caught at him in a way he had experienced only in the great cathedrals of Earth. It was impossible to resist such a voicing of joy, impossible not to accept this celebration of renewal as his own. The pressure in his chest was his own desire to exult, to laugh and sing without restraint.

Hands urged him gently forward. The throng thinned in front of him. He glimpsed Kav Daven shin-deep in the middle of a water-filled terrace. The priest's bony arms were outstretched, his head thrown back in blissful benediction. Stavros eased toward the front rows of celebrants. Kav Ashimmel waited behind Kav Daven, wearing a pale tabard embroidered in red and gold. The long ends trailed in the muddy water. The rest of the PriestGuild ranked behind her, a hundred strong, in rows ascending the tiers. The senior priests and journeymen filled the first rows. Behind them, along the ridge above the highest terrace, the apprentices raised banners of triumphant yellow and red. Liphar stood among them, banner held high, his dark young face transcendent with joy.

"Can you believe it!" Susannah exclaimed as she appeared at Stavros's side.

He nodded, absorbed by the bliss on Kav Daven's face.

She grabbed his sleeve and pulled him through the press of bodies to the front of the crowd. "I mean this. Look!"

Stavros looked. He had not noticed at first, but in addition to water and priests, the terraces were full of bright yellow shoots. The tallest reached to Kav Daven's thigh and already showed strong secondary leaves uncurling from the stalk like the fronds of a fern.

Susannah was struggling to remain coherent. "That seed went in less than four days ago! There wasn't a sign of life out here yesterday! These things shot up in a matter of hours!'' She paced toward the bottom earthwork and back to him, gesturing. ''I swear they've grown measurable centimeters since I've been standing here!''

''Wow,'' he breathed, for lack of a more appropriate reply.

''But that's impossible!'' Megan accused as she pushed in beside him.

Stavros's instinctive glance back to Kav Daven met the old priest's blind eyes directly. It shook him thoroughly. The impression of sight without seeing was stronger than ever. A touch of amusement seemed to curl the priest's bloodless lips.

Ashimmel ignored the Terran outburst of astonishment. She nodded to an acolyte, who scurried up the terraces into the ranks of waiting apprentices. The ranks parted smartly to clear a broad space along the ridge. Two dozen senior apprentices, Liphar among them, passed their banners to a neighbor and fell into a dance formation, filling the open space with three interlocking circles. The younger apprentices began a high-pitched rhythmic wail. The journeymen priests joined in a lower key. The circles broke and reformed, revolved and broke again.

Kav Daven held Stavros's eye. The linguist waited for explanations to come to him, but the priest was once more perturbing his reality in a way that defied simple understanding. The chanting built a wall of sound around them.

Then from the cliff top, the wooden horns blared a new and dissonant note. The singing stilled. Kav Ashimmel looked puzzled and annoyed, but Kav Daven's amusement broadened into an elfin grin. He nodded slowly to Stavros as if sharing a joke, then lifted a parched hand toward the cliff, an invitation to observe.

Stavros turned. At first he could see nothing unusual, just the amber brilliance of the rock and the green sky beyond. Bright spots of motion spaced regularly along the scarp indicated the nine teams of horn bearers, each manning their giant instrument.

The throng rumbled. Then a sharp-eyed young ranger cheered and pointed. Others saw now, and a chorus of cheering broke out. Stavros felt himself once again propelled through the crowd, this time back toward the cliffs. Hands patted his back, faces smiled at him, congratulating.

Behind him Megan murmured, ''Oh my loving god.''

Then he saw it. Motion along the horizon of the cliff between two of the horn emplacements. Spots of dull color against the sky, beginning to descend the easternmost ledge. He made out two figures, no, three, tall Aguidran unmistakable in the lead, the third in white nearly invisible against the pale hot rock. They supported something dark between them.

"It's Ronnie!" Susannah exclaimed. "She's found them!"

Stavros swore without thinking. "And one of them's walking!" He turned back to find Kav Daven still smiling and thought with dread and disappointment, *Doesn't he understand this is the worst thing that could happen?*

Echoing his dread, Megan muttered beside his ear, "Just pray the live one is Danforth."

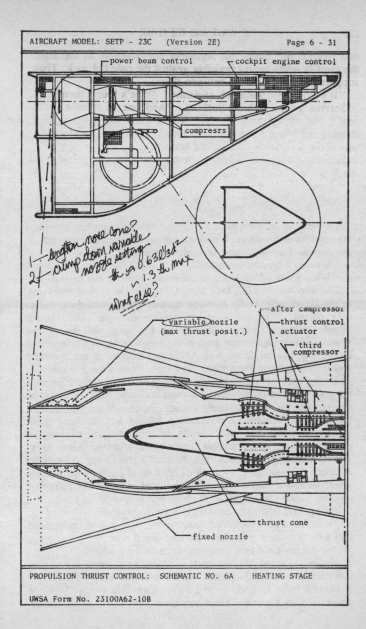

power beam control

cockpit engine control

compresrs

1 — lengthen nose cone?
2 — crimp down variable
        nozzle setting
        # ≈ 8.63 2¾ 3d²
        ≈ 1.3 th max
        what else?

after compressor

thrust control actuator

third compressor

variable nozzle
(max thrust posit.)

thrust cone

fixed nozzle

PROPULSION THRUST CONTROL: SCHEMATIC NO. 6A   HEATING STAGE

UWSA Form No. 23100A62-10B

27

"Are you out of your mind?" Megan latched onto his speeding arm and hauled back on it with all her weight, jerking him out of the crowd. Stavros swung around, surprised.

"We can't let him in there!"

"What good is making a scene going to do?" she hissed.

The noisy throng fell back instinctively at the arched entryway to the Physicians' Hall. Massing against the smooth rock walls, they parted to let the stretcher bearers through. The Master Healer followed, already rolling up the long sleeves of his smock. Susannah hurried after him, grasping her white medical kit. A step behind them, Kav Ashimmel stopped at the archway and turned to face the crowd. She raised her arms for silence. The long tails of her ceremonial tabard and the stained hem of her robe dripped muddy puddles onto the stone floor. The din in the crowded tunnel abated only slightly. Several of the journeymen priests nosed among those standing nearest her, hushing them sternly. Beyond this small circle of intimidation, pockets of cheerful debate raged around wager-holders calling home bets. The remaining apprentices in Ashimmel's train slipped away to circulate through the crowd out of her line of sight as the Master Priest launched into a ringing speech that claimed the return of the lost Terrans as a sign of the renewed power of Lagri.

"Meg, you don't understand," Stavros groaned.

"I understand, better than you realize. But I also understand that a doctor can't refuse to treat an injured man."

"So let her treat him downstairs, or in the Lander!"

Megan regarded him tolerantly. "Now how are you going to make sense of that to Susannah when Physicians' is all equipped?"

Stavros tried to pace in the tight space left to them by the crowd. "That's just it!! He'll see all of that, the . . . ah, damn.

Damn!'' He fell silent, leaning against the rock with his head bowed and his hands balling into fists.

Liphar elbowed through the throng to join them, looking busy and concerned. He stuffed a well-fingered strip of paper into a pouch under his mud-spattered ritual garb and a pencil into the thick of his curls. He glanced at Stavros, then at Megan, then back at Stavros, frowned and made it obvious that he was holding his tongue.

Megan waited out the stalemate for a moment, then sighed and shook her head. ''You've got to learn to keep a lower profile, lad, if you want to slip anything past them.''

Stavros's eyes flicked up at her but he offered no comment. Liphar shifted uneasily, keeping an ear open to the transactions going on among the wagerers nearest them.

''I mean,'' Megan continued in a voice like a foot inched out to test thin ice, ''Say we go in there and simply *contrive* to keep him from noticing anything . . . unusual.''

''Ummm,'' said Stavros neutrally.

''Well, to begin with, what sort of unusual might that be?''

Ashimmel ended her speech with a flourish. Gathering her dignity and what small entourage remained to her, she swept off, plowing a pathway through the noise and congestion. Much of the crowd fell in behind her, the excitement over for the time, but a goodly number remained behind, still negotiating over whether the terms of this particular wager or that had been met. Liphar drifted in their direction, pulling the pencil out of his hair. Stavros glued his eyes to the floor in a panic of conflicting thought. He knew it would be a great relief to share the burden of his secrets, but he found it hard to break his habits of mistrust.

''Did you listen to her?'' he stalled, tossing a contemptuous gesture at Ashimmel's receding back. ''She'll have the whole place opened up to him.''

''As long as it suits her,'' replied Megan dryly. ''If the weather turns bad again, we could be out on our ears, right? It was smart of you to go after Kav Daven, though. That shows at least some political acumen.'' She glanced up as Weng hurried toward them with a bedraggled McPherson in tow. Megan nodded toward the archway. ''That way, Commander.'' She turned back to Stavros. ''So what should I be looking for in there?''

Stavros took his chance on impulse, caught in a sudden rush of hopelessness. ''Little things,'' he murmured with a shrug.

"Like a pressurized hot-water system, like . . ." *Piped-in gas?*
"You'll know when you see it."

Megan nodded thoughtfully. "Okay. So let's go."

"You go," he said quickly. "I've got to deal with Aguidran
about getting the Sled hauled in. Didn't I hear him say he'd been
in contact with CRI?"

Megan nodded again.

"That means we have at least one functioning antenna out
there." Stavros looked away from her stare. "Look, Meg, you're
right. I can't be trusted in there with him. Low profile, you
know?"

He urged her toward the archway. She went, but her brief
backward glance promised that her demands for a fuller explanation were merely postponed.

"Ph'nar khem," Liphar muttered, returning to Stavros's side
when she had gone. The corridor was nearly empty but for a
knot of hopefuls lounging near the entry, their wagers apparently
depending on the skill of the doctors inside. "Kav Ashimmel
wrong say Lagri bring this."

"You said it." Stavros rubbed his brow, searching for a
coherent plan of action. He paced back and forth a bit while
Liphar watched in sympathetic silence. "The only thing I can
think of is to bring it before the Kethed. Do you know when the
next meeting is?"

Liphar shook his head warningly. "Big voice of Kethed,
Ashimmel."

"So we get to the other guild heads separately," Stavros
proposed. Megan's remark about political acumen haunted him.
This sort of maneuvering was her second vocation, not his,
though he had not noticed that she had been keeping *her* political
profile particularly low. But that, he realized, was because she
had nothing at the moment to hide. "Can you talk to them,
Lifa?"

Liphar's mouth tightened in concern. Stavros realized he was
asking the young apprentice to work behind the back of his own
guildmaster, but he could think of no other solution.

"Then just tell them of my concern. Tell them I must talk to
them before it's too late. Then they can call a Kethed and decide
the issue."

Liphar nodded unhappily. Stavros knew he would not refuse
the request. He squeezed the little Sawl's shoulder in guilt and
gratitude and sent him off. With a final nervous glare in the
direction of the Physicians' Hall, he trotted away to find Aguidran.

28

"A touch more light on this one, if you can, Ghirra." Susannah blotted her forehead on her sleeve, wishing for a good o.r. nurse, then found Ghirra's youngest apprentice ready at her elbow with a clean cloth. She let the boy dry her face more thoroughly and bent to inspect the last of the serious wounds. Ghirra adjusted the reflector on the battery lamp that Susannah had clipped to the hub of the oil chandelier. The big spoked wheel swayed on its stout rope and the hard glare of the Terran lamp flashed in and out of the darkened corners of the hall like a berserk searchlight. The anxious faces gathered around the operating slab raised hands to shade their eyes.

Megan slipped in while Susannah stood aside for another apprentice to bring a fresh bowl of the long absorbent fibers Ghirra used as a sponge. Megan smiled at Susannah and remained standing, taking stock of the room. Ghirra's operating chamber was the smallest of the four adjoining caverns that formed the Physicians' Hall. It was tall and narrow. In the shadow of deep shelves cut into the rock, ranks of glass jars glinted in long neat rows. The patient lay on the central of three waist-high marble slabs.

Susannah nodded Megan to a stone bench set along one wall. "We'll be a while here," she said, gathering up a fiber sponge. The Master Healer reached a long arm to steady the swinging lamp, then leaned over the patient to take a closer look. His surgical assistant Ampiar, a slim, serious woman, hovered nearby.

The wound was a near-critical puncture high on the right side. A shard of metal had cut deeply but at an angle that allowed it to just miss the lung. The shard had been removed in the field, but bone fragments from a shattered rib remained. The tear had partly closed itself. Infection had set in. Susannah swabbed away the purulence with Ghirra's herbal disinfectant. She probed for the fragments, then applied an antiseptic from her own supplies. Ghirra shared a guttural comment with Ampiar and wrinkled his nose. Susannah nearly apologized for the flat medicinal smell that cut so crudely across the healthy pungence of his herbal infusion.

When the wound was cleaned, she set a small section of rubber tube in it to drain any excess fluids, and closed as neatly as she could. There would be a nasty scar, but the patient's entire body was hot and sandpaper-dry. There were more pressing considerations than cosmetics. Her mouth tightened in dissatisfaction with the aesthetics of the closure, but she moved on immediately to a shallow gash that needed only minor stitching. She cleaned it out, and as she reached for a suture, Ghirra's hand met hers halfway with the instrument already prepared.

"Thank you, Doctor," she remembered to murmur. As an intern, she had suffered through many months in chill operating rooms before she had learned to detect the gratitude that lay unvoiced behind the operating surgeon's mask.

Danforth stirred weakly under her hand.

"He's waking up!" McPherson squawked. She pushed in against the stone table until the plastic sheet crackled. Ghirra frowned absently and spread the wrinkles smooth. He had not objected when Susannah had laid the sheet out to cover his polished marble. Plastic seemed to intrigue him.

"Soon," Susannah soothed as she completed a stitch. "But not just yet. Don't worry. If the gas runs out, Ghirra has other ways to deal with pain."

"I prefer him out cold, this one," said Weng from Danforth's head. She tipped the valve on the small field canister of nitrous oxide and set the mask to his nose and mouth. "Still a quarter full," she reported. "Stand aside, Lieutenant."

"You won't improve Tay's chances by leaning all over him, McP.," chided a cheerful voice from the next table. Clausen sat jauntily upright, legs swinging over the edge as if at a sporting event. The white therm-suit he had donned three weeks earlier was dusty and stained but still intact, except for the sleeves. Those had been cut away at the elbows and folded back to make neat cuffs. A sandy gray beard furred the prospector's sunburned cheeks. He looked gaunt but healthy. Only the stout stick leaning by his knee suggested that he had not walked home completely on his own power. He sat calmly peeling back the emergency sealant from a small gash on his forearm. Lying on the slab

beside him was a bulging leather knapsack with wide padded
straps. Its heavy brass buckles were tarnished from their weeks
in the open.

The young apprentice Dwingen brought a bowl of hot water
and gestured a shy offer to help Clausen wash out his wound.
The prospector twisted away abruptly, then relaxed and smiled at
the boy wolfishly. "Nothing personal, you understand."

"He doesn't speak English, Emil," said Megan as she slumped
onto the hard cool bench.

"Well, he must learn, my dear Megan, he must learn."

Megan watched him with distaste. Looking about the room,
she had seen nothing to worry Stavros so far. Ghirra's setup was
clean and simple, and perhaps it would take a doctor to appreciate how skilled the Master Healer's long-fingered hands truly
were, how he and Susannah worked together with the smooth
rhythm of doctors long familiar with each other. In Megan's
opinion, the worst of the situation was that Clausen had survived
his ordeal with little more than fading bruises and a healing scab
or two. There was the minor matter of his ankle, swelling again
now that he had stayed off of it for a while, but that was nothing
compared to Danforth, who had been stretchered in unconscious
with both legs set in field splints. Danforth was sliced up,
battered, broken and delirious with fever. Megan's suspicions
were habitually tender and this would have had them more than
usually aroused, were it not for the fact that Danforth and
Clausen had been allies since before the expedition began.

*Damn Clausen, anyway. Just like my brother, who won every
fight he ever lured me into.* And like her brother, Clausen
seemed to possess more lives than a cat, and had that same
unshakable self-esteem that both fascinated and repulsed her.
Why is it such confidence is never put to good uses? she mused
darkly. Clausen turned his smug grin on her, and she glanced
away, studying the glass-stocked shelves to avoid glowering
back at him like the vengeful sibling she had been in her youth.

The operating chamber made up in height what it lacked in
width. It had a clerestory like the FriezeHall. A narrow band of
amber noon sunlight fell from the high windows onto the operating tables. Megan thought this a rather melodramatic gesture on
the part of the builders, suggesting as it did that the tables were
favored by nature. But she had to concede that any and all light
is useful in a cave, and admired their cleverness in focusing the
sun appropriately for at least part of the long Fiixian day. The
second cavern adjoined directly, separated only by a thick linen

curtain fastened by rings to a horizontal pole. Through the center split, she could see a long double row of pallets set on low platforms of glazed white brick. Now they were mostly empty. Anyone well enough to crawl was downstairs celebrating. One old man reclined with his back to the curtain. In a far corner, a young mother nursed her recently delivered infant under the watchful eye of the Head Midwife, Xifa. Megan stretched her legs and turned her attention to deciphering labels etched on jars filled with substances beyond her imagining. Her eyelids drooped. By her wrist chronom, it was four-twenty in the morning, ship's time. So many of the important events in the Caves seemed to take place in the middle of the Terran "night." She wondered how Susannah and especially old Weng remained so steady of hand on so little sleep.

Little Dwingen came toward her balancing a bowl heaped with bloodied linens. Megan drew in her legs to let him pass. He went through a narrow archway at the end of her bench. Megan slid down and peered around the corner. A white-smocked teenager tended a row of steaming ceramic caldrons. Dwingen emptied his load into a deep sink and turned a large brown wheel that protruded from the wall above. Steaming water flowed into the sink. Megan nodded to herself and studied the caldrons. Tiny blue flames danced beneath them.

Oh ho, she thought, suddenly very much awake. *Gas? Is it possible? Is this what Stav couldn't bring himself to tell me about?*

She estimated Clausen's line of sight and judged that he could not see through the archway from his slab. If he were to try walking around, she would have to get imaginative. Megan stretched out her legs again and left them there.

"Okay," murmured Susannah, completing a final stitch. "He's as clean and tight as I can get him for now." As she checked the drip taped to Danforth's arm, Ghirra laid two fingers on the wrist. He followed a few moments of concentration with a faint shake of his head.

"I know," said Susannah. "He's very weak. But the antibiotic ought to bring that fever down—that is, if your bugs are anything like our bugs."

"Buggs." Ghirra savored the consonant as he let his spread hands hover over Danforth's head. "Yes. Explain this, you." He moved his hands down to the chest and laid them lightly over the heart. "But if this not succeeds, we try . . ."

"None of that yucky stuff in the jars!" exploded McPherson.

Susannah shot the little pilot something uncharacteristically like a glare, but Megan noticed that the corners of Ghirra's wide mouth twitched to conceal a smile.

Picks up more than he lets on, this handsome one.

Weng was scandalized. "One more such outburst, Lieutenant, and you will be ordered to duty in the Lander!" She poised the respirator like a weapon.

"Worry not, McP.," said Clausen airily. "You'd be surprised at the useful little medicinals these primitives stumble upon sometimes."

Susannah's hand froze on the lid of her portable autoclave. She let it down very carefully. "Almost as surprising as the emergency care some amateurs can manage in the field."

So. She's got a tongue on her when she decides to get protective, Megan noted. With her eye still on Ghirra, she saw him flick a long-lashed measuring glance at the prospector. Her slump deepened. *Ah, yes. We'd forgotten what it was like to have Emil sniping around all the time.*

Clausen chuckled. "Did the best I could, Doc. The boy would have died without it, you will admit." He blinked at McPherson and grinned.

"You did very well, and we're all grateful," put in Weng sternly.

Susannah turned her back. Ghirra readjusted the battery lamp to light the full length of the slab, then nodded to Dwingen, who waited with a bowl of minted hot water and clean strips of linen. He washed and dried his hands while McPherson penitently helped Susannah peel off her bloody surgical gloves. Again, he let his hands hover over Danforth's body, this time with his eyes closed. His long fingers barely skimmed the white oversheet. As he reached the right leg, just above the knee, he grunted.

Weng looked interested. McPherson's expression implied native mumbo-jumbo but she held her peace. Susannah watched unsurprised as solemn Ampiar fitted her with a clean pair of gloves. "Needs to be reset," she agreed. "The other's fractured below the knee but it seems to be healing. The alignment was undisturbed."

Ghirra's hands skimmed the left leg briefly and he nodded.

"Thanks to my expert splinting," Clausen reminded her.

"Of course," Susannah replied, this time with only the slightest show of sarcasm. She folded back the oversheet to expose Danforth's legs. The right knee and thigh were scabbed and discolored. Carefully, she probed the kneecap.

Clausen pushed himself along his table to the end nearest Megan's bench. "Tay'll be the worst sort of invalid if he ever wakes up," he confided loudly. "Should have heard him out there at the wreck, whining and complaining."

"Yeah, for shame," Meg growled. "Pain is such a lot of fun."

The prospector tilted his bullet head. "Now, now, my own sweet Margaret Meade, do you take me for a sadist? I kept him well stoked up with the Sled's supply of painkillers. It wasn't the pain that bothered him, it was the boredom of having to lie there while I was out scrabbling around in the rain and dark. By the time dawn arrived, the fever'd gotten him." Clausen patted the leather knapsack at his side and announced to the room at large, "I do hope he comes around long enough to find out he was right."

Susannah continued her murmurings with Ghirra over the resetting of the leg. McPherson remained riveted to their every movement. But Megan slid upright, alerted by the gloat in Clausen's voice.

"Oh?" she asked, she hoped casually.

"It's here, like he said it would be."

"It, Mr. Clausen?" inquired Weng without diverting her focus from the anesthesia.

The prospector grinned. "Lithium."

The word fell among them like a lead weight.

There we go, thought Megan. *The Sawls' eviction notice.*

"What we came here for, remember?"

"What *you* came here for," Megan amended.

Clausen's grin slipped toward impatience. He had expected a livelier reaction.

"Look." He hauled the mud-caked pack up onto his lap and unbuckled a side flap. Several chunks of glittering rock tumbled out. He caught one and held it overhead like a victory cup. "Lepidolite. An excellent lithium ore. Pretty little sucker, eh?"

The rock was pale translucent lilac, like a summer dusk. It was studded with crystalline outcroppings of quartz mixing with flat plates of silvery mica. As Clausen twisted it in the light of the battery lamp, deeper hues of rose and lavender appeared in veins along one side.

Megan thought of the sparkle-eyed goddesses in the FreizeHall.

And so, another world falls to the miner's shovel. No wonder the bastard's so cheerful!

The familiar inevitability of the moment was like a stone

dropped on her chest. Always she indulged in private optimism, hoping that the prospectors would find nothing to interest them, and always they did. Clausen would call it progress, so sure of his right by might that the dissolution of entire cultures by his hand was taken as a necessary part of the forward movement. Perhaps it was also proof to him of his superiority, that he survived and they didn't.

It doesn't really matter now what he sees here and what he doesn't, she thought heavily. *The outcome is preordained.* She was going to have to tell Stavros. Better he should hear it from a sympathetic party than be forced to suffer this inhuman gloating. There would be enough of that in the days to come.

Clausen juggled the sparkling rock from palm to palm. "I think it's a big strike, too. I've got to get back out there, of course, with instruments, to measure the size of the lode before I make an official filing, but I located at least one decent vein showing in the side of a ravine below our crash site. Pretty good for working in the dark!"

Weng nodded, still intent on the operating table. "This is good news, Mr. Clausen."

Clausen regarded her ramrod back with amusement, then threw up his close-cropped head and laughed aloud. "Why, you bet your ass it is, Commander!"

"Shhh!" hissed McPherson, and then she groaned aloud as Susannah grasped Danforth's thigh top and bottom around the break and wrenched it into alignment. Megan felt the crunch to the very roots of her teeth. It was too much. She rose swaying from the bench.

"Excuse me," she mumbled and fled from the hall.

Ghirra stepped back from the table with a look of relief on his tired face that slowly drained away to dismay as he saw the glittering rock held high in the prospector's hand.

29

Aguidran made her office at the head of the long wooden table that occupied one end of the RangerHall. It was the one relatively clear space in the Hall, the rest resembling the cargo hold of an old sailing ship on the homeward leg of a long voyage. Tall racks stuffed with gear hugged the walls. A jungle of ropes and strapping hung from the lowish ceiling. Piles of sacking and big wooden cabinets fought each other for floor space.

The Master Ranger sat in a wide leather-bottomed chair while Stavros hovered at her back. On a rough-edged sheet of the grainy paper the Sawls used for everyday, she scrawled a hurried sketch of the wreck site: a brief plateau surrounded by steep ravines and rock slides in the southern mountains, the Grigar.

Grigar. Stavros dissected the word instinctively. *Lagri-egar. Lagri's Wall.*

Aguidran paused, studied her work, then drew a circle to indicate the downed Sled. She angled the paper and used a blank corner to begin a detail of the Sled itself. Clausen could have supplied a more technical assessment of the Sled's position and condition, but Stavros could not imagine getting close enough to him to ask. A quick glimpse had been bad enough, as the prospector glided into the Caves grinning like a ghost come back to haunt.

Smug bastard. Smug as a sunning crocodile, Stavros thought.

He beat his fist gently on the stout back of Aguidran's chair. She looked up, frowning, her concentration disturbed. He backed away abashed, and paced a little.

Perhaps it was time to give Megan's notion of low profile some serious consideration. For instance, his absence from Physicians' was sure to be noticed, by Weng at least, though perhaps not by Clausen.

*No. He'll notice. He'll want to know where his damn gear is
stowed. Fuck 'im. I'll tell him I had to sleep sometime.*

Aguidran growled privately and rubbed out a line to redraw it
in a sharper curve. Her visual memory was keen and her hand
practiced at conveying scale and spatial relationships. But her
diagram of the Sled suffered from a lack of comprehension of the
machinery. Stavros squinted at the drawing sideways, trying to
coax the rough charcoal lines into three dimensions readable to
his brain. The stubby triangular body of the vehicle was apparent
enough. Despite its bent or perhaps missing stabilizers and its
crumpled tail fin, it seemed miraculously intact.

*Sonofabitch managed a cleaner landing than should have been
possible in weather like that!*

A relay runner appeared at the table with several minutes'
worth of verbal messages and a rare written letter to deliver.
Aguidran pushed her drawing aside with a grunt of relief to listen
to the runner's recitation and dictate replies to him at a memoriz-
able pace. The letter she set aside. Stavros suspected something
of a confidential nature, the only reason he could think of to
eschew the convenience of the runners' prodigious trained
memories.

When he could reclaim her attention once again, Stavros
convinced the Ranger to attempt a rendering of the rear section
of the Sled, where the all-important communications equipment
was housed in its transparent blister. Pulling over another sheet
of rag paper, Aguidran tried gamely if impatiently. But without
knowing the function of the intricate shapings of rod and mesh
and wire, it was impossible for her to clearly delineate their
form. The sketch rapidly degenerated into a smudged-out study
in abstract. Aguidran crumpled the rough, spongy paper into a
ball and lobbed it into the darkness behind her. It landed with a
dull plop among the dead ashes in the fireplace. She gave
Stavros a look that implied several cycles' worth of more pressing matters that required her attention. Stavros relented, nodding
his gratitude. He eased the site drawing out of the scattered
stacks of lists and notes and allowed the Ranger to attack the
mountain of paperwork that had piled up while she was away on
the search. It occurred to him that she probably hadn't slept
either since she returned.

He looked around for a perch that was out of the way but still
within the circle of light from the overhead lamp wheel. Short
backless benches with flat leather pads lined the long sides of the
table. Stavros pulled out a bench and sat, laying the drawing in

front of him to make sense of and memorize. The two benches next to him were occupied by three youngish guildsmen, no longer apprentices but still required to put in their time at copying and bookkeeping. Two more sat opposite, and all five shared a huge inkwell that squatted in the center of the table like a glass sea urchin. One muttered to himself as he counted. The girl next to Stavros chewed the end of her quill and occasionally glanced around at the others as if measuring the extent of their progress against her own. In the shadow of the inkwell sat five equal stacks of flat stone counters.

Unh-huh, thought Stavros, and wondered idly what the bet was. First to finish? First to finish a page? First to run into a snag and be forced to disturb the Master Ranger? Stavros yawned. He was having difficulty concentrating. The trestled table drew his eye down its enormous length, out of the pool of lamplight, through the darkened jungle of equipment toward the cool glow of daylight that leaked up from the cave mouth to peek in at the entrance arch. The table was a double arm's reach wide. Its thick planks had been planed and sanded and oiled until the seams were visible only in an abrupt change of the grain. Stavros smoothed its golden surface with a reverent finger and recalled his love affair with the winch.

Perhaps I was a tree in a former life. . . .

He imagined a guild meeting, with the hall alive with torch- and firelight, with every one of the guild's ninety-odd full members comfortably seated and the storage racks and ceiling hooks groaning with the load of apprentices eager to observe the goings-on and dream about the day when they could claim a place at the table.

A draft slipped down the long low cavern to lift the corners of his paper. It brought warm air and earth smells from the cave mouth, and the faint echoes of the continuing celebration at the foot of the cliffs.

Concentrate, Ibiá. Is the Sled salvageable?

A senior ranger came through the archway with a FoodGuild clerk. They stepped around fat bundles of rope fiber, deserted beside coils of half-twisted rope when the call to Planting had come, and stopped at the table. The FoodGuilder dropped a sheaf of mud-stained papers by Aguidran's hand and left. The ranger stood mopping his brow while she dipped her pen to scratch a series of numerical entries into a cloth-bound ledger. Stavros left his bench to fish the sketch of the antennas out of the ashes. The arch of the fireplace was as tall as he was. From the center of a big frieze over the mantel, the Sisters beckoned him with their jeweled eyes.

I know what you want, he answered them, *but you can't have it, not yet. Belief does not come that cheaply.*

He turned his back on them and flattened the wrinkled paper against his thigh, then spread it out on the table in the light.

Okay. So Clausen said he'd contacted CRI when the storm cleared, so there's one functioning antenna at least, the omni probably, not the high gain, or he would have tried picking up the power beam to fly the damn Sled out of there and we would have heard about that.

He gazed at the larger drawing once more. Lacking Aguidran's knowledge of the surrounding countryside, he needed a larger frame of reference to fit the site map into. He would need more complete directions to the wreck. He gathered his courage and went back to Aguidran to explain his problem. She returned him a steely glare, but pointed with her pen to a boxy wooden cabinet halfway down the hall, hemmed in almost to disappearance by overflowing storage racks. She snapped a number at him, then turned away to listen as the patiently waiting ranger gave his report.

Stavros went to the cabinet and pulled open its man-high double doors. The interior was divided into several hundred numbered pigeonholes. More than half of them contained what appeared to be slim rolls of fabric. Stavros located the number Aguidran had given him, toward the middle right of the cabinet. He slid the roll from its cubicle and carried it to the table. Unknotting the faded ribbon ties at either end, he unrolled the fabric gingerly. Spread before him was a yellowing map, carefully inked on vellum and attached to a cloth backing, with flaps that folded around to protect the delicate edges. The backing had been neatly mended in several places. The map was so worn that the vellum had entirely lost its curl. It lay perfectly flat.

He left it on the table and returned to the cabinet to ease several other rolls partway from their slots. From their varying colors and states of repair, he judged them to be of vastly differing ages, some dark and threadbare with use, others as fresh as if they had been inked the day before. He pulled one of the older ones at random from the top row of pigeonholes and brought it back to the table.

It lay very limp in his hands. He opened it carefully and spread it flat. Two large circles greeted him, side by side, filled with various markings that could indicate features of terrain.

A world map? he thought, with some astonishment. *And hemispherical at that.* By his memory of it, it was not until the advent of spaceflight that the inhabitants of Earth had been unalterably convinced that the apparently flat ground they walked on was actually a section of arc. He studied the double hemispheres again. Every area was complete in its detail. Particular attention had been paid to a slanted quasi-equatorial band, and two isolated points, one low in the southern latitudes, circled by the squiggle marks of mountains, the other in the middle of a vast body of water in the northeastern quadrant. Stavros thought it peculiar that he had heard no tale-chants or histories of the intrepid Sawl explorers who had brought back such a wealth of detailed knowledge about their planet. Even more intriguing was the focus on those two widely separated points. Lagri was said to make her home in a mountainous desert far to the south. Valla Ired, it was taught, lived in the great northern ocean.

Would they actually put that down on a map? This way to the godhome? It would have struck him as comical if there weren't something bland and understated about the map that treated those two markings as just another bit of fact.

He made a mental note to study this map further and question Aguidran when she could find the time. He rolled it carefully and replaced it in the cabinet, then went back to the table and the map the Master Ranger had directed him to.

He found it cryptic in the extreme, he being more at home with circuitry diagrams than with cartographics. The double hemispheres had been far easier to orient himself in, but that, he reflected, was because their layout was familiar to him from Terran world maps. This other he found deliciously exotic. As the days progressed and he slipped closer to accepting Sawlian reality as his own, an object like this, with its obscure symbolisms and hen-scratch notations could still bring him up short and remind him he was living inside an alien culture. He studied the yellowing chart for a while, then gave up. He gathered it up and brought it to the head of the table.

Aguidran took it from him brusquely but handled it with great care as she cleared a space for it among her layered papers. She called an instruction to an apprentice who was clambering noisily around the storage racks among the ropes and tarps and stacks of blankets. He set down the keg he was struggling with, climbed down and brought her a sheet of crinkly paper from a file of wide drawers beside the map cabinet. Aguidran smoothed the translucent paper over the map and traced out the route she had taken, starting with the several circles that marked the Caves. Her wide mouth quirked in an afterthought and she added a smaller circle for the Lander. Her dotted line wove through canyons and ravines and up into the mountains. *A circuitous route*, thought Stavros, wishing the second Sled had not been washed away. *But then, we'd have working antenna and . . .* And then what? He wasn't quite sure. He wasn't ready to think that far.

Aguidran went back over her line of travel, inking in landmarks such as the Red Pawn and the Talche, called the Knees, a low range of knobby mountains directly east of the Caves. She drew a broad serrated oval to represent the Dop Arek, then labeled the mountain ranges like the Talche and the Grigar in her spiked script. Next to the Cave circles, she wrote "DulElesi" with a final flourish. Her calligraphy had all the big-bellied curves that she did not, but Stavros was sure that such hinting at concealed softness was illusory. Each letter finished with a sharp serif or downturn that more than reinforced her external image. But her writing was clear and strong, far easier to decipher than the ancient crabbed markings on the original map. Aguidran regarded her work with amused pride, then flicked an impatient hand at Stavros, and sat back and stretched.

Stavros took the map and the tracing and wandered back to his bench. The route now defined made the salvage trip a reality. Based on McPherson's preliminary report, he figured they'd need two and a half days to get there, maybe a day for the salvaging, then the return. Six days, if they didn't try to bring back the Sled. He hoped Aguidran or maybe the Engineers' Guild would lend him some men to manage that miracle. He laid the tracing on the table and leaned over it, squinting thoughtfully. Though the Ranger's route dipped to the south, it snaked back to the east again. The crash site was actually due southeast. Stavros guessed he might be able to save some time if he cut east across the southern arm of the Dop Arek instead of struggling through the rougher terrain directly to the south.

Of course, Clausen is going to want to come along. That thought filled Stavros with dread, but he could see no way around it. *Sure beats leaving him behind to run rampant in the Caves. . . . He'll probably want the Sled made a priority, too, so he can haul it in and get it fixed,* he guessed. *Tough shit. Communications are my duty, first and foremost.*

As he maundered on about Clausen, his nose sinking lower and lower toward the map, the slap of running feet broke the hall's industrious silence. A young courier from one of the relay teams charged through the main archway, took a flying leap over the bundles of rope fiber and sprinted the length of the hall to skid to a halt at her superior's elbow. She spilled her report breathlessly, and Stavros had the satisfaction of seeing genuine surprise touch Aguidran's weathered face. She made the runner repeat her story more slowly, then pushed back her chair abruptly and strode muttering from the hall, trailing the excited courier behind her.

Stavros hastily folded his copy of the map and shoved it into his waistband. He took two long steps after them, then caught himself and ran back to roll up the old map and stow it away in its numbered slot. The journeymen at the table noted their guildmaster's hurried exit with mild interest and returned to their work.

In the outer corridor, Stavros had to twist aside sharply to avoid slamming into Megan.

"What are you *doing* here?" he demanded, his legs dancing to be off after Aguidran. "You're supposed to be . . ."

"I couldn't take it up there," Meg interrupted. "What's going on?"

"You shouldn't have left him alone!"

"He's got a bum ankle. He's not moving around much. Why's everybody running around all of a sudden?"

"I'm on my way to find out," he called as he sped off toward the entry stairs.

A small but noisy crowd had gathered at the cave mouth. Stavros counted half a dozen priests, Ashimmel among them, several of Aguidran's couriers and the Master Ranger herself, towering over the others, listening with stern eyes while they all tried to speak at once, like a gaggle of kindergartners. Only Ashimmel remained quiet, standing a bit aside, puffy-eyed as if she had just been awakened. She had not even taken the time to don her embroidered regalia. Stavros thought she looked older, less substantial in her civilian tunic and pants. It was no mystery to him why priests throughout the galaxy assumed some kind of fancy dress.

He took up an unobtrusive post along the wall near the opening. He had nearly managed to isolate from the pandemonium the one phrase that seemed to be on everyone's lips when Aguidran hushed them with a bellow and elbowed her way out onto the ledge. Ashimmel did likewise, standing with the Master Ranger but pointedly not beside her. The other priests drew up in formation behind their guildmaster, and the crowd fell silent, waiting.

Puzzled, Stavros stared out across the plains. The ravaged Dop Arek stared balefully back. Below, the tent city still sported its brightly colored streamers, cheerful arms waving in the breeze while an army of FoodGuild apprentices bustled about cleaning up. The planted terraces were now solid beds of waist-high yellow stalks beginning to uncurl their segmented leaves. The larger open fields were showing rows of amber spikes. The little vegetable plots bristled with new growth. Even the far gullies and rises of the plain were softening under a pale lemon fuzz. The air was warm and fragrant, the sky a clear watery green shading toward azure overhead. The salmon sun was approaching zenith.

What the hell are they staring at?

He studied the intent faces and understood from their unfocused gaze that they were not looking at all, but listening. Then Aguidran's head jerked up and swiveled to the northeast, toward the mountains that bounded the plain, which the Sawls called the Vallegar, or Valla's Wall. Stavros listened and heard it also, a low slow grumble of distant thunder.

Megan nosed in beside him, swallowing a yawn. "So what is it?"

He nodded northeastward. "Thunder."

"Bad?"

"I doubt they'd make this much of a fuss if it meant a little summer shower."

Megan chewed her lip and joked half-seriously, "So which Sister do we have to root for this time?"

"Rain coming would be Valla's fault," he replied blandly.

The crowd stirred into motion as Aguidran issued brisk instructions to her couriers. One jogged back into the Caves. The others sped out along the stairs and ledges to alert the weather watch. Aguidran folded her leather-clad arms and turned to face Ashimmel.

Megan eased herself down the wall and sat. "The crops'll never survive the kind of rain they come up with around here."

Stavros crouched beside her. "And if that crop isn't harvested, we may all starve."

"Well . . ."

He shook his head emphatically. "Liphar told me the last of the seed stores went into the ground this time. The previous harvest, before we arrived, wasn't good."

"Bad weather."

"Correct."

"Rash, though, to use up all the seed," Megan commented.

"It was either that or risk a harvest too small to feed every-one," he defended, as if it were his own harvest.

"They need more land under cultivation," said Megan.

Stavros nodded impatiently. "Fine, Meg, but think of it this way: they'd have to not eat part of a harvest that barely feeds the population as it is, in order to have more seed left over to expand the planting."

Megan rubbed her forehead. Her eyes were pink with exhaustion. "Susannah understands all this growing stuff better than we do. Maybe she could help them out." She dragged both hands down across her eyes. "Speaking of which, there's plumbed gas in Physicians'. Did you know that?"

Stavros's mouth tightened. "Suspected it. I'd seen it . . . elsewhere."

"But you didn't see fit to tell us."

He nudged her silent. Aguidran's conference with Ashimmel had flared into heated debate. Ashimmel was completely awake now, arms waving and gray curls flying as she stalked about the cave mouth inside of a circle formed by her priests, with Aguidran at its center. The long sleeves of her tunic flapped like pinion feathers as she jabbed her hand alternately at the sky, then down at the planted fields. The Master Ranger stood her ground calmly, talking through the priest's harangue in a voice of iron, ticking her arguments off on her long brown fingers like so many items on a shopping list.

Stavros eavesdropped intently. "Something about going or not going," he translated. "Ashimmel insists on staying in case the storms return."

"Sounds logical," Megan ventured.

"Yes, but you know, it isn't like Aguidran to be unreasonable. I can't quite understand where she means them to go, but it seems to involve a lot of people."

"A lot?"

Stavros frowned. "Like . . . everyone?"

"Everyone?"

He nodded, as mystified as she, and continued to listen. "Sounds like something they'd normally do but now Ashimmel doesn't think it's the right time."

"Everyone," repeated Megan. "Well, what they do, they do tend to do en masse."

"Shhh. Wait. I think they've agreed. Oh." He shrugged. "They've agreed to wait awhile and see if anything comes of the thunder."

The argument ended abruptly. Ashimmel looked dissatisfied as Aguidran moved away to squint fiercely at the Vallegar and listen. Then, with a final frown, the Master Ranger turned on her heel and mounted the stone stairs into the Caves. Ashimmel followed more slowly, after murmured discussion with the other priests. Several of them settled themselves cross-legged at the edge, their eyes fixed on the northeastern horizon.

Stavros leaned back against the rock and felt a corner of the folded map bite into his hip. He sighed. *The Sled. The damned Sled.*

"And *now* can I have two seconds of your undivided attention?" demanded Megan.

He looked at her blankly. Between one moment and the next, he had forgotten she was there.

"Here's the bad news: Emil's found his lithium."

Stavros didn't move. "What's the good news?"

"There isn't any."

He blinked, then shut his eyes and was glad to be near to sitting down. "Already? But how?"

"Leave it to Emil Clausen to go prospecting in the middle of a hurricane." Megan bowed her head. "He came back with big chunks of it in his knapsack."

"Lithium."

"Some ore he seemed happy with."

"Shit."

"I couldn't agree with you more."

"Shit, shit, shit!" He pressed his hands to his temples. *Work, brain! This is it! What do we do now?*

"Wish to hell there was something we could do," Megan muttered.

He looked up at her, because she sounded in earnest.

She shrugged. "Well, it has been done, you know, once or twice."

"*What?*" he demanded, impatient with her cautious approach.

"Getting a world declared closed to development. Urhazzhle, for instance, or the Double Moons. But in those cases, life signs had been detected long before the landing parties arrived on the scene. A friend of mine"—Megan smiled ruefully—"from the Bad Old Days spearheaded the case for Urhazzhle. The lawyers got a head start on the commercial interests, for once. But both of those were advanced civilizations, thriving planet-wide, not like this.'' Her shoulders drooped as she leaned back against the wall. ''Remember Feingold's Star, the fourth planet? Nah, you're too young. Well, CONPLEX found something they wanted there, too, and had an indigenous population of half a million moved to the next planet closer to the sun, where they promptly became wards of the corporation because the planet was too hot and dry for them to practice their traditional agriculture. In some CONPLEX report I read somewhere later, the rapid decline of that population plus their alcoholism and high crime rate is laid to the natives' 'failure to adapt' appropriately. Plus ça change, plus c'est la même chose.''

But Stavros felt an absurd resurgence of hope. ''You mean, if the Sawls could be shown to be sufficiently advanced . . . ?'' Picturing the BathHall in all its glory, he stared at her so piercingly that she smiled, resigned and sad.

''I don't think gas and running water are enough to build a case, Stav. Fusion or spaceflight is more what the courts have in mind, being stuck into using themselves as the standard to judge by.'' She paused thoughtfully. ''There was one world where the enormous size of the population won the case. I mean, there *are* regulations, laws on the books that are repeatedly ignored. But who knows what they are or how to find out about them at this distance or even what evidence would be required to prompt legal action? We'd need a court injunction against CONPLEX and a team of first-rate counsel.'' Megan made a mocking grimace. ''And you'll never guess who alone among us is the oh-so-proud possessor of a law degree.''

Stavros didn't need to ask. ''Sonofabitch,'' he stated.

They sat for a moment in silence, watching the equally silent huddle of priests, while Stavros waited for his brain to stop pinwheeling about the insides of his head. As his thoughts calmed, he said, ''But wait, Meg. CRI might have that information in her library files.''

''If we could get to CRI.''

Suddenly, the working antenna in the Sled assumed a new importance. ''Yeah, and we'd have to do our search in secret, too. Can't tip Clausen off until we're sure of our case.''

''You'd also have to file a protest before he gets his claim staked, if I remember correctly.''

''Jesus.''

Megan shrugged. ''I know. I wasn't trying to offer you any hope, just discussing the extent of the tragedy.''

Stavros felt the map again, prodding sharply at his hip like a goad. "So he hasn't staked it yet? Not while he was in contact with CRI?"

"Said he had to determine the extent of it first."

"What if I could keep him from doing it for a while?"

Megan chuckled bitterly. "Convince Emil to postpone 'Progress'?"

"Keep him from being *able* to do it, I mean." He leaned forward, suddenly eager. "Meg, if the comlink stays ostensibly broken, he can't report his claim. Meanwhile, we do our research. Is your lawyer friend still around? If we can pull together the rudiments of a case, we can put it to him. Send a drone back to Earth with a message."

"We'd never get the legal wheels moving in time," resisted Megan. Then she peered at him sideways. "How could you keep it broken?"

Stavros laughed softly, excited. He was past praying that he was right, that Megan was the one he could trust. She was, after all, the prospector's natural antagonist. "Meg, I know it's five a.m. by your schedule and you're dead on your feet, but I'm making us some coffee, real Nescaf, and then I want you to talk this over with me real carefully. We've had our disputes, but basically we agree on the basic issues, the, ah, *moral* issues. If, and I say if, there turns out to be something legal we can do to save this world for the people who live in it, just how illegal are you prepared to be in order to get those legal wheels in motion?"

Megan sighed, closed her eyes, and he feared she was trying to decide how to refuse him most gently. But finally, a dreamy smile flitted across her face, expressing not just her exhaustion but some flicker of memory that caused her to look up at him with a younger woman's eyes.

"Stav," she murmured, "just because it's law doesn't make it right."

BOOK FOUR

BOOK FOUR

"First let me talk with this philosopher.
What is the cause of thunder?"

KING LEAR,
Act III, sc. iv

30

While Susannah went with Ampiar to prepare a bed in the ward, the Master Healer lingered over Danforth, resting his hands lightly on the fevered head and seeming to concentrate while watching Clausen out of the corner of his eye. Danforth lay unconscious, breathing shallowly. Weng packed up the anesthetic kit. McPherson hovered at Ghirra's elbow, taking in the expression of deep peace on the patient's ebony face.

"He looks dead," she mourned.

Ghirra rumbled gently, a wordless negative.

McPherson stared up at him soberly. "Well, he could still die, couldn't he?"

"Yes," Ghirra replied simply. "Always we can die, M'Furzon."

Clausen chortled. "A real philosopher." He yanked the last of the plastic sealant from his arm with a tight grunt of pain. The wound reopened and began to bleed. Clausen clamped his hand over it and looked annoyed.

Ghirra noticed Clausen as if for the first time. He left Danforth and brought over fresh linen and a bowl of hot water. He eased aside the bulging knapsack as if it too might need his care, and set the water down at Clausen's side. Then he stood back and waited, as blood seeped through Clausen's fingers and dripped onto his white-clad thigh.

Clausen grinned at Weng across Danforth's still form. "There's always a bright one in every bunch, eh, Commander?" He offered Ghirra his bleeding arm. "You win, friend. I'm all yours."

Susannah and Ampiar returned with a light cloth stretcher as Ghirra finished cleaning and wrapping Clausen's arm.

"This guy's not bad," the prospector noted to Susannah as she passed. "You ought to take him on as a trainee."

"Interesting," Susannah returned curtly. "That's just what I've been hoping he'd do with me."

Four pairs of arms were required to shift Danforth's limp weight onto the stretcher. Ampiar pushed aside the linen curtain as Ghirra and Susannah carried him into the ward, McPherson in close attendance.

"She'd rather have him charged up and ordering us all around again," Clausen commented not unkindly. He slid from his slab, supporting himself on his stick, and hobbled after them. Weng followed more slowly, observing the details of the hall.

Clausen stopped briefly to peer through the open archway at the end of the big stone bench. He saw several apprentices stripped to the waist, stirring vast clay caldrons with long wooden poles, bathed in clouds of steam. He shook his head and limped onward. In the ward, the newborn chastised its mother with a screeching wail that was quickly hushed as she returned it to her breast.

As Weng moved through the linen curtain in Clausen's wake, her attention was drawn to a second archway just to the other side. The opening was low and narrow, nearly hidden in the curtain's stiff folds. She lingered as the others went ahead into the ward.

A faint light burned inside, a small oil lamp on a wooden table in the center of the room. Weng went in and stood looking into the shadows at tier after tier of polished wooden shelves sagging under the weight of enough books to fill a small Terran library.

Along one wall, the shelving gave room to a long waist-high counter. A confusion of glass glimmered in the darkness, cylinders and tubing and long-necked spheres, and tall jars with etched labels. Thick books lay open among the glimmer. Weng crossed the room noiselessly to squint at the dimly lit pages. Columns of faded Sawl numerals marched across yellowed vellum, numbers and letters in vertical array, like mathematical formulae turned on their sides. Weng reached with careful fingers to turn a page. More numbers, some embedded within geometric figures: circles, triangles, six- and eight-sided polygons. Gently, she lifted the front half of the book, keeping one finger at the original mark, to open it at the beginning. She leafed through it intently. There was a long passage of text, then more numbers. Fastened to the third page, carefully bordered by thin silken bindings, was a brown and spotted fragment from a far older volume. It contained a chart and notations, so precisely and regularly formed that it might have been a scrap of a printed page. The figures in the chart were again laid out in vertical columns, but in noticeable eight-part groupings. Weng frowned at it, turned her head to study it sideways, and frowned again.

"Why can't he be downstairs with the rest of us?" McPherson's querulous complaint drifted in from the ward along with renewed infant wails. Regretfully, Weng opened the book to its original place, took a last look around and glided out of the room.

Danforth lay on a clean pallet in the middle of the ward.

"He can," Susannah was saying, "when you can supply better round-the-clock nursing care than Ghirra can up here, and still manage the rest of your duties."

McPherson glanced uneasily down the row of beds at the new mother and her attendant midwife, and grimaced her acceptance.

"The Sled, McP., the Sled." Clausen hobbled around among the shining tiled pallets. "And my lithium. We've got to get right back out there. The distraction will do you good." He raised his face to the slice of sunlight streaming through the wide glass panes of the clerestory. Reflections illuminated the arched ceiling, groin-vaulted in a nearly gothic manner. The prospector rubbed his new-grown beard. "Nice room, this," he murmured to Weng as she rejoined them. "I'd like to see what else they've been hiding up here."

"Our first efforts must concentrate on equipment recovery," Weng stated, ostensibly for McPherson's benefit. "As soon as we've all had some sleep. We must trust Dr. Danforth's recovery to Dr. James and to our friends here." She smiled graciously around, catching Ghirra's eye. He dipped his head imperceptibly in return.

Clausen limped back to McPherson and curled an arm around her shoulders. "She's not in as bad shape as you think, McP. I had her nearly to the ground before we lost power. A little tinkering, you'll have her zipping around in no time."

McPherson resisted being coddled. "You're out of your mind," she countered and shrugged away his arm. "I was out there. I saw the damn thing and she's totaled. Besides, we can't even get power or comlink working *here*, never mind get a Sled in the air!"

"This is not the best place for an argument," reminded Susannah with a glance at the unconscious Danforth.

"Aw, he can't hear anything!" McPherson retorted, but her voice was subdued and she turned to leave the room. Clausen

caught up with her, laid a hand on her shoulder to slow her down
to his hampered pace.

"The Sled's omni is working fine," he consoled her, as they
passed through the curtain. "The high gain's down but it's
probably just a little shaken up. I didn't dare go into the housing
in all that rain."

"Emil!" Susannah called, and got no answer. "You really
ought to let me look at that ankle," she insisted and strode off
after him.

Ghirra smoothed the linen bed coverings, murmuring briefly
with Ampiar, then turned back toward the operating hall. Weng
walked alongside.

"I wonder, GuildMaster," she began.

Ghirra slowed, inclined his head politely.

"I wonder if I might spend some time in your library?"

When he looked puzzled, she indicated the narrow archway
with a wave.

Ghirra smiled. "Lyberry?"

Weng nodded. "*Books* are kept in a library."

"Ah," said Ghirra.

An old man in a multipocketed apron thrust himself through the
curtain, nearly colliding with Weng. He stared at her accusingly,
then bustled off muttering. Two apprentices followed breathlessly. They apologized to Ghirra with big eyes, then hurried
after the muttering ancient. Susannah came through the curtain
shaking her head.

"All I did was ask him for some cussip to soak Emil's foot,"
she explained to Ghirra in mild exasperation. She turned to
Weng. "That's Ard, the Head Herbalist. I don't know how
Ghirra puts up with him!"

"Cussip. I will get," Ghirra offered.

"He said something about the weather and growled at me,"
Susannah elaborated.

Ghirra threw a questioning glance at Ard's back, but he
nodded to Weng in answer to her request. "Welcome you my
. . . lyberry, Commandur."

"Thank you, GuildMaster. When I have a moment, I will take
you up on that. Perhaps you would care to visit mine sometime,
in the Lander? It is not so big as yours but you might find one or
two things of interest. I don't believe you have been down to our
Lander yet, GuildMaster."

"I will come," Ghirra assured her graciously.

"Excellent. Then I will be off. Dr. James, I hope you intend to get some rest as well?"

"I will, Commander. Soon as I finish here."

Ghirra accompanied Weng through the curtain while Susannah joined Ampiar at the patient's bedside. She put a hand to his hot papery skin.

"Still burning up," she said. Ampiar murmured her worried assent. Susannah smiled and patted the solemn healer's hand. "Do what you can. I'll check in later."

She returned to the operating hall to clean up her instruments and found Ghirra standing beside Clausen's pack, with a chunk of the frosty lavender rock balanced with caution on his palm, as if it were a holy relic or a snake that might bite him.

"What is it, Ghirra?" She had seen him approach a shattered limb with greater equanimity. He looked up, searching her face as if desperate for an answer but reluctant to reproach her for a trespass he was not sure she shared. Clausen and McPherson stood in the little antechamber leading into the hall, noisily debating the condition of the Sled and plotting their next move. "What?" she asked again, keeping her voice low.

He tilted his palm slightly. The rock flashed star-specks of lamplight. "What does he with this?" he asked gravely.

Susannah opened her mouth to answer, but caught herself as she realized how loaded that answer would be. The Master Healer might as well have asked to see what was inside Pandora's Box. She felt a slight stab of resentment. It should not fall to her to have to explain the prospector's intentions, to thus seem to share the blame. That job belonged to someone official, like Weng, or Clausen himself. But then, as she imagined Clausen making his announcement, she realized what a construction of half-truths it would be, no real answer at all. Ghirra deserved better than that.

But how do you tell someone such a thing? Well, Ghirra, he wants to dig up your planet?

It wouldn't be the entire planet, of course, only what was commercially viable. Susannah had seen strip-mined worlds before. Why now this attack of queasy weakness? Some of the mining companies even terraformed after they were done, usually at the request of the vocal Terran colonies that inevitably sprang up around a mining effort and stayed on to expand and thrive. Susannah pictured one of those colonies and suddenly found herself unaccountably close to tears.

"He wants to dig it up," she heard herself say. Her voice

came out flat and hard. She hoped the notion would strike him as mere offworld eccentricity and that the confrontation could be postponed.

"Why?" Ghirra pursued, as if the thought were not at all inconceivable.

Susannah's weakness threatened to become physical. "He says it's lithium. He wants it . . . some . . . to take away with him." *Coward*! her inner voice shouted. *COWARD*!!

"Lithy-um."

"Yes. To study, you know? Emil studies rocks, like I study plants?" She mimed her little field microscope and wished herself a thousand light-years away.

Clausen's voice floated in from the antechamber. "If we can get enough of these little guys on it, we can haul it right in . . ."

Ghirra nodded thoughtfully and laid the chunk down among its brethren, then thought again and picked up a smaller one. He wrapped it carefully in a square clean cloth and slipped it into his pocket. He said nothing more about it as he helped gather up the used instruments and linens, but Susannah could sense a hidden smolder of dissatisfaction waiting in him.

He has an ear for the truth, this quiet man, and he knows I have not said it to him. Half-truths, just like Emil.

She told herself that situations like this were precisely why she made sure never to get too personally committed in the field, and in the same thought, realized that her nearness to tears probably meant it was already too late.

If only Emil had come back empty-handed!

But that was again postponing the inevitable. She rethought how she might phrase the prospector's intentions to make them seem less dire in their consequences, a way she might tell the truth and at the same time disassociate herself from it. She failed.

Heartsick, she tried to make light of the issue by ignoring it. She summoned her best tone of professional intimacy as she hefted an armload of linens and followed Ghirra into the side hall the healers called the hotroom. "Taylor's a strong one," she said, dumping the linen into the long stone sink. "If we can get that fever down, I think he'll be fine."

"Yes," Ghirra agreed coolly. "Nhe khem. He has luck."

"Luck?" She tried smiling at him. "He has *us*. Two good doctors."

He returned her smile but a polite distance had settled into his eyes. He loosed the tie that held back his long curls and turned away, calling for his apprentice Dwingen, who came running out of the ward eager for a task. Ghirra bent and murmured briefly in his ear. The child nodded and sped off toward the outer corridor. Looking pensive, Ghirra went back into the operating hall. Susannah tagged after him, already feeling cut adrift from the fraternity that had finally been her support and solace through the long night of storms, when she had faced the growing conviction that she would never see her home again. Again she felt the resentment rise in her.

All this over a damn rock! Or is it just because he knows I'm not dealing straight with him?

But she knew it was childish to expect trust to be given where it wasn't being offered. Why should the healers offer her the intimacy of their fraternity if she would not offer a commitment in return? Laying out clean linens on the slabs, she watched Ghirra deftly remove the obsidian-flake blade, one of his own, from her scalpel. He squinted at it and set it aside in a bowl with other used blades. These would be passed along to various craft halls that required a sharp but no longer surgical edge. The metal clamps and handles he placed in a ceramic basket pierced with triangular holes that would fit on top of one of the steaming caldrons in the hotroom.

He does nothing without purpose, nothing without good reason, she thought and recalled his uneasiness as he handled the rock. *It's not just me that's bothering him, then*, she decided, *it's something about that rock.*

31

Stavros trotted briskly toward the PriestHall. The coffee recently shared with Megan had grabbed his nervous system like a football and was running with it, but his heart's noisy anticipatory pounding spoke of adrenaline as well as caffeine. He had gained an ally in his secret battle to protect the Sawls. An ally and the rudiments of a plan, both at once.

He saw Liphar in the corridor ahead, standing outside the PriestHall archway in a huddle of debate with four fellow apprentices.

Looks like a union meeting, Stavros thought, but he heard none of the usual excited chatter, only a hiss of urgent whispering. He grinned and waved as Liphar glanced up. Liphar did not grin back. His already anxious expression awoke to near panic. As Stavros drew up beside him, the young man leaped on him, hushing him as he tried to speak. Half pushing, half dragging, Liphar herded him away from the huddle, away from the PriestHall, down the corridor and into the open double doors of the Woodworkers' Hall.

Two surprised guildsmen drew back from the doorway and nearly dropped the large crate they were carrying. Liphar's mumbled apology was inaudible over the racket of sawing and hammering from inside the hall. He slipped past a stack of crates, hauling Stavros behind him. Sawdust and wood shavings covered the stone floor. Several apprentices pushed at the rubble with brooms, only to have their neat piles scattered by the busy scuffing feet of the journeymen. Racks of rough milled planks lined the walls. Stavros sucked deeply at the sweet heady scent of cut wood. The quartet of long workbenches that filled the center of the cavern were near to being buried in a mountain of crating, most of them already well used and being repaired.

Bright new wooden pegging or replaced slats showed hard white against the darker aged wood.

Now Liphar managed a grin, an unconvincing one which he threw at those guildsmen who bothered to look up at his sudden appearance. Woodworkers' was one of three or four guildhalls with two entrances. Stavros guessed they were used to being used as a shortcut between two main corridors. Liphar kept going, snaking a rapid path among the stacks of finished crates. Finally Stavros tired of being hauled around without explanation. He let his weight drag the smaller man to a halt.

"Lifa, what is going on?"

"Hssst! Hssst!" Liphar insisted. His feet slipped in the sawdust as he tried to pull Stavros onward. "Ibi! Please, come you!"

Stavros relented. At the far end of the hall, a second set of carved double doors yawned open. Crates were piled inside the doors and out in the corridor. A senior woodworker with a list stood among a bustle of apprentices, checking the stacks, directing the movement of crates from one stack to another, matching up the individual guild seals burned into the side of each crate. In the corridor, a handful of Glassmakers loaded their guild's refurbished crates onto a big hjalk-drawn flatbed wagon. Stavros had never seen a hjalk being used in the upper caverns. The Glassmakers seemed to be in an abnormal hurry to finish the loading and be on their way. Thinking about it, Stavros realized he had never seen Woodworkers' in quite such an uproar either.

Liphar ducked around the crates and out the door. He sped past the wagon with a backward glance to assure himself that Stavros still followed. The linguist jogged gamely after him.

In the opposite wall of the corridor was the entrance to Keth-Toph, the grab bag, all-important guild whose name literally meant "LifeGuild." The Terrans tended to refer to it by the more prosaic nickname "Heat and Light." Liphar slowed, glanced up and down the corridor, and slipped through the open archway. Stavros shrugged and followed.

Keth-Toph was an island of serenity compared to Woodworkers' and the peripheral corridors. From a tiny deserted antechamber that served as the local light station, Liphar led the way through a maze of narrow shelf-lined caverns. The shelves were stocked with a now-dwindling supply of brown soap and tallow candles, bundles of lampwick, ceramic lamp bowls and glass chimneys. One long cavern held row after row of tall graceful jars for lamp oil. Less than a quarter of them bore the wax seal

that indicated they were still full. A larger cavern off to one side
was pitch-dark but reeked of dried dung cakes. They passed
through a small messy workshop for the repair of lamps, also
deserted, and came into the central guildhall, a large circular
cavern dominated by the traditional broad table with numerous
backless stools for guild meetings. In a gesture worthy of the
eccentricity for which Keth-Toph was famed, a single-bowled oil
lamp hung over each and every stool. Against the wall, a ring of
giant caldrons, encrusted with use, hung over soot-blackened
firepits. The hall was empty and the fires cold, but Stavros could
imagine, from the touch of it that lingered, the stench and heat in
the RoundHall during the darktime rendering of fat for soap and
candle making.

Liphar finally came to rest, leaning against the great central
table under one of the three oil lamps that remained lit.

Stavros folded his arms, breathing heavily. "Well?" he demanded laughingly.

But the young Sawl was not playing games. He shook his
head and began to pace while he caught his breath.

"Okay, Lifa, what's going on? What's all the secrecy, and
what's with the crates in Woodworkers'?"

"Anu!" exclaimed the Sawl unhappily.

Stavros considered this. "Anu" referred both to the giant
wooden priest-horns and to the thunder whose sound they imi-
tated. Thunder was said to be the war horns of the goddesses,
blowing the challenge, the call to battle. But the priest-horns
were reserved for ritual use. "Thunder?" he replied. "Yes, I
heard it."

"Sisterfight maybe, too soon!"

"Lifa, the thunder was very far away."

Liphar shook his head, unconsoled. "Ashimmel, Aguidran,
very worried, very mad both!"

"Yeah, at each other." Stavros tried a smile. "Just like the
Sisters."

"Aguidran want go. Ashimmel say no, bad khem go now!"

"Go where?" Stavros thought to distract him from his tightening spiral of anxiety.

"Ogo Dul," replied Liphar as if it were obvious. As he read
Stavros's surprise, he stopped pacing and spread his arms wide.
"Big markethall," he explained. "Go there, we. Make trade
always."

"And that's what all the crates are for. But it sounded like
Aguidran was saying *everyone* goes."

"Yes," said Liphar. "All go, we. Some stay with crop."
Then he added with a touch of returning mischief, "No good
stay here. No fun. Many beautiful lady, Ogo Dul."

Stavros grinned, his mind balking as he tried to imagine five
thousand men, women and children picking up and trekking off
simultaneously, like an army on the march, in search of markets
and mates. The logistics were staggering. But suddenly he saw
possibilities for a magnificent cover for the salvage operation he
had decided he must carry out in secret. On the other hand, if the
entire population deserted the Caves, who would be left to keep
Clausen from invading them unchallenged?

"What about the Kethed?" he remembered. "Did you talk to
any of the guildmasters?"

Liphar's anxious frown returned. "No Kethed now. After
come back Ogo Dul." He lowered his voice even in the deserted
hall. "All guildmaster no want hear bad khem now." He pushed
himself off from the table and began to pace again. "Anu bad
khem, Clausen bad khem, Ashimmel say no go Ogo Dul.
Guildmaster say *need* go, say need trade very bad, no food, no
other thing. FoodGuild big mess, not know go trade food, stay
here keep crop. All guildmaster very worried, no listen Ashimmel,
no listen bad khem. Big mess, Ibi!" He stopped and murmured
desperately, "Too soon now, anu!"

Stavros's head swam with the complexities of politics. "You
mean, the guildmasters won't listen to anything that might stand
in the way of this trading trip, even if we're trying to warn them
for their own good, plus we have to keep Ashimmel thinking all
Terrans are terrific or she'll use us as an excuse to get the trip
called off? So who do we go to, to both keep the Caves protected
and go to Ogo Dul?"

Liphar peered into the shadows and moved closer, as if
Ashimmel herself might be listening from concealment in one of
the giant black caldrons. "Must talk Aguidran, you," he
whispered.

"But she's not going to want to hear about any bad khem
either. She wants to go to Ogo Dul."

Liphar squirmed visibly, then spoke in a rush. "Aguidran not
same, others. Guildmasters see only food and trade. Ashimmel
hear anu, bad khem, get most worried, want stay in Caves
always. Aguidran not same. Aguidran hear anu, get mad." He
hesitated, then seemed surprised to hear himself whisper,
"Aguidran get mad Rek."

"Mad at the Sisters?" Stavros worked hard to repress a smile.

He liked the image of the weathered Ranger howling her rage at the heavens.

Liphar nodded disapprovingly, but then he added, "Aguidran not think Wokind come Valla Ired."

That was Liphar's reasoning, then. Aguidran wanted the trade trip but was unlikely to link the "bad luck" of Clausen to the threat of bad weather. The unspoken implication was that she was also unlikely to link the recent retreat of Valla Ired to the Terrans' very visible show of support in the StoryHall. She would deal with the Terran issue as independent from the weather. And at the moment, with the trade trip in dispute, she had the ear and support of the craft guild heads.

Stavros looked at Liphar with a new respect for this willingness to balance priestly convictions with a sensitive nose for pragmatic considerations, despite the anxiety it caused him to do so. Stavros knew his next question would cause him even more, but knew he would ask it anyway. Thus he absorbed one more lesson in his crash course in political maneuvering: one can always rationalize using one's friends for the sake of the Cause.

"Will you talk to Aguidran with me?"

But Liphar had foreseen the request and had already decided. He nodded miserably. To prove that the risk did not go unnoticed, Stavros asked, "What would Ashimmel do if she found out you were speaking against her word?"

Liphar shrugged. "Very mad, she." But he would not elaborate, and Stavros decided there were limits to the discomfort he was willing to impose. He squeezed the young man's shoulder and wished he were not doing it so often out of guilt. "Then let's get it over with," he said gently.

They slipped out of Keth-Toph. Liphar did not want to use the exterior route to the RangerHall for fear of running into a weather-watching priest on the stairs or in the cave mouths. They took the corridor inward instead and cut through a busy domestic sector to reach the wide inner tunnel that connected all the third-level entries along the back of the guildhalls. The narrow streets of the living quarters were crowded with the two-carts that had not been winched to ground for the planting. Families had turned their caves inside out, deciding what to pack and what to leave behind. Some carts stood already packed, among piles of household goods waiting to be carried down to carts below.

Stavros eyed the size of the piles. "Lifa, how *long* is this trade trip?"

"Go on lighttime, stay trade some darktime, come back darktime-lighttime."

Stavros calculated, came up with about an earthmonth. "Long time," he murmured, subdued. Coming out of the living quarters into the main corridor, they approached a group of FoodGuilders engaged in a furious argument about the wisdom of going on with the trade trip. They still wore the aprons they had stained while preparing the Planting Feast. They looked hot and tired and confused by their own impassioned choosing of sides. Liphar hurried by them with averted eyes and whipped gratefully around the next corner into the tunnel that led to the RangerHall.

At the entry to the RangerHall, the Master Healer's apprentice Dwingen stood chewing a finger and fretting. As they came up, he looked hopeful and asked if they had seen the Master Ranger or knew where she was. When Liphar shrugged, the boy returned his finger to his mouth and then asked if they agreed that the best thing he could do was return right away to Physicians' and tell his guildmaster that Aguidran was nowhere to be found. Stavros smiled. Clearly this thin child had no patience for standing around corridors wasting time in waiting.

Liphar nodded his assent in a grown-up fashion. The boy grinned his thanks and went speeding off. The older apprentice hesitated at the tall arched entry. Stavros beamed a steady encouragement, then led the way.

"Come on," he said. "We might as well wait for her inside."

"Stav! *Stav!*"

Startled, he turned. Liphar ducked inside the archway. Megan hurried toward them from the cave mouth.

"You'd better come down," she called, not waiting until she reached them, "before Emil and Aguidran tear each other limb from limb."

Danforth woke with the abruptness of one freeing himself from a long drifting sleep. His eyes and head hurt. His hearing felt preternaturally sharp. The incessant hellish drumming of the rain on the hull of the broken Sled had ceased. He had a sensation of comforting hands resting on his forehead, warm and loving, as his mother's hands used to feel. He could not move his head but willed his eyes to focus. Amber sunlight hung in the air above him, exciting the little dust motes into their frenetic dance. He watched them for a while, forgetting about the hands, and wondered if his arm would be there if he tried to raise it.

Can't move.

He tried to call out, but his voice still slept. His jaw worked.
He was a fish gasping for air. He could express only an inarticulate gargle. He became aware of the hands again, soothing,
calming his panic.

Relax, T.D. It'll come. He told himself he'd had worse dreams
than this. Gazing beyond the motes in their shaft of sunlight, he
saw a huge wooden wheel suspended in shadow. Glints of sun
reflected off glass and glazed ceramic. Beyond that was stone
vaulting and darkness.

Where the hell am I?

He swallowed. His throat awoke to the relief from dryness.

"Hello?" he croaked. He was rewarded by an answering
rustle. The hands withdrew their gentle pressure from his brow.
He was not sure until they were gone whether he had imagined
them and the comfort they brought.

"Wait!" he protested hoarsely. He had discovered his arms
and they were enveloped in tubes and bandages.

"You wake, TaylorDanforth," said a quiet voice.

A man appeared from behind his head to crouch beside his bed
and press cool fingers to his wrist. Against the pale beige of his
collarless smock, the man's skin was dark, Danforth thought
nearly as dark as his own. His long ringleted brown hair was
gathered into a tie at the back of his neck. He stood, gingerly
moved the rolling IV stand out of Danforth's line of sight. He
looked tall and thin leaning over the bed.

"Who're you?" mumbled Danforth. His sudden wakefulness
was slipping away from him. *Water through a sieve*, he thought,
drifting.

The brown man smiled as he crouched again at Danforth's
side. "I am Ghirra Ogo Dul. I am a doctor."

Danforth closed his eyes in relief. "And I was sure I was
gonna die out there. Christ!" He opened his eyes again and
turned his head with effort to study the man more closely.
"Don't know you, do I? Did they send in a rescue crew from the
Orbiter somehow?"

The brown man considered for a moment. "No," he replied
finally.

Danforth tried to place the man's odd accent. "You from one
of the other ships?" Even this impossibility seemed minor compared to the miracle of being alive. For a moment he was lost to
a memory of pain and despair in endless cold and hammering
rain, and then the man was talking to him, bringing him back
from his drift.

"Do you know what this is, TaylorDanforth?"

Danforth squinted dutifully, fighting the drift. He made out a handful of lavender sparkle.

"Pretty rock," he murmured. "Pretty."

"Do you know what it is?" the man repeated, but now Danforth saw other white smocks hovering at the periphery of his vision. His drifting stopped abruptly.

Oh shit. A goddamn hospital!

"Am I offworld?" he demanded in a waking panic. "Did they send me *home*?"

Please god, they can't have sent me home!

The man restrained him gently as he struggled to sit. "No, you must rest still, TaylorDanforth." He beckoned one of the white smocks to him, a woman with brown skin like his own. He murmured briefly and sent her away. Danforth picked out familiar syllables.

"Susannah? Is she here? Am I still on Fix?"

"Phiix, yes, you are," the man soothed.

Danforth felt the hands again as the man returned to the head of his bed. The hands did not move, merely rested lightly on his skin, radiating comfort. "Then who are you?" he repeated thickly, closing his eyes again against the confusion.

"I am a doctor," the man replied, and Danforth slept.

Megan stayed in the cave mouth to observe from a distance. Stavros slipped down the long stone stair, squint-eyed in the sunlight. He took advantage of the cover of a detail of apprentices loaded down with bales of cloth stamped with the red interlaced sign of the WeaverGuild. The rough outer wrappings creaked and smelled of musty straw. He dipped into their shadow and glanced back up the steps, hoping for a glimpse of Liphar, lost in the bustle behind. The young man had stopped to share the load of an elderly rugmaker who had taken on more than any single soul could dream of managing on the steep stair. Stavros could not find either of them in the confusion of goods and people inching down the stairs.

Above, the cave mouths yawned darkly against the amber cliff. The winches were again in use, throwing moving shadows on the pale rock. The PriestGuild had watchers stationed at half a dozen entries, their attention fixed on the skies while an earthyear's worth of hard work in the craft halls moved past them toward the cliff bottom. Stavros did not see Ashimmel among them and was obscurely relieved.

Maybe it's not so serious yet, he decided.

Two ascending shadows passed. All five of the cliff-top winches had been pressed into service to speed the loading. Descending crates of pottery and glass slid past emptied pallets rising to be refilled.

Aguidran will have her way by default, thought Stavros. *Not even Ashimmel could halt this momentum now it's begun.*

Progress down the stairs was slow. The Weaver apprentices struggled with their bales. Stavros peered around them down into the seethe of activity at the cliff bottom. The tent city had been dismantled, packed and returned to storage. The rock flat was crammed with a motley assembly of half-loaded wagons, all sizes and shapes, from single-family two-carts to the twenty giant red-and-blue FoodGuild wagons. Off the far edge of the flat, the hjalk milled in the sun, waiting, their fleshy hooves buried deep in the cooling mud. The flooded fields and terraces gleamed like a vast shattered mirror. FoodGuilders bent solicitously among the yellow stalks. The water was merely ankle-deep now and the tallest crops were uncurling broad fleshy leaves.

With little effort, Stavros picked out the dapper figure of the prospector, face to face with the Master Ranger, she leaning against a tall-sided wagon, her arms negligently folded across her leather-clad chest, he doing the talking, with his bullet head set at its most amiable angle. McPherson hovered uncertainly in between.

Stavros yawned convulsively, wishing he had downed another caffeine jolt before walking into his first real skirmish. Doubt assailed him. His role had been only hastily rehearsed with Liphar and Megan. Would the prospector suspect? Seeing Clausen and the Ranger subtly arrayed for conflict brought home to him how suddenly the battle lines were being drawn, almost without the awareness of the participants. It was crucial to keep the struggle *sub rosa* as long as possible. He hoped the first Clausen would know of it was when he finally was able to stake his claim, only to find a legal action had already been filed. The scene to come must be played with calm and confidence.

As cold-bloodedly as Clausen would in my place.

Stavros consoled himself with the reminder that he had been playing roles all his life, though perhaps not as consciously. It was only the new degree of self-control required that should concern him.

The congestion eased as four Basketmakers who had taken

their time on the stairs made it to the bottom, balancing tall wobbling stacks of their most intricately woven wares. The flow carried Stavros along more quickly than he'd hoped. From his concealment behind the bobbing cloth bales, he saw Aguidran shrug and glance significantly at the sky. Clausen's answering gesture to McPherson was rueful but just abrupt enough to reveal impatience. They both looked brushed and refreshed, the pilot in clean whites warmed to pale gold by the sun, Clausen in neatly pressed tans, leaning on his rough crutch as if it were a gentleman's walking stick.

Stavros hit the bottom step and sidled through the crowd. Nearing, he heard: "So where is our Ship's Linguist when I need him?"

"Right here, Emil." *On cue*. Stavros took a deep breath and moved away from the line of weavers into the open.

The prospector swiveled gracefully. His sunburn was already deepening to a healthy tan. His new beard had been carefully trimmed to the same brusque length as his sandy hair. One raised brow took in without further comment Stavros's bare feet, blousy linen pants and long ropy vest tied across a naked chest.

"Stavros, my boy! Didn't see you at my triumphal homecoming. Feared you'd been washed away with the flood!"

You wish, Clausen. "Sorry, Emil. Been real busy, with all this going on, the Planting, the packing." He noted Aguidran's baleful look and hoped he could manage to affect innocence. Liphar's fist nudging the small of his back fortified him. He nodded in response, then said to the prospector, "You having a problem here?"

Clausen smiled. "Well, this gentlelady and I seem to be having some trouble making ourselves understood," he replied smoothly.

"She's being weird," complained McPherson. "Usually she gets me just fine."

Stavros kept his smirk under wraps. Aguidran could forget that she spoke Sawlish if it suited her purpose. He suspected that Clausen had resorted to this oily charm only after failing in his assumption that the Ranger could be ramrodded. That being roughly equivalent to charging full tilt into a force field, Stavros wished he'd sneaked up earlier to witness the collision.

Even the old charm looks a little burned around the edges. Is it possible, Clausen, that you've met your match?

"What is it you want her to understand?" he asked earnestly, thinking, *Oh, Christ, Clausen'll never buy this act from me!*

Liphar had gone over to chat with Aguidran. His part in the plan was to convince her to play along until they had a chance to properly explain themselves to her.

"It's very simple, really," Clausen replied. "I need as many of her men as it takes to haul that Sled in here for repairs."

The prospector's presumptuousness was outrageous, but Stavros kept his nod carefully neutral. "I'll see what I can do, Emil."

He approached Aguidran with elaborate courtesy, using the most rapid Sawlish he could muster. It would not hurt his pose as the crucial go-between to appear more fluent than he really was. Meanwhile, he was learning something else, as he felt himself ease into the role with more confidence than he'd expected: the accompanying power rush was considerable, now that he actually had the prospector at a disadvantage. It was more than the heady weight of responsibility, which he had felt and nearly bungled during the evacuation of the Lander. It was about control, of people and situations.

I've had enough trouble just controlling myself *in the past. . . .*

Aguidran's eyes slitted in response to his obsequious formality. They met Liphar's briefly, then returned to his. Her reply was terse and equally rapid.

Stavros breathed a private sigh of relief and turned back to Clausen. "Doesn't look good for now, Emil. She says she's already been put way behind schedule by going out after you and Taylor. She has to get the trade caravan on the road as soon as possible in order to reach Ogo Dul by darkfall." He dropped his voice and tried a comradely tone. "This is a major undertaking for her, you understand, packing up the entire population and all the market goods, plus supervising the provisioning." He hoped the overworked old Master of the FoodGuild wouldn't hear that last untruth. "She just can't spare anyone right now."

Clausen's expression remained patient. "The entire population. All right, I'll bite. What or where is Ogo Dul?"

Stavros consulted Aguidran briefly. Then, attempting to sound unamazed by information that was still very recent news to him as well, he replied, "A city on DulValla, the great ocean to the north. She says it's ten throws—that's a local unit of both time and distance, equivalent, as far as I can gather, to about twenty kilometers of travel in a thirty-hour cycle. So, about two hundred kilometers away, somewhat less than thirteen of our days' travel."

Clausen nodded tightly. "One way."

"You mean there's *cities* out there?" broke in McPherson.

"A number of them." Stavros used the tone of brotherly

reproof he could not direct at Clausen. "On a world this big, it would be unusual if this tiny settlement were the only population."

"Well, I didn't mean . . ." McPherson began, then shrugged and fell silent.

"This is interesting news," said the prospector. "I would have expected actual cities to have shown up in my remote sensing data."

"They're probably not cities as we think of cities," Stavros temporized. He gestured up at the cave openings. "Would DulElesi have shown up as a settlement? Particularly under thirty feet of snow?"

Clausen pursed his lips. "And what is the population of this Ogo Dul?"

When questioned, Aguidran shook her head unhelpfully. Liphar piped up with a suggestion that sounded like a guess.

"They don't keep close track of such things," Stavros replied, his mind's eye filling with the volumes of extensively detailed records that swelled the library of each and every guildhall. *But this is just the beginning of the lie*, he thought. "Liphar says that the tunnels of Ogo Dul spread through many miles of the coastal cliffs. His population guess is several hundred thousand at least."

"How many other such . . . settlements are there?" asked Clausen casually.

Stavros let this require more extensive consultation. Clausen did not fidget as he waited, leaning on his stick. McPherson scuffed the mud-caked layered rock with the white toe of a clean boot. The answer Aguidran gave him surprised him. He would only have to stretch the truth to make it sufficiently impressive.

"In the most livable zone, the equatorial regions, she says there's a settlement every ten throws in any direction. Widely but evenly scattered, it would seem. She reports word of hardy pockets of population to the north and south, but cannot vouch for them herself." Stavros pictured the world map in the cabinet of the RangerHall and wondered if Aguidran was telling *him* the truth. Certainly *somebody* had had access to very detailed information that included the northern and southern regions, in order to draw so complete a map.

Clausen continued his relaxed interrogation. "And again, the reason for the trip?"

"To trade in Ogo Dul."

"And this requires the entire population? Not very efficient."

Stavros shrugged helplessly. "That's the way they've always done it."

"Of course. We wouldn't want to upset tradition." Clausen stroked his beard with a cupped palm. "Well. Perhaps we could arrange something for when she's done organizing this . . . caravan."

"The problem is," Stavros began carefully, "most of her rangers have duties with the caravan en route." He pumped meek apology into his tone. "But give me a minute. Maybe with Liphar's help, I can make her understand your . . . that is, *our* urgency." *That is, make her understand that I must get to the wreck first, in secret, to get my hands on the omni before he does, that we must stall the repair of the Sled and comsystem as long as we possibly can. . . .*

He conferred with Liphar and Aguidran. The Ranger listened to their murmured explication impassively. Stavros knew it was unsatisfactory but he didn't have time to supply all the details. He asked mainly for her cooperation until he could explain himself more fully. Clausen waited, sharing an occasional things-we-have-to-go-through glance with McPherson. His only sign of impatience was his free hand twitching at his side, worrying the seams of his spotless canvas slacks.

When they had finished, Aguidran shifted, rubbed her nose thoughtfully, then growled a curt order that Stavros meet her in the RangerHall at the start of the next shift. Stavros turned to Clausen, thinking, *This is too easy. What if he understands every word we've said*? But that was impossible. He spread his hands. "She says she'll think about it."

Clausen's mouth tightened imperceptibly. "And how long might that take?"

Before Stavros could ask, Aguidran pushed herself away from the side of the wagon and stalked off through the maze of wheels and cart traces and stacked crates and bundles, scattering low-voiced orders right and left.

Stavros called up apology again. "I think I can let you know first thing in the morning, ship's time. Let her get this sorted out and we'll try her again later." He pretended to speak to Clausen's compassion. *As if there was any.* "It's real tense for her just now, being behind schedule and all. They need this trade trip badly, so there's a lot of pressure. You heard there's been thunder up in the northeastern mountains?"

Clausen nodded indolently. "Heard it myself."

"But Aguidran'll do the best she can for you. Remember, she risked her life and those of her guildsmen, going out to search for you guys in the middle of the storm."

The prospector looked politely unimpressed. "So McPherson has told me." He smiled and Stavros suffered a flashing image of crocodile jaws parting to expose a row of needled teeth. It terrified him. He struggled to remain composed while Clausen continued, "Well, I'm a patient man. In the interim, McP. and I can spend some time and effort on the high-gain dish. At least they saw fit to haul that back before they got too busy." His smile relaxed a bit, became a grin as he let it fall on McPherson. "Time we got the Lander powered up again, eh? I for one could use a hot shower." He grasped his cane and turned, signaling the pilot to follow, then slowed to remark pleasantly over his shoulder, "You won't mind, I'm sure, since you've found so little time to work on it yourself?"

"No. Be my guest," Stavros replied, returning what he hoped was a smile. But he felt thrown on the defensive and could not help adding, "You're going to need a welder."

"Shouldn't be too much of a problem," called the prospector airily as he limped away with McPherson in tow.

No? Stavros frowned. It bothered him that the man could manage to saunter even with a cane. *Be just like that sonofabitch to have a cutting torch hidden in his goddamn pocket!*

At his side, Liphar stared after Clausen and muttered the first deprecatory comment Stavros had ever heard him make about his offworld visitors.

"You said a mouthful," Stavros agreed, and then, "You think it worked? With that guy, you can't tell." Thunder rumbled beyond the plain, so faint it sounded like distant waves. His knees weakened as the anxiety of the moment ebbed. He caught Liphar's shoulder, his balance wavering. "Lifa, we ought to grab a few hours' sleep before we get much further into this." He sighed deeply, a release of tension. "And *then* we go explain ourselves to Aguidran."

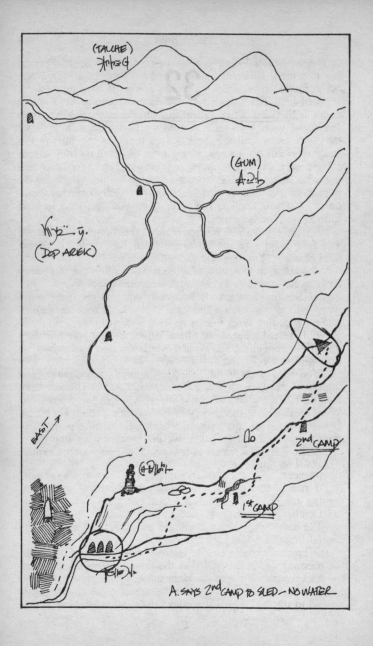

32

Thunder was rumbling across the Dop Arek in earnest by the time Ghirra's runner found Susannah in the shade of a giant FoodGuild wagon, stating her case to a somberly pensive Weng. The wagon's freshly painted wheels, red rims with blue spokes, stood as high as their shoulders. The wagon itself was a healthy twelve feet to the top of its arching canopy. At its rear, four FoodGuilders struggled to find space for a last load of grain sacks. They grumbled their frustration at each other, distracted by the oddly discrete pockets of green-black cloud gathering in the distant northeast.

Susannah spoke with quiet reasoned intensity. Megan hovered in the background, pretending to study the intricate pinning system for the wagon's removable wooden canopy. She limited herself to the occasional added comment or grunt of support. It would be better for the implementation of the conspiracy, as she had already come to think of it (not without irony—a conspiracy of two?), if she did not seem to have too urgent a stake in Susannah's request.

"We'd be insane not to take advantage of this opportunity, Commander," Susannah was pointing out as the Physicians' Guild runner trotted into the wagon's shadow and pulled up, panting and damp from the heat.

"Derelict," Megan elaborated.

"The data on population dynamics and intermingling could be crucial," said Susannah.

The courier waited, loath to interrupt but brimming both with his message and with anxiety as the thunder rumbled louder in the background. The FoodGuilders shoved the last sack into the back of the wagon and slammed the rear gate shut. One came around to the side with a thin stick. He squeezed behind Susannah and Weng to check the water level in the huge wooden kegs lashed to the belly of the wagon.

"Who knows how long it'll take Ronnie and Emil to fix the Sled? Here's an ideal chance to expand our zone of inquiry immediately."

Weng dipped her silver head. "All you say makes perfect sense, Dr. James. My concern is that expeditionary personnel and resources not be spread too thinly while we are still in a state of emergency."

"Meg and I can't help with fixing the com or the Sled. If the population departs, Meg's left with nothing but her notes. If I go, I can at last begin my biological survey."

"Which was your primary mission objective," Megan reminded her, hitting on the word 'mission' with what she hoped was not too heavy a hand.

"And we wouldn't have to use expedition resources," said Susannah.

Megan patted the red and blue striped side of the towering wagon. "Tyril says two or three more people isn't going to overburden the FoodGuild's resources."

"Two or *three?*" Weng inquired.

Megan shrugged. "Figures approximate."

A particularly loud boom of thunder, like a distant cannon, burst, spurred the waiting courier into action. He moved himself into Susannah's line of sight and fidgeted impatiently. When she noticed him, he delivered his message in a rush so that only its general sense was intelligible.

"Okay?" he finished, with the word that seemed to be every Sawl's first and favorite word of English. When Susannah nodded, frowning with concern, he waved and ran off.

"Ghirra wants me upstairs to check on Taylor," she said to Weng. "Hope nothing's wrong. Will you give this all some thought, Commander?"

"Indeed, Dr. James. In fact, I'll come up with you and consider while we walk."

Coming out of the wagon's shadow afforded Megan a better view of the plain tops of several acres' worth of other wagons and carts. The packing had slowed as guildsmen set down their bundles and gathered in nervous groups to observe the rumbling activity over the plain.

"Now that's really odd," Megan remarked. She heard the clink of stone counters among the watching guildsmen.

As Susannah and Weng slowed to look where she pointed, a

single clot of darkness detached itself from the lumpy bank of cloud hanging over the sawtoothed profile of the far-off Vallegar. With surprising speed, the cloud scudded southward over the Dop Arek, growling thunder and spitting tiny forks of lightning. Megan felt a breath of hot wind ruffle the back of her head. Halfway across the plain, the cloud seemed to lose substance and momentum. Within seconds, it had dissipated. The Sawl watchers cheered, invoking Lagri's name and passing their counters back and forth. The hot wind died and sprang up again as a second cloud detached itself and a third, each seeming to reach a little farther across the plain before dissolving.

The Terrans watched open-mouthed.

"Small wonder they ascribe intent to the weather," Megan exclaimed. "Just look at it! I'd like to hear Taylor's explanation for that!"

"Hopefully he will live to give us one," Susannah commented, turning back toward the Caves. She hurried off with Weng through the crowd of wagons and gathering watchers.

The Master Healer was not in Physicians' when Susannah and Weng arrived. Ampiar stood by Danforth's bed, her sober face touched by sunlight from the clerestory as she gazed down at him with quiet satisfaction. The planetologist looked very limp and still.

Susannah put a hand to his skin. Worriedly, she checked his pulse and put her head to his chest. Then she breathed a sigh of relief. "He was so cool, I thought . . ." She grinned at Weng, amazed. "It's impossible, but the fever's broken already."

"Congratulations, Dr. James," the Commander nodded.

Susannah noted Ampiar's look of pride. She shook her head and smiled. "Just like Ghirra, to take care of the problem first, and then send for me."

"The intemperate herbalist Ard is worth his keep," Weng observed.

"Yes," Susannah agreed, her voice soft with bemused wonder. "But mostly it's Ghirra himself. I never believed much in the laying on of hands until I spent some time watching him work. Even then, I assumed it was mainly the patients' total faith in him that helped them to heal. But Taylor has no such faith. . . ." Disturbed, she frowned and fell silent.

Weng pursed her thin lips. "But faith is a strange thing, Dr. James. We find it where we least expect it."

"I suppose, Commander, I suppose," Susannah replied, but her frown remained.

33

Aguidran stood at the cold hearth of the RangerHall, her arms braced against the high carved mantel, her dark head thrown back to stare at the frieze that marched across the wall. She held her lean body stiffly, as if in pain. Stavros halted by the head of the long table, reluctant to break into what seemed to be a moment of private angst or doubt. He held Liphar back and waited, while at the other end of the hall, guildsmen came and went noisily, stowing equipment into canvas packs, lifting down coils of rope and masses of leather harness from name-plated pegs. Senior journeymen moved among them, checking lists of provisions and personnel assignments.

At length, the Ranger turned her head to regard them unblinkingly. Stavros thought he heard a quickly repressed sigh. She pushed away from the mantel and came toward them. "O rek," she muttered to Liphar, shaking her head in casual disgust.

"Gisti," he intoned, awed that her unusual candor was addressed to him but disapproving of her tone. He slid his blue-green amulet back and forth on the thong around his wrist.

"Anu?" Stavros asked, already decided that Aguidran was more worried about the thunder than she wanted the priests to know.

Liphar nodded. "Remember, you, I say too soon Valla now. Big trouble she come now. She come now, Lagri too weak. Bad for us. No food, no Ogo Dul."

Aguidran turned aside to answer a guildsman's question. Stavros recalled what Liphar had spoken about easily enough once, but had refused to discuss of late, perhaps out of superstition. The too rapid return of one Sister to strength after a defeat was considered a sign of the rise of that Sister's power toward domination over the other, a domination that historically brought famine and devastation to the human population.

"Can the FoodGuild trade at Ogo Dul for supplies?" he asked.

"Yes. There they grow big. . . ." Liphar formed quick ovals with the thumb and forefinger of both hands, drawing one end outward.

"Big fish?"

"Phish, yes." He bladed one hand and sent it on repeating S-curves through the air. "More big, our phish."

Stavros looked forward to the idea. The fish grown in the deep cave pools of DulElesi were no doubt nourishing, but they were tiny and bland. Ogo Dul's being on the water might provide something considerably more interesting.

"But Ibi," Liphar continued. "If Valla too strong here, she more strong there, you see?"

He means closer to Valla's territory, Stavros mused. *No hope then for the battle being locally contained.*

Aguidran sent the guildsman on her way with a growled word of encouragement. She stalked up to the head of the table, dragged her chair back and sat, gesturing them sharply to follow suit. Stavros slid onto a bench and laid his hands palm down on the golden wood.

Here the defense enters its first plea. Better make it good, Ibiá.

But it turned out to be unnecessary to remind the Ranger that Clausen's movements must again be restricted. The image that Stavros had used to warn the Guild Council weeks ago, that of the prospector scaling the walls of the FriezeHall to pry the jewels from the Sisters' eyes, had remained a potent one. Besides, one direct encounter with Clausen had been enough to arouse Aguidran's enmity. She was contemptuous of Ashimmel's self-serving nonchalance regarding, as she said, the Visitors. (Stavros noted that the tall Master Ranger did not use the Terrans' cave nickname "Wokind"—"heads-above-our-own"—for the obvious reason.) She assured him that Clausen would be kept under surveillance by her own guild. What little had been revealed to the other Visitors in the presumed safety of Clausen's absence would now be covertly guarded. As well, she would bring pressure to bear on the other guild heads in the Kethed and see that a home guard was authorized, drawn from all the guilds. Those who stayed behind must seem to be a random selection of the population.

So Stavros could go after the working antenna on the Sled without fear of disaster. But again, he needed the Ranger's help to do so: advice about the route, provisions and equipment, but most important, her compliance in his cover story. Probably she would grant him supplies long before she would fill Clausen's request for the services of her rangers, but she must also lie for him, not only to other Terrans but to any Sawl, such as Ashimmel, who might through ignorance or for political reasons give the plan away. Liphar did not think Aguidran would lie unless she understood the reason to be a good one.

Before even touching on the possibility of lying to protect his purpose, Stavros was faced with the difficulty of explaining the significance of the object he claimed to need so desperately, as well as why he needed to obtain it without the others (except Megan) knowing. He had never felt more professionally inadequate as he searched for words dire enough, trying to express the concepts of the Sled and long-range communications in nontechnical metaphor, and getting nowhere.

Then he recalled a long rambling session with Liphar in the BathHall, when he had worked himself up to a peak of intimacy and confessed his otherworldly origins. The anticlimax had been shattering. The young Sawl had accepted Stavros's descriptions of Earth and his flight across the light-years with unperturbed interest, as if it were one of his own tale-chants. The linguist's disappointment had soon faded to amusement.

If the goddesses walk the world and play games with the wind, what's so remarkable about spaceflight? Magic is magic is magic.

Liphar had added further that he was not surprised to hear that the Wokind came from the sky, for hadn't the ranger sentinels seen the Lander descend with their own eyes? He was far from associating such skyward origins with divinity, as the ancestral Catholic in Stavros had assumed. The Sister-goddesses of Fiix did not live in the insubstantial heavens but on the good solid ground where any worthy deity belonged.

So instead, Stavros offered the Master Ranger a straightforward description of the Orbiter, explaining that the object he required from the wreck would allow him to talk with the people on this other "lander" in the sky without actually going there. Liphar received this information with his usual deferential acceptance, but Stavros thought that Aguidran regarded him with some skepticism. But she let it pass as he moved on to the real issue, that Clausen must be kept from communicating with this other

ship even though he himself was clamoring to do so. He did not
know where to begin to explain why the Orbiter could communicate with Fiix, given the aid of the antenna, but could not
communicate with the strange place he called Earth. He did not
know how to make the exact nature of the danger clear, when a
true understanding required knowledge of the bureaucratic workings of an interstellar civilization from one who was clearly
dubious that it existed in the first place. How could he explain to
the Master Ranger what the word "lithium" meant?

Stopped by the limits of verbal language, Stavros shaped his
hands into a lump that might resemble a rock. He was launching
into an explanation that there was a rock that Clausen wanted
and would do anything to get when he saw Aguidran glance up
and smile. It was a small smile, rather tired, but it brought to her
brown face the softness he had sworn could never be there. It
dazzled him.

Who. . . ?

He turned to find the Master Healer striding toward them
through the stacked-up packs and piles of supplies and equipment.

That one, Stavros thought disgustedly. *The smiling ladies'
man.*

But Ghirra was not smiling. His linen smock flapped like a
cloak around his tall frame. His brown hair, loosed from its
usual tie, stood out from his long face in a mane of curls.
Aguidran rose to meet him, an arm outstretched to grasp the
hand he offered. The small bundle he carried he set with some
ceremony on the table. He had bent to undo its cloth wrappings
when he recognized Stavros through the screen of his Sawlish
clothing. Ghirra had obviously taken the linguist for another
guildsman. He straightened, let his hand casually sweep up the
still-wrapped bundle as he drew his sister aside. Aguidran listened to his hurried murmur, her own smile fading. When he
was done, she leveled at Stavros a long and speculative gaze.

Stavros looked down in confusion. *What have I done?*

Ghirra awaited his twin's response, his handsome face grim as
he eyed Stavros guardedly.

He doesn't like me much either, noted Stavros with a creeping
satisfaction that faded as he began to wonder if this was proof of
some involvement between the Master Healer and his Terran
colleague. He pushed this inappropriate worry from his mind as
Aguidran guided her brother back to the table with a firm hand.
She slipped the cloth bundle from his grasp, set it back on the
table and urged him to continue the unveiling. Ghirra hesitated,

disapproving, then did as she bade him. He folded aside the corners of the fabric to reveal a ragged triangle of sparkling lavender rock.

Stavros sensed the familiar slippage inside his head. He gripped the hard edge of the table, seeking reality reinforcement, then stared at the rock and back at his hands that had been so recently struggling to describe a rock. And not just any rock. A rock of exactly this color and crystalline formation.

That rock! That's lithium! It has to be!

At his side, Liphar molded a gasp into words. "Guar rek!"

Aguidran nodded gravely.

The rock was as Megan had described it: pale, coolly glittering against the soft fabric and polished wood, very beautiful.

Ghirra must have lifted it from Clausen's pack. Why did he bring it here?

Stavros glanced up to find the Master Healer studying him with that same speculative gaze that his sister had pinned him with a moment earlier. He felt like a moth on a specimen board and returned Ghirra's scrutiny purely out of self-defense.

Apart, he had seen brother and sister as opposite extremes: stern Aguidran who was never heard to laugh, and handsome Ghirra, always with a smile and a gentle word for the world. But seeing them together, it seemed that they drew in toward some invisible center to mirror each other more exactly. Ghirra now, taking on some of his sister's hard-edged gravity, came to share the power of her presence. Stavros was forced to consider him seriously, even to wonder how he could not have done so before. He had never, as Susannah had suggested, gone up to the Physicians' Hall to observe the Master Healer at work.

Because you're a jealous fool, that's why. . . .

Stavros waited, half resentful, half abashed. Finally Ghirra picked up the triangle of rock. Reaching his long arm across the table, he set it down between the linguist's hands.

"Do you know what this is?" he demanded softly.

The precision of his English wording unsettled Stavros's resistance further. He eyed the healer tentatively, reluctantly impressed. "I think so. I think it's a lithium ore."

"Lithy-um," Ghirra repeated. "Yes. She said this."

Liphar reached to touch a hesitant finger to the rock. "Guar rek," he murmured lovingly.

"Guar rek?" Stavros had not heard the phrase before.

But Liphar was lost in his contemplation of the rock. He

cupped both hands around it protectively, smiling into its crystal-line facets.

"This is old words," said Ghirra with gentle dismissal. "Priest words. Now we say 'gorrel.' "

Gorrel. Food? Gorrel rek. Food of the goddesses? Oh, come on. Yet a sure instinct told Stavros that here was a mystery ripe for revealing. "Old words?" he asked.

"The PriestWords," Ghirra repeated, and this time Stavros heard the phrase differently, as a true descriptive rather than a dismissive. "They are from long time ago."

A root language, preserved like Latin through the priesthood, though bearing less resemblance to the modern tongue than Latin did. The "old words" must be very old indeed. The seemingly alien and untranslatable words imbedded in many of the songs and rituals had led him to suspect as much, but he thought it curious that no one before Ghirra, not even Liphar, the priest-in-training, had been either willing or able to confirm his theory. His estimation of the Master Healer rose another large notch. " 'Guar' means 'food'?" he asked. "The rock is the Goddesses' food? I don't understand."

Ghirra sucked his lean cheek, clearly seeking an improved translation. "SisterBread," he stated at last. His shoulders hunched loosely and dropped. "Old words."

Liphar's nervous fingers had returned to their telling of the malachite bead on his wrist, but his concentration remained with the rock. *Old words!* Stavros reined in his excitement. If he could just keep the information coming, at some point it would begin to make sense. A key to translating all those untranslat-ables could be a key to the origins of the Sawl mythohistory. "I'd like to know more about these 'old words,' GuildMaster. Can you enlighten me?"

But Ghirra straightened away from the table without answer-ing and came around to straddle the end of Stavros's bench. So close, he was a substantial presence. Though the healer was as lean as any Sawl, Stavros could imagine in him, as in his sister, a physical strength to contend with. Stavros half turned to face him, sharply aware of Liphar at his side and Aguidran leaning against the table with folded arms. He slid a hand along the edge of the bench to push against Liphar's thigh.

Liphar glanced up, distracted from the rock by the sudden silence and the tension in Stavros's grip. "Ibi . . ." he began placatingly, but the Master Ranger hushed him brusquely.

Ghirra reached, wrapped the rock in his lithe surgeon's fingers and held it up for emphasis. "What does he with this?"

Stavros swallowed. Ghirra's manner implied no threat, but rather a moral imperative to tell the truth. "You mean Clausen?"

"Clauzen, yes. Why does he want this?" The Master Healer set the rock down on the bench between them and sat back a little, folding his arms in an exact reflection of his sister behind him. "You know this?"

Stavros met the healer's direct, thoughtful gaze, then dropped his head in relief. *At last*! He knew he could make this man understand. "Yes, I know. I was just trying to explain to Aguidran. . . ."

"Explain to me."

Now that there was a chance the full implications of his news might be understood, Stavros dreaded the moment when those implications took hold in the healer's consciousness. He imagined the reproach and horror and rage. He nodded weakly and plunged in. "That rock, the substance in that rock, the lithium, is very valuable on . . . where I come from. We don't have very much of it there and we need it for our . . . industry. Here on Fiix, it would seem, there is a lot of it. Danforth's probe . . . his, ah, studies told him that from the distance of my home world." He paused. Ghirra was listening intently, nodding encouragement. His expression told Stavros nothing of what he understood and what he did not.

Stavros sighed, a release of long-stored tension. "Emil Clausen works for a company—that's sort of like a guild—a group of powerful men. They sent him here to dig up all this rock and take it home with him, where it will make both him and them a great deal of profit."

"All." The healer refused himself the laziness of incredulity.

"Every ounce and gram he can get his hands on." Stavros sighed again, though it felt almost like a sob as the words began to spill out unconsidered. "And he's not going to go after it with a wooden pick and shovel, believe me. He'll bring huge machines in here that can extract every last molecule of lithium and anything else he happens to want from this planet's crust, and the parts they don't dig up, they'll use as a trash heap or a spaceport or a parking lot—"

Ghirra raised a restraining hand. "Please. I do not understand this."

Stavros took a breath but barely slowed. He could not now, until he had purged himself of the burden of this dreadful knowledge. He swung his leg over the bench and stood. The movement was a release. "Imagine the land all torn up, the Dop Arek shredded for as far as you could walk in a hundred cycles. Imagine parched mountains of rubble, the growing fields reduced to dust, the air unbreathable, watercourses rerouted, polluted. Imagine noisy, dirty shanty towns and cities springing up all over like diseased fungi. GuildMaster, you won't recognize this world when Clausen gets through with it. He'll make it unlivable. He may even try to round you up like a herd of hekkers and pack the whole population off to some other planet!" He paced to a stop in front of Aguidran, pointing up at the invisible sky. "Which is why we can't allow him to tell anyone out there that he's made his lithium strike on Fiix!"

The Master Ranger sucked her cheek impassively.

"He would not do this in his own Caves," Ghirra murmured.

Stavros laughed harshly, pacing again. "It's already been done. Long ago, by those before him. There's nothing left on Earth except more people than you can imagine, all choking to death on filthy air in buildings built from the resources of other planets."

Ghirra was struggling with an understanding. "Suzhannah say to me one time about a box. This box has words inside. Knowing."

Stavros stopped pacing. "Knowledge," he corrected reflexively as his estimation of the Master Healer rose yet again. Ghirra was making the connections even faster than he had hoped. "The box is called a computer," he added.

"Also she say the box . . . the computur, talks. It talks words to friends far away." Ghirra waited for Stavros to nod his agreement, then added cannily. "But the . . . computur does not talk now."

"No. It's broken, from the storm."

"Clauzen cannot talk to these far friends now."

Stavros blinked, but no, he had heard the healer correctly. Hope surged through him once again. First Megan, now this remarkable Sawl. Allies were appearing out of nowhere just when Clausen seemed to have won the battle without even a skirmish. He wanted to shout for joy and relief but contented himself with matching Ghirra's slow, intelligent smile. "And we'll have to make sure it stays broken until we can figure out a way to stop this man. I was just working that out with Aguidran." He could not hold back his astonishment any longer. He faced Ghirra earnestly. "GuildMaster, what made you suspicious? About the rock, I mean, and Clausen? How did you *know*?"

Ghirra picked up the rock and weighed it on his palm. "I know nothing. But this rock . . . I see Clauzen wants it very much." He rotated his hand and the chunk of ore flashed lamp-light. He glanced up at Aguidran as if seeking her approval of what he was about to say. "But also *we* need the SisterBread."

"Yes," breathed Liphar, who had been listening with increas-ing confusion and dismay. He recited a line of what his tone suggested would have been a prayer, if the Sawls had prayers.

" 'The Sisters gave to us, ah . . . before the wars,' " Stavros translated roughly, " '. . . their bread, that we might live, ah . . . survive'?" He looked to Ghirra for confirmation. "Is that right? What does it mean? How can a rock be bread? Why do *you* need lithium?"

"That is many questions, 'TavrosIbia," Ghirra replied. He rose from the bench, looking pensive. "Suzhannah would not say about this."

"You asked her?"

"Yes." Ghirra was studying him again.

Susannah's still determined not to get involved, is that it? he wondered regretfully. *Then I was right to keep all this from her.*

"She has orders not to talk about it," he lied.

"Ah. And you do not?"

"I do." Stavros shrugged. "We all do, but . . ." The truth was, no one had thought such orders were necessary. He felt the sudden pressure of time. He wondered how long he would be able to keep his campaign against CONPLEX a secret and what Clausen would do to him if he found out. "Look, GuildMaster . . . Ghirra . . . you don't have to tell me why you need the lithium if it's knowledge you don't trust me with. It's enough for me to know that you need it, and that there's more at stake than I even suspected."

"Why only you?" Ghirra asked softly.

"What?"

"Why only you know this must not be?"

"Not only me, Ghirra. Megan has seen this happen on other worlds. She was set against Clausen and his company from the beginning. And we can bring some of the others around in time. But meanwhile . . ." His urgency pushed him onward, past all the answers he wanted, all the questions he was dying to ask. "If you will hear me out, Megan and I have a plan. . . ."

34

"Taylor, I'll put you in a walking cast when you're damn good and ready for one, and not before! Do you want to limp like Quasimodo for the rest of your life?"

"Hell, no." Danforth fretted while Susannah changed the dressings on his wounds. A bowl of herbal infusion steeped fragrantly beside the pallet, its thin curl of steam rising into the shaft of sunlight that fell across his bound and splinted legs. "All these locals running around doing who knows what to me . . . and *you*! At least you're done with the tubes and wires!" he grumped.

"You have 'these locals' to thank for being *compos mentis* so quickly," Susannah returned.

"And I'm grateful, so get me the hell out of here!"

Susannah sat back warningly, then began to pack her bandaging supplies away in a woven rush basket. Danforth's big hands grabbed for hers and held them tightly. "Susannah, for the love of god, I really am grateful but I'm going nuts up here in this stone hole! I feel like I've died!"

"You nearly did," she reminded him.

"Granted, but I'm alive now and I need to get *out* of here!"

Susannah laughed gently. "Taylor, we did miss you around here. Our impatience quotient has foundered drastically while you were away."

He pushed her hands away from him. "Okay. Go ahead. Torture me. Sabotage my bloody career!" He struggled against the nest of sacking that supported his back. "CRI's down, I can't read shit in this lousy light, I haven't the vaguest idea what's going on outside. . . !" He tried to sit up, gasped and eased himself down, tight with agony. "Whew."

"Tay. Please. In addition to breaking both legs, you nearly lost a lung."

Danforth clamped his eyes shut in frustration and lay quiet for a while as Susannah continued packing. "He does have fine hands, that healer man," he said finally.

"I know."

Danforth sighed. "So how long, do you think?"

Susannah tried to sound encouraging. "You'll have to stay on your back for a good while yet, but I don't think you need twenty-four-hour care now that the fever and infections are gone. I'll speak to Ghirra about getting you moved out of here. Question is, where?"

"I've got to be outside," he insisted weakly.

"Well, Weng's reestablished base camp under the Lander. I don't know how she'd feel about you being around to distract Ronnie into playing nursemaid." She patted his hand and gave his dark cheek a motherly stroke. "But I'll see what I can do." She rose, but he held her hand to stay her.

"Is it still clear out there? No clouds?"

She sat down again, smoothing the blanket with her free hand. "Some clouds, coming and going." She did not want to tell him the exact nature of the clouds' coming and going, for fear he would demand to be taken outside immediately.

"Ronnie told me there'd been some reports of thunderstorms?"

"Thunder, very far away across the plain. No storms."

"Yet." His breathing slowed as he slipped at last toward sleep. "You know, I had a lot of think time out there before the fever got me. Decided I've got to hit the problem of this place from a whole new angle. *Tabula rasa*."

"I know what you mean," she agreed truthfully.

"Patterns. Gotta look for existing patterns. Stop worrying about what it *should* be. There's something missing from the model, some process, maybe unique, that I should have been looking for instead of trying to force it all into some familiar shape."

"Ummmh." Susannah eased her hand free as his hold relaxed. She stood, gathering up the bowl and dirtied dressings.

"Susannah?" Danforth murmured sleepily. "You happen to notice what direction the wind was coming from?"

She smiled at the big man lying as quiescent as a child. "No, Tay, I didn't. Around here, you'd best ask a ranger or a priest for that kind of information."

And this unanswerable seemed at last to drag him into sleep.

As Susannah headed for the hotroom with her bowl and basket, Weng called from the narrow arched entry to Ghirra's lab. "Something to show you, when you get a minute, Dr. James."

"Be right with you, Commander."

She found little Dwingen in the hotroom and put the sterilization of her equipment into his charge. She went back to the lab, where Weng stood in the middle of the floor, gazing up at the crowded bookshelves and stroking her chin as if she were a bearded old man.

Susannah slumped into Ghirra's padded chair with a dramatic sigh. "Well, Emil was right about the kind of invalid Tay's going to be. Can you deal with him down at the Lander, do you think? He can't stand being left alone with nothing to occupy him."

"Bring him down, by all means, if he's well enough," Weng murmured abstractedly.

Susannah decided that Weng was always at her most amenable when most of her brain was off in the higher reaches of contemplation. "Have you had a chance to think about our request to go with the trade caravan, Commander?"

Weng pointed up at the rows of dark volumes. "Do you have any idea what's in all these books?"

"Yes. Those are the Birth Records."

"Ah. Every birth is written down, then?"

"According to Ghirra, yes. And I've seen Xifa entering new births. It's practically the first thing she does as soon as she's sure the mother and child are delivered safely. It's not exactly eugenics but they are very careful to avoid inbreeding."

"Yes, I recall Dr. Levy mentioning that." Weng's black eyes narrowed. "I wonder how far back these records go."

"Again, according to Ghirra, all the way."

"All the way to what?"

"Well, the beginning of their recorded history, I guess."

"That could be a very long time, Dr. James. Tyril's Weaver-Guild records barely scratch the surface at twelve hundred earthyears, by my rough calculation."

Susannah was ashamed to admit she had not given the matter serious thought. "Twelve hundred . . . ?"

Weng had returned her attention to the bookshelves. "If we could determine what constituted a generation, we would have only to count backward. Indications are that this is a very old civilization, Dr. James, far older than we at first imagined. And here's a remarkable coincidence for you to ponder.''

She went to the glass-crowded lab counter along the back wall and brought a heavy book to the table. She set it in front of Susannah, then laid some sheets of her own notes beside it. Pointing at the bound-in ancient diagram in the book, she said, ''When I first saw this, something about it struck me as familiar, though it isn't anything I have seen before, of course. But the thought kept coming back to me, and I did a few scribbles, and finally it came to me: it's partly grouped in eights, you see? Twos and sixes. And notice this.'' She turned the old book sideways. ''Do you see?''

Susannah shook her head, mystified.

Patiently, Weng sifted through her own notes, extracted a sheet and laid it on top of the stack. ''Is this familiar to you?''

''Of course. That's a periodic table.''

''Excellent. Now if you remove this block containing the rare earths from the middle and place them down here, as is sometimes done . . .''

Susannah reconstructed the table in her mind's eye. ''Oh, my goodness.''

Weng gave her best Cheshire Cat smile. ''It was the eights that got me. You know that the rules of atomic structure dictate a return to a similarly structured atom every eight elements. And . . .'' She let a fingertip glide reverently down the ancient scrap of page. ''If we consider the elemental family structures to be oriented this way, the space that has been left here could be a diagrammatic pause for the transition metals, etc., starting with number twenty-one, and so on. This peculiarity here could analogue the horns that hydrogen and helium create in our own table.

''But, Dr. James, most remarkable of all: remember that this restructuring of our own periodic table still contains the full range of noble gases, which in the history of our science were not discovered until after the advent of absorption-line spectroscopy and the analysis of stellar spectra.

''Now, the question I must immediately put to our Master Healer is this: if this aged Sawlish diagram does indeed represent the families of the elements, when and through what method was it assembled? Dr. James, it preserves the same number of slots as our most modern table, *plus a few more*!''

Susannah allowed the skepticism which she had always considered healthy to slow her astonishment. ''Spectroscopy and

periodic tables require a more precise grasp of atomic theory
than I would have expected here, even of Ghirra."

"Have you ever asked?"

"Well, no, but . . . Commander, are you sure about this?"

"Not in the least, but the coincidence is seductive, is it not?"
Weng stood back, arms folded and black eyes glittering. Susannah could not recall ever having seen her so visibly excited.
"Consider the implications, Dr. James! The most recent addi-
tions to our own table are no longer found in nature. They had to
be manufactured for proof of their existence."

"Manufactured?" Susannah shook her head with an uncomfortable smile. "Sorry, Commander, you just ran past my credibility limit. Try it out on Taylor—he's ripe for anything, I
think."

"You worry for my sanity, Doctor?" said Weng dryly, her
quiet intensity undimmed.

"And mine as well. I have enough trouble fighting off the
various local implications of the paranormal, between the
seemingly sentient weather and Ghirra's, shall we say, less
traditional methods of healing. Now you're going to have me
thinking my wild ideas about genetically engineered plants and
animals might have some basis in possibility."

"Is there anything that doesn't, Dr. James?"

Susannah laughed. "Mind games, Commander. Shame on
you."

Weng's raised eyebrow was like a faint shrug of disappointment. "Well, then, I shall keep my games to myself, until
further proof presents itself. And that, Dr. James, brings me to
your request. Go with the caravan, by all means. Observe carefully. Discover everything you can."

"For the sake of *my* sanity, Commander?"

Weng said nothing, only smiled again, so privately amused
that Susannah would have been but mildly surprised if the Old
Lady did fade away to leave nothing but her smile behind.

35

The big yellow infirmary wagon gave shade enough for ten. As little Dwingen and another Physicians' apprentice, Phea, looked on amazed, Susannah hauled pillows and blankets and wicker boxes out of the back for the third time, in preparation for packing it all back in some new way that would allow everything to fit.

"A Sawlian periodic table?" murmured Megan dubiously from her seat beside the rear wheel. She polished her little field compass on her shirt, opened it to watch the needle maintain its sure hold on Fiixian north, pointing towards the Vallegar. Hemmed in by the tall canopied wagons and the bustle of people and hakra carts, she could not see the mountains or the cloud bank slouching about their summits like a street gang massing for a riot. The sky above the white cliffs remained unclouded turquoise.

"And a very up-to-date one, at that," Susannah replied. "Well, she admitted it was a wild shot, but she was so entranced by the idea, she said yes to the caravan without a fuss."

"But not without her reasons," Megan advised. "Did she mention keeping an eye out for anything in particular?"

"Discover anything you can, she said." Greedily, Susannah considered the empty field cot, a hekker-skin stretcher supported by a folding wooden frame. It was lashed unfolded along one side of the wagon, taking up a great deal of room, but the first of Ghirra's list of instructions had been to reserve sufficient space for the transport of serious injuries. Dwingen and Phea fidgeted silently in the sun, waiting for her to require their assistance. Though she was Dwingen's senior, Phea, a short and solid child, was equally as wide-eyed. "I'll tell you the first thing I intend to discover," Susannah added, "and that's how to mend this awkwardness with Ghirra over Emil's rocks. What sort of taboo do you think we stumbled on there?''

Megan shrugged, kept an uncharacteristic silence, then said, as a long and subtle thunder roll tumbled over the plain, ''You know, this word 'arrah' that we've been blithely using to denote 'weather' doesn't really mean that. It means 'struggle.' There is no word for just plain weather, or climate or anything neutral.''

Susannah nodded distractedly, clutching a basket full of linen. ''About the first thing we learned was that the Sawls don't think of climate as a natural phenomenon.''

''I know, but have you really thought about what effect that has on them, seeing themselves as pawns in the midst of an eternally ongoing war? There's nothing they can do to end it, as they see it, not good works or prayer or sacrifice, none of the traditional offerings.'' Megan stretched neck and torso ostrichlike to listen without rising as the thunder died into the clatter and uproar of the packing and loading. ''Tyril assured me quite calmly the other day that the arrah would end when the 'darkness' lifted from the Sisters' eyes, and until then, the best the Sawls can do is try to keep one Sister from winning. What 'darkness'? says I. *The* darkness, she replies, as if I had asked a Baptist, what Satan?''

Susannah put down the linens and dragged her own medikit out from between the legs of the lashed-in cot. ''There's not much talk of the Goddesses up in Physicians'.''

''Probably because they're said to have no interest in the fate of the individual. Their only power over life and death is through the havoc they wreak with the climate.'' Megan blotted her cheeks and neck with a moist square of cloth. ''Speaking of which . . . it's going to be hot as blazes out on the plain.''

''Oh yes.'' Grunting, Susannah yanked at a heavy wooden box until Dwingen could bear it no longer and leaped in to grab a corner. Phea followed eagerly, and Susannah left them to struggle the box into the dust while she concentrated on the problem of the wagon. It had looked gigantic when empty, and cheerful enough in its fresh yellow paint to remind her of a circus wagon. It was long and narrow, very like an old Conestoga in construction but for its hard bentwood canopy and its lack of metal underpinnings. It was larger than any of the other guild wagons but for the FoodGuild's twenty red-and-blue giants. Like those, it had been winched down from the Caves in three pieces, and would require double teams of hjalk to haul it when fully loaded.

If I can ever get it fully loaded. . . .

She was beginning to despair, feeling sweaty and dust-coated, when Phea touched her arm. Politely, the apprentice pointed under the big wagon, which rode high off the ground to make room for an ingenious suspension system made of leather and oiled hardwood. Susannah looked, then groaned softly. Above the rear axle was a large built-in shelf with several tough woven straps hanging loose. Earlier, against Dwingen's meekly proffered advice, she had buried three odd-sized wooden boxes at the bottom of the load. They contained the store of dried herbs that Master Herbalist Ard was sending both for use and trade, and Susannah had wanted to be sure they were safely stowed. Suddenly it was obvious that the boxes had been built specifically to fit on the secure but easily accessed shelf in the undercarriage.

Ghirra had not demurred when she offered to oversee the packing, even though Xifa and Ampiar were in charge of supplying the guild for the trip. *Pushy offworlder that I am . . . is this another of our Master Healer's subtle lessons?*

But Susannah had made the offer only to please him, trying to win back the confidence which had been so clearly eroded by the issue of the rocks. She supposed that point had been reached in the expedition's relations with the Sawls when the initial good will of both sides had been exhausted and their cultural differences began to appear as obstacles rather than novelties. She was sure that with a little extra diplomatic effort, the difficulties could be worked through, but she felt sad and isolated nonetheless, and irritated with herself for botching the job of loading the wagon.

She was somewhat relieved to notice that behind a nearby wagon, an aging potter was suffering a similiar dilemma with his loading. He, however, had the good humor to offer a wager to the apprentices assisting him. Susannah overheard him swear jovially that a spot would be found for every last bowl and tankard. One eager girl eyed the stack of straw-wrapped pots waiting to be packed and accepted the bet with a cunning grin.

Susannah sighed and set Phea and Dwingen once again to digging out the herb boxes. Megan chuckled hugely, looped the braided lanyard of her compass around her neck and rose. Thunder kettledrummed across the plain, and the guildsmen at the Potters' wagon stopped their work to glance over their shoulders at the sky.

"I suppose it's possible," said Susannah, "that Aguidran'll get the whole population packed up and still have to call it off at the last minute.'' She searched for clouds overhead and found none.

"That's what Ashimmel's pushing for," Megan agreed. "Look at her down there with TiNiamar, like a fly buzzing in his ear, poor old guy. She's been at him for hours.''

Between the lines of half-loaded wagons, Susannah could see the Master Priest pacing toward them in the hot sun beside the elderly Master of the FoodGuild. One hand solicitously supported his elbow, though the old man's step was agile. The other gestured sharply in the direction of the cloud-shrouded Vallegar. TiNiamar's round face was prune-dark and wrinkled with worry. His head inclined as if unwillingly to Ashimmel's exhortations.

"She figures as goes the FoodGuild, so goes the rest of the Kethed," Megan continued. "If she can get him scared enough that Valla might sneak by Lagri's defenses with a storm that'll devastate the crop, she'll swing him to her side. She's already won over the Papermakers and Keth-Toph.''

Susannah frowned lightly. "Neither of whom really need the trading in Ogo Dul. Their products are both made and consumed at home.''

"Precisely.''

Susannah noticed how carefully the guildsmen working at their wagons observed the pair, gathering together when they had passed by to murmur and shake their heads. The old potter sent one of his apprentices scrambling to the top of his wagon's arched canopy, where she perched as a lookout to report on the movements of the cloud bank now barely visible across the plain. Among a group of smaller wagons farther along the lines, families halted their packing as the two guild masters approached, only to take it up again as soon as they had passed.

Beyond the cluster of family wagons, to one side of the great stone stairs, a few brightly colored festival pavilions remained erect, nestled against the rock of the cliff. As Ashimmel and TiNiamar turned to pace back down the line, they interrupted their ambulatory conference to nod courteously to Weng, who was observing the commotion of wagons and goods from the canopies' filtered shade. Weng returned their greeting, then resumed her own intense conversation with a person beside her wearing clean ship's whites, whose face was in shadow, back to the brilliant sun. Judging from the incline of her head, Weng was engaged in being gracious.

Susannah squinted into the shadow. "Well, I'll . . . Meg!'' She pointed. "Look who's back in uniform!''

Megan looked, then chortled with gentle irony. "He's trying to convince her that going to Ogo Dul is more vital to his official mission than fixing the comlink."

Susannah stared. The Sawl clothing he had assumed so many weeks ago had obscured the shape of his body. His back was to her, the close-fit Terran shirt clinging damply to his skin. His dark hair was wet, slicked back behind his ears, clipped closer to regulation length but raggedly, as if without benefit of a mirror. Susannah could not help but notice the trim white triangle formed between shoulder and hip. She sucked her lip speculatively.

The potter's apprentice atop her guild wagon called down a report that was followed immediately by a dull crack of thunder, loud enough and lengthy enough to perceptibly still the hubbub of packing and loading as every Sawl on the rock flats glanced over his or her shoulder, shuddered and went back to work with newly frantic energy.

"Pretty loud, that one," Megan commented.

Susannah pulled herself away from her rediscovery of the ship's linguist to renew her own assault on the infirmary wagon. She shoved at a stack of boxes next to the field cot. The pile of blankets on top cascaded onto her head. Dwingen succumbed to a fit of giggles which Phea tried unsuccessfully to discourage.

"The Sawls call it Valla's Ice," Megan continued.

Unaccountably annoyed, Susannah shoved a tangled heap of blankets into Megan's arms. "Fold these, will you? Make them small." She made a gesture of surrender to the two apprentices and stood aside while they willingly jumped in to finish the packing themselves.

"The thunder, I mean." Megan sat on a crate, pulling a blanket onto her lap. "Because it sounds like an avalanche."

"Did you mention spectral little Dutchmen with giant bowling balls?" Susannah asked, while Stavros's sun-bright image teased at her mind's eye.

Megan made a slow fold and smoothed it flat as if to press the blanket into miniature. "You don't trade mythologies with these folk—they're liable to take you literally. They'd end up sure our thunder's made differently from their thunder."

"Perhaps it is." Susannah smiled. "So you've given up on holding out for metaphor versus belief?"

Megan nodded glumly. "Stav is right, much as I hate to admit it. The Sawls believe their goddesses are real. Actual physical beings."

Susannah smiled again. "Perhaps they are."

The anthropologist made a wry face. "Wouldn't that just show us all."

They heard another profundo rumble that could have been a legion of cartwheels groaning across the stone terrace. This time work came to a true halt. Aguidran appeared, flanked by her two most senior guildsmen, strolling down the line of wagons as if nothing more in the world were on her mind than the pleasant sunny day and the proper ordering of the wagons for the trek. The Master Ranger offered a somber nod in response to Megan's grin of commiseration. She gave the inside of the yellow wagon a cursory inspection, growled briefly at Phea and Dwingen and continued on her way, picking up speed so that she and her aides contrived to reach the bottom of the cliff stairs just as several elder craftsmen from the allied guilds of Weavers, Leatherworkers and Basketry openly confronted a retinue of priests descending from the cave mouths to broadcast their latest dire warnings. Debate flared into argument instantly, but was snuffed almost as instantly by the Master Ranger's barked advice to the guildsmen that their wagons needed attending to if the caravan was to depart on schedule. Ashimmel stalked out of the press of wagons, having deserted TiNiamar the moment raised voices were heard, only to find the argument dispersed before she could make use of it. The Ranger and the Priest flicked dismissive glances at one another and went off in opposite directions. As if on cue, an entire phalanx of rangers gathered to work up and down the long lines of carts and wagons, checking the loads, tugging at ropes and harness, kneeling to inspect wheels and axles, the mountings of running lanterns and water supplies.

"And there you see the traditional division of Church and State," muttered Megan, turning back to her lapful of blankets. "Though not your traditional spiritual versus temporal, since both priest and craftsman in this society consider their bailiwicks to be totally temporal, here and now."

"Hadn't you gotten the impression they had that division nicely worked out?" said Susannah, who had watched the argument with some surprise.

Megan shook her head. "Recently they've begun to air their differences in public. The cracks always show most during times of crisis."

Under the canopies, Stavros finished his discussion with Weng and stepped out into the sunlight. The flash of white caught Susannah's eye. She studied him as he walked in her direction, his attention drawn aside to the scattered tendrils of debate drifting through the crowd at the bottom of the stairs. He listened as he walked, frowning slightly as if the incident were an inconvenient intrusion on some other train of thought. His step was purposeful but oddly, for Stavros, unhurried. It seemed to Susannah that he carried himself with a taut confidence that she had not seen in him before. The energy in him was collected, for once not spinning off like sparks from a flywheel.

When he glanced around to find her watching him, his impulse toward a smile was damped immediately by awkwardness as he retreated behind his usual misunderstood whiz-kid glower. He allowed her a nod and dropped his eyes as he approached.

"It's all fixed with the Commander," he announced quietly to Megan.

"At what price?" she returned, still folding blankets.

Absurdly, Susannah felt rejected. In the space of a second, the man had become a boy again.

Did I do that? she wondered.

"She wants Danforth's terminal moved back down under the Lander," he replied with only mild disgust. "He wants to be out where he can keep his eyes on the skies, since he hasn't got CRI to do it for him."

Megan smirked. "Never trust a weatherman who refuses to look out the window."

"Taylor is not a weatherman," returned Susannah, surprised at how defensive she sounded.

Megan's smile was sly. "Closest thing we have at the moment, next to Ashimmel and her cronies." She turned back to Stavros. "Will that leave you the equipment you need?"

"All stowed away," he replied with studied casualness. "It's not much, but I'll manage."

"You're taking a terminal along with the caravan?" Susannah asked, mostly to force entry into a conversation that did not seem to want to include her. She thought he looked momentarily furtive.

"No, well, the translator. I'll need power packs for the translator."

Megan glanced from one to the other, tight-lipped, about to say something, deciding finally on silence. She bent her head and reached for the last blanket. Stavros stood with his hands on his hips, as if uncomfortable to be there but not yet willing to leave.

"Has Clausen stopped yelling yet?" Megan asked eventually.

There's something going on here, Susannah realized. She was missing everything but the innuendo. From her oft-assumed position of neutral observer, she had acquired a nose for the subtler currents of alliance and coalition, rather like a magnetic field detector, but it was not clear yet where the poles were in this particular alignment.

"Clausen doesn't know yet," said Stavros. "He's been too busy fussing with the comlink. I warned Weng that he thinks we should all dump our own jobs to help him, but she agreed that until the Sled's recovered, wagon train is as good a way to explore the planet as any. All thanks to the Commander's dedication to Mission."

Megan finished folding the final blanket. "Any luck with the com?"

Susannah read definite smugness in Stavros's shrug.

"Not so far," he answered, and as his glance flicked toward her and away, she recalled that she had already accused him of purposefully delaying the repair of the comlink. This time she saw defiance in his response rather than guilt. The implication of challenge piqued her.

"So it must have been to encourage the Commander's dedication to Mission that you reported in looking like an Academy recruiting poster," she teased. She took the pile of folded blankets from Megan's knees and stood with them hugged to her chest. For reasons she was not entirely proud of, she let her gaze be frankly appraising. "I believe you even shaved."

She had wanted his attention, and got it. He looked briefly startled. His hand strayed unconsciously to his jaw. "Yah," he admitted with an embarrassed half-grin. "Guess it must have worked, eh?" For a moment, the boy slid away and the man stared out at her with a look as intimate and hungry as a hand slipped between her thighs. Then it was gone, and the boy returned, as he caught himself and backed off, moving away from her, aware of having been discovered. "Gotta find Aguidran," he muttered and stalked off down the line of wagons.

Susannah found herself gazing at the ground, sure that she must be blushing. She turned to the wagon with her armload of blanket and began shoving them into every available crevass.

Megan nodded to herself, then wagged her head. "Susannah, Susannah," she chided. "Why don't you just get into bed with the lad instead of torturing him this way?"

"Oh, Meg . . ."

"Take him or let him go. The boy's in pain."

Susannah resumed the obligatory protest, then stopped herself. "You think so, really?"

"You expect me to believe you never noticed?"

Susannah stowed a final blanket in silence. "Never took it seriously," she said finally. "I mean, he's young and . . . well, I guess I thought he'd be a bit much to handle, being the way he is, and you know, that stuff always gets in the way of the work . . ."

"But?"

"Well, he is rather a pleasure to look at, and . . ."

"And sometimes it's hard, out in the middle of nowhere." Megan's laugh was nostalgic. "That's gotten me in trouble, too, in the past."

"Sometimes you just can't help . . . well, I don't know."

"My, that was coherent."

"I don't know," Susannah repeated. Her shoulders hunched, then relaxed. "Hell, maybe I should."

"Well, if you do," offered Megan, sobering, "don't expect it to be casual with him. Life is not yet a game to Stavros."

Susannah nodded pensively in reply. All her pragmatic instincts told her to avoid this complication.

And yet . . .

And yet, he was there and she was lonely, suffering from the recent chill among the fraternity of physicians. But would it be fair to him?

In the distance, the thunder cracked and built into a rolling boil that finished with a dying basso flourish. The clot of priests at the bottom of the stairs sat in a circle on the dusty rock and began a low-voiced chant.

"I think," said Susannah, "that I'd better give this long and careful thought."

"Don't think about it for too long," Megan advised.

"Why?" Susannah laughed, but Megan's serious eyes stopped her. "Meg, time seems to be the one thing we have plenty of."

Megan nodded as if unconvinced but would not elaborate.

Stavros searched down one line of wagons, then doubled back along another, heading for the stairs. He put Susannah from his mind with an ease that was becoming practiced. The plan and its various unresolved details dominated his consciousness. He was impatient to be on his way to the Sled, committed in action as well as in thought. He wondered if a few light questions to Weng on the subject of extraterrestrial-development legalities would attract her undue attention.

She was gone when he reached the stair bottom. He found a ranger group leader bundling up the poles that had supported the last of the festival pavilions. The canopies themselves lay folded on the rock, ready to be stowed in heavy canvas bags. He chatted with the group leader, a youngish maternal woman, especially cheerful for a ranger, and secured the aid of two guildsmen for the hauling down of Danforth's equipment. He felt better for not having bothered the Master Ranger with minute details. He helped the woman tie up the pole bundles, then stood with her on the bottom step, where the planted terraces were visible over the sea of multicolored wagon tops. The thunder was in retreat for the moment. A haze of damp heat hung over the flooded fields. The ranger pointed across the wide Dop Arek at the cloud bank hugging the Vallegar and spoke to Stavros about Valla's habits of battle strategy and what Lagri might be expected to do in response. She discussed each Sister's arsenal as familiarly as if she had the care of it herself. She described Valla's Water Soldiers to him in precise detail, and allowed that Lagri's counterforce of fire was one of the best defenses but was difficult to manuever on the attack. Stavros was not sure, but he thought he was begining to detect a greater tendency among the rangers than among others to use this battle-related vocabulary when speaking of the Arrah. The priestly vocabulary more often emphasized the formal gaming aspect of the conflict, though it was no less aggressive in its imagery.

On his way up the stairs, he met Ghirra coming down, ahead of four burly Sawls who were stretchering Danforth out into the open air and sunlight. Stavros leaned against the cliff to let the stretcher pass.

"Weng's letting me go," he murmured as the Master Healer paused beside him. Ghirra nodded, careful eyes on his patient. Danforth lay quietly, gazing up at Stavros as the stretcher went by.

"Hello, Ibiá," he said slowly, noting the other's spanking clean whites. "Someone throwing you a party?"

Stavros returned a thin smile. "Your homecoming, Danforth," he called with a ready hostility that left him shamed. The planetologist was painfully thinner, weaker. His handsome ebony face seemed hollowed and a bit haunted. Stavros asked the stretcher bearers to wait and descended the three steps to Danforth's side. "I'm bringing your stuff down now," he offered more gently, refraining from reminding the injured man that it was no thanks to him that there was any equipment left at all.

The two faced each other in a silence made awkward by the acrimony of their last confrontation. Danforth glanced away first.

"Ibiá, I . . ." he began.

Thunder rumbled. Danforth's head swiveled toward the sound. The stretcher bearers cast worried looks up at Ghirra, who gestured them onward.

"Wait!" Danforth exclaimed. "Hold it! Ibiá, get them to stop."

Stavros also looked to Ghirra, who shrugged and nodded, watching with interest as the planetologist searched for the source of the thunder. The bearers unfolded the stretcher legs and set it down atilt across two wide steps.

Danforth struggled against the webbing that held him into the stretcher. "Pull me up here, Ibiá!" he demanded impetuously. "Untie these damn straps! I can't see a thing!"

"You must not move this way," said Ghirra, coming down the steps to calm him.

"I've got to see!" Danforth insisted.

Ghirra bent and loosed the straps that pinned Danforth's chest. He let Stavros draw the big man up so that he leaned against the physician's chest as Ghirra knelt beside the stretcher. Danforth's jaw clenched as they moved him. His knuckles whitened, grasping the sides of the stretcher.

Stavros put his hostility aside as he felt Danforth's weakened muscles bunching against the pain. "Easy, now," he soothed.

"Damn!" Danforth wheezed. "Doesn't get any easier!"

"You try too much," said Ghirra sternly. "You must sleep more to heal."

Danforth let out a breath. "Doc, I got too much to do!" He squinted at the distant Vallegar. The lurking cloud bank had retreated but the thunder remained. "Ibiá, are my eyes going with the rest of my damned body, or is the sky out there clear as a baby's ass?"

"It is now," Stavros affirmed.

"And what's that yellow fuzz all over everything?"

"Vegetation," replied Stavros blandly. "Cultivated on the terraces out there, wild on the plain. A shipweek ago, the ground was waterlogged mud. Now the crops are shoulder-high in the fields. The wild species seem to grow considerably slower," he added, conceiving at the same time the unlikely hope that Susannah had not yet noticed this, which would allow him the opportunity of bringing it to her attention.

But Danforth was new to the phenomenon of near-instant growth. He stared at the fields in wonder. "One shipweek!" he breathed. "Christ!"

"Oh no," the linguist corrected. "Lagri and Valla Ired." He shared a crooked smile with the Master Healer, helped him ease Danforth down again and continued on up the stairs.

Later, he rode the winch pallet loaded with Danforth's equipment. He dropped past the long flights of stairs, clinging to the ropes as the pallet swayed with the speed of its descent. The steps were once again impassable, as the herdsmen led out the dairy cattle. They nosed cautiously out of the cave mouths into the light, blinking, five or six hundred rangy long-haired beasts, crowding along in ragged double file. Their hornless heads were lowered, intent on the steps. They needed no encouragement to stick close to the cliff side of the stair. At the bottom, a group of herdsmen urged the leaders off the last wide steps where they wanted to halt for a leisurely look around. Apprentices yelled and shoved at their flanks to hustle them off along the line of wagons to join their larger cousins, the hjalk, in the muddy flat at the far end of the rock terrace.

Stavros clucked at the hekkers sympathetically as he slipped past them, clinging to the winch ropes. The herd was part of his cover. Traditionally, they accompanied the caravan for the first two throws across the Dop Arek, following a more southern route than would lead straight to Ogo Dul, so that in the middle of the third throw, the herd could be turned aside and driven up into the foothills of the eastern mountains, the Talche, to graze those richer pastures until the caravan collected them on its return trip.

This time, in the rest period before that third throw, while the caravan lay camped and, he hoped, sleeping soundly, the plan was for Stavros to vanish with Liphar into those same hills, from there to make their way in secret through the Talche to the site of the disabled Sled. It would take longer to reach the Sled this way, but it provided the advantage of surprise and a substantial head start. Only after the dairy herd was settled in their new pastures would Aguidran return a small number of her rangers to the Caves to help Clausen haul the Sled in for repairs.

The winch bucked, swung precipitously toward the cliff, but slowed and swung back short of impact. Stavros barely noticed, preoccupied with his plan. It sounded viable as far as it went. It was what would happen after he'd salvaged the antenna that was most in question. He was not schooled in law or lawyer's rhetoric, yet he would be on his own when he reestablished contact with CRI. Megan had insisted that she would be a physical burden to him, that to go underground as he must would require being able to move fast on the spur of the moment. She would go to Ogo Dul and return to remain as his mole in the enemy camp. He must do the research himself without benefit of her long experience in such matters. He must patch together the skeleton of an argument convincing enough to lure her people's advocate into taking the case. Finally, he must fox CRI into sending an FTL drone to Earth in secret with his message. From there, they could only hope that the lawyer would be won over enough to begin proceedings immediately, so that when Clausen did file his claim (Stavros knew he could not hold off that inevitability forever), he would run smack into an already full-blown court case.

As Stavros played through his various alternate scenarios for the hundredth time, the pallet touched ground with a gentle shudder. A borrowed hakra two-cart awaited him, along with his volunteer help, two young ranger apprentices whom he did not know. He wondered whose household goods now lay in the dust until the return of their conveyance. The apprentices helped load the equipment into the cart, then set off ahead of the shaggy little hakra to guide it along the road through the fields to the Lander.

Stavros followed, with a backward glance at the continuing pandemonium of packing. While the last of the hekkers started their ungraceful clatter down the stairs, the bulk of the herd still milled about among the wagons, kicking up dust clouds and resisting the best efforts of the herdsmen to get them moving toward the mud flat. The big hjalk were being led up to be strapped in their traces, team after team of them, pushing a path through the dust and lowing hekkers and the swarms of little hakra carts. The winches rose and fell with last-minute bundles of goods to be made room for in already overstuffed wagons. Children darted back and forth among the beasts and vehicles with armloads of clothing and utensils.

Along the edge of the rock flat, their bright red and blue reflecting in the watery mirrors of the nearby terraces, the twenty FoodGuild wagons waited in a trim impressive line, fully packed and ready. TiNiamar huddled with Aguidran and his senior guildsmen at the head of the line. At the back of the rear wagon, two older women wearing the guild's red and blue stripes on their tunics lounged against the big wheels, playing stones.

Stavros held back at the top of the path and let the ranger apprentices go ahead with the cart. He stood in the still heat, tugging at his damp shirt, already anxious for a chance to shed the close Terran clothing.

Taking the entire population to market! he reflected. There were carts and wagons as far as his eye could see, at least a hundred large hjalk-drawn wagons of various sizes, and six or seven times that number of smaller hakra carts and wagons, nearly five thousand men, women and children on the move together. *What a glorious madness!* If he had been able to observe this process beforehand, the evacuation of the Lander might have seemed merely efficient instead of miraculous.

In his heart, he saluted the ambitious spirit of the venture, then squared his shoulders mentally to face the base camp at the Lander, where he had not set foot since before the storm.

Ocher dust billowed from under the cartwheels ahead as the already drying road dipped down through the plantings. In the mirrored fields, sheaths of fernlike fronds were thickening into stout fleshy clusters. Behind the terrace earthworks, the tall yellow stalks sank muscular roots into mud topped by several inches of warming water. Broad furry leaves shaded the path where it narrowed, the lower foliage shading from yellow to amber and orange between bright lemon-colored veins. Food-Guildsmen hurried barefoot between the rows, peering into the fat leaf whorls, scattering dried manure from sacks slung across their chests.

The road narrowed again at the turnoff to the Lander site. The wheels of the hakra cart just fitted between the earthworks that hemmed in the path on either side. Stavros brushed leaf stalks aside as he passed, and glanced up through the foliage to see the Lander towering above him. He felt like a runaway, caught and forced to return to a home he no longer wished to claim.

The Lander was now resting in a barren circular clearing, surrounded by a velvet yellow wall of vegetation. The mangled high-gain dish lay between two of the landing struts, five meters of mud-splashed metal, half in, half out of the cooling shade of the underbelly. Stavros gave it a sidelong casual inspection, as if it were old news, though this was as close to it as he had been since the Engineers had found it and hauled it in. Sections of its golden mesh and several of its umbrella ribs had been ripped away during its tumble in the flood. Other ribs had been bent like hairpins, their mesh interstices shredded and hanging loose like dead skin.

McPherson glanced up at the rattle of cartwheels and freed one hand from the rib she was straightening, long enough to wave. Clausen crouched in the sun near the center of the dish, in a pie slice between two barren ribs, contemplating the stump of the sheared-off central post, all that remained of the receiver mounting. His expression was unreadable behind his mirrored sunglasses as he watched Stavros approach.

Stavros was disproportionately relieved to see the lean profile of the Master Healer seated beside Danforth in the shadowed Underbelly. A small section of the space had been once more partitioned into private quarters, using crates and storage lockers brought back down from the Caves. But Danforth's bed had been set up beside the third landing strut, where he could watch the sky protected from the ferocious sun. An arrangement of blankets and bundled tarps allowed him to sit upright, propped against the trusswork of the strut.

Stavros halted the ranger apprentices beside the cart and eased into the shadow. Table-sized crates were pulled up around the bed, already littered with pictures and data sheets. Danforth seemed diminished, his dark skin almost pale against the thick stack of tarps, but he was busily sorting the pile of photos nearest him into several smaller piles laid out around him on the bed. Weng sat to one side, taking careful notes as Danforth read off time and location from the bottom of each photo. Stavros noted that the Master Healer, seated silently at Danforth's shoulder, held a photo in his hands which he studied with a deeply thoughtful intensity. Two fingers rubbed wonderingly at a corner of the glossy plastic.

"The mass cloud movement would seem to be diagonal," Danforth was muttering as Stavros approached. He tipped one photo at an oblique angle, then grabbed up a second and a third to match them side by side until he had a handful like a fan of cards. "Northeast to southwest? Bearing no relation to the planet's rotational poles . . . okay . . . well . . ." He nodded to Weng. "Put a flag on Sequence L-Beta 374-29 through 34."

He tossed the photos aside to greet the arrival of his equipment with a mixture of impatience and relief. Weng looked merely relieved. She unobtrusively dropped her hand to flex out an attack of writer's cramp, and Stavros decided that playing secretary to her second-in-command, no matter how much she favored him or the work he had come to do, was not exactly her idea of the first order of the Captaincy. But her usual groundside pastime did require a computer. Stavros was sorry that his purpose required her to remain bereft of her music for a while longer, but meanwhile, Weng apparently welcomed any task that put idle time to good use.

"Over here, over here," Danforth urged as Stavros signaled the cart in to unload. Grimacing from the sudden movement, Danforth gestured to the crates nearest his bedside. "Ibiá, pull those over closer. Lay that stuff out on the ground—no, wait, I need that pile! Stick it over here."

Weng rose and silently stood aside. Ghirra watched without a change in his pensive gaze.

"He's already back in stride, I see," Stavros murmured to Weng as he moved in to set up the terminal. Guiding the ranger apprentices in quiet Sawlish, he felt like the local repairman from the native quarter called in to fix the colonists' holoset.

"At last! A toy to quiet our restless invalid!" Clausen strolled in out of the sun and stood with his hands in his pockets, an avuncular grin curling beneath his mirrored lenses. Stavros watched Ghirra withdraw further into himself, and turned his own back as if absorbed by the equipment.

"No fresh data until we get CRI up again," Clausen continued. "A shame really, but then there's plenty of backlog for you to clear up, eh?" He leaned against the landing strut at Danforth's side and said, *sotto voce*, "Six weeks of numbers you read and stored away, Tay?"

"It was all coming in too damned fast," Danforth admitted peevishly. "And it kept changing on me. Without CRI, I can't run the high-resolution models, but even with this little terminal, I can do some tinkering with the input data on simpler models, see what it takes to get them to match the weather patterns we're actually observing. That should tell me whether I'm right about there being a whole term missing from the big model." He looked for support to Weng. "Our mystery factor."

Weng nodded and Clausen clucked sympathetically, but his silvered eyes focused on Stavros's unresponsive back like a homing weapon. "Don't you feel honored, Tay, that our Ship's Linguist has taken time from his very vital work to do you this favor?"

Stavros ignored him. Danforth, for his own reasons and to Stavros's surprise, let the opportunity for a dig go by. Clausen stretched his grin into a jovial smile and winked at Weng.

"This's more time than he's given so far to fixing the comlink, am I right, Commander?"

"I was made Com Officer by default," Stavros reminded him quietly as he straightened to lift the monitor into place. "I didn't volunteer for the job." He made an elaborate business of adjusting the screen to Danforth's convenience, testing the planetologist's unusual silence. Danforth's eyes resting on him were carefully neutral. Stavros realized he could no longer deal with Clausen and Danforth as a single entity. The relationship had shifted during their long night out in the storm. Stavros allowed Danforth a moment of honest if unexpressed empathy. Two weeks in the dark with Clausen had probably been no picnic, all injuries and fever aside.

"Tut, tut," admonished the prospector cheerily. "Was I complaining? I need something to keep busy with myself until I can get back to the Sled. . . . By the way, Stav, my boy, I hear you're joining the exodus, and quite an exodus it is, I must say."

Here it comes, thought Stavros, preparing his arguments for the omni-precedence of Mission.

"Mr. Ibiá asked my permission and I gave it," Weng interceded coolly. "After all, Mr. Clausen, you are the person most experienced with the electronics of the comlink. It seemed most efficient to let Mr. Ibiá get on with his real work."

Clausen nodded, all patient understanding. "Whatever you think is right, and of course I'm flattered. But there was also the matter of securing help to recover the Sled."

"I believe Mr. Ibiá has managed to arrange that," Weng replied.

Stavros fitted the last jack and flipped the switch on the battery pack. His rough-cut hair was drying and falling in his face. He shoved it back, making it seem a gesture of impatience rather than nerves. "I did the best I could for you with Aguidran, Emil," he began earnestly, thinking how second nature the dissembling had already become. Astonishingly, Ghirra chose this moment to rise and wander around to Clausen's side of the landing strut, coming up beside him to play the responsible healer who insisted on checking the progress of all of his patients' wounds. Only the seriousness of the situation kept Stavros from laughter.

"I got her to agree to send back the extra contingent of rangers assigned to the dairy herd, once the herdsmen have them settled in the summer pastures. That should be as many as a dozen rangers, and they should be able to make it back within, oh, four shipsdays after the caravan leaves, which will be very soon now, within the day."

Clausen did some fast calculating, distracted as he was by Ghirra's gentle but insistent ministrations. "By which time, it will be dusk again."

"Late afternoon," Stavros conceded. "You'll make it out to the Sled by nightfall easily enough, maybe even get it ready to be hauled out. The night will slow down your return, but the rangers work well in the dark, and you can be doing some of your repairs along the way. As long as the weather holds, you should be okay."

The mirrored lenses stared at him a moment as Clausen shook off Ghirra's hand with a small sharp jerk. Stavros heard a soft mirthless chuckle. At first, he couldn't imagine who it had come from.

Danforth?

Then the prospector laughed also, and pulled off his sunglasses to rub his eyes with apparently amused exasperation. "Well, my boy, in that case I shall have to feel encouraged, shan't I?" He turned the friendliest of smiles on Ghirra, who waited like a stone at his side. "Are you done with me, honored doctor? I'm quite all right, as you can see, and I really must get back to work." Ghirra stood aside, and Clausen nodded a cheery adieu to them all, then strolled back into the sun.

Stavros hoped his gratitude to the Master Healer was clear in the look he gave him.

Weng stirred. "While you have a moment, GuildMaster . . ." She drew Ghirra away to her worktable deeper in the Underbelly. Stavros sent his apprentice helpers on their way to return the borrowed cart, then fussed a bit more with the equipment setup, conscious of Danforth's steady quiet attention.

"Ibiá," said the planetologist at last. "I've got one bit of advice for you out there."

Stavros met his glance and caught the disappearing remnant of a bitter smile.

"Take a hat," Danforth advised. "The hardest one you can find."

"Mr. Ibiá, perhaps you could be of some help."

Stavros turned aside on his way through the shaded Underbelly to join Weng and Ghirra at her crate-top workplace. She had hemmed her space in with tall storage lockers, creating a three-sided cubicle whose cramped dimensions and molded plastic walls recalled a shipboard cabin. The single folding camp chair faced into the cubicle, into the plastic walls, presenting a stubborn back to the hot sun and the dust and the velvet yellow foliage beyond the Lander's shadow.

Ghirra hovered at the cubicle opening, uncommitted to entering the angular plastic space. For the first time removed from his own frame of reference and set against this aggressively Terran background, he seemed less substantial, thinner, browner, smaller, yet so much richer and more complicated. Stavros sensed his entire data set for the Master Healer reordering yet again. He noted a certain fragility of expression in Ghirra's long fine-boned face, visible only when the golden smile had been put away. He marked it for a sign of deep-set doubt, and longed to know the precise nature of the Master Healer's personal dilemma.

The doubt rose closer to Ghirra's surface as he attended politely to Weng's inquiries. He held a sheet of limp Terran paper in his hand, delicately, as if he would prefer to be without it but had no wish to offend the alien Commander.

"Mr. Ibiá," began Weng brightly as Stavros approached. "I have asked the GuildMaster if he would explain in his own language what this is." She handed Stavros another piece of paper. A neatly drawn but mysterious diagram dominated the page, joined columns filled with oddly distorted Sawlish characters. Jottings in Weng's hand filled the borders of the sheet. "From his own library," she added. Weng was clearly excited.

Stavros looked to Ghirra.

"I cannot," said Ghirra quietly.

"Guild lore?" guessed Stavros. "Not to be revealed?"

Ghirra shook his head, a mixed gesture of pride and apology. "Physicians' keeps no secret. I cannot because I do not know it. It is from the very old books."

Stavros looked back to Weng. She had obviously received this answer already.

"GuildMaster, if you will?" She gently plucked the other paper from Ghirra's fingers and passed it to Stavros for his perusal. Stavros gave it a grunt of puzzled recognition.

"Periodic table?"

"Correct. Ours. Can you explain it to our Master Healer?"

Stavros tried, lacking a major part of the appropriate vocabulary. Ghirra listened impassively, looking very like his stern sister, as Stavros talked of the nature of matter, then launched into a basic outline of atomic theory. Hoping to settle on a viable word for 'atom,' he paused.

"Imael," supplied Ghirra.

Stavros cocked his head at the uncommon diphthong.

"Old words," Ghirra added tightly. "This is a Priests' Truth, what you say." And he continued the explication on his own. His description was highly metaphorical, like a complex tale-chant. The theory contained within the poetry was broadly drawn but essentially intact. Most significant to Stavros, the more technical specifics, such as the atom and its parts and characteristics, were all named in the ancient ritual language that Ghirra had called PriestWords.

When Ghirra had finished, Stavros translated for Weng, who expressed her satisfaction with a sublime smile.

"A *priests'* truth?" he asked Ghirra. "You do not believe this?"

Ghirra's delicate tension increased but his tone remained carefully reasoned. "How do I believe what I do not see?"

This man has the soul of an empiricist, thought Stavros. *No wonder he's contemptuous of the priests.* He handed back the Terran periodic table. "Through this you can see. It offers the truth of numbers."

Weng took the second sheet from him and gave it to Ghirra as well. "And through this," she stated. "In your own tongue."

Stavros grasped the connection at last. "That?"

"I believe so," she replied. "The more I study it, the surer I am."

"From the *very* old books, Ghirra?" he asked in a near whisper. "And you cannot read them?"

Ghirra's eyes were lost when he looked up from the two diagrams he held side by side. "Dho imme rek," he murmured helplessly.

Stavros felt the now familiar awe that prickled him whenever he heard the Sisters sincerely invoked. He had unwittingly plumbed the bottom of the physician's anti-PriestGuild skepticism, and touched belief. Unwilling belief, it was, belief crying out for a more satisfactory explanation, but belief enough to cause Ghirra to stare at Weng with new eyes.

To Weng, Stavros explained, "The ancient books come from the Goddesses, he says."

"Toph-leta," Ghirra added faintly.

"Life-gifts," Stavros translated.

Weng finally absorbed the Sawl's now very evident distur-

bance, but could not be discouraged from her course of inquiry.
"I apologize if I have caused you discomfort, GuildMaster. I
merely seek confirmation of a thought that perhaps once, a very
long time ago, your society was a different one." She chose her
words carefully now, eschewing all value judgments. "It is not
unheard of that a civilization has once been more extensive,
perhaps more mobile, perhaps lacking the raw materials necessary to space flight but with more time and interest for the
pursuit of the sciences. That diagram, if it is what I conjecture,
might be seen as proof of this. Do you have history of such a
time?"

"Science," said Ghirra softly. The word was not unknown to
him. Stavros supposed there would have been talk of science
with Susannah in Physicians', though perhaps on a more practical level. The healer seemed to recover his composure by a
sudden effort of will. "No. No history. The Sisters only."

Weng pursed her lips, disappointed but not discouraged. "The
veil of time is always thicker than we hope for."

"Weng! Come look at this," called Danforth from the confines of his bed.

Weng did not refuse the interruption. She took the diagrams
from Ghirra's hands and laid them on her worktable. "Perhaps
we will speak of this again, GuildMaster. I thank you for your
time." She nodded to them both and glided away to answer
Danforth's summons.

Stavros did not move. He waited. Ghirra was silent for a long
time, head bowed, mulling over some private difficulty. His eyes
when he raised them were profoundly troubled, seemed to wish
to bore into Stavros's soul for an answer.

"Ghirra," Stavros offered humbly and meant it. "Anything . . ."

Ghirra considered. "Yes," he decided. "It is time." Having
made his decision, he relaxed a bit and let his smile uncloud his
face and touch it with anticipation. "Come, 'Tavrosibia. There
is a thing I must show you."

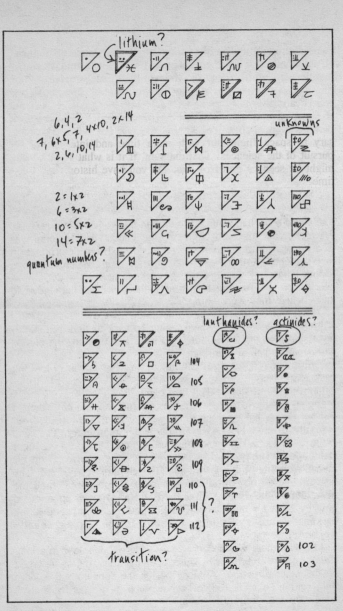

36

The cloud bank had returned to shroud the Vallegar in a massive fog as Stavros followed Ghirra up the stairs. The physician was in a hurry, his troubled manner transformed into determination that hardened further with each upward step. When they met Liphar coming down, breathless, pointing at the clouds, Ghirra barely slowed. Turning to run after them, Liphar demanded to know where they were going.

"Eles-Nol," Ghirra replied in Aguidran's growl.

Liphar stopped dead. Stavros glanced back to find him standing slack-jawed in the middle of a step. Behind him, the clouds had begun to roil and darken.

"Ghirra. . . ?" Stavros stumbled, moving upward, looking back at Liphar.

Ghirra did not stop. "Tell him come."

Liphar sprang forward at Stavros's signal, shaken but eager to follow. Ghirra led them up to the second level, then headed out along the exterior ledges toward the easternmost entry. The cave mouth was a small one and deserted. Ghirra hurried up the inner stairs and into the tunnels. Once inside, Stavros gave up on his mental mapping of every turn and allowed himself to be led. The last time he'd gone blind into the maze of corridors behind the main tunnels, he'd ended up at the BathHall. He was encouraged now by Liphar's nervous bird-dog twitch, as they paced along darkened empty corridors, to hope for something equally wonderful.

At length there was a door, a low wide wooden door in a long stretch of wall unbroken by other openings for as far as he could see in either direction. A niche beside the door housed a large light station. It appeared to be not much in use, as its shelves were crowded with unlit lamps.

The thick planking of the door was carved into decorative panels and strapped with thin curlicued bands of precious iron. Its heavy barrel hinges were of hardened wood. The carvings told a tale in shallow relief, spread over five consecutive panels, to be read from top to bottom. Stavros touched the crude granular iron reverently, then the oiled wood. In the smooth stone above the doorframe was carved the wave-and-flame motif of the PriestGuild. Ghirra lit a lamp and held it up to light the topmost panel.

"It is the story when Valla forget . . ." His surgeon's fingers mimed a one-handed tying of a knot. "She forget tying the clouds on the Vallegar." He lowered the lamp. On the next panel, the staunch figure of the goddess, long curls and garments flying, pursued across fanglike mountain peaks a herd of amoebic shapes that had grown heads and tails.

Stavros smiled in spite of himself, and was relieved to see a broad grin stretch Liphar's face as he read the panels. This was his first hint that not all the SisterTales were deadly serious. "So Valla can be forgetful . . . What happened?"

Ghirra consulted the door. "It's hard to explain," he stated finally.

Stavros started, hearing Susannah's exact intonation in his reply. *The man's a superb mimic! No wonder his English is so good.*

"I'll bet Lagri took full advantage of that," he suggested.

Liphar finished reading with a laugh, pointing out the bottom panel. "That time much wager lost!"

Ghirra's smile was tolerant, but clearly implied that he had not come this far to reread old legends. He lowered the lamp to check its oil reservoir, then passed it to Liphar. He grasped the stout door handle and pulled. The huge door swung on its hinges without a sound.

Inside was a small chamber, disturbingly reminiscent to Stavros of a ship's airlock. A second, less decorative panel with practical wooden knobs confronted them, set in a faceless wall. Liphar cradled the lamp protectively, nodding his readiness as Ghirra reached for the door.

It opened with a whoosh that sucked at the insides of their ears. Beyond the opening was darkness and the deep hollow moan of air rushing upward. A place of infinite possibility, of genuine storybook mystery. Stavros's spine tingled. He was already having a very good time, despite Ghirra's somber mood, and knew he would have to watch himself carefully.

Liphar went in first, with the lamp. The flame danced against the glass chimney like an imprisoned djinn. It lit up a brief landing, and a wide spiral stair that curled both up and downward from where they stood, wrapping around a giant hollow sheath of tubing, fat white pipes like those in the BathHall, slimmer ones of glazed terra-cotta, and bundles of still-thinner pipe, greenishly translucent, all surrounding a dark inner shaftway whose height and diameter could only be hinted at by the howling insistence of the updraft.

Lamp in hand, Liphar started down the stairs. His earlier surprise at their destination had been subdued by his obvious eagerness to get there. Stavros followed at Ghirra's signal, and found himself hugging the outer curve of the wall, wishing for handholds or a railing. The singing void of the shaftway was visible in long night-black gaps between the runs of pipe. He could feel its vertiginous presence like a worm in the pit of his stomach, and for the first time in many days, he worried for his grip on his old panic reflex. It was one thing to go with the excitement of the adventure, another entirely to disgrace himself before the Master Healer, whose opinion had begun to matter a great deal to him. Beyond the few steps within the circle of Liphar's lamp, the stairway dropped into darkness. Stavros put a hand to the wall for psychic anchoring and discovered that it was extraordinarily smooth, like polished marble.

Or glass.

It glimmered faintly in the lamplight, seamless, crackless, without bump or blemish. His fingertips were mesmerized by the perfection of its arc. No anchoring to be found there, not in such dreamlike flawlessness. Then he began to notice the heat.

The updraft was not just warmed, as if from the cozy body heat of the inner living quarters. It was hot. And dry. The impossibly smooth glass wall, enclosing them like a giant crystal tube, was warm to the touch.

Stavros's control slipped another notch, almost without his noticing. His brain conjured a mammoth furnace waiting below. The literary image of a descent into hell brought a curve to his lips. He followed Liphar with building excitement, down, down and around in endless dizzy spirals, until the heat and his growing giddiness and the rush of air lifting his damp hair awoke a seductive thrilling in him.

And he knew he had missed walking the edge, during these many days of keeping himself wrapped tight, of driving himself without rest for the sake of his newly assumed purpose. In this singing darkness, it was hard to recall the responsibilities of the daylight, easy to forget why the restraints were necessary. He regretted that such fearful pleasures required the sacrifice of his dignity, but as always before, the precipice drew him and he made the trade willingly. He heard music and let it vibrate through his internal spaces. The mystery of it enveloped him, the mystery he had waited to see revealed. He was descending into it, step by dizzying step, with Liphar his Virgil, the flame held high to light the path. He laughed in great gulping breaths and felt he must kneel in gratitude for this revelation, but as his knees buckled, a strong arm caught him from behind. A slight muscular body supported his fall and pressed a practiced hand to the back of his neck to force his head between his knees until the dizziness passed.

When Stavros could breathe evenly again, Ghirra eased him against the wall and tipped his chin into the lamplight, firmly prying back an eyelid, brushing back his hair to feel his brow. He pressed both palms to Stavros's temples and let them rest there. Their gentle pressure seemed to suction the panic from behind Stavros's eyes. He groaned and struggled to sit upright, to shake off these hands with life and energy all their own. He inhaled deeply, met Ghirra's calm gaze, then let his head slump to his chest.

Ghirra read his shame accurately. "Sleep you need," he commented with faint disapproval.

"Ibi?" Liphar knelt beside him in concern. He, who knew Stavros better than any other Sawl, was no stranger to these moments, yet this had seemed worse than a mere outburst of panic.

Stavros raged inwardly at his own weakness. "I'm hopeless, Lifa," he whispered.

"No," stated the healer with casual conviction. "But you hear too well the voice inside, 'TavrosIbia."

Stavros looked up at him, astonished. "Yes. How did you know?"

Ghirra smiled gently. "Ibi, it is my work, as the words are yours."

Moved, Stavros nodded, though the gesture felt hugely inadequate.

"And I say sleep you need." Ghirra grasped his arm. "Come, you walk now, yes?"

"Yes. My thanks, GuildMaster." Stavros stood with their help, then eased himself free to stand alone. That Ghirra should treat his fit of imbalance as merely exhaustion-induced was somehow stabilizing. ''I'll be fine now,'' he assured them, for of course he would be, until the next time he was indulgent enough to let his unconscious take him by storm. He *was* tired, but mostly of his own weakness, that he had indulged for so long, that kept him now from truly trusting his own ability to cope with responsibility. He thought of his purpose, of Megan's plan, of the Sawls' future, all dependent perhaps on his success or failure. How could he presume to take on such responsibility for others if he must always rely on having a McPherson around to slap him out of panic, or a Ghirra to hold him back from the void? Praying for strength, Stavros swore there would be no more indulgences.

Maybe Ghirra's right. Maybe what I've needed all along was a little more sleep. The absurdity of it made him laugh, and the laughter too was steadying. He urged Liphar onward and followed with a firmer step.

Moving downward, he counted stairs, and the tiny landings where other levels and half-levels accessed into the shaft. At major intersections, sections of the central pipe column bent away from the shaft, crossed over the stairs and vanished into horizontal tunnels of their own. The black gaps leading to the void widened.

He wondered where he was. They had entered the shaft on the third level, the level of the RangerGuild and the MeetingHall, among others. Stavros had kept track that far before surrendering to Ghirra's lead. So far they had passed three major landings on the way down the shaft, the second or stable level, the unused first level and . . . *and what*? They were now on a stretch of stair that had descended unbroken by landings or openings of any sort for quite a while.

Well below plains level, then, Stavros guessed. *Have to be*.

And then, surprisingly, there were others on the stair. Two old women came toiling upward in the heat, sharing a lamp and identical peaceful expressions. A young priest bounded past, a tiny lamp clutched in one hand, his embroidered wave-and-flame tabard bouncing against his chest. He panted a hurried greeting to Liphar without breaking his breathless ascent. As they continued downward, the roaring of the updraft lessened but the darkness and the heat did not, until a deadening of the echoes announced the bottom of the spiral and a cooler crossdraft floated past to refresh them.

Liphar stopped on the last step and held up the lamp. Above

their heads, the pipes angled out of the shaft to run along the
high ceiling of a corridor that led out of the shaft and slanted still
deeper into the rock. At the bottom of the shaft was a broad
circular depression. Stavros stepped down into the middle of it
and stood gawking upward in wonder. He could see nothing but
fat pipes fading into a central core of darkness, but the configu-
ration struck resonances with other more familiar structures, such
as the lift shaft of the Lander or the inner service columns
common to the high-rise architecture of Earth. But what might
be common on Earth was on Fiix such a miracle of engineering
that even his wonder seemed inadequate.

He looked to Liphar, then to Ghirra with a feeble shrug. "So
big. And so . . . perfectly round."

Ghirra motioned him out of the shaft bottom with a laugh.
"Wait, you," he promised. He took the lamp and led the way
down the tall ramping corridor. Heat radiated from the suspended piping but the cooler draft continued to whisper across
their faces. In the bouncing lamplight, Stavros could see that
unlike the more rough-hewn excavations of the upper caves, this
corridor had exact corners. Floor and walls and he assumed the
ceiling, invisible in darkness, met at clean right angles. Their
surfaces were as utterly smooth as the wall of the shaftway, but
they were not glass, rather a pale granular stone. The floor
hollowed slightly toward the center of the corridor, a mark of
long wear and the passage of countless footsteps. The walls bore
faint areas of darkness at the heights of hip and shoulder. Stavros
touched the staining.

"Old, old, old," he murmured, and knew Weng's speculation
was right. Some other Sawls, some former technological giants,
had built these corridors. What had become of them? How could
the Sawls have no memory of such a glorious past? Could it be,
as Ghirra implied, that their historics were completely buried in
myth?

A gargle passed through the pipes overhead, some liquid
message speeding uplevel. He felt no drips, heard no hiss of
escaping steam. The joints were tight and clean.

Still. After how many hundreds of years?

Ahead, there was light. Ghirra extinguished the lamp, and
carried it swinging at his side to the light station at the end of the
corridor. The light leaked through a pair of towering double
doors, one of which was ajar. Ghirra pulled it open and motioned Stavros in.

He entered a vast space suffused by a cool greenish glow. A

vast space but not an empty space, so that an understanding of its monumental size could only be grasped from the number and enormity of the objects within it. These objects were cylinders, at least fifteen meters high and six or seven wide, like mammoth Doric columns but too broad and too closely spaced for their purpose to be mere support. Stavros had a flashing vision of the PriestHall and thought he understood now what architecture it attempted to mimic. From the entrance, their surfaces appeared smoothly glossy. As he moved in among them, dwarfed by their bulk, Stavros saw that the shine was actually a glint off fine vertical ribbing. Light penetrated the furrowed surface until swallowed within the depths of the material. The cylinders were greenly transparent if viewed sideways along their curve, but opaque if looked at straight on, attempting to peer into their interior.

More glass, thought Stavros. He knocked the ribbed surface with a tentative knuckle.

"This is Eles-Nol," Ghirra said with quiet ceremony.

"What is it?"

The Master Healer shook his head. "First, you look." He let his arm sweep the hall, then pointed upward.

A grid of slim pipes was suspended from the ceiling to join the tops of the cylinders to the bundles of smaller pipe entering from the shaftway. Stavros traced the route from cylinder to corridor and back again. The fatter pipes, the terra-cotta and white, continued on between the rows of cylinders without connecting. Liphar danced at Stavros's side, urging him onward, but Ghirra stayed him, waiting for Stavros's reaction to what he was seeing. He touched the linguist's elbow and led him around one immense circular base. On the far side, a slender glass pipe dropped from above, nestled in the ribbing. It passed through a low tiled shelf set with a small ceramic valve. Embedded in the shelf was a glass disk with a tiny hole in its center. Ghirra crouched, reached under the shelf and drew out a hand-sized box. It was a more elaborate version of the wood-and-emery strikers carried in the base of every large oil lamp. The physician twisted a valve gently and put the striker to the glass disk. At his spark, a flame jumped up, hot yellow and orange, then as Ghirra adjusted the valve, settled into a pencil-thin blue spear. He rose and stood back. Liphar whispered a small priestly incantation and settled himself on the floor in front of the flame.

"Gas." Stavros gazed around, trying to take it all in slowly. "Storage tanks. Giant *glass* storage tanks." He decided that

nothing he might learn about the Sawls would amaze him anymore. He reached down and passed his finger quickly through
the flame and felt the compact sear of its heat. "I saw this in the
StoryHall."

"Yes. Shallagri," replied Ghirra, none too reverently.

"The Breath of Lagri," Stavros translated. "But you have it
in Physicians' as well."

"And in the StoryHall of Valla. Then the priests say the small
fire is the color of her eyes." Ghirra stooped and adjusted the
flame more to his liking. "But in Physician's, we use to make
sterile. Also to cook the medicines." Practical uses, his half-
smile implied.

"Natural gas?" asked Stavros. *Clausen'd sure like to know, if
it is*!

"Hjuon. I do not know how you name it."

"Where does it come from?"

"It is there, in the nol, the rock. From the Goddesses, the
priests say."

"And you say?"

For an answer, Ghirra laid a gentle hand on Liphar's shoulder
to break the young man from his contemplation of the flame.
Liphar smiled up at them as radiantly as if Lagri herself had been
speaking to him. Ghirra bent to close the valve and the flame
died. "Come. More there is."

He allowed Liphar the choice of path through the towering
forest of cylinders. The air was still abnormally warm but not
unpleasant. A faint continuous whispering filled the hall, reminding Stavros of the sighing of a quiet sea at night. As they
wandered, they passed several cylinders where the tiny gas flame
burned in its glass disk. At each flame, a silent Sawl or two or
three sat cross-legged, staring into the blue fire with the rapt
concentration of deep meditation. Farther along, they met a trio
of elderly priests walking along the rows, chatting quietly like
monks in a cloister. They nodded a serene greeting and passed
on. Liphar's nervous pace had relaxed into calm elation. He led
them proudly, without urgency, finding a joy in his surroundings
that Stavros could not help but envy. Even Ghirra seemed willing to let their progress take its own time. The green lumines-
cence of the glass was restful, the soft warm air as comforting as
sleep. Stavros held back a sigh. Once he had stood in a redwood
grove at dawn. Not until this moment had he sensed a deeper,
older peace.

Then, as they came around the glimmering base of a cylinder, they faced a series of wide steps leading down to a stretch of open floor. At last, the astounding dimensions of the hall were fully visible. A half acre away, within a space the height of a five-storied house, sat three final cylinders. They were larger than the others by half, and set in a close triangle around a circular tiled platform. Laid into the stone floor in slabs of white marble, so that each cylinder sat within a circle, was the same three-ringed symbol that decorated the floor of the FriezeHall. But here, the circles were unbroken.

Again, Ghirra drew Stavros's attention to the tops of the cylinders. A halo of heavy white pipe hung above each domed summit, receiving the big white pipes entering from the shaft-way. The halo connected with the cylinder at several points around its perimeter. The smaller terra-cotta pipes ran directly to the cylinders' sides. From the apex of each cylinder's dome, a single greenish pipe rose and angled across the vast open plaza to join the network above the storage tanks.

At Ghirra's nod, Liphar led them down the wide shallow stairs and across the plaza to the steeper steps of the circular platform. A horseshoe of pipes filled the space between the platform and the three cylinders, making connections with them here and there, then running off behind. From the top of the platform, a triangle of railed wooden gangways arched over the horseshoe of piping, one to meet each cylinder. The smooth-milled ancient wood seemed worlds apart from the sleek tech of the glass and ceramic, yet within the confines of the giant underground cavern, curiously at home. Where gangways and cylinders joined, there seemed to be a hatch in the glass. At least Stavros could see what might be handles, though no openings were apparent.

Liphar laid a thin hand on Stavros's arm and guided him up the steps as if bringing him into a Presence. Ghirra followed almost reluctantly, hands shoved into the pockets of his smock. A circular structure dominated the center of the platform. It was nearly two meters across, waist-high, like a drum of greenish glass, but topped with a clear glass dome. Stavros leaned over to peer through the thick transparency of the lid, and saw a rosy lavender sparkle.

Ah.

Wordlessly, Ghirra drew his hand from his pocket and placed a glittering triangular chunk of rock on top of the glass.

"Guar rek," whispered Stavros, pronouncing the old words for Liphar's benefit.

"Yes," said Ghirra. "The SisterBread."

He drew Stavros aside, to the edge of the platform. They watched as Liphar pressed himself against the glass with reverent longing, his arms outstretched to embrace the dome.

"When he is made priest," said Ghirra, his wide mouth touched with distaste, "He is allowed to feed the Goddesses. Now he cannot." He traced a finger across his palm. "His hands are yet, ah . . ."

The physician used a Sawlish word that Stavros thought meant "free" but now considered amending to "profane." He pictured the layers of scar tissue on Ashimmel's, on Kav Daven's palms, the heavy repeated scarring that scoured the palms of every full priest. Stavros's jaw tightened uneasily. He had never thought it his place to ask what rite of passage the scarring represented. "Feed the Goddesses?"

Ghirra motioned with his thumb from the domed glass drum with its hidden amethyst treasure to the trio of cylinders, then out along the piping and across the plaza. The sequence was clear. The guar was placed in the cylinders by the priests, and the gas came out.

"What's inside the cylinders?"

Ghirra shook his head. "The priests say, the Goddesses."

Of course. Stavros could only nod helplessly.

Now here is a meshing of science and religion you need a chemist to unravel. A reaction, obviously . . . lithium plus something equals a gas. Plus what? What gas? CRI could have the answer in a nanosecond . . . but then, so could Clausen.

Ghirra watched his amazement with evident satisfaction but seemed to be waiting for something more.

For what? A response? God help me, an explanation? Stavros circled the platform, seeking an understanding of the system as a whole. "The gas comes from here." A sweep of his arm took in the forest of cylinders. "It's stored there." He considered the fat white and terra-cotta pipes, recalling the heat in the shaftway. "And there's forced hot air as a by-product, and hot water, carried up to the BathHall." He looked back to the cylinders. "From the cooling system surrounding the reaction vessels inside the glass." He let out an explosive breath. "Wow."

Ghirra smiled, still waiting.

"And where does the lithium . . . the guar come from?"

"From the nol. Come." Ghirra returned to the dome for his chunk of ore, then paced down the steps of the platform and around the nearest cylinder. Behind the glassy bulk, the vast cavern ended in a wall pierced by three openings. Three arched tunnels led off into blackness.

The nol, puzzled Stavros. *The rock . . . ah. The bedrock.*

"Mined from right under the cliffs?" he exclaimed.

"Yes. The priests dig there, very deep." Ghirra held out the ore in his hand. "But it is not like this. The guar from the nol burns."

Burns? A vague memory from grade-school chemistry returned to him. A tiny sliver of pure soft metal dropped in a beaker of water, with rather spectacular results. *Pure*? It would have to be, he guessed, to produce a worthwhile reaction in the cylinders. Stavros started to chuckle. *Holy shit! Pure lithium! What a joke on Clausen that he might be sitting right on top of the biggest strike of them all*! But with his smile, he felt his stomach knot against the implications of this discovery. If the prospector found his way down here, it was all over.

"Burns?" he asked aloud, thinking again of Kav Daven's palms. "Do the priests carry it barehanded?"

Ghirra nodded, frowning slightly. "It is the way."

Stavros met his gaze. "And you disapprove." *But of course. How could a healer with proven subtle magic in his own hands, be expected to approve of a painful disfiguring practice*?

The physician shrugged. "The priests' way," he repeated. "It is not my way. But it brings the hjuon, and the hjuon is our life."

Yes, acknowledged Stavros. *Without this source of energy, heat and hot water and, in places, light, the Sawls would be reduced to the primitive life we first assumed.*

He spread his arms wide, overwhelmed at last into laughter. "Ghirra, this is *astounding*!" He spun around, taking in the wonder of it. "How long has this been here? Who *built* it?"

The healer's frown deepened, and for a moment, Stavros worried that in his high enthusiasm, he had committed some rudeness or worse. But he thought Ghirra unlikely to respond to sacrilege. And he realized that had he asked the question of Liphar, the apprentice priest would have reflexively answered that the goddesses had made it and that would be the end of it. For Ghirra, it seemed, an answer did not come so easily.

"It is here," the Master Healer equivocated, stoop-shouldered, staring at the marble floor.

Stavros sucked his lip. Ghirra's expectant silence pulled at him like a rope knotted around his chest. "It's here?" he repeated softly. "It just exists, like the books, from the Goddesses?"

He paused, prayed that his assessment of the Master Healer was correct, and said, "That's not good enough, Ghirra. Not from you."

Ghirra's head jerked up to pin Stavros with Aguidran's hard stare.

Uncanny, thought Stavros. He forced himself to start breathing again. "It's lazy thinking," he pursued.

The physician paced away a bit, slouching, his hands shoved deep into the pockets of his smock. Stavros followed, and waited beside him when he stopped to stare again at the floor.

"The priests do not like our idea," Ghirra said at last. His lowered voice rumbled with intimations of heresy that Stavros found irresistible.

"*Our* idea?"

"My idea and Aguidran's." He raised his head to gaze thoughtfully at the dark arches of the mine tunnels.

"What is it?" When Ghirra didn't answer, Stavros said earnestly, "My sponsors don't like my ideas either, or they sure as hell won't once they find them out. Our plan to prevent Clausen's claim could put me away for the rest of my life. And if you're worried about Liphar, he won't hear a word of your ideas from me."

Ghirra drew in a long breath. "It is not an answer," he began.

"Ideas lead to answers," Stavros returned.

"It gives only greater mystery." He dealt out the words deliberately, in a tone that was almost bland. But a fierce glimmer had risen in his eyes. "The First Books tell of the Creator who gave us the Sisters from her womb. But I know also there is knowledge in the old books, as your Commander says. And I think, maybe the books and Eles-Nol, all this was made by those who made the Goddesses."

Stavros felt an echo of Weng's earlier disappointment. *Well, he did say it wasn't an answer.*

But then the fuller implications of this deceptively simple remark began to sink in.

"Wait. *Made* the Goddesses? Like they were some kind of machine?"

"Machine," said Ghirra, as if that thought were new to him.

"Ghirra, are you suggesting some race of super-techs, that came, built all this and left?"

The Master Healer looked cautiously blank, unsure whether his idea was being received or ridiculed.

"I mean," Stavros continued, "not a supernatural Creator or

goddesses at all, but a human civilization with supremely developed science and technology, that would be capable of all kinds of miracles. They could build any machine they'd want. They could control the natural processes." He let the glorious vision swell in his mind. "Changing the climate would be nothing to them! They'd have matter transport, interstellar travel in an instant! They'd remake entire planets, move suns!" He stopped as his vision foundered in incredulity. He met Ghirra's hungry look with a sigh, and his heart went out to him. He understood the true nature of the physician's heresy at last. It wasn't the existence of the Goddesses he questioned, it was their divinity. The man was a scientific visionary. Leonardo da Vinci must have suffered a similar pain imagining wonders so far beyond his technological grasp. "Science fiction," he finished softly.

"Fiction?"

"Dreams."

Ghirra's warm fierce eyes leveled on him. "You can do these things!"

"I . . . *what*?"

"You. You . . . wokind can do these things!"

Ah, god, if only! "No, Ghirra, I . . . ." With a shock, it came clear. "You think it's *us* who made the Goddesses?"

"You can read the Toph-leta!"

"Weng was *guessing* at it! Ghirra, listen to me! Do you even understand what all those things are?"

Ghirra dismissed his own ignorance with a wave. "You say about miracles. It is a miracle that you come here!" He gestured sharply upward. "From the sky!"

Well, I'll be . . . someone finally noticed. "Not a miracle, Ghirra. Technology. Science."

"*This* is science!" Ghirra cried, spreading his arms to the vast space around them. He whirled on Stavros, eyes alight with frustration, then caught himself abruptly with a hunted glance at the tiled platform, where the young priest-to-be still rested in deep communion with the precious contents of the glass drum. Ghirra let his body sag and said no more.

Stavros thought he might weep for having to deny the desperate hopes of such a man. "Of course it's science," he agreed softly, hoping this affirmation might ease the strained stoop of Ghirra's shoulders or soothe the anguish in his eyes.

But Ghirra had stunned even himself with his outburst. He remained withdrawn, limp and silent.

Stavros stood beside him awkwardly. The man's great dignity

prevented him from offering physical contact, as he could with Liphar, an arm thrown across his shoulders for comfort. He saw Ghirra's dilemma as the mirror of his own. While he plumbed his Terran-bred soul for belief in the irrational, in the magic of the Fiixian goddesses, the physician fought that same belief because it would not satisfy his questing intellect. Ghirra's life would be far easier if he could believe that gods were gods, and question no further.

And yet, their dilemmas in being opposite could also be seen to be the same. Stavros took a breath and with it came the sensation that in bringing him here, by sharing his heresy, Ghirra had unknowingly thrust him across an invisible threshhold. He felt himself to be the Sawls' man now, past loyalties and commitments not just set temporarily aside but forgotten. He found joy in this new sense of community, and more important, he found strength. The Master Healer would be not just a political ally for his struggle but an intellectual one as well. Stavros' worries of inadequacy eased. He let the breath out slowly.

"Ghirra, I don't know how much of what I'm going to say will make sense to you now, but I'm going to try it anyway.

"Earth science, Earth technology, *my* technology, could accomplish what's going on in this room. We'd use other methods and materials, but we'd get it done. And yes, that technology can bring us from our own world, one farther away than either of us can imagine in terms of man-miles, and it can set us down on worlds like yours, and allow us still to talk from world to world.

"But Ghirra, there are many, many things it cannot do, and believe me, we are not capable of building machines that wage war with the weather as your goddesses do. If Valla Ired and Lagri are products of some super race's technology—and mind you, that idea had never occurred to *me*, so you're already way ahead of me in that regard—but if they are, then that race is already the next thing to gods, or goddesses, anyway."

He moved a step or two, so that he could face Ghirra directly. "Do you see what I'm saying? Ghirra, you carry the powers of healing in your own hands. Is that science or miracle, knowledge or belief? I also claim to be in search of which is the truer truth, but maybe after a certain point, the distinction is moot. You can dispute your goddesses' divinity without mourning its loss, as long as you can believe in the wonder of their accomplishments. Science or miracle becomes a mere matter of personal definition." He tried to coax back a hint of Ghirra's smile. "But don't ever breathe a word to Megan that I said it doesn't matter."

The joke was lost on the Master Healer, but the basic argument was not. He shook off his slump, fists clenched with resentful vehemence. "No, Ibi, you are wrong, this saying it doesn't matter! These hands can do no miracle. Always here we live or die by the Sisters' game. A hundred generations we struggle and grow, but one time Lagri weakens or Valla sleeps and we are nothing again."

Stavros was taken aback by the Master Healer's evident outrage. "You believe in the legends of devastation, then? Liphar has hinted that there are signs of another on its way."

"I cannot know what I do not see," Ghirra replied tightly. "But yes, I believe the legend is true. And the priests say it, this is the way. We can do nothing. And they say true, if the Goddesses are as they say. So they teach, accept this, until the Darkness passes."

Ghirra tossed his head angrily, his long curls slashing the air. "Accept! If there is sickness, I do not say 'accept'! I fight the sickness! Accept? Accept always the deaths? Our friends, our children? My mother and my father in the storm? Accept that we must always struggle to put food and warmth in our caves? If the Goddesses are as the priests say, we must accept. But if they are not . . ."

He dropped his voice but the words still rushed forth with an intensity born of righteous anger. "This, Eles-Nol, the priests say comes from the goddesses. I say, now you say also, it is *science*. It is tech . . . technology." He spread his hands, appealing to Stavros. "Why not the Goddesses also? If this what they give is science, they may be science also."

Stavros saw where the physician's rage at his helplessness in the hands of the Goddesses had led him. He gave a grunt of admiration.

"And then," Ghirra continued fervently, "we can ask, why does this science help us sometime and kill us sometime?"

"You're right, of course," said Stavros. "Technology shouldn't kill you, but Ghirra, it wouldn't be the first time. Often people have the skill to make machines before they have the understanding of their consequences or how to use them—"

"If it is machines," Ghirra interrupted, "it can be not-made, yes?"

"Not made? *Un*made?"

"Yes. If the winch on the cliff top will not turn, the guildsmen say not 'accept.' They *un*make it to make it new again."

"They repair it." Then Stavros amended himself, loving the

play on words. "They *fix* it." This time the laughter bubbled up uncontrolled. "Ah, Ghirra, what a wild-assed, outrageous, spectacular idea! To fix the gods! Throughout its history, my race has struggled to change itself to suit its gods. Sacrifice, penitence, celibacy, charity, reform, good works. But here is a man who would change his gods to suit himself!" He beamed at the amazed Master Healer and shook a fist at the distant ceiling. "Hear that, you Sister-ladies? Watch out!"

Ghirra shifted, moved away. "You laugh now at my idea."

"No!" Stavros pursued him. "No. My life on it, Ghirra. Forgive me if it seemed that way. It doesn't even matter if the idea is true or not. I . . ." He fumbled for the right word. "I exult in it, GuildMaster, and in you for thinking it, because I'm sure Weng is righter than she could ever suspect about an older advanced civilization on Fiix. And it's not some other race she means. It's you. The hints are there in what you call the Old Words, that contain technical names for all the parts of a theoretical construct such as the atom. Your ancestors spoke that language, and if your idea *is* true, the super-race who made these god-machines were surely your ancestors. Perhaps you have only the leftovers of their technology, but you've inherited all of their vision."

Ghirra took this in silently, staring at the floor, but Stavros thought he stood a little taller than he had a moment before. And so, for Ghirra and for himself, the linguist made a promise, as mad and wild as the vision that prompted it.

"I'll find your goddesses, GuildMaster, man-made or divine. You'll have an answer, and if we are able, a solution."

Ghirra's head sank deeper into his shoulders, but after a moment, he raised it again and began to laugh softly, a delighted release of tension that offered never to hold the young man to his impossible promise, but thanked him sincerely for the giving of it. Stavros stared, then broke into an embarrassed grin to share the physician's gentle laughter.

"I guess that does sound pretty presumptuous," he admitted as reality descended. "Especially from one who's just insisted he's incapable of miracles."

The two men offered each other rueful smiles and shook their heads.

"We might be able to do it, though, you know . . . with a little work," Stavros added. "And a little science. A little Terran science." He was still smiling, but his eyes earnestly begged the Master Healer to keep some small faith in the plausibility of his promise. "Even though we're not the super-race you'd hoped for."

Ghirra's mild nod said he was ready for anything but expecting nothing.

At least I don't have to worry about disappointing him further, Stavros mused soberly. *Nowhere to go from here but up.* He turned to look at Liphar, still rapt in his meditations. "Meanwhile, the wagons will be leaving soon, and Lifa and I have a job to do out there."

Ghirra nodded again, and together they walked back to the platform to collect the priest's apprentice from his reverent dreams of the day when he would be allowed to feed the Goddesses.

37

The crack and roll of thunder echoed up the tunnel to the cave mouth. The three separated by the entrance to the Meeting Hall, Ghirra to assure himself of the final readiness of the infirmary wagon, Liphar to prepare for the leavetaking rituals, though the thunder made him tight-lipped with doubt.

Stavros headed for the Black Hole to pack the few necessities he would be able to carry for the second, secret leg of his journey. He trotted through the dim corridors, eager to be moving at last, eager to prove his worth to the Sawls. Later, he found himself whistling as he rustled about the darkened sleeping platform, stowing away his less portable belongings, settling the load in his pack more to his liking.

"You also work well in the dark?"

Stavros looked up. Clausen stood at the cavern entrance, a battery searchbeam in one hand. He stepped in, flashing the beam into the hidden recesses, picked out the cold firepit, the stone sink, the sleeping platform, the tiny oil lamp burning at Stavros's side, as well as the assurance that the linguist was alone. "Your neighbors indicated I might find you here. Obliging little folk."

He moved farther into the cavern, stopped at the firepit, nosed a casual boot into its ash. "Quite a storm brewing out there, from the looks of it. Right up out of nowhere, like the last time. This wagon train of yours may never get off the ground."

Stavros fastened a final buckle on his field pack and stood. He slung the pack across his back, abruptly tired of fencing. "What's on your mind, Emil?"

Clausen sighed, wandering deeper into the cavern. The lamp swung offhandedly at his side but the beam slid deliberately from floor to sink to pipes and on around the wall. "I'm glad you asked," he began in a comradely tone. "Because I'd like to work this out in a friendly fashion." He stopped his wandering, rested one suede boot on the sleeping platform and let his lamp beam settle at Stavros's feet. "Stav, what the hell happened while I was out there in the bush? I don't recall we had such adversary relations before that, you and I." He paused with a smile that might have included a wink had Stavros been looking at him. "No more than your usual with the rest of the world, that is."

Stavros stepped off the platform and crossed to the sink. Such a direct confrontation was unexpected. "Don't know what you mean," he replied lamely.

Clausen chuckled. "I could almost believe that, Stav. And not wanting to tarnish your reputation as a young hothead, it still seems to me you could be a little more accommodating here and there. I'll let the issue of the comlink go by. Weng's right there. I'm best qualified to fix it. But when I ask for your help with the locals . . ."

"Emil, I've been doing the best I can."

"So you keep saying," Clausen replied, "but I know you can do better."

"I'm a linguist, Emil. Labor relations is not my job." Standing at the sink, packing his razor and soap in a side pouch of his pack, Stavros heard the prospector come up behind him. The lamp flashed on the wall and steadied as it was set down on the floor.

Right, Stavros thought. *Now I get the lecture about remembering the source of my funding.*

Clausen grabbed his arm, twisted hard to spin him around and threw his weight against his chest. Stavros was flung spread-eagled against the wall. The back of his head slammed into solid rock. Pack, razor and soap clattered across the floor.

"Your job is what I fucking well say it is!" hissed the prospector.

Stavros gurgled, heaving, the wind crushed from his lungs. His vision blurred. Clausen shoved a skilled arm up against his throat, pinning his head to the wall. The other hand came up gripping a silvered laser pistol, a small personnel weapon of the sort expressly forbidden on board spacegoing vessels. "The truth is, you don't like me much, am I right? And you're doing everything in your power to get in my way."

Stavros sucked for air dizzily, struggling to understand how this could have happened so fast. Cool metal kissed his temple.

The arm across his throat pressed harder, making him acutely aware of the fragility of his windpipe.

"Am I right, Stavros, my boy?" Clausen repeated more gently, his tone almost paternal, while his forearm increased its grinding pressure.

"*No!*" Stavros choked out, and his desperate lie sounded like terror. He struggled to free his breathing, but the smaller man had him expertly immobilized. "You sonofabitch!" he flailed, hearing himself whine like a wounded animal. "Get your fucking hands off me!"

Clausen laughed and stepped back gracefully, releasing Stavros as easily and unpredictably as he had taken him prisoner. The little laser gun swung to level at Stavros's chest. "Well," said Clausen with satisfaction. "That at least answers one of my questions."

Stavros sagged against the wall, gasping, and made no move to lunge after him. Clausen shrugged and lowered the pistol to his side. "So tell me, son, what's your beef? Surely we can work this out. What have I done to offend you, so wet behind the ears from the university?"

"Nothing," growled Stavros. He rolled along the wall and slumped against the sink, panting with shock and rage and humiliation.

"I have something you want, perhaps?" asked Clausen slyly.

"Nothing," rasped Stavros again, this time truthfully. Clausen had money and power and Stavros had always been sure he wanted neither, power particularly. Now he wondered if that was because he had never before been so aware of how little he possessed.

Clausen found the three-legged Sawlish stool that had served the computer work station. He dragged it into the beam of his battery lamp and sat, one leg crossed over the other, the laser resting comfortably on his knee. "You academics," he began tiredly, "just don't seem to understand the realities. This is not fun and games, boy, you get me? I'm putting your career on notice. As of right now."

When Stavros held his sullen silence, Clausen shook his head. "I can make you or I can break you, Ibiá. It's as simple as the old cliché. So why make it the latter when the former could be so much more satisfying for both of us? Believe it or not, I get no kicks from having to shove you boys back in line."

Stavros glared back at him, hating the prospector for his calm while he himself still fought for a measured breath. What price, what form of bribe would Clausen offer for his loyalty? He was almost curious enough to open negotiations. The lamp beam backlit the prospector's seated form with cold bright glare, leaving his face in shadow. He sighed and uncrossed his legs. The pistol flashed a sharp glint of reflection into Stavros's eyes.

"And then," Clausen mused, "there are always those unfortunate accidents that occur on these uncharted worlds. . . ."

Stavros gathered the shreds of his self-possession and laughed. "Don't you think you've threatened me enough already?"

"Evidently not," replied the faceless voice. "Or in the midst of all the heavy breathing, did I miss your promise to get in line? You know, I've seen all this before, boy, these petty alliances with the locals. It's always some idealistic youngster like you who gets himself in over his head. You should take a tip from Megan Levy. You don't catch the old pros like her messing about, no matter how much they'd like to smear my ass from here to Centauri."

Stavros held himself very still, pinned by the searchbeam, afraid that his slightest move might surrender whole paragraphs of meaning to Clausen's canny hunter's instincts. *How much does he know?*

"On the other hand . . ." The prospector rose and his shadow leaped against the wall. "This is getting a trifle tiresome, as impasses often do. I could put a bolt through your skull right now and be done with you, but then there'd be some awkwardness to deal with." He reached for the lamp and hefted it, training the beam into Stavros's slitted eyes. "And I prefer to think you're as bright as they say you are, and will learn to value your future health as a working professional more than a few local acquaintances." He paused, waiting. "Do I get the help I need?"

"You'll get it," Stavros growled, to be rid of him.

Clausen backstepped toward the cavern entrance. The searchbeam held steady, then dropped. "Excellent thinking, son. Well, go on, then. Have a good trip and get out of my hair. CONPLEX and I are delighted your work means so much to you, but don't let it get in our way, eh?"

No bribe. No bribe at all. The offer was simply his life.

"Does the Commander know you smuggled an illegal weapon on board?" Stavros spat after him helplessly.

"Tut, tut. Smuggled?" Clausen balanced the pistol on his palm with a snicker. "This little guy's classified as a tool, my boy, officially listed with the contents of my emergency kit, and you should be glad of it, since you yourself said I'd need a welder to repair the dish." He raised the shining gun and laid the stubby barrel alongside his nose. "You might be able to nail me for assault and battery, though I think you'd be hard put to offer evidence, but illegal possession? Never. The Company doesn't want me running around unarmed." He switched off the lamp as he reached the doorway. "Predators, you know," he whispered and ambled off into the darkness, laughing.

Megan found him still slumped against the sink, head sunk to his chest. The little oil lamp sputtered on the sleeping platform. In the sink, the faucet dripped into an overflowing stewpot.

"Aguidran says it's time, Stav. You all packed?" she called from the entry. She had put on fresh-pressed khaki field clothes. Her compass swung around her neck. "Stav?"

He didn't move.

"Stav?"

His head lifted, barely. "I just had a visit from Clausen," he said thickly.

"Yeah, he told me you were up here."

Stavros shifted, coughed. "Did he also tell you he'd slapped me up against the wall like I was nothing, like some ball of shit, and shoved a gun in my face?"

"Ah. So soon," Megan responded quietly.

Stavros glared at her. "Christ! Is that the best you can do?" He pushed limply away from the sink and muddled about gathering up his pack and soap and the shattered pieces of his razor. He clutched it all to him, looking dazed, then sank in a dispirited heap onto the steps of the sleeping platform. The pack tumbled from his grip as he dropped his head into his hands. "I couldn't stop him, Meg," he mumbled. "He could've fucking killed me."

Megan went to him quickly, sat on the step beside him and slipped an arm around his back. His sweat-drenched shirt was cold against his skin. "Oh my poor innocent," she soothed. "Of course he could have. And would have, if he'd been feeling threatened enough." She rocked him for a moment, then asked, "How much does he know?"

Stavros muttered something inaudible, then took a breath, dragging his hands across his eyes. "He's not on to you yet. I think mainly he's noticed me getting in his way a lot."

Megan patted his shoulder as she drew her arm away. "Well, it could have been worse, god knows. He may think a simple threat will be enough to scare you into line.'' She sat back. ''Weather's acting up again out there. Aguidran seems to want to go ahead anyway.''

Stavros remained sunk in his gloom. ''So goddamn helpless. . . !''

With a sigh, Megan leaned her elbows on her knees, matching his posture. ''Look, Stav, I'm sorry. I thought you understood when you got into this that Emil is the real thing. He plays stakes in the gigabillions, and he plays them for keeps.''

Stavros raised his head to stare into the darkness of the entry. ''That sonofabitch'll never get his fucking hands on me again.''

Megan eyed him. ''My goodness. You sound as if no one's ever knocked you down in your life.''

''Not like this! Not with so little chance to hit back!'' He roused himself long enough to slam a fist helplessly into the air. ''Sonofafuckingbitch! How could I let him get the jump on me so easily?''

''Whoa. Hold it,'' Megan warned. ''Keep that young Mediterranean blood of yours below the boiling point. You have to stay as cool as he is, or he'll have you. He'll have all of us. We're too few and too weak to risk giving ourselves away with impulsive action. We need you, Stav, and we need you calm and quiet and undercover. You can't let this become a personal grudge match, or your anger will be another weapon in his hand.''

Stavros pretended not to hear. '' 'Bloody, bold and resolute!' '' he quoted, then muttered recklessly, ''Of course, the real solution is to get rid of him. A little trip at the edge, a casual push, and . . . splat!''

Megan pursed her lips. ''It could come to that with him, in self-defense. Are you ready to kill a man, Stav?''

''You got a better solution? That's what he'd do to me, if nobody were around to notice!''

''I asked if you were ready to kill a man.''

''I'm ready to stay alive,'' he returned harshly. ''Shit, now who's the innocent?''

''Stav,'' she chided gently, ''listen to me. You're rightfully pissed at the man for proving his power at your expense, but it's no cause for suicidal vows of cold-blooded murder. He is, as they say, armed and dangerous. You are neither. So put away your bruised pride and remember the real enemy. If by some miracle you did manage to get Clausen before he got you, CONPLEX'd just send in another like him. He's not exactly unique out there in the megacorporate universe. Emil Clausen is basically a highly paid errand boy. The power he wields is only local, and he's smart enough to know it. That infernal confidence of his is based on accepting both where the real power lies and his place in its structure.''

"Is this political science class?" Stavros sneered.

"Know thy enemy as thyself," Megan returned. "And never let it get personal.''

He shook his head, relapsing into gloom. "The innocent and the professor . . . fine pair of conspirators we make. What in holy hell are we going to do against the likes of him?''

"Hey, I said calm down. I didn't say roll over and die." Megan smiled and nudged him playfully. "Listen, I've seen much worse than us going up against the biggies. How do you think revolutions get started?'' She touched his chill arm. ''The point is, you can't give up on the legalistic approach just because you got messed around a little. Face it, you're likely to get messed around a little more before this is all over, but next time, you'll be ready for him. Adopting his methods is not the answer. The laws have been written to keep power like Clausen's in check, and sometimes—rarely, I admit, but *sometimes*—you can even make them stick.''

"Meg, laws and revolution are a contradiction in terms.''

"Not if what's revolutionary is to invoke the laws as they are *written*. Stav, don't jeopardize the chance for real change for the sake of your ego.''

Stavros shrugged her off. "I won't! Christ, Meg, I'm not a child!''

Backing off, Megan wondered. In a way, the incident was fortuitous. Clausen had unwittingly provided a naive and idealistic young man with a bloodless first blooding that left only his pride gasping for its life in the sand. Only much later would he understand how lucky he had been that Clausen did not yet see him as a real threat. Still, Megan had her doubts about Stavros's ability to learn the lessons of self-control fast enough to save himself and save their plan. It was all mad, of course. After years of talk and no action, she had chosen this out-of-the-way planet to make a stand and this volatile raging boy for her ally. It was bad practice. It was flexing muscles left too long unused. She was still unsure why she had done it, but suspected the answer could be found in her fear that she might not be given another chance in her shortening life to take action where it mattered.

And then, of course, there were the Sawls.

It was too late to do anything about it but worry, and pray their conspiracy was not as hopeless as it might seem. She gathered up Stavros's pack and shoved it onto his lap. "On your feet, comrade," she ordered stoutly. "We've got a caravan to catch."

38

The living quarters were dark and the corridors deserted. Megan and Stavros met no one until they neared the PriestHall, but the hubbub could be heard several tunnels away. Turning the corner, they found the corridor outside the Hall filled with apprentices, chattering excitedly as they helped each other into ceremonial tabards. The wave-and-flame sign of the PriestGuild glimmered on every proud chest. The chatter, interspersed with wrangles over the assignment of various banners and flags, mostly concerned the threatening weather and the dubious wisdom of going ahead with the leavetaking rituals.

Stavros looked about for Liphar and was relieved not to find him. He was still shaken and angry, and Liphar would read him clearly and be worried. The merest thought of what Clausen had done to him threatened a new attack of debilitating outrage. As he edged Megan through the busy crowd, he glanced through the columned arch to the interior of the Hall. He saw as much noisy milling confusion inside as out. The majority of the PriestGuild, evidently convinced until the last minute that the ceremonies would not take place, now rushed to ready themselves. Mutters of thunder still rolled in from the nearby cave mouth, but Stavros doubted the priests could hear themselves over the din in the Hall, much less sounds from the outside. His eyes strayed unavoidably to their hands, chilled by their unnatural gleaming smoothness as he thought of the guar and the Master Healer's uneasy acceptance of the painful ritual that brought life and comfort to the Caves. He longed to tell Megan about the guar cavern and its power plant, but remembering the cool touch of Clausen's laser against his neck, he decided that among the prospector's less formal credits was probably a master's degree in extracting information. For Megan's sake, Stavros would keep that information to himself.

"The PriestGuild seems to have accepted the inevitable," Megan remarked as they sought a path through the mob of chattering apprentices. Stavros ducked to avoid a silken banner hoisted clumsily by a boy too small to control its weight. Just as they had worked themselves free, Kav Ashimmel came striding down the corridor with the harried members of her entourage scuttling along behind her, fresh from a final consultation with the weather watch. Stavros touched Megan's arm to slow her, and glanced back as the apprentices stilled to their guildmaster's approach. Her usual scowl tinged with reluctant optimism, Ashimmel announced that the sky had cleared and the ceremonies could proceed. The apprentices cheered. With a wave that seemed to imply some responsibility for this change of fortune, the Master Priest turned and stalked into the Hall.

"Well, hallelujah," said Megan as they hurried toward the cave mouth. "I wasn't sure how we'd explain your disappearance if the caravan had been called off."

"Or how I'd get to the Sled if the weather turned *really* bad."

A group of journeymen Engineers crowded the cave mouth, bustling around a tallish young apprentice dressed in white. They all talked at once as they fixed the folds of her tunic, fussed with the arrangement of her beribboned hair. The young woman's eyes shone while she patiently withstood their ministrations and advice. To one side, two guildsmen polished a large plaque painted with the guild's triangular seal.

As Stavros stepped out of the shade of the overhang, he thought he heard thunder again. But the turquoise sky stretched unbroken all the way to the Vallegar. One or two discrete spots of cloud still lurked about the sawtooth peaks. Stavros grinned crookedly, picturing them with with heads and tails, lashed to the mountaintops as Valla had neglected to do in the tale carved on the entrance to Eles-Nol. And he thought again of Ghirra's dilemma, which he had made his own, and of the elating sense of the Possible he had felt, standing among the giant shining cylinders. The elation was gone now, crushed by Emil Clausen's all too efficient arm. What remained was a reckless promise that Stavros could no longer conceive of being able to fulfill.

"It's the priesthorns," said Megan, thinking his sober frown a response to the baying thunder-sounds that richocheted from the cliff tops. The sun was hot on their faces. Below, the dust rose in a giant ocher cloud from the rock flat, as eight hundred wagons and carts jostled for their assigned positions in rows that stretched along the cliff bottom for a solid half kilometer. Farther to the east, the dairy herd nosed among the plains ravines where the newly sprouting vegetation softened the drying mud with a dense yellow carpet. Rimming the eastern horizon were the blunted mounds of the Talche, the Knees. *Whose knees, Valla's or Lagri's?* Stavros mused with therapeutic irreverence as he and Megan started down the stairs. He noticed two more little cloud scouts lingering about the Talche, as if reconnoitering the terrain. They moved even as he watched them, sliding farther south, clinging to the profile of the lavender hills like low-flying aircraft.

Weird shit, he thought, and wondered why it had taken him so long to see it that way.

The Engineers' guildsmen came clattering down the stairs behind them, surrounding them with excited greetings and swallowing them up in their midst, urging them to greater speed. The priesthorns ceased their random thundering and segued into a thrilling basso call that stilled the racket below and drew the population away from their last-minute frenzy. They gathered along the rock terrace in front of the rows of wagons, leaving a wide strip of open ground between themselves and the cliff face. Stavros hurried along with the Engineers, bringing his mind to focus on the coming ritual as a distraction from his self-pitying gloom. He lost Megan in the throng at the bottom of the steps. He looked for Susannah or Weng, but if the other Terrans were there, they were well hidden by all the confusion.

The ceremonial horns fell silent. The dust cloud settled about the wagons as shouts and chatter and the rattle of harness and cartwheels died into an expectant hush. Stavros searched his pack, located his pocket recorder and eased himself with his observer's presumption into the front ranks of the silent crowd. By now accustomed to his polite but aggressive curiosity, the watchers parted to give him room. Crouching in the hot sun among the children and the elderly, he activated the recorder.

The cave mouths waited, black and empty maws in the sheer fall of sun-bright rock. Then the horns sounded again, first one, the westernmost, followed by the others in sequence toward the east. When all twelve boomed a single drawn-out chord, the caves overflowed amid a burst of plainsong. Across the third level, twelve dark entries glittered, and with a swirl of color, twelve honor guards of apprentices carrying bright banners marched out of the shadowed mouths to begin the processional descent along the connecting ledges to the stairs. A pair of musicians followed each cluster of banners, and next a cohort of priests, all moving in single file to the beat of skin drums and the shrill of woodwinds.

The priests had donned their longest, whitest robes, simple long-sleeved shifts over which they wore soft tabards and shawls of earthy red. Unlike the apprentices, they bore no PriestGuild seals. Their hems and sleeves were embroidered in the colors of flame, the hot salmons and vermilions, the golden yellows and the crimsons that honored Lagri, whose dominance they hoped to encourage until the trade caravan had returned and the crop could be harvested. They poured out into the sunlight in a blaze of finery, and behind them came another glowing rank of banners and the rest of the apprentices, dressed also in white. The younger ones carried triangular flags in Lagri's brightest colors. The older ones supported tall fringed standards, painted or sewn with picture tales of the goddess's past victories over her sister-rival. Last in line came a master apprentice from each of the guilds. Their white tunics sparkled like sea foam as they moved to the staccato beat of the drums. Each carried a carved or painted plaque bearing the symbol of his guild. As they marched, they sang, priest and apprentice alike. A hundred voices joined as one brought the masses assembled at the cliff bottom to their feet to raise a throaty chant of exultation.

Stavros rose with them, surrendering his gloom to the crowd's contagious enthusiasm, adding his voice gladly to theirs while still remembering to clip the recorder to his belt and adjust the volume.

A stout figure clothed in white appeared at the mouth of the highest cave. Even with the distance and the glare of the sun, Stavros could tell from the redoubtable posture that it was Ashimmel, putting on the kind of show for which she was famous. There was no sign in her stance that she was anything but ecstatic about the forthcoming departure. She stood alone for a moment, arms spread with palms up as if humbly receiving the accolade of the throng. Then she lowered her arms and moved toward the ledges to begin her stately descent.

Behind her came a line of open sedan chairs and litters carrying the members of the guilds too elderly or infirm to walk. Each was supported by a pair of strong white-clad apprentices from the elder's own guild. The litters were draped in white. The chairs bore white canopies and their side panels were decorated with carved polychromed friezework. The last and largest was a high-sided chair carried by two pairs of priests. The wave-and-flame seal gleamed on both side panels. The curved white canopy was tied with streamers that fluttered in a diaphanous curtain around the sides and back, in colors that honored both Valla Ired and Lagri. The Master of Ritual was nestled inside, seeming as slight as a child in the huge chair's embrace. His blind smile lit up the inner shadow.

The procession zigzagged down the cliff face to the rhythm of the music and the joyous chanting of the crowd. When they reached the bottom, the guild apprentices lined up facing the throng, the hundred priests and their apprentices behind them, banners and flags raised in a rainbowed wall at their backs. The freshly painted guild seals glistened in the sun. The elderly were set down next to the seal of their guild. Their bearers retired into the ranks behind. When Kav Daven's chair had left the final step and was lowered lovingly to the ground, the horns on the cliff top sounded a final note, a long tumbling call that fell like water into silence as the chanting ceased within the space of a breath.

Stavros forgot the recorder at his side. He could not hope to preserve the quality of that intent silence, filled as it was with wind sighs and the flap of ribbons and banners, with the silken murmur of long priestly sleeves, with the lowing of the distant dairy herd and the wavelike rustle of the yellow stalks in the fields behind the wagons. There was every sound in that silence but the nonsound of five thousand people waiting motionless, enrapt.

The sedan chair's ancient joints creaked as the Ritual Master inched his bony legs over the edge and climbed down into the sun. No one stepped forward from the ranks of priests and apprentices to offer him support. He stood a moment, balancing, smiling as if it were a game to relearn the art of existing upright. He was not wrapped in the ceremonial white but in his own soft brown layers that made Stavros think of wilted leaves. His head swung in a gentle arc as he oriented himself with the preternatural hearing of the blind. He took a few shuffling steps, an experiment, then stopped and beamed at the crowd, a jester's grin, as if he would follow this act with juggling or a few jokes. Instead, he took a few more steps, firmer now, advancing as far as the front ranks of children so that he could bend, an old tree swaying stiffly in the wind, to touch fingers with those sitting nearest him. The children chattered at him and softly called his name and there was no disapproving adult around to hush them,

but Stavros, who felt like a child himself, in awe of the old
priest's mystery.

Kav Daven smiled again for them and shuffled back a step.
Then he straightened, impossibly old and frail, and began to
walk along the long line of enthralled watchers, a solitary brown
figure moving through heat and dust and silence. The standing
watchers sat as he trudged by them, so that his passing was like a
slow wave receding across a sea of heads, a relief of waiting
tension. Stavros wished briefly for his videogun, but knew that
he would need no machine to recall this moment. His own
flesh-and-blood brain would retain the memory in all its vividness.

When the Ritual Master had passed by him on his journey
along the line, Stavros backed through the crowd and made his
way through the press of smaller carts to climb the slatted side of
the nearest big wagon for a better view. He searched for Liphar
among the ranks of apprentices and found him not far from
Ashimmel's retinue of senior priests who had gathered in a
semicircle around her. Liphar looked scrub-faced and solemn in
his knee-length white tunic. His long brown curls had been
combed and braided with red-and-orange ribbon. Feet braced,
his head high, his hands behind his back tightly clasped the tall
shaft of a triangular banner sewn with the wave-and-flame seal
of the guild. The long orange point of the banner fluttered just
above his head. The silky threads of the embroidery shone very
blue and red in the brilliant sunlight.

Glancing down the front line of wagons, Stavros noticed the
yellow mobile infirmary in the middle of the row. Megan had
found herself a grandstand view. She sat hunched in the driver's
seat, scribbling in her notebook with a tiny pencil stub. McPherson perched beside her, whispering eagerly into her ear, laughing
occasionally and pointing. Ghirra leaned beside the tall rear
wheel, intent on the ceremony. Susannah watched beside him.
Danforth lay in his folding stretcher, propped up against the
wheel rim. Weng stood with them, slim and erect, her white
uniform outshining even the white of the priests' robes. Clausen
was nowhere in evidence.

Stavros frowned, suddenly distracted from the joy of the
ceremony. He realized that Clausen's absence would now always
hold the threat of his arrival, until the grudge was repaid or the
man himself was light-years removed, or dead. In his mind,
Stavros refought his moment of humiliation. He rehearsed all the
things he could have done to the prospector if only he'd been
able to wrench free a hand, an arm, a leg, anything. And he

would have done all of them, even with the cool steel of the laser pressed to his throat, anything but suffer that awful impotence that Clausen had forced upon him, with hardly a visible effort.

And Stavros decided that Megan was wrong after all to think that the personal injury bore no relation to the larger issue. CONPLEX might be the ultimate power, but Clausen was here and it was not. Local power is the only important power when one man threatens another with death. But the real lesson to be taken from this individual violation was that Clausen would treat the Sawls with the same arrogance and casual violence he had shown to Stavros. He would grind them under his heel without a thought.

Just as the Goddesses march rough-shod over the Sawls in their blind determination to subdue each other.

Stavros had a sudden gut understanding of Ghirra's raging at the Sisters, that before had been merely intellectual. If it was possible to "believe" an emotion, as opposed to "knowing" it, Stavros felt himself to be a true believer at last. He had felt himself as helpless in his own rage as the Master Healer was in his. It was the same rage, after all, the rage of the powerless against the powerful. Did Clausen see himself as godlike in his power over others? Stavros had no doubt that the directors of CONPLEX nurtured vast Olympian notions.

Remembering made him restive. What was to be done? He could not imagine backing away from his commitments to Ghirra, to the Sawls. He would be left without purpose, meaningless. So it seemed he must throw himself against the rocks for their sakes, though it might do them precious little good. He felt no resentment, only sadness that he had made promises he could not fulfill.

Clinging to the side of the tall wagon seemed suddenly an unnecessarily conspicuous and vulnerable position. *This is what it's going to feel like, being hunted*, he thought. He unclipped the recorder from his belt and replaced it in his pack, then eased himself down from the wagon. He could see over the heads of the seated crowd well enough, but also feel protected by them.

He wandered close to the infirmary wagon, past two wagons belonging to the Leatherworkers' Guild. A bevy of apprentices perched on the curving canopies, whispering excitedly. The hjalk teams, bored with standing, bent their heads to watch him pass. Stavros found a vacant wheel to lean against, and returned his attention to the ceremony.

Incredibly, the old priest's pace had quickened as he progressed along the line. A glad tension built within the crowd as he neared the end. When the priest had several hundred meters left to travel of that long half kilometer, the tension became a sound, a low eager humming as if from a swarm of bees. Kav Daven covered the final distance in a miraculous swinging walk, his wilted-leaf clothing floating around him with a rhythmic life of its own. His stride was more like a curious lope than the deliberate putting of one foot after the other. Every eye was on him, and the humming increased its pitch and volume.

He reached the end and stopped. From behind the lead wagon, Aguidran emerged. She was dressed in her dark road leathers but over them she wore a white sleeveless robe with the RangerGuild insignia embroidered on a wide soft collar. She approached the Ritual Master, made a formal bow of greeting, which he returned, then came to stand beside him. He raised his right arm, palm up, and offered it to the sky, the white cliffs, the wagons and lastly the waiting crowd. The Master Ranger followed the motion of his hand with a narrowed piercing glance that seemed to penetrate into every corner and heart.

When the priest's salute was completed, Aguidran extended a leather-bound arm to him. He laid a feathery hand on her steady wrist, and the rising hum climaxed in joyous song. The crowd surged into motion. Kav Daven and his ranger escort started slowly back along the line of people and wagons. The priests and apprentices broke rank to fall in behind, banners and long robes flying. Following them, the musicians started up several tunes at once, and the populace rose from the dusty rock to mob after them in cheerful, chanting disorder.

Stavros found himself once more being swept up by a throng of celebrating Sawls. He was drawn away from the wagons as if caught in the current of a laughing stream. Hungry for the soothing touch of communal joy, he let himself be filled by the sensual rush of music and song vibrating around him. He drifted forward with the watery surging of the crowd, at ease, laughing with them, humming when he lost the words, enjoying his surrender. And then, into the center of his vision moved the mismatched pair, the ranger and the priest, approaching with measured step.

Caught up in the tide of elation, Stavros felt the familiar signs, the slippage, the slight quaking of his reality. He shook his head to clear it. *Not again*, he told himself firmly, *not twice in one day*. And still, as priest and ranger approached, all else blurred around him into an aura surrounding them with misty brightness.

He fought the urge to move closer, considered clinging to the nearest arm, digging his feet into the ground. Yet move he did, as if compelled. Without his asking, a path to the front of the crowd was cleared for him, for he moved like a sleepwalker, intent but humble, grateful to find space among the others sitting to receive Kav Daven's greeting. It seemed suddenly appropriate to him, given the hopelessness of his future purpose, that he drop to one knee to ask a blessing for his endeavor. He hoped Ghirra would not be disappointed in him for giving in once more to his inner voices. He knelt, dropped his pack to the ground, and bowed his head.

Kav Daven worked his way slowly along the line, touching fingers, greeting those he knew with soft words and laughter. Aguidran paced beside him in patient silence. When he came to the kneeling offworlder, he stopped. Stavros dared not raise his head to meet those sightless eyes. He saw feet, booted and sturdy, Aguidran's, and others, Kav Daven's, gnarled and brown and bare, dusted with ocher. He heard murmurs, a grunted exclamation of surprise, a discussion and a rustling, and then more feet appeared, women's feet in thin white sandals, a pair on either side of the gnarled ones, as the booted feet withdrew. He wondered why he could hear such quiet sounds through all the uproar, and then realized.

The singing had stopped.

He started to a touch, cool fingers brushing aside his long hair to rest against the nape of his neck. Thumb and little finger slipped inside his collar to lie along his shoulder in a protective caress, almost sexual in its intimacy. Stavros shivered, too much in the grip of his compulsion to resist.

"Ibi, this is not needed," murmured Ghirra's voice above him.

"I must ask his blessing," Stavros replied with the last ounce of will left to him.

"Leave this, Ibi. It is not needed."

Stavros shook his head. He thought the Master Healer sounded sad, and did not understand why the asking of a simple blessing should disturb him so.

Ghirra sighed. "I will help, if you must do this thing. The pain I will help. Give him your hands."

Pain? Do what thing? Stavros put out his hands, confused by old memories of the altar rail.

The pairs of white-sandaled feet shuffled uneasily. Stavros waited head down with palms outstretched. He heard another muttered discussion, and a voice raised in protest that he thought was Ashimmel's. It was silenced by a low singsong command in words Stavros could not understand. But he recognized their throaty diphthongs and their ancient cadences. *Old words. PriestWords.*

It was Kav Daven, he guessed, who had spoken, though the voice was firm and smooth, a younger man's voice.

The priest's silken scarred palms folded themselves around Stavros's outstretched hands. He pressed them palm to palm, then gently spread the thumbs so that the hands were cupped. The strength of the priest's hands surprised Stavros, for they seemed to have no bones in them.

Not strength, he thought. *Power. Powerful. Full of power. Ah, for a touch of such power in my own hands to serve my cause!*

Stavros rested his hands within the priest's willingly.

Or rather . . . will-lessly.

It was strange to be so aware, of the Kav's soft hands, of the sun's heat, of the rustle of the white robes around him, of Ghirra's light touch on his neck, so *aware* and yet so unable to act. Helpless again, but willingly. Aware enough to feel self-conscious. So aware and yet in such confusion.

The priest's hands cupped his own. The old man bent low. Stavros could feel the whisper of breath against his ear as Kav Daven spoke.

Do you will this calling?

Stavros heard the old words and the sense of them as if with two separate parts of his consciousness. His voice returned to him long enough to answer.

''No, Kav.''

The sun weighed heavily on his head and back. Its light was thick and amber, like honey. *What is happening*? he asked himself, amazed at last.

Who wills it then?

''Kav, I know not.'' This at least was true, though it frightened him to hear his voice replying as if it were someone else's.

Ghirra's fingers twitched against his skin, then steadied. There was a quiet stir behind, someone approaching through the crowd. Aguidran's booted feet moved suddenly from behind Kav Daven and stepped to Stavros's left side as Ghirra shifted to his right. He felt their strength as a single presence, brother and sister protecting him.

From what?

He looked up then. A flash of silvered lenses in the crowd jolted him with unreasoning terror. He jerked backward against the fingers at his neck, and Ghirra's free hand gripped his shoulder, steadying him before the rage that quickly displaced his terror could seize control. The rage felt clean in him now, sharp as honed steel, a weapon to draw quick and fatal blood. But Clausen kept his distance, his slouch confident, his mocking smile implying he was merely there to observe the native antics.

Kav Daven murmured, drawing Stavros's attention back to him. The sudden fear had cleared his head. The weapon of rage seemed once again a double-edged blade as thirsty for his own blood as for Clausen's. As he set aside both fear and anger to concentrate on the old priest, the sense of compulsion eased. He could see Kav Daven clearly, no longer through a mist of awe. He could focus on his own paler hands held between the knotted brown fingers. He felt no need to look anywhere else. He forgot Clausen for a time.

The Kav spoke again, and a PriestGuild journeyman in embroidered red and white came forward, holding a small cloth-swaddled bundle. The loose white wrappings masked the shape of the object inside, but to Ghirra's tight-lipped mutter, Stavros merely nodded. He had known what it must be the moment he saw it.

Guar. The rock that burns.

Stavros's entire being drew in to focus on the shining scarred flesh of the old priest's palms.

Do you accept this calling?

"Tell him no—you can still," whispered Ghirra urgently.

Stavros tried to answer the healer's sincere concern, but his voice had left him once again.

"You understand this, Ibi, what he means?"

He could not move his head.

Do you accept?

No . . . but how can I do otherwise?

How could he refuse a visitation of Power that came swooping down from a place unimaginable to take without asking, to sweep him unsuspecting along into the cosmos like so much stardust?

What is happening to me? a part of him asked again, more desperately, while another part bid joyful welcome to this manifestation of Power beside which Emil Clausen and CONPLEX and all the mundane issues of money and politics were reduced to insignificance.

Kneeling with hands extended, in the age-old supplicant's posture, Stavros was granted an instant of true knowledge. He saw himself as through the wrong end of a spyglass, with the harsh objectivity of distance: a romantic silly young man on his knees, in the grip of the incomprehensible and afraid in his soul for his sanity. He thought of the Catholic saints and martyrs, wondered if this was how it was with them, no climax of faith at all but an accidental visitation of terror, like a window opened into the Void that only faith could close again.

His back arched as the voidwind rushed through him.

"Ibi?" Ghirra's voice was strained.

"Ah . . ." he managed, a gasp of ecstasy and fear. He felt the parts of himself, already imperfectly joined, breaking up like a ship on the rocks, scattering timbers, sails, rigging, all.

Do you accept?

"You understand this, Ibi?"

"Yes!" he answered, to silence their questioning, that kept drawing him back from the Void.

The elation singing in him only hastened the breakup. Internal vibration stretched the last ligaments of his consciousness toward a final snap that would fling the scraps of his being to the farthest corners of the universe. He found it hardest to bear that his physical body would remain after his mind had shattered. If this disintegration must be, he would prefer it to be total.

"Too weak, I am," he murmured, failing.

Ghirra's fingers searched the side of his neck, checked the pulse point, then moved upward to probe beneath the curve of his jawbone. Already surrendering his sanity, Stavros offered up his life as well to a pair of hands whose delicacy concealed a strength that could snap his neck with a single motion.

Kav Daven smiled. He leaned over and spat into Stavros's cupped hands. He gently drew his own hands along Stavros's palms, spreading the moisture and reforming the cup. Then he turned to the bright-robed journeyman and received the white cloth bundle. He let the wrappings fall open, and with both hands raised the chunk of guar for all to see.

The throng murmured its approval.

Silver-white metal flashed in dull gleams, enough like mirror to rouse a spark of will in Stavros's yielded consciousness. He remembered Clausen.

A hot magma of rage boiled up within him. Dizzy in its heat, he thrust his cupped hands forward. With the sureness of the sighted, the blind priest lowered the guar, transferred it and its wrappings to one palm, then placed his other hand in a little dome over the metal. With a deft twist, he rotated the palms, balled the white wrapping in one fist and let the knobby fingers of the other close around their silvery burden. His ancient face showed no change, no sign of pain. The white cloth he slipped between the brown layers of his clothing. Finally, he joined both hands around the guar and rested them lightly within the bowl of Stavros's hands. He bent lower, swaying on ancient legs, kissed Stavros on the brow and opened his hands.

Stavros felt no impact as the guar dropped into his palms, but the moisture of the priest's saliva made the pain instantaneous, and as excruciating as molten metal poured onto his skin. He shuddered, knowing he would not be able to bear it, but a moment later, knew he must, as Clausen moved into his line of sight, insinuating himself through the crowd as if something had suddenly stirred his interest.

He must not weaken, must not let the rock fall. He must deny himself the oblivion of the Void a little longer. But the pain seared him. He felt the guar, greedy for moisture, eating wormholes in his palm, and had no idea where he would find the strength.

His throat made noises he could not control.

Ghirra's fingers pressed hard into the curve of his jaw. It was no longer a caress but a sharp businesslike probing that at first hurt almost as much as the corrosive guar. Stavros moaned in a delirium of agony. Then the pain eased, marginally, or his tolerance of it increased. Kav Daven's brown hands embraced his once more, and squeezed them gently to flatten their curve, so that the guar was imprisoned more tightly. Stavros could feel nothing but a fiery locus of agony in the center of both palms that would have had him screaming like an animal, begging to be released, but for the steady relieving pressure of the Master Healer's hand.

But even the pain itself was steadying, now that he could imagine enduring it. He was not so shipwrecked as he thought. What the touch of Power had riven in him, the pain drew together again as he marshaled his resources against it. No mere physical pain could be as annihilating as that wind from the Void. Suffering the pain in order to conceal the guar became reason enough for Stavros to recall his scattered parts and renege on his surrender.

There was movement to his right, a flash of silver, then an instant of scuffle. Ghirra's hand was ripped away from his neck with a speed and economy of movement that left Stavros no doubt who now stood behind him. The crowd backed off in surprise, giving room to Aguidran as she moved to steady and restrain her brother. Stavros had no time to consider the simmering of his rage. Its heat was mild compared to the fire in his palms. He braced himself, sucked air as his deadened nerves rewoke, and clamped his hands still tighter about the source of his agony.

"You all right, Stav?" demanded Clausen loudly.

Stavros held himself still, erect, silent. He let his anger harden around him like a wall of cooling lava.

"Stav, can you hear me?" The prospector put a hand to his shoulder, bent closer and hissed, "Open your hands, Ibiá. I want to see what you've got there."

Stavros made his shoulder relax within the prospector's grip. He let the pain be his center, his hardening rage his shield. He was on his own, braving it without benefit of Ghirra's analgesic touch. Calm enveloped him, cool as an evening breeze. His rage became brittle in its chill. He dared a smile, though it came with effort, and looked up to find it shared by the old priest. Stavros shivered, but this time with joy.

Not helpless! No!

He began to laugh softly. He let the anger crack and fall away like a molted shell. He needed it no longer. He had never felt so whole, so in control as he did this moment, giving his entire self willingly to the pain that its secret might remain concealed. If this was the guar ritual that welcomed an apprentice into the priesthood, though the Master Healer might think it barbaric, Stavros now thought he understood its purpose.

Clausen shifted, pressing his knee sharply into Stavros's back. It was no surprise to the linguist when the sleek chill of the laser pistol slid up like a metal snake to nestle behind his ear.

"Open them, boy. *Now*. No one will know any better when I say I was too late to stop these native pals of yours from making you a human sacrifice."

Stavros kept his smile focused on Kav Daven. The Ritual Master returned it as if nothing out of the ordinary had occurred, as if there were only the two of them alone beneath the hot amber sun. At last, he nodded. He laid his fingertips to the top of Stavros's rigid hands and broke their seal by gently uncrossing the thumbs. His smile widened as he spread the palms apart.

Stavros stared as his rational universe turned inside out once again.

The guar was gone.

His palms were intact. No blood and stink and charring. No ghastly burns. The skin was as clear as if freshly scoured.

My god, he thought. *A miracle*.

But that could not be. He knew that miracles were a proof of faith, and his faith was anything but proven.

He heard gasps and murmurs and exclamations of surprise all around him, and Clausen's muttered oath beside his ear. He gazed down at his hands uncomprehendingly, held still in Kav Daven's grasp. They hurt as if the burns were real. He tried to flex his fingers and sent agonizing shocks of pain up both his arms. His mind felt the burned tissue ooze and crack, but his eyes saw only clear olive skin.

"What does this mean?" he asked the old priest fearfully.

Kav Daven regarded him with satisfaction. His smile grew inward until he seemed to be smiling to himself alone as he drew his fingertips slowly across the linguist's uninjured palms. He nodded again, a finish to the ritual, and drew his hands away. As he turned to go, Clausen was on the old man like silent lightning, imprisoning his fisted hands at the wrists.

Stavros forgot his pain and bewilderment. Without thinking, he launched himself at Clausen's back. But his legs would not hold him. Real or unreal, the ordeal had drained his strength. He stumbled, and Ghirra, released from his sister's grasp, caught him before he fell and held him back.

"Leave him alone!" Stavros snarled at the prospector, struggling vainly against Ghirra's restraints. The ghostly agony returned to sear his palms. He sagged back against the Master Healer, cradling his arms against his chest.

"Tut, Ibiá," Clausen remarked over his shoulder as he gripped Kav Daven's scrawny wrists with surprising gentleness. "Hurt a blind old man? A coward's act. Do you think that ill of me?"

Firmly but kindly, as if dealing with a child, Clausen pried open the fingers of first one and then the other of Kav Daven's hands. The old priest did not resist. He gave the prospector his jester's grin and proudly extended his hands, palm up.

Clausen seemed surprised that the hands were empty. "Now you see it, now you don't," he muttered, and stared at the silky scar tissue for a long moment, stroking it once with a curious finger before he released the priest's hands and stood back.

"A thousand pardons for doubting you, ancient sir," he said with a twisted smile and a little bow.

"Aren't you going to beat him up?" Stavros growled.

Clausen scoffed. "If you think what I gave you was a beating, Ibiá, you don't know the meaning of the word."

He watched as Kav Daven turned away once again, still smiling but shaky. The old priest extended a frail arm to Aguidran, who was instantly at his side. The Master Ranger gave Stavros a single piercing glance, then the pair resumed the interrupted march along the line toward the waiting sedan chair. Ashimmel followed, looking perturbed and solemn, the other priests and flag-bearing apprentices falling in behind her. They moved more slowly than before, for Kav Daven showed signs of fatigue and there were many left who wished to exchange greetings with him. The chant was raised again, with some confusion at first, then building to its previous joyous intensity as the throng followed after the priest and his escort, streaming past with only the occasional awed smile for Stavros or nod of support. The whole incident happened very fast, and most of them had not seen enough of it to be amazed.

Clausen sighed, his hands in his pockets, one of which Stavros knew must conceal the little laser gun. "Besides, that blind old man outfoxed me fair and square, and I have to admire that. We must treat the elderly with respect, Ibiá. They have seen so much in their lives. I hope there's someone tough as me around to admire me when I'm that age."

"You'll never live that long," returned Stavros sullenly, wondering what the hell the prospector was talking about.

Clausen gave him a nasty smile. "Neither will you, at the rate you're going. You'd better pray this traveling circus gets itself on the road while you still own your skin." Jiggling his hands in his pockets, he nodded in the direction of the wagons. "Ah. Here comes the Ladies' Auxiliary, to see to your welfare. What are you going to tell them, Ibiá?"

"That you bulled your way in when a high priest was showing us the honor of including me in a harmless ritual."

The silvered glasses flashed as Clausen shook his head wonderingly. "Perhaps I've misjudged your intelligence, Ibiá. Well, suit yourself. You've had ample warning." He shrugged and strolled off to lose himself in the crowd.

Ghirra released him, and Stavros slumped forward onto his knees, unsure if he would ever have the strength to stand again. He thought it odd that his body should feel so weak when he felt so strong inside. He heard a rumbling growl from above that he thought was the priesthorns resuming their call. He held his burning unmarred hands out to Ghirra in wonder. "What does this mean?"

The Master Healer grasped him by the elbow and hauled him roughly to his feet. The crowd was slowing, halting, gathering in groups to stare apprehensively at the sky. Stavros held back to follow their gaze, but Ghirra guided him abruptly away, ignoring Susannah's and Megan's calls as they approached, losing them in the milling confusion. Stavros's feet scuffed in the dust, his legs threatened to fold.

"Ghirra, what. . . ?"

The Master Healer dragged him into the shadow between two close-set wagons and released him ungently. Stavros slumped onto a wicker crate, still staring at his hands.

"How did you do that?" Ghirra demanded harshly.

The physician's anger confused him. "The guar . . ." he said helplessly.

"That is not how it goes with a calling!" Ghirra growled.

"I did nothing . . . Ghirra, I . . ."

Ghirra paced away angrily, glancing between the wagons, tossing a black look at the sky as another booming roll shook the air.

Not the horns, Stavros realized. He looked up to see a single dark cloud puff speed by overhead.

Ghirra paced back, grasped one of his hands firmly and turned it palm up to study. He drew his finger across the palm as Kav Daven had done, but with far less satisfaction. Stavros winced.

Ghirra's eyes narrowed. "This hurts you, still?"

"Yes," Stavros whispered. "Though not so much now."

Ghirra looked incredulous, but his touch eased as he held the offending hand.

Stavros realized the Master Healer suspected him of fraud.

"The pain was real, Ghirra, I swear. I *felt* it! Even with your . . . help." An insight reached him. "Will you do that for \.iphar when the time comes for him to hold the guar? For all the apprentices?"

Ghirra nodded. "When they are called. It is nerve damping," he muttered, in Susannah's diction but with his own tone of professional dismissal. "Simple tricks. But those who hold the guar are not like this." He explored the palm more gently, pressing the joints, stretching the clear skin as if willing it to show a crack, a sear, a blister, some sign other than obviously radiant health.

"Kav Daven didn't seem surprised at all," Stavros reflected vaguely.

"He makes some game, this Kav." Ghirra pushed the hand aside, murmuring deprecations about the PriestGuild that sounded more perfunctory than heartfelt.

"Ghirra, please believe me," Stavros begged.

The physician buried his hands in the pockets of his smock and stood rocking gently on his heels. His eyes seemed to have absorbed an echo of Stavros's pain. "But, Ibi, if this is true, where is the science in this?" he demanded quietly.

Stavros foundered. "I don't know," he admitted. He recalled his mad promise once again. Was this "miracle" a sign of the divinity of the Sister-Goddesses or was it, as Ghirra suggested, a trick of Kav Daven's? What "game" would the old priest be playing with an offworld stranger? Stavros could not shed the sensation of having received that very blessing he had knelt for, that his purpose had been somehow sanctified. For there was more than just the disappearance of the guar to be explained. How would the physician react to claims of inexplicable visitations of Power that offered self-knowledge and sudden cures for long-term mental instability in return for visions of annihilation? How to explain the falling away of his helplessness and rage in the face of this new calm and strength of purpose? Stavros prevaricated, for his friend's peace of mind. "Back on Earth, you know, there are all kinds of religious fanatics who can dance on burning coals with no apparent damage to the skin. And on Ba-hore, the fertility rites include flame-walking." He held out his palm with an unconvincing grin. "I'm small change compared to that."

Ghirra regarded him without humor. "Are you a religious fanatic?"

Stavros dropped the hand into his lap, into the protective curl of the other, so that the lingering phantom pain was held centered in his body. "Of course not," he said. "Though this is the sort of thing that could make you one. . . . I don't know. Mass psychosis? Belief and knowledge again, Ghirra."

"Science or miracle," echoed Ghirra unhappily.

Stavros discarded his efforts at easy explanation. They would not satisfy the Master Healer any more than himself. And then, unable to withhold it any longer, he added softly, "But, Ghirra, I must tell you, I felt such . . . joy out there, despite the pain. I feel . . ."

"There you are!" called Megan from the head of the wagons. Beside her, Susannah peered in at them with concern.

"Stav? You all right? Ghirra, is he all right?"

". . . whole," Stavros finished lamely. The more he tried to express it in words, the more it began to sound like simply growing up.

"There's one hell of a storm brewing out here again," Megan warned.

The pain in Ghirra's eyes softened as his healer's instincts responded to Stavros's fervent relief. "I am glad for you, Ibi," he replied.

Susannah came into the shadow of the wagons. "What happened, Stav?"

Megan followed. "All happened so fast."

So fast, yes . . . but it felt like forever.

With their entrance, the moment of Power had passed into history. But it had left a residue of Power behind. Stavros could feel its workings through the pain in his hands. Now it remained to him to integrate his miracle with the reality around him, either to find a "scientific" explanation, or to simply let the miracle live within him as an anomalous moment of mysticism that was all the more precious for having no explanation. He knew Ghirra would not be happy with that solution. He forced himself to resume using his hands as if they were a normal part of his body, ignoring the ghostly fires in his palms.

"Nothing much," he replied easily. "Just a little send-off ritual."

"The sun," Ghirra offered to Susannah. "But he is better now."

Megan found a free crate to sit on. The wicker creaked. She eyed it dubiously and got up again. "A send-off ritual that includes Terrans?"

Stavros nodded, spread his hands in a Sawl-like shrug. "Kav Daven's gesture to ecumenicism."

Thunder cracked overhead. Through the space between the tall wagons, Stavros saw shadows scudding across the bright face of the cliff.

"May have all been for nothing," commented Megan darkly, following his glance. "Shall we get back out there to watch Ashimmel have the final word after all?"

Ghirra's concern had already shifted to the sky. He lingered long enough to see Stavros pull himself successfully to his feet, then moved out into the open. Megan followed. Susannah waited while Stavros tested his balance.

"The sun, indeed," she sniffed. "Are you sure you're all right?"

He was relieved to hear no pity in her voice. He found his physical strength returning, even while the pain remained to haunt his palms. "Oh yes," he smiled at her, wishing he could tell her why and what had happened and about the new strength he had found. "Better than I've ever been."

Susannah laughed. "No need to exaggerate for my sake. I believe you."

She led the way to join Megan and Ghirra.

The chanting had stopped. The assembled population stood silent, backed against the cliff face where it was possible to gain a view of the northeastern horizon over the tops of the wagon lines. Stavros saw McPherson corral two Sawls to help carry Danforth up to where he would be able to see. Weng stood with Ghirra and Aguidran in the front ranks of the crowd. Megan had found Tyril and was holding the baby while the weaver comforted a frightened older child. Seeing them gathered there, Sawl and Terran, he felt suddenly as possessive of them as a father, and a part of them as well. *My people*, he thought happily. Glancing higher, he spotted Clausen sitting on the cliff stairs, halfway up the second flight. He smiled with relief to see no less than three of Aguidran's biggest rangers spread out across the first step of the next flight up.

How foolish to have let myself think I was doing this alone!

Shadows sped past as Stavros crossed the dusty rock. Reaching Ghirra's side, he turned to look out over the plain.

"Oh my loving god," he breathed, and realized once again that Clausen and his megacorp were only part of the survival problem.

Valla's forces had massed for the attack.

A towering cloud front advanced from the Vallegar, at the measured inexorable pace of crack infantry. The clouds cut a straight line across the full eighty-kilometer width of the Dop Arek, stretching from the far western hills to the knobby Talche in the east. Along the leading edge marched a Himalayan range of thunderheads, their distant cloud tops shining like golden helmets in the sun, their bottoms roiling brown and black and spitting forked lightning like a den of dragons. The plain beneath was sunk in darkness shattered by the nightmare flash of green and yellow.

"No rain out there," Stavros observed to Ghirra.

"She saves the water for her Sister," Ghirra replied tightly.

Stavros recognized the physician's undertone of rage and despair. The crops were not yet ripe. There was no help for them. The wagons were hard-roofed and shuttered tight. They were as safe as it was possible for them to be outside the Caves. Still, it felt wrong to stand by and let destruction happen. He had learned that helplessness came from within as well as without. He glanced around at the stilled crowd. "Shouldn't we *do* something?"

"What, Ibi? Tell me what can be done!" Ghirra glowered and gestured at the approaching cloud bank helplessly. "The storm comes again. No trade in Ogo Dul. The food dies in the fields. We die in our Caves. You see how it is with these Sisters, Ibi?"

Stavros gripped the physician's hunched shoulders with a compassionate hand. For once, it was he who had comfort to offer. Though the pain in his palms still lingered, he found it mattered little whether he used his hands or not. "Yes, my friend, but please, it's not over yet."

"No," Ghirra agreed darkly. "Lagri waits her time."

The cloud scouts sped northward past the sun to be swallowed by the approaching darkness, as if recalled to deliver their report. The front continued to advance. Stavros noticed Kav Daven's canopied sedan chair, left out in the open between the crowd and the line of wagons. He saw one bare gnarled foot nosing through the front curtain of ribbons.

High above the Dop Arek, the fast-moving little cloud puffs detached once more from the main front, this time scudding straight across the plain. Behind them, the thunderheads discharged a brilliant electrical display and roared a deafening challenge. The thunder hit the cliffs and rolled off in echoing crescendos as palpable as shock waves.

A warm breeze lifted Stavros's hair. Ghirra straightened expectantly.

"Now we will see it," he declared.

The breeze picked up, gusting at first, then steadying into an unnaturally even blow like the wind from a stationary fan. Its temperature increased. Static sang like cicadas in the hot dry air. The assembled throng jostled with eagerness and dread, loving the anticipation of battle, fearing the outcome. Softly they invoked Lagri's name. Stavros heard several fatalistic wagers being exchanged.

The cloud scouts approached in a neat and widely spaced row, a cautious vanguard. They slowed as they neared the southern edge of the plain. Suddenly there was a wavering of the air around the easternmost scout. Like a desert mirage, it shimmered and vanished. The next in line quickly met a similiar fate, and the next, while the others reversed themselves and fled back toward the main column.

The black towers of cloud kept up their slow steady advance. The strange shimmering of the air spread itself east and west in a line parallel to the oncoming cloud. It extended itself as high as the tallest thunderhead. The front became a dark distortion behind a plane of dancing air. The hot wind blew with eerie consistency at Stavros's back. Its static tension played like fingers on his skin and made him shiver. The wavering line across the plain uncannily resembled the silvery undulations of a force field, though his brain ached to imagine the energy required to sustain a field barrier eighty kilometers long.

"What is it?"

"The fire," said Ghirra. "Lagri's tshael."

"Heat weapon." Not totally irrelevantly, Stavros thought of Clausen's laser.

"Now Valla will answer," the Master Healer predicted.

A roil of motion erupted behind the shimmering curtain of heat. Blinding shocks of lightning lit the distorted darkness. Thunder cracked and rolled and shook the rock they stood on. The heat barrier glowed and rippled like an opalescent curtain blowing in the wind. Sparks danced along its curves. Giant hissing clouds of steam billowed up along its length. A child began to wail in the rear of the throng. Stavros's eye was caught by a movement in Kav Daven's chair. The old priest was rising once again from its shadowed depths.

He climbed out of the chair with agonizing slowness, balanced on his unsteady legs, shuffled a few steps away from the chair, then straightened, facing the plain. He stood like a sentinel as the heat curtain glowed and billowed and the steam clouds mushroomed up to obscure it in a dense white fog suffused with light. And then he began to dance.

He twisted and turned in the same boneless minuet that had accompanied his tale-chant in Lagri's StoryHall. In a single voice, the populace raised a keening wail that sent chills snaking up Stavros's spine and drowned out the boom of the thunder. The diffused flash and glow of the heat barrier turned the veil of steam into a wall of light. The brightness increased until it hurt to look at it. Steam clouds rolled overhead, obscuring the sky and dimming the sun until the fog was the brighter glow.

Then, as Kav Daven danced, the hot wind stilled and died. A heated deadly calm settled in against the cliff face. The crowd held a collective breath. Just as the tension became unbearable, a touch of chill brushed past, a cooling current of dampness from the direction of the plain. The white fog coalesced into a low-slung cloud cover that gathered about the cliff tops, and finally it began to rain, no violent torrent, no slashing downpour, but a soft warm springlike rain that tasted sweet on the tongue. It settled the ochre dust and brought a shine to the wagon canopies and the yellow leaves in the fields. The wall of light glistened like a million rainbows through the gentle shower, and then the hot wind sprang up again in one sudden shuddering gust. The light wall broke up into a rain of sparkles. The sun brightened. The white fog thinned and vanished. The towering front was gone. The sky above the wide Dop Arek was empty, restored to its singing turquoise clarity.

A murmur of delighted awe swept through the throng. Kav Daven lifted his brown hands to the last drops of gentle rain, then slowly shuffled back to his chair and hauled himself inside.

Celebration broke out along the rock flat. The priesthorns bellowed from the cliff top. The jubilant populace danced and cheered and congratulated each other for their narrow escape. Aguidran mobilized her rangers at once to hurry the final preparations for leavetaking. The guild masters rushed to see to the hanging of the guild seals on the sides of their lead wagons. Even Ashimmel looked pleased and relieved, and took it upon herself, still dressed in full regalia, to bend low to check the harness of all the teams pulling the PriestGuild wagons. The other Terrans gathered in quiet astonishment around Danforth's stretcher as McPherson and Susannah tried to calm the apoplectic planetologist.

Stavros thought to himself, *Truly, anything is possible*. He grinned happily at Ghirra. "Slipped by that time, GuildMaster."

Ghirra nodded solemnly, then relented. He let his face relax into a smile that bled the worry from his eyes. "That time, 'TavrosIbia. But next time. . . ?"

"Ibi!" Liphar was breathless at his elbow, fumbling the tall banner he carried into the crook of his arm to snatch up Stavros's hand and stare at his palm with something akin to reverence. "Ibi, a wonder!"

While Ghirra looked on with bemused pride, Stavros threw one arm about the young man's shoulders and hugged him tight.

"Yes, Lifa, a wonder!" he declared joyfully.

With the other hand, he seized the brilliant orange banner sewn with the wave-and-flame, the PriestGuild symbol for the Warrior Sisters, and raised it high above the crowd. Pain flared into molten agony in his palms. The shaft of the banner hummed like a tuning fork within his grip. Stavros heard the voidwind howl at his back, felt its power brush him and was not afraid. His people were around him and he had a job to do for them. He hugged Liphar closer and turned his pain into an ecstatic roar of triumph.

"EMBRIHA LAGRI!!" he proclaimed.

Along the cliff face, five thousand voices echoed his call.

And in the shadow of his chair, Kav Daven smiled.

ABOUT THE AUTHORS

M. BRADLEY KELLOGG lives in New York City and designs scenery for the theater. Her first novel, *A Rumor of Angels,* was published by Signet in 1983.

WILLIAM B. ROSSOW is a space scientist with NASA, studying planetary atmospheres and climate. He lives in New York City with Lynne Kemen and their two cats.